Praise for Lind...

"Linda Thomas-Sund... ...Moons series constantly entertaining, and *Immortal Obsession* is a compelling romance with intriguing scenarios."

—*CataRomance*

"Linda Thomas-Sundstrom's well-written, action-packed novel will keep readers entertained from start to finish."

—*RT Book Reviews* on *Guardian of the Night*

"*Golden Vampire* will wrap you into a story that you will not want to put down."

—*Night Owl Reviews* (Top Pick)

Praise for Linda O. Johnston

"Ms. Johnston has a winner on her hands with this installment of the Alpha Force series."

—*Fresh Fiction* on *Undercover Wolf*

"*Back to Life* is a crafty tale, where the unseen paranormal element packs a powerful punch. Ms. Johnston gives readers a strong romantic suspense with life-or-death situations, and adds a sizzling dose of chemistry to heat up the pages."

—*Darque Reviews*

"In this exciting continuation of the Alpha Force story line, Quinn is a likable character, both sexy and strong, and Kristine's clever moves in crisis show an intelligence that will appeal to readers."

—*RT Book Reviews* on *Undercover Wolf*

Linda Thomas-Sundstrom writes contemporary paranormal romance novels for Harlequin. A teacher by day and a writer by night, Linda lives in the West, juggling teaching, writing, family and caring for a big stretch of land. She swears she has a resident muse who sings so loudly, she often wears earplugs in order to get anything else done. But she has big plans to eventually get to all those ideas. Visit Linda at lindathomas-sundstrom.com or on Facebook.

Books by Linda Thomas-Sundstrom

Harlequin Nocturne

Red Wolf
Wolf Trap
Golden Vampire
Guardian of the Night
Immortal Obsession
Wolf Born
Wolf Hunter
Seduced by the Moon
Immortal Redeemed
Half Wolf
Angel Unleashed
Desert Wolf

Harlequin Desire

The Boss's Mistletoe Maneuvers

Visit the Author Profile page
at Harlequin.com for more titles.

DESERT WOLF
LINDA THOMAS-SUNDSTROM

PROTECTOR WOLF
LINDA O. JOHNSTON

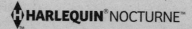

HARLEQUIN® NOCTURNE™

Recycling programs
for this product may
not exist in your area.

ISBN-13: 978-0-373-20858-6

Desert Wolf & Protector Wolf

Copyright © 2017 by Harlequin Books S.A.

The publisher acknowledges the copyright holders
of the individual works as follows:

Desert Wolf
Copyright © 2017 by Linda Thomas-Sundstrom

Protector Wolf
Copyright © 2017 by Linda O. Johnston

Printed in U.S.A.

CONTENTS

DESERT WOLF

Linda Thomas-Sundstrom

To my family, those here and those gone,
who always believed I had a story to tell.

The Desperado ghost town is far from empty...
but its inhabitants aren't ghosts.

Chapter 1

There was no man in the moon.

Every werewolf knew this.

The moon was female and a temptress. Her kiss was cool and her love ran hot. For Weres, Madame Moon was everything—lover, mistress, redeemer, betrayer. She bestowed power, strength, enhanced senses, lightning-fast reflexes and pain…terrible racking pain that long ago had turned former Texas Ranger Grant Wade inside out, but seemed normal to him now.

Tonight, the moon took up a good portion of the wide expanse of the star-filled Arizona sky and called to Grant with a seductive, silvery promise that made his shoulders twitch.

Only two other things Grant knew of felt anything remotely like this gut reaction: beautiful women and fine, aged whiskey…neither of which were present at the moment.

"Wait." Holding back tremors that were bubbling up inside, he addressed the moon. "Not yet. Soon."

The night was still warm after that day's unforgiving desert sun. Shirtless, wearing only jeans and boots, Grant rolled his shoulders to ease the growing aches of his imminent shape-shift. As a pure-blooded Lycan version of the werewolf species, shifting was part of his heritage. He liked it.

But he needed a little more time before he could do so, and he needed to keep his voice for a while longer. Long enough to corral the trespasser he was hunting out here, a rogue who brought trouble too close to home and was slippery as hell.

"Where are you?" Grant whispered to his prey. "What are you?"

The interloper whose arrival he anticipated could be human, though Grant doubted it. As a rule, humans weren't partial to acts as grisly as this crazy son of a bitch's grotesque taste for the raw meat of neighboring cattle. Disappearing animals had garnered the attention of angry ranchers with rifles, and those ranchers would be on the prowl tonight to protect their herds.

No. He suspected it was a half-crazed werewolf doing the damage. And if that scenario turned out to be true, the rogue had to be removed from human radar as quickly as possible. Werewolves had kept their presence and identities safe for over a thousand years and couldn't afford to blow it all now.

But damn...

The whole raw meat thing surrounding the freak he was after was a strange twist on abnormal. No werewolf Grant knew of went after cattle on the hoof. Most Weres, including him, preferred their burgers well done and on a bun.

These days, most Weres were as civilized as their human counterparts—at least 99 percent of the time. Humans just wouldn't like the fact that some police officers, nurses and even ER techs could actually be more than they seemed each time a full moon rolled around.

This trespasser was messing with those secrets. Grant couldn't afford to let angry ranchers get too close to his place of business. Keeping neighbors out of his hair and away from Desperado was imperative to protect the special beings harbored behind the old ghost town's shuttered windows.

Grant raised his head, sniffed the air.

A bittersweet scent left a tang on his tongue. Moonlight ruled the desert tonight in an almost-full phase. His inner wolf was expanding, waiting in anticipation, as the moon rose above the trees.

Unlike most Weres, Grant didn't have to give in to the moon's mystical allure. He could refuse the call if he chose to. A special gift had been twisted into his heritage, giving him the ability to shift with or without the moon calling the shots, when resistance for many others of his kind was futile.

"Just a few minutes more," he mused, almost ready for his transformation. Wolf blood made him faster and more flexible. It also made him lethal.

The first claw popped out as his fingers uncurled. The rest of them followed in rapid succession, long and razor sharp.

Pressure inside him was building. Ten seconds was all it would take to complete a full shape-shift. His unique abilities, combined with the purity of his bloodline, made him alpha of his own desert pack. Rattlesnakes and crazed lunatics aside, he was probably the most dangerous creature in the area.

"As for you," he said, speaking to the interloper he waited for. "Are you an unlucky bastard who'd been in the wrong place at the wrong time? Were you infected by a bite or scratch from a bad wolf and surprised when the next full moon came around? Because it seems no one has taught you how to behave."

Even after a bad bite or scratch, Grant knew, if a human being had been a good human before, he or she would be a good Were now. And good guys weren't cattle rustlers.

"You would have garnered sympathy if you had come knocking. Now look. The problems you've been causing have to be dealt with." The secrets hidden inside the town called Desperado were at stake and Grant was uncomfortable with how close to Desperado's gates he was standing. "So, come on. What are you waiting for?"

He searched the area for a hint of the trespasser and spoke again. "I am leader, watcher, gatekeeper, secret holder, guardian and reluctant ruler of a pack of like-bodied, like-minded Weres. Do you purposefully taunt me?"

His patience was wearing thin. Grant glanced once more at the moon then did a quick scan of the mountain range, sifting through the night smells in search of anomalies.

The air was loaded with unique fragrances only found in the West: a combination of sand, brush, over-heated rock, animals, cactus and the trees that tenaciously clung to the hillside despite a general lack of water. All those smells fit neatly into his mental data banks.

Except for one.

That one stood out like a shout.

Wrapped in the breeze was the unmistakable odor of

blood. There had been another fresh kill, the third in as many passing months. That pissed him off.

"Damn fool." His voice rumbled. "Who the hell do you think you are to put all of us in jeopardy? It's only a matter of time before we find you."

The fact that the creature out there had so far eluded capture was also an anomaly with a wolf pack on the prowl. The only question to consider was whether this trespassing idiot would turn out to be adaptable if offered a choice.

Grant turned upwind. His shoulders twitched again. *"If you're a Were, and in the vicinity, you should be able to pick up my thoughts."* Grant silently sent the message over the telepathic channel most werewolves used to communicate. "Barring that, maybe you can hear my voice."

He detected no response at all.

"Okay. All right." Grant raised his face to let the moonlight soak in. "It's time to up the ante."

Waves of cold penetrated his bronzed skin and sifted downward, layer by layer, to take control of muscles and nerves. The pain the cold brought was immediate and terrible, but was quickly replaced by a searing heat that would fuel mounds of muscle.

Grant welcomed the discomfort. He welcomed the wolf. Vestiges of his human shape began to shred as he became one with the song that sang to him now. Wolf music. The call of the wild.

I am Lycan, alpha and a servant of the moon. Whatever the hell is going on around here needs to be set straight.

Muscles trembled as they began to expand. Grant's jeans felt tight. His boots felt cramped and his face stung. With his last speaking breath, he warned, "Time to face the consequences of your actions, whoever you are," knowing that any rogue wolf with half a brain would run the other way.

Cheekbones rearranged with a rub of ligaments. Vertebrae crackled with sounds no human would ever want to hear. Rabbits scurried. Coyotes whimpered and tucked their tails as Grant Wade, now half man and half wolf, straightened up in the light…his transition punctuated by gunshots in the distance.

Hell, had ranchers found that rogue?

Voiceless now, his body corded with tense, fine-tuned muscle, Grant issued a roar that echoed along the red-rock canyon walls behind him…and began the steep slide downhill.

Chapter 2

Paxton Hall wrinkled her nose as she stepped off the plane.

She pressed her blond fringe of bangs off her forehead and squinted at the scene in front of her. The jet had parked its little tin-covered ass in the middle of nowhere, it seemed to her. Unlike private airports in the East, this Arizona stopover would require a long-distance sprint across an acre of molten tarmac in the blazing sun to get to the terminal. And she was wearing heels.

"We'll unload the luggage," someone said from behind her. "You can pick up your bags at the gate."

Swell. Her bags were going to get a ride. Maybe she could hitch a trip to the terminal along with them.

"Thanks," she said, watching heat rise from the asphalt like a wavering mirage. She hadn't forgotten the extremes of Arizona weather and the scorching wind that made everything look barren, but being born here wasn't an automatic passport to feeling familiar with it now.

Paxton didn't reach for the metal stair rail, which would have been a sure way to scald her fingers. She was seriously reconsidering the viability of this trip, not quite sure why she was in Arizona. She had her own gig in the East and a nice rented town house. Her income was steady, if not fabulous, and good enough to support her current lifestyle.

So, why did she really need this Arizona property her father had left her, other than for a trip down Nostalgia Lane and the small chunk of change a couple of hundred acres in the middle of nowhere might bring when it sold?

Except that she couldn't actually sell it, as things were, since her father, God rest his soul, had left the old tourist attraction that sat smack in the center of all that land she had inherited to someone else. Someone unrelated to the family. An unfamiliar name in the will.

Who the hell was Grant Wade, anyway?

How was she supposed to sell a parcel of land that circled, but didn't include, the central piece?

"Safe journey," the attendant said politely, interrupting her thoughts. "Will you need anything else, Ms. Hall?"

"No. Thanks," Paxton returned absently as she headed down the steps with a tight grip on her briefcase.

That man… Grant Wade…would either have to buy her out or turn the Desperado ghost town over to her so she could sell the place and be out of here—back to civilization, green grass and cool breezes. When she was in Maryland, coming here had seemed like the thing to do. Now that she was here, Paxton hoped she hadn't been wrong about that.

She'd worn a skirt, which allowed hot air to flow up and over her thighs as she stepped onto asphalt so overheated her heels seemed to sink in. With that hot caress on her naked legs came flashbacks…memories of sweltering desert heat on her face when she was a kid and how much she had liked the soaring temperatures back then. A very long time ago.

She remembered the distinct smells of heat-scorched land and the way her young skin had first burned before becoming a sun-kissed gold as summers wore on. Here in Arizona is where her wildness had first blossomed and where she had learned to ride and run. It's where her mother had died, right before little Paxton had been sent away to a distant relative on the East Coast, away from this place and far from her dad.

Those old memories were more reminiscent of bad dreams now. But the tingle at the base of her neck signified something more complex than just reminisces and the firing up of a few random nerve endings. It brought home the fact that she had never seen her dad again after leaving this place. Not even once. She hadn't heard from him—no birthday cards, Christmas packages or calls—in all that time.

Twenty frigging years.

And now Andrew Hall was dead, and she was back where she started. The land of sand and sun. Because of that, Paxton was determined to be trouble incarnate if Mr. Grant Wade didn't listen to reason. She was going to bury her fear of confrontations and make Grant Wade assume *trouble* was her middle name.

Got that, Wade?

Besides, the man had to be at least sixty-five years

old if he had been her father's friend. That land might be a burden for an old guy. She'd done some research, of course, but the only person the internet had turned up with that name in this part of the United States was a Texas Ranger nowhere near an advanced age. So her Grant Wade had to be an old guy who had inconveniently stayed off everyone's front page.

Paxton squinted as she scanned the tarmac, where the damn heat waves were manifesting into the form of a man—one lone man in all that wide-open space, seemingly walking toward her.

Shielding her eyes with a hand, Paxton wondered whether to keep walking and meet this guy or stay in place and fry in black silk on the hot asphalt.

She kept walking.

Behind her, she heard the luggage cart pull away from the plane. From somewhere far off came the static sound of a speaker. Those things were inconsequential. Her eyes were trained on the man who walked with the casual, apparently single-minded intention of meeting up with her. Had to be her, because at the moment she was the only one out here and he wasn't headed to a parked plane.

Who was this guy?

The stranger was tall, lean, and wore a wide-brimmed hat. Broad shoulders balanced a narrow waist. Long legs were clad in jeans, and his boots made soft thudding sounds on the pavement. A silver buckle on his belt flashed in the sun the way diamonds flared beneath jewelry store lighting.

Those things screamed the word *cowboy*.

A white shirt with the sleeves rolled up to his elbows showed off sun-bronzed skin. As he approached, Paxton saw that enough top buttons on the shirt were open to lay bare a triangle of skin that attracted her attention for a little too long. When she looked up, he was close enough for her to see his wide, engaging smile.

And his face...

Christ almighty. It was chiseled, angular, with taut skin that fell somewhere on the golden spectrum. This guy, whoever he was, seemed to have inherited a lucky combination of genes that made him both elegant and rugged. The whole package suggested a new classification of the term *handsome*. Even if he was a cowboy.

"Paxton Hall?" He stopped a few feet from her and removed his hat, showing off a mass of shaggy auburn hair.

He was fine to look at, sure, Paxton noted. But what could he possibly want?

"Ms. Hall?" he repeated, with a slight variation.

"Yes." She continued to shield her eyes. "That's me."

The hunk's smile was as brilliant as the rest of him, and that was saying something. Fine lines shot out from the corners of his eyes in honor of some years in the sun without detracting from the overall hunky look.

Paxton wished she could see the color of those eyes, hidden behind his sunglasses, and wondered if they'd be blue. Light blue eyes set in sun-darkened skin would have topped the whole thing off nicely.

"I've come to escort you to your hotel," he said in a deep voice that ran ridiculous circles around Paxton's impoverished libido. It was obvious to her that she hadn't taken enough time lately to explore the ramifications of having been without a boyfriend for several months now.

Plus...didn't every woman have cowboy fantasies?

"Your hotel," he repeated, probably wondering if she had hearing problems.

There was just something about his voice and how suggestive it was of star-filled desert nights and the almost unearthly scent of night-blooming flowers. Two sentences from him and Paxton was thrown back in time to when she had first noticed things like those strong, sweet Arizona scents.

Or maybe it was all just a side effect of the stifling heat.

"I didn't call for a taxi service," she said.

He nodded. "I thought you might like a ride."

"Because?"

"It's hot." He was still grinning, and that grin was contagious.

Paxton smiled back.

"I totally agree about the heat. But I'm pretty sure you didn't answer my question about not calling a service," she said.

"Your attorney mentioned that you might be headed this way today."

Okay. That made sense. She felt better.

"In that case, yes. Thanks. I'd like a ride to…" Paxton paused, mid-speech. "I didn't book a hotel, sure there are plenty of them."

He nodded again. "No problem. I'll take you to one. I think you'll find most of the accommodations around here acceptable."

He was staring at her, not exactly rudely, but with the kind of lingering appraisal that brought on a blush. He'd be taking in the black silk shirt, the high heels and the private plane her attorney had let her use because several well-off clients needed to hitch a ride back to Maryland. This guy would probably be thinking he'd have to book her a suite in a fancy boutique hotel.

Hell, she couldn't afford a suite. Not that she wouldn't

like one. Cash wasn't exactly tight, but it was on close watch. She didn't get paid for extra time off from her gig as a nurse in the ER, and her return trip to Maryland was on a commercial flight, in coach.

"That would be great," Paxton said. "Any hotel will do. I'm not fussy and I won't be here long."

She just needed to get out of this heat and into different clothes. Big thanks would be due to her lawyer for thinking about her enough to send a gorgeous chauffeur.

That smile he was still offering? Dazzling. Yet Paxton's instincts warned her that the guy's smile hid something. A trace of concern, maybe? Concern for what? That she'd be a prissy Easterner for whom the extremes of comfort were paramount, when that was miles from the truth?

If they spent any time together, he'd find out how unprepared she was for this trip into her past. Her black silk shirt hadn't been the greatest idea for day wear in a sun-drenched state. Cowboy would note that, too. She had worn it in honor of her father's recent passing, in spite of the fact that she hadn't really known her dad.

Briefly, Paxton closed her eyes, thinking that anyone would have assumed she'd have gotten over that kind of loss, along with old abandonment issues. But being here in Arizona again was causing a sudden emotional upheaval. Just a few steps off the plane had been all it took to bring the old days back.

"This way," the cowboy said, stepping aside, waving his hat at the terminal. "I hope you don't mind riding in a truck."

So, no real chauffeur then. Just a favor from someone her lawyer knew.

"That would be fine," she returned. "Would you mind confirming my attorney's name?"

"Daniel Dunn, Esquire."

"Do you know Dan personally?"

"As well as anyone can know a lawyer by phone."

"Great." Paxton moved forward, eager to get to the terminal. If this guy knew her lawyer, he had to be legit.

"Do you think we could get something cold to drink on the way to the hotel?" she asked.

"It would be my pleasure to make that happen," her escort congenially replied.

Though she didn't glance sideways, Paxton was aware of every move the guy made. He purposefully shortened his strides to accommodate hers. Having him beside her was both a boon and another unsettling feature of this trip. Speed hampered by the height of her heels, Paxton felt doubly foolish and out of place. She no longer belonged here. She was trespassing on the past—both its ideals and its pain.

What the hell was I thinking?

As they entered the small terminal, her companion placed a hand on her elbow to guide her toward the bags. His touch was electric, empathetic. Paxton wanted to lean into him for the kind of support she needed to get through this ordeal, when giving in to the urge to fold up like an accordion would have been the end of her.

Gently, he steered her toward her luggage, the two small bags she had seen fit to bring for a weekend in the desert. Her companion lifted the bags easily and reached to take her briefcase. She gave him a firm head shake, preferring to hold on to the paperwork she'd need for a quick sale when the reclusive Grant Wade agreed to her terms.

"There's a watering hole down the road," this guy said. "The truck is right out front."

When she glanced at him, he added, "It's a café. We can get something to drink there or take it to go."

Paxton nodded. She followed her guide through the revolving doors and onto the street where a large blue truck sat parked at the curb. Like the cowboy beside her, its lines were tall, long and sturdy. Chrome wheels and other fancy stuff were missing. The hood was covered in dust and there was a baseball-sized dent in the passenger door. This truck was a working man's transportation, not merely a vehicle meant to prove male bravado.

After tossing her bags in the back, her makeshift chauffeur came around to open her door. Getting in while wearing a short skirt took some feminine know-how when the truck's cab was so high off the ground.

Once she was inside, Paxton stuck out an arm to stop the door from closing and faced the guy helping her. "I really am grateful for the ride. And I'm sorry I seem to have lost my manners. I didn't ask your name."

"Wade," he said, the dazzling smile no longer in evidence. "Name's Grant Wade."

Chapter 3

Paxton Hall wasn't what Grant had expected, and that came as a surprise.

She looked the part of the spoiled young woman he had expected to show up, and she dressed well, but Paxton didn't really seem spoiled. She'd brought one bag and an overnight case that not too many fancy outfits would have traveled well in. She had been happy to let him choose her hotel and had allowed him to guide her along without complaint.

And she was beautiful. Incredibly beautiful. Though he'd seen a few pictures of her in Andrew Hall's file, in person, Paxton Hall was a whole new deal.

He liked all the details ringing up—the big eyes that were an unusual amber color, the porcelain skin and the kind of oval face that begged a second and third look. Dark blond hair was cut in a swingy, shoulder-length style and appeared to be natural in color. Very little makeup muddied her face, just a swipe of something dark on her eyelashes and a hint of rose on her cheeks. In his estimation, she didn't need even that.

She was antsy, her discomfort easy to read. Being beside her made his nerves buzz. Back in the terminal, when he had touched her arm, that buzz had been transmitted to a spot way down deep inside him.

The feminine perfume she wore didn't help with his initial response to her, either. Some kind of woodsy aroma trailed her, almost completely covering up a more elusive scent he couldn't yet place. Everything about Paxton Hall, all those details, were laced with a layer of subdued anxiety and anger. Because of him, in part.

He slammed her door and walked around the truck, acknowledging that Paxton was surprised by this unexpected meet up. She knew his name now, but he'd had the advantage of getting to see what she was like before she found him out and the arguments he anticipated began.

Did she consider him the enemy? A problem to be solved?

He had told the truth about her lawyer giving him a heads-up on her visit and knew Paxton would have questions. Plenty of them. Most of those were questions he wouldn't be able to answer, due to secrets he had to keep, though she deserved some kind of explanation for what was written in that will.

The reason for her visit was a no-brainer. Paxton Hall wanted to sell the land her father left her and have nothing more to do with her early Arizona upbringing. But her father had left him part of that acreage in order to make sure a sale didn't happen, so surely Andrew Hall must have foreseen that some sort of contact between his two heirs would take place.

As an ex-Ranger with connections, Grant had been tracking Paxton since her father's death a few weeks ago. And here she sat, in his truck, putting *traitor* and *Grant Wade* together in the same unspoken breath. She'd be thinking that the man she had been trusting to get her settled for the night had turned out to be more like the personification of sabotage.

Grant climbed into the cab and rested both hands on the wheel. Without looking at his guest, he said, "Would you like to talk now or wait a while?"

"Now," she said breathlessly.

Her attention on him was unforgiving. His Were senses told him Paxton's heart rate had kicked up a notch and that Paxton Hall had expected someone else attached to the name Wade. Someone different. She was trying to reconcile his image with her former ideas about who might turn up to potentially oppose her.

"If you're uncomfortable, I can call you a taxi," he said.

"I've been uncomfortable since I read my father's will, as you must already know."

Direct and to the point. Grant liked that, usually.

She turned on the seat. "You are that same guy?"

"One and the same, if you're talking about Andrew's legacy," Grant replied. "If you're talking about anything else, I probably didn't do it."

Levity wasn't going to get him anywhere. He didn't have to look at Paxton to feel the animosity creeping into her tone.

"Why?" she demanded.

Pretending to misunderstand what she was asking would have been lame, so he said, "It was important to your father and to others that the property wasn't sold."

"Why?" she repeated.

"I can't tell you about the specifics of that right now, other than to stress your father's desire for me to hold on to the town."

"You're talking about an old tourist attraction that's been closed for twenty years. I fail to see why hanging on to a defunct ghost town wins out over selling the place," she argued. "Surely you have better things to do than keep track of it."

"Not many people would understand my reasons for staying here," Grant said. "Your father did."

She zeroed in on that. "You knew my father well, then?"

"Truthfully, I didn't know him much at all."

The way she drew back told him that Andrew Hall's daughter hadn't considered that kind of an answer. Had she imagined he had goaded Andrew into handing him the town? Finessed Desperado out of a tough man like Andrew Hall?

"What you're saying doesn't make sense," she eventually remarked. "Maybe you can explain things better?"

Grant nodded. "We had a deal."

"You and my father?"

He nodded again. "Our deal was that I would inherit the town when he passed, and that I'd take care of it and never sell the land Desperado sits on or allow anyone else to sell it."

That slice of the truth would sound absurd to the woman sitting beside him. The whole truth could never be spoken, of course, though Grant could see Paxton was firm in her resolve to get to the bottom of her father's strange bequest. He just couldn't let her find that reason. Paxton Hall, along with all the other humans on the planet, had to be kept from learning Desperado's secrets—and his.

That much, at least, was clear to Grant. What wasn't immediately clear was how he was supposed to oppose her when Paxton was here, in his damn truck, with her pale face and her black clothes that reflected her consideration for a man she hadn't really known.

"Why didn't he just leave the whole thing to you?" she asked.

"I'm not sure, actually. That would have made more sense."

And it would have kept Paxton away, maybe, a fact that he had considered since meeting Andrew Hall. He had a glimmer of an idea that Paxton's father might have sent her away in the first place so she didn't learn about the werewolves in residence here, and that Andrew's ongoing silence had furthered the cause of shielding his daughter from truths too difficult to explain.

"Will you sell it to me?" she asked.

And there they were, at a standstill. Checkmate. Paxton would assume her request was reasonable, and it would have been if things had been different.

Grant started the engine. "Do you still want that drink?"

"I'd rather you answered my question."

He looked at the white-faced woman who couldn't have been more than two or three years younger than his twenty-eight. She looked even younger than that, though. Paxton truly was an eyeful, though that couldn't matter in their negotiations.

"Maybe you'll want to turn right around and go home when I reiterate that I'm not going to sell," he suggested. "Why waste money on a hotel when more time here won't get you what you want?"

"You might change your mind," she countered stubbornly.

"Not going to happen, Paxton. I made a deal."

The heat inside the car was harsh. Moisture had gathered at Paxton's temples, dampening her hair. The black silk was starting to stick to her in ways Grant shouldn't have noticed.

In any other situation, he would have liked a close-up with Paxton Hall. As things stood, the best case scenario would be for her to go away mad and never look back. She might try to file a lawsuit in order to force him to sell, but her father's attorney wasn't going to condone a move like that.

"Look," he said. "I don't want to make an enemy of the daughter of the man who left something valuable to me. So how can we resolve things before that happens?"

"Too late," she said, reaching for the door handle, "if you refuse to see my side of this argument and either buy me out or sell."

Grant reached to take hold of her briefcase, stopping Paxton from opening the door. "Stay," he said, removing his sunglasses.

She turned her head. Amber eyes lighted on him, connecting with his gaze. Earnest eyes. Wounded. Haunted. Wild.

A stunning jolt of something extraordinary hit Grant in the chest and then melted downward as a second jolt, larger than the first, hit. He had seen eyes like those before and didn't want to face what that meant. He didn't want to face *her* with what that meant.

What he saw in those eyes quite possibly changed everything—his future and hers.

Paxton Hall was a Were.

He had no doubt about it.

Still, Grant could see that she was ignorant of that fact and therefore didn't know what was in store. He believed this because he couldn't feel the thing she kept hidden inside her, in the dark. Her scent had kindled his discovery. Those big eyes of hers said it all.

Grant broke eye contact and dropped his hold on the briefcase, stung by the realization of who and what Paxton really was. Worse yet, the air in the cab suddenly seemed charged with wayward electricity that had nowhere to go due to the fact that his inner wolf had been awakened by the directness of Paxton's gaze.

"What I mean is that we can get to know each other better if you stay as planned," he said, wondering if he could let her go at all now that he knew what eventually would happen to her. "Maybe then we'll both understand where we're coming from."

Everything about this new turn of events was dangerous, he realized. Remaining close to Paxton could be bad when wolf might call to wolf, setting free what now lay curled up inside her. Letting her go without an inkling of what she was would be equally dangerous. Her wolf had to show sometime and was long overdue. For wolves, timing was everything.

She studied him frankly as she thought over his suggestion. Her eyes never left his face.

"Will you consider buying me out?" she asked.

"We can talk about that and the reasons I can't agree to doing what you ask."

Grant's mind whirled with things he wanted to say, but couldn't.

I now think your father might have been keeping Desperado for you, leaving it in my care, he wanted to tell her. *For when you...in case you needed help and a place to go for a while, among others just like you.*

No way could he tell Paxton any of that, since he was only now beginning to understand it himself.

Had her father meant to bring her here for this reason, intending for his heirs to meet? Could Hall have masterminded all of this to ensure his estranged daughter's first transition from human to Were was in safe hands? Grant Wade's hands?

"How about if we discuss it now?" she said.

Grant shook his head. "Give me a few hours to think things over."

She released the door handle and sat back, unable to mask her hopeful expression. "All right. A few hours."

He couldn't help but notice how small she looked in the truck. Although Paxton had to be at least five foot five, she was a shade too slim and as willowy as the trees along the riverbed.

She wasn't lighthearted. Hints of sadness weighed down her shoulders. Did she possess a strong Hall family backbone under all that silk?

It seemed that Andrew had also kept Grant in the dark about a few minor details concerning this legacy. And now, secrets on top of secrets had left him in the hot seat.

Grant reached for the gearshift, mulling things over.

Most likely Paxton didn't know that her father had followed her life from behind the scenes, and how much Andrew must have loved her.

Sooner or later, Paxton's wolf would make an appearance. There was no way to postpone that event forever, no matter where she lived.

And that made Andrew Hall one tricky son of a bitch.

"You believe I'm your enemy, but we're actually more alike than you know," he said, growing more uncomfortable as the minutes passed. Because, hell…

Just one long glance at those golden eyes of hers had done more than make him realize what kind of DNA she carried. It had also done him in. Captured him completely. Put him on her side. Whatever haunted her, now haunted him.

His wolf wanted to growl in protest over the burden laid upon him, because the wolf had a heads-up on what her innate sense of sadness might actually be.

Paxton Hall was a she-wolf in waiting, and her timing couldn't have been worse. With a full moon due the following night, she'd be too close to a shape-shifting pack. If she were to face another wolf up close, that meeting might bring out the secrets kept from her all this time. And it wouldn't be pretty.

It seemed like more trouble had landed in his lap, and that these next few hours were not going to be easy to get through. He had asked Paxton to stay when it now might be imperative to keep his distance from her. He wanted more than anything to take her in his arms and offer comfort, something she hadn't ever gotten from her estranged father…and that, too, could be dangerous for her.

Damned if I do. Damned if I don't.

With one more glance at Paxton, Grant said, "I think I'll need that drink."

The look she returned made his stomach tighten.

"Make mine a double," she said.

Chapter 4

As Grant Wade pulled the truck away from the curb, it dawned on Paxton that there might be a downside to remaining in his presence.

From where she sat, on the opposite side of the truck, she still felt the impression of his hand on her elbow, left over from when he helped with her bags. When she had looked at his face, searching for more hints about his character, what she'd found was a man who might not be as happy to accommodate her visit as he seemed.

They were at odds about Desperado, and Grant Wade showed signs of discomfort. Although he rested one arm casually on the window frame and the other on the wheel, those bronzed forearms were corded with tension.

Were those arms sexy? *Yes.*

Did that matter? *No.*

So, why had she even thought of questions like those?

Truth was, Paxton wondered what that smooth golden skin would be like to touch and chastised herself for thinking she'd like to find out.

Her reactions to Grant Wade were as automatic as breathing. In her defense, most women liked strong, sexy men who didn't overtly try to overpower with all that testosterone. Men who could easily take control of any situation, yet sometimes knew better than to try. Handsome men at ease in their own skins who radiated self-confidence and looked exactly like Grant Wade did, from Stetson to scuffed boots.

Weren't those things tied to what constituted wet dreams for women? Because surely she was going to have a dream like that about this guy tonight, no matter how far apart they stood on her father's deal.

"Name your poison," he said to her as the truck rolled past a few strip malls and gas stations, its engine purring like a well-tuned tractor.

"Iced tea. Heavy on the ice."

He gave her a sideways glance.

"I don't think alcohol would further my cause much. Do you?" Not wanting to relax, Paxton leaned back against the leather seat, liking the masculine smell of the truck. The trip to Arizona had been taxing. She would have given anything to be able to close her eyes.

"Hotel choices," he said. "Big or small?"

"Cheap."

He nodded.

"Then you'll give in and buy me out of all that acreage. Or vice versa," she added.

"You're pretty confident one of those two things will happen?"

"Aren't you?"

Her companion didn't reply to that question and angled the truck into a parking space beside a small road-side café.

"Hungry?" he asked.

"Famished, actually."

"I hope you like burgers."

"Not unless they come with fries."

"Then you, my fine lady, are in luck," Grant Wade said as he turned off the engine. "Though you will have to sit across from me."

"I'll manage somehow," Paxton returned.

The café was nearly empty this time of day. A few small tables ringed a linoleum patchwork floor and three faded red booths hugged the windows. The only waitress in sight, dressed in faded jeans and an apron, eyed them curiously when she and Grant slid into a booth. After Grant returned the glance, the waitress ambled over.

"I guess I'm conspicuously foreign," Paxton said when their order went in.

"This is a place for regulars. Anyone new is suspicious."

"Maybe she likes you. She's staring."

"Nope. Shirleen is just curious. She has imprinted with…" He stopped there without finishing the strange remark.

"Does that mean she's engaged to someone?" Paxton asked.

Her cowboy nemesis took a swig of the iced tea Shirleen had brought over. "Yep. Western slang for people coupling up."

Paxton didn't share how much she might have liked to couple up with Grant Wade after first laying eyes on him, since that wasn't going to happen. She hoped to get the paperwork signed and be back on a plane.

They ate in silence, an unspoken truce, of sorts, with the curious waitress looking on. Grant didn't seem to notice the scrutiny, but Paxton couldn't get much of her burger down. She was relieved when Grant took care of paying the bill. By the time they headed for the truck, evening was settling in with a pink glow on the horizon.

"It's quite beautiful," she said, staring at the landscape for a few minutes before getting into the truck. "I had forgotten about that. Maybe I was too young to notice."

"You remember being here?" Grant Wade asked.

"I remember a few small things. Mostly unimportant stuff."

"Like pretty sunsets?"

She nodded. "Yes. Like that."

"There's no place better for showy horizons than this one," he said.

"Not even in Texas?" she asked, testing her new theory on Grant Wade being that former Texas Ranger.

"Similar, but not the same," he replied, opening her door and playing the gentleman card well. He added, "You know about Texas?"

Paxton shrugged.

"Know thine enemies?" he suggested.

"Hopefully you aren't one of them."

"Hopefully not," he agreed, waiting for her to climb in. "We just shared fries."

More silence ensued as they drove to the edge of town. What more was there to say without getting back into the argument over the property? Grant had asked for time to consider everything she had suggested. That was fine, if he didn't take too long.

"I'd like to go there tomorrow," she finally said when

a tiny motel on the edge of a wide expanse of desert came into view.

"Back to Maryland?"

She shook her head. "Desperado."

He took a beat to reply. "I'm not sure that would be a good idea."

"You'll be driving over my property every time you go in or out of that old town. I think you owe me a look, don't you?"

His hesitation wasn't subtle.

"I can always rent a car," she persisted. "I wouldn't be trespassing if I stopped at the gate. I won't bother the ghosts."

When he offered no comment, Paxton got the impression Grant Wade might be hiding something out there in the desert that he didn't want anyone to discover. Had he found gold?

"You said *valuable*," she noted.

He glanced at her.

"You mentioned that my father left you something valuable."

"Did I?"

She waited him out, wondering what kind of actual reason there could be for keeping her away from the old town. Maybe Grant was planning on reopening Desperado as a tourist attraction and didn't want to mention that. Perhaps his deal with her father had been to make the old place live again and earn Grant Wade, former Texas Ranger, a decent living. If so, the deal was terribly shortsighted, since everyone involved had to realize that no one could reach Desperado without her permission granting the right-of-way.

Surely her father's lawyer would have pointed out to Grant that buying her out would be to his benefit? The truck had stopped without her noticing. Grant got out, took her bags from the back and again came around to open her door.

"Small and cheap," he said with a nod to the motel.

Funny, Paxton thought. That's exactly what she felt like as she watched Grant Wade enter the lobby of the two-story U-shaped building ahead of her. Small and cheap. She'd sell the land for a song if it meant getting back to her life without taking Grant Wade up on whatever emotion he hid behind those sunglasses.

Reluctantly, she followed Grant to the lobby, trying hard not to stare at the way his jeans emphasized his magnificently compact backside and how his auburn hair, badly in need of a trim, brushed his shirt collar. Taking stock of those things made her uneasy. Still, she had to assess her opponent and hope that the best person would win this argument.

As the hot wind caressed her face, Paxton felt even stranger, in a déjà-vu kind of way, as if it wasn't actually possible for a person to get over their beginnings.

She looked at her feet, then tipped her face toward the motel's neon sign. Her gaze flicked to the light of the lobby's open doorway, filled at the moment by Grant Wade. He was waiting. But what, exactly, was he waiting for—the woman to tag along behind him, or the completion of a deal in his favor?

Maybe she was just projecting her own thoughts on the matter, because, damn it, the man was messing with her sense of justice. Grant Wade, in the flesh, suddenly seemed like the perfect guy to manage a ghost town in the Old West.

And he was looking at her in that way he had, making her feel as though she was the only woman in the world on his mind.

Chapter 5

What did Paxton think he was going to do with the old ghost town?

Grant had taken to swearing under his breath and did so repeatedly in honor of the situation he found himself in now as he stood on the threshold to Paxton's room. Half the space in that room was taken up by a bed, and in a perfect world, he and Paxton might have worked through their differences on top of it. Of course, they weren't going to do any such thing. He had to get in and get out without lingering.

Cautiously placing one boot inside, then the other, Grant set Paxton's bags down on the carpet. With his hands now free, he thought seriously about reaching for her and got the feeling she might have been willing to have that happen.

Then again, maybe not.

Besides, he was needed elsewhere.

Open curtains at the window allowed the evening moonlight in. That light was a reminder that he'd need to be on guard again tonight for the return of the slippery rogue he hadn't been able to catch in the months before. His pack would already be prowling near the hills, careful to avoid ranchers doing the same thing. After four months, most of the valley was in an uproar.

Paxton stood in the doorway behind him. She hadn't followed him inside. Her watchful gaze burned a hole in the back of his shirt, and that was bringing up all sorts of wayward emotions that were never good for a werewolf to have in a closed space.

"Well, guess I'll head out." Grant brushed his hands on his jeans as if wiping away the idea of an imminent and untimely appearance of his claws. He was usually good at compartmentalizing his emotions.

"My thanks are piling up," she said when he turned to face her. "Pretty soon I'll be the one owing you a meal."

Grant nodded. "No thanks are necessary. It's an awkward situation we're confronted with. I'll be the first to agree."

She remained in the doorway, blocking his exit. Maybe Paxton was afraid of what he might do if she came inside. Maybe she could read his mind about that bed.

"I'll need a car," she said.

"You can have the truck if you need to go somewhere."

He fished in his pocket and tossed her the keys.

"I'm going to Desperado in the morning," she reminded him.

"I'd advise against it, Paxton, unless I'm riding along."

Palming the keys, she said, "How will you get home if I have these?"

"Friends."

"Do you live nearby?"

"I live on the ranch near Desperado's gates, as you quite possibly already knew."

"In my old house?"

Grant noted how her voice had lowered. She'd likely be remembering the house she grew up in. *My* house, she had said. Did she think of it fondly?

He said, "It's still there. A little worse for wear, but standing. I've made some necessary repairs."

"After you sell, or I sell, will you go back to Texas?" she asked, which Grant thought was pretty cheeky for someone facing an opponent in a motel room located in a state she hadn't set her stilettos in since she was six years old. Just how far would her confidence take her, though?

He didn't glance again to the window. Didn't need to note where the moon was. He was looking at Paxton with his wolf's eyes, watching her unfasten the top button of her shirt because she was used to a more moderate climate.

Sensing his attention, she dropped her hands to her sides. "That was not an invitation."

Ignoring the comment, Grant pointed to the floor-model air conditioner. "Press the button on the left and you'll soon feel better."

Paxton's cheeks colored slightly. He noticed that, too. Now that dusk had come and gone, and darkness had arrived, moonlight flooded the motel's balcony behind her as she tossed his keys back to him.

"See you tomorrow," Grant said, with his hat in his

hand like every good Texas boy under a roof. "Breakfast?"

She shook her head. Paxton's hands were shaking, too. Why? Were her quakes a sign of pent-up anger? Maybe the moon was finally affecting her in some small way?

That was bound to happen sometime.

Moving to the window, Grant closed the curtains halfway to mute the moonlight. A random thought crossed his mind that moon children all over the world would be tuning in to that bright silver disc in the sky.

But this wasn't the time for explaining anything about that to the woman across from him. She wouldn't have believed him, anyway.

"I'm leaving. It's safe to come inside now," he announced, heading for the doorway she hadn't yet entered.

They were face-to-face, very close for a few seconds before Paxton stepped back. Close enough for Grant to feel her warm breath on his chin and to observe the tight line of her full, lush lips. There was no eye contact between them this time, which was for the best. Any further connection with those haunted amber eyes of hers, and he might have…

Well, he might have forgotten about who she was and why she was here, and also about proper decorum with strangers.

"Breakfast?" he repeated to scatter the images of what he might have done in this room with Paxton Hall if she had been anyone else.

"I'll meet you out there," she said soberly. "At Desperado. I'll find my way."

Her black silk shirt had opened just enough below her collarbones for him to get a quick view of Paxton's flawless ivory skin. It was rare to see pale people in the West, and the contrast between the black silk and the porcelain skin beneath it seemed to him a metaphor of sorts. All this time, she had assumed she was human. How could she have thought otherwise if things had never been explained to her? But the silk was only a top layer. Peel that back, and what lay beneath would reveal the real Paxton Hall.

Bathed in moonlight and the slanted glow from the motel's neon sign, Paxton seemed vulnerable and alone. Her mother had died long ago. She'd never known her father. Grant hated to leave her, but he had to.

After one quick brush of his hair with his fingers, Grant set his hat on his head, feeling the need to offer Paxton something, even if what he was about to say might sound trite.

"You're not alone. I want you to understand that," he said.

Confusion crossed her features.

"I'll take you there tomorrow," he continued. "I'll take you to Desperado first thing in the morning."

Relief softened her expression. Happy with that, Grant added, "Whatever you might be thinking, I'm not the enemy."

Another step brought him close to her. After a second quick glance toward the window, he lowered his voice. "No one here is out to hurt you. Please remember that."

Daring to touch her, Grant placed a finger against her lips, fighting an overwhelming urge to replace those fingers with his mouth. But that kind of unanticipated incursion would have ended any future dealings they might have. He got that.

Her lips were soft against his fingertips, though. And she didn't back away from his touch.

Damn those haunted eyes of yours.

Damn those lips.

He almost said those things out loud.

Hiding a shudder similar to the one he saw pass through her, Grant spoke again. "Good night. Sleep well."

It took all of his willpower—every last ounce of it—to leave her there and keep walking.

In the back of his mind, he was sure she wanted to call him back.

Fighting the impulse to shout for him to return, Paxton watched Grant go, believing the sincerity in his voice when he'd said all those things about her not being alone. Instincts seldom led her astray and were telling her now that Grant Wade would have capitulated about the property if he had been able to. Something held him back, some part of the deal he'd made with her father that hadn't been made public or available to her. Besides the mess she had found herself in, it seemed there were more secrets to uncover.

"Is it gold?" she mused. "The grand reopening of Desperado?"

If either of those things governed his deal with her dad, why hadn't Grant just come out and mentioned it? They both stood to gain from public access to the old ghost town. Land value surrounding a viable business would make her property worth more. And if that were the case, maybe Grant would make enough money to eventually buy her out—if, in fact, he was short on funds at this point.

That had to be the sticking point here, right? Money? Otherwise, owning everything would be of benefit to him. Truthfully, she didn't give a damn about his plans for the old place. Right now, she just wanted nothing more than to go home and forget about all of this.

Her cowboy stopped when he reached the truck, and turned around. He didn't wave. He wore no smile. His only offering was a quick nod in her direction before he climbed into the truck. After that, he sat for some time before starting the engine, as if he might be reluctant to leave.

Did he have more to say?

Did she?

Paxton waited until the truck backed out of the lot, feeling caught up in the treacherous thrill of having been close to Grant Wade for a minute or two. His brief touch had contributed a lot to the current heat spell.

She was burning up, on fire and hog-tied until she got what she wanted.

Behind her, inside the room, the air conditioner waited for her to punch the button. Overhead, the small neon sign buzzed. Moonlight flowed across the desert in the distance, unbroken by barriers and buildings, having risen above the mountain range.

She remembered damp skin and unrequited longings, as if those feelings had merely been temporarily buried somewhere. Rushing back to her were more remembrances of heat, wind and moonlight, along with memories of running through the brush howling like a coyote and pretending to be one of them.

Paxton closed her eyes.

Somewhere near those distant mountains the buildings of a decrepit town nestled. The place had been legit once, a real mining hub that had fallen on hard times when the mines were tapped out. In the forties, movies had been made there with bronco-riding cowboy stars. At present, who knew what kind of shape the place was in? Twenty years had passed since she played on those dirt streets, and the buildings had been older than shit then.

The truck had disappeared. Only the hum of neon was left in a quiet night. Paxton wanted to raise her face to the night sky in search of a nonexistent breeze, and experienced a sudden feeling of abandonment that was both odd and absurd since she had just met Grant Wade.

"If you're hiding something that affects this decision, I need to know what it is," Paxton whispered. "I won't care. I swear I won't care. I just need the truth."

Her mind turned toward a darker theory.

Knowing she'd be going to see Desperado in the morning, had Grant set out tonight to clear up whatever he was hiding? There was plenty of time between now and sunrise for him to accomplish whatever he had in mind. Hide things. Keep his secrets from her.

Backing into the room, Paxton closed the door and stripped to her underwear. She pressed the button on the air conditioner and waited impatiently for the machine to kick on. Cool air felt good on her hot, bare skin. So good, she almost discarded the plan she was formulating.

Almost.

Chapter 6

Grant pulled over a block from the motel, let the truck idle and sat awhile in thought. Should he go back? Forget that last look on Paxton's face and move on?

She might not have realized how good his eyesight and hearing were. He now figured that she suspected money was a deciding factor in his holding out on a sale. She didn't trust him. Her wary expression made that obvious. But how far would she go to get what she wanted? "You won't do anything crazy?" he muttered, hoping he was right.

Though there had been a glint of wildness in her eyes when their gazes connected, Paxton didn't seem the type to blatantly ignore his warnings about a visit to Desperado being ill-advised. Still, the look she had leveled at him from the motel balcony left him unsure about how far her defiance might take her.

"Pain in the ass is right," he mumbled.

What an idiot he was, Grant decided, for worrying about the woman when there was a more important situation at hand that required his full attention. His pack would be hunting the rogue tonight, hoping to find where the bastard hung out, and he needed to be with them.

Turning the wheel, he put the truck in gear and stepped on the gas, heading for home. When the last of the city lights finally dimmed behind him, Grant breathed easier. Out here, in the open, he was more at ease. Far from the city, he and his pack were free to be what they were, and that kind of freedom was rare for his kind.

"Did you really think I'd open Desperado to the public, Paxton Hall?" he muttered, as if she still sat beside him.

Reopening the town was about as feasible as getting down and dirty with Paxton tonight in that motel room would have been. As for any other bright ideas, the only one pestering him at the moment was his desire to run his hands over Paxton's incredibly soft blond hair.

"No secret there."

Enough desert fragrances came through the open window to dislodge the scent that had taken root in his lungs. Paxton's alluring, woodsy sent. It was no joke that his thoughts kept returning to her. She also was part wolf, and he had never met anyone quite like her. Nevertheless, Paxton couldn't be allowed to see behind Desperado's walls unless she was a fully formed shewolf in on the secrets of his kind.

"Will your first shape-shift happen here, Paxton Hall?"

What would she think about the fact that behind Desperado's facade lay cages, ropes, chains and other devices used for aiding the transition from human to

Other without hurting the Were or anyone else? And that when he found creatures in need, he brought them here to help them avoid the trauma of becoming a were-wolf in a human world?

This is what he did and what he was needed for.

"Somebody has to do it," he said aloud before realizing he was again speaking to the absent Paxton. Grant supposed he was, in a way, apologizing for the uniqueness of her father's will and how it had affected her.

"Like it or not, I have to watch over you now that your father sent you to me."

Maybe one of those cages would have her name on it if she sought answers so close to the full moon. Possibly Paxton was here for a reason altogether different than she assumed.

But having Paxton and a dangerous trespasser here at the same time was bad news any way he looked at it. And if, without knowing it, Paxton had arrived in time to set her wolf free, and Andrew Hall had sent her, then he owed her father another round of respect for executing that plan so perfectly.

Pushing the truck to eighty on the open road, Grant voiced one more thought before vowing to shut his mind down. He spoke a final word to Paxton through clenched teeth.

"I'll be here for you, no matter what you think of me."

And then, hearing the echoing report of gunshots, he jammed on the brakes.

Minutes had gone by since Grant had left her, and as luck would have it, the proprietor of the motel had a car to rent. It was an old station wagon, the likes of which Paxton had only seen on late-night TV.

Dressed in an old T-shirt and jeans, she plugged into her cell's GPS and drove along the highway for several miles before turning off on a smaller, unsigned road where she lost sight of other cars. Desperado wasn't in her GPS app, but the ranch next to it was. If she was careful, she might avoid Grant Wade's current residence and find Desperado on her own, though darkness might make locating the entrance to the town difficult.

Her goal, though, was to spy on Mr. Grant Wade.

The back of her neck tingled as she drove over ruts in the road. Thoughts of how many rattlesnakes existed per square yard of desert sand would have made anyone shudder, but she didn't plan to get out of the car. All she wanted was one look at the town from the front gate leading to it, to see if there were lights. She had to know if Desperado was as vacant as it was supposed to be, and if Grant had nothing to hide.

Honest to God, she hoped Grant had been straight with her. He seemed like a good guy. She got no bad vibes from him, just the odd sense that he was keeping something to himself. Some secrets were okay. She didn't need to access his life, just his plans for Desperado.

Paxton blew out the breath she'd been holding. She couldn't stop thinking about Grant. Only a fool wouldn't have envisioned what life with a man like that could be like, and she was no fool… usually…except for maybe right now, as she drove on a dark road in the middle of nowhere just to prove a point.

Men weren't always accommodating or trustworthy. She knew that firsthand. So it was important she made sure the man her father had left Desperado to had nothing to hide and therefore might be coerced into either selling his inheritance or buying her out. The key word here was *selling*.

Wondering if all these thoughts about Grant were truly rooted in business, she pounded the wheel with both hands. After meeting him, she was no longer sure. Still, plan B was to go after that sale tomorrow and then go home.

"Too damn dark," she said aloud to ease the discomfort of being alone so far from civilization. The road made the going slow at twenty miles per hour. It had to have been ten minutes since she passed another car, and so far, she saw no twinkle of distant lights.

She'd traveled fifteen miles from the motel Grant had put her in, and damn it, Desperado was out here somewhere. In the old days there had been signs leading to it and paper maps that an ancient tourist attraction might have been noted on. Current technology wasn't always so hot for things that had fallen off the radar.

Her phone, on the seat beside her, beeped, giving her a start. Paxton stopped the car and found that her battery was getting low. She sat there a couple of minutes more, trying to get her bearings and breathing in the delicious desert smells she had never really forgotten.

Reaching again for the gearshift, she hesitated, listening, hearing a noise that hadn't come from inside the car.

Rustling brush? Desert animal?

She jolted upright as a terrible thud came from the roof of the car, sounding as if something heavy had landed there.

Her muscles seized. White-hot streaks of adrenaline shot through Paxton as her pulse began to pound with a new, raw kind of fear.

She cried out when another thud came, this one from

the hood of the car, and again when something dark and shapeless peered at her through the front window.

Fear froze her in place. Her frantic mind worked to dig up an explanation for what that dark thing could be, and what was going on. Hell, was it a bear?

She was shaking so hard, the keys in the ignition rattled. Her heart exploded with wild, erratic beats she felt in her throat.

Damn it. Did Arizona even have bears?

Breathing became difficult. Each new effort she made to take in air only partially sufficed. No scream would come now. Paxton thought she might pass out. The thing on the hood had its big eyes trained on her, and those eyes looked nothing like a bear's. Those eyes looked sort of…human.

And then, as if she had merely blinked this beast away, it was gone, leaving behind a loaded silence filled only by Paxton's racing heartbeats as she sat there, unable to move.

Eventually, a survival instinct nudged her to get going and hightail it out of there before that awful thing came back. Finding Desperado in the dark now seemed like a ludicrous idea. What had she been thinking?

What was that thing that had landed on the hood?

Slowly, with adrenaline continuing to push her, feeling returned to her body. Enough of her focus returned for Paxton to acknowledge that although she had been born in this desert, she'd long since become citified.

She didn't like that realization. Didn't like feeling weak or vulnerable.

Her thoughts fluttered in much the same way her heart did.

In Hollywood horror movies, she recalled, the chick in this situation would have opened the door and stepped out of the car to see if there'd been damage to the roof and hood. That would have been a *duh* moment because, in the movies, monsters always returned to finish off their prey.

She didn't intend to become a bear's next meal. Swallowing the fear that clung to her like an unwelcome guest, Paxton shoved the car into Reverse. Backing onto the dirt lining the narrow stretch of road, she two-fisted the wheel into a U-turn without looking back.

Icy licks of fear chased away any thoughts she might have had about Desperado and Grant Wade. At the moment, she needed light. She needed people. Dents in the car were nothing when compared to the perks of civilization. She doubted that even a bear that had built up an appetite for humans could outrun an old station wagon.

At least, she hoped not.

Chapter 7

Grant drove the last stretch of road leading to the ranch like a NASCAR driver. Relief came when he turned into the driveway between two large posts still supporting the Hall sign—a reminder that this ranch was part of Paxton's legacy.

The house itself was dark, but one outdoor light illuminated a portion of the yard leading to the front porch. Another light flooded an area beside the barn, showing him that he wasn't alone. The black sedan parked there was Shirleen's.

Before he stepped out of the truck, she was beside him, utilizing the kind of speed built into most Weres. Shirleen still wore her apron, which told Grant she'd been in a hurry to get here from work.

"It's back," she said with a hand on the truck's door frame.

"Back?"

"I tried to tell you in the café, but you were busy," she said.

"Tell me what, exactly?"

"That rogue bastard's trail was found this afternoon in the hills."

Grant knew that none of his pack would have fired the shots he had heard, which meant the ranchers were already onboard tonight, just as he'd feared.

"What kind of trail was found?" he asked.

"An old campfire. I don't want to tell you what else was in that fire."

"Bones," Grant guessed, praying he was wrong.

"Yep. Bones," Shirleen replied.

"Cattle?"

Shirleen's face tensed. "Human."

Grant was out of the truck before the meaning of that word fully sank in. He didn't have to ask Shirleen to repeat what she'd said, or quiz her. She wouldn't have said it if she wasn't sure.

Part Native American, she'd been born and raised just twenty miles from Desperado, and she was their resident expert when it came to finding things in these hills. Being bitten by a werewolf in her eighteenth year had sent her Grant's way just twelve months ago. What had been bad luck for her turned out to be the welcome addition of an expert tracker to this pack.

"How old is that campfire?" he asked, heading for the house with Shirleen in his wake.

"A month at least. We had missed it because the sucker used an old mine shaft and then sealed it up afterward."

Over his shoulder, Grant said, "Those bones. Do you recall hearing about any disappearances? Has there been any mention of missing people at the café?"

Besides waitressing to pay the bills, Shirleen's job at

the café was to gather information that might be important to the pack. Like a missing hiker or two, the theft
of horses or more about missing cattle. Lots of conversation went on in that diner, which was a hangout for
regulars and local law enforcement. Waitresses weren't
usually given much notice during discussions like that.

"No disappearances were mentioned," Shirleen said.

"Hell." Grant headed for a box of battery-operated
lanterns kept stored at the ranch in case Desperado's
streets needed illumination after dark. "We don't have
time to pursue that beast tonight. The priority is to shore
up Desperado."

"Why?"

"Andrew Hall's daughter wants to see the place."

Shirleen leaned against a wall with her arms crossed
over her chest. "That's the girl you were with?"

Paxton Hall is anything but a girl, Grant thought,
remembering the sexy paleness of her skin. He kept
that to himself.

"One and the same," he said.

"Of course, she doesn't know anything that goes on
here? Right?" Shirleen pressed.

Grant gave her a wry look in response to that question.

She said, "There aren't any new Weres coming in,
so the cages will be empty when the full moon rolls
around tomorrow night. There haven't been any newbies for a few months now."

Grant turned from the box of lanterns. "Yes, and all
of a sudden I'm wondering why there haven't been any
newcomers needing our unique kind of hospitality."

Shirleen pushed off the wall. "You don't think…"

"It's a viable theory, right? That rogue might be waylaying Weres before they can reach us."

"You're suggesting this rogue might be eating a

werewolf or two for supper, as well as cattle, and that's why the bones in that campfire belong to a human? Because a Were's bones would look human if it wasn't furred-up at the time of its death?" A look of utter disgust crossed Shirleen's face.

"Either that, or our elusive bastard nabbed a hiker. I guess the bones will tell us if I'm right, if the right person looks at them. Did you move those bones?"

"Ben took them."

"Good. Ben should be able confirm if my suspicions are viable. It's handy to have a vet around."

"What are you going to do, boss?"

Grant eyed Shirleen thoughtfully. "I'll have to see to it that Hall's daughter doesn't stay too long or get too nosy."

"I meant about tonight and cleaning up the town."

Grant's gaze moved to the truck, and he wished he could avoid Shirleen's question. Strange sensations ruffled inside his chest. He'd felt this same kind of sensation only once before, and that was the first time he'd seen Paxton Hall.

What did those strange sensations mean now?

Hell. Could Paxton be in trouble?

Handing the box to Shirleen, Grant strode to the door. "Take these to Desperado for me. I'll be there as soon as I can. Make sure things are closed up tight. Guard the place."

He had smelled trouble the minute his boots hit the dirt. Trouble resonated in his bones, and he knew why. Christ, yes. He knew why.

Paxton Hall's connection to him was strong enough to enable him to almost see her. That's the way wolf to wolf communication went. Because of their attraction, a special bond had been forged. They seemed to be linked together by invisible chains that were proving to be stronger than the usual male-female kind of animal attraction. How else could he know what Paxton was feeling right that minute?

Bonds. Wolf to wolf chains binding us together...

Grant now began to fear he might have inadvertently imprinted with Paxton, settling into place an attachment that couldn't be broken by either party, no matter how hard they might try. Imprinting brought a whole new meaning to the phrase *until death do us part* and upped the degree of attraction to full-on hunger. Mental and carnal hunger.

He hungered for her that minute.

Damn it all to hell, he wanted to shout. Through that connection to her, he knew that Paxton had not stayed at the motel. Contrary to his warnings, she was out there somewhere in the dark, along with a madman, a bad wolf with a taste for cattle, humans and maybe other Weres. A beast that hunted for sport and ate its prey.

Deep in his mind, the sound of Paxton's startled cry echoed. His heart began to race, as if matching hers, beat for thrashing beat.

"Okay," Shirleen called out as Grant jumped into his truck. "We'll take care of things here."

With blood pounding in his ears and the back of his neck chilling up, Grant was beyond caring about Desperado. He had to get to her. To Paxton. That's the way imprinting worked. There was no other option. No way to avoid her call.

With his boot to the pedal and his lips moving with a litany of unuttered curses, Grant headed at breakneck speed back toward the city.

Paxton hit the highway with relief and with her heart hammering. Her knuckles were white from her grip on the steering wheel, and she kept repeating out loud how sorry she was that she had left the motel.

Though the highway was pretty much deserted, two cars heading in the opposite direction passed, and Paxton was finally able to take a deep breath. Cars meant the city wasn't far off. But as their headlight beams bounced off the sizable dent in the hood of the station wagon, she rang up the cost of the repairs she was going to have to pay for. Worse yet, she'd have to try to explain what had caused it.

She had to be right about the bear.

Skin tingling with remnants of leftover adrenaline, Paxton kept her attention glued to the road as the speedometer inched upward. Lightheaded from lack of sleep and from being scared half out of her wits, she spoke again out loud to cover the sound of her heartbeats.

"If I didn't actually want to think more of you, I might start to believe you set this up on purpose, *Dad*. So, what's this deal you made with Grant Wade going to turn out to be?"

When a voice replied to her question, she nearly spun the car off the road. But the voice was inside her mind, and likely a remembered thought in one word. *Stay.*

Grant Wade had asked her to stay. Given that he might be hiding something from her, why would he have then issued an invitation to go there tomorrow and then advised her not to visit Desperado?

"Which is it, Wade? Stay or go?"

Her fear was just beginning to evaporate when she noticed a set of headlights behind her, closing in fast. Turning the wheel, Paxton hugged the right side of the road to allow the car to pass. Instead of doing so, it pulled up alongside and stayed there long enough for her to get a clear picture of the man inside that blue truck.

Grant.

Satisfied that she'd seen him, he backed off the pedal. The truck pulled in behind her, as if the man driving it knew what she had been through and was extending his job description to encompass the term *bodyguard*.

Swear to God though, Paxton was glad to see him.

The café where they'd shared their late-afternoon meal was the first building she saw. She pulled into the lot and turned off the engine. Grant was beside her in a flash and opening the door. Concern darkened his handsome face as he leaned in.

"What happened?"

"Bear. I think a bear jumped on the car."

He hadn't looked at the dent in the hood or the one that had to be on the roof. Grant Wade's focus was on her.

"Are you okay?" he asked.

Paxton heaved a sigh. Having this man here with her made her feel safe. She didn't recall ever having felt completely safe before.

"I'm fine," she lied, not quite sure her legs would hold her up if she got out of the car. "Just scared."

"Coffee?" he suggested.

"So you can scold me in public for driving into the desert?"

"You're not a kid, Paxton. You could have been hurt." She nodded, in full agreement with that last part.

"Coffee?" Grant repeated. "Or something stronger?"

She offered him a weak smile, still gripping the wheel. Seeming to read her tension, Grant reached in to unlock her grip. He helped her out of the car and to her feet, his touch providing the same kind of charge she had experienced earlier.

She supposed she was a sucker for feeling anything at all for this tall stranger, and countered those thoughts by telling herself he merely made her feel silly about going out there.

"Come on." His tone was gentle but firm.

When Paxton didn't immediately start walking, he pulled her closer to him with a snap of one arm. Their chests met. Their hips met. Grant didn't appear to think this was awkward, when, for her, their two bodies meeting in a parking lot where other people might be around seemed almost obscene.

Truly, Grant Wade—solid, somber and handsome in the extreme—was likely every bit as dangerous as that damn bear. His hold on her was light, yet supportive. His pulse was pounding as hard as hers. And he was every bit the solid he-man male she'd imagined he would be.

Was he going to kiss her? She knew he was thinking about it.

Would she allow such a thing?

With cars coming and going from the parking lot around them, Grant acted like they were the only two people here. She was in his arms and couldn't shake herself free. Hell, she didn't even try.

Her cowboy's eyes didn't meet her questioning gaze. Nor did his mouth come anywhere close to hers. He continued to steady her quaking limbs…and she was a sap for thinking he might have had other plans.

"You think you saw a bear?" he asked, reminding her of what she'd said.

She nodded. "Yes. Big, dark and like nothing I've ever seen."

"It got that close?"

There was no way to miss the trepidation and concern in his voice. Each word he spoke made his chest rumble. However, Paxton couldn't figure out why he was so concerned about her when her father's will stated that if anything were to happen to her, the land she'd been left would go to guess who, along with Desperado.

"It looked at me through the windshield before taking off, and nearly wrecked the car," she explained.

Grant's hold on her loosened. She didn't ask him to wait another minute before letting her go. Didn't confess to needing his strength a while longer. What right did she have to expect anyone to save her from her own stupidity?

"I shouldn't have tried to follow you," she admitted.

His voice lowered. "It was a regrettable move, but not entirely unanticipated."

Had he read her so easily, then?

Maybe that's why he had found her out there on the road. He had expected her to act like an idiot. Expected her to spy on him.

"Do you know about the bear?" she asked.

"I haven't heard of one, but we'll be on the lookout after this."

"Then why did you advise me not to go out to Desperado on my own, if not because of that bear?"

"The desert can be a dangerous place for other reasons."

"Such as?"

"Snakes." He hesitated before adding, "Wolves."

"The threat of snakes and wolves is what made you warn me off?"

"In part."

"There are more parts?" Paxton got the fact that Grant Wade didn't appreciate being questioned when she was the one who had been caught in an unfortunate act of defiance.

Just one more question, she told herself.

"Were you driving back to town? That's why you saw me?"

He returned a question for a question. "You're sure it was a bear you saw?"

She pointed at the car. "What else could it have been? No wolf or coyote I've ever heard of is that big."

Paxton was sure that having coffee while sitting across from Grant in a lighted café was not going to make her feel better about that dent in the hood. In fact, she felt foolish any way she looked at tonight's events... and that made her angry.

"I'm all right," she repeated. "I should probably get back to the motel and face the fire about this accident."

"I'll follow you," he suggested. "I can talk to Dev, the manager of the motel, about the car."

"My insurance might cover the damage, if anyone were to believe how it happened."

Her self-appointed cowboy bodyguard smiled weakly and said, "I'll take care of it."

He hadn't let her go and seemed as reluctant as she was for him to do so. And, okay, she had to admit that having his arms around her was nice. But she also got the feeling Grant was waiting for something. What? An invitation for that kiss?

Stupid girl. How inappropriate would that have been? How absurd was it to wait for a kiss that was not going to happen, in light of them still being strangers on the opposing sides of an upcoming round of litigation?

The thought had barely receded when Grant Wade rested his mouth on hers.

Chapter 8

It wasn't the smartest move, Grant knew. In fact, kissing Paxton was the polar opposite of smart. He just could not help himself.

The kiss was meant to be a further comfort for her, but didn't turn out that way. Desire to devour the woman in his arms filled him the second his lips touched hers.

She was soft, and tasted good. He held her lithe body to his, thinking it might have been a fluke that she kissed him back. A kind of stunned reaction. Whatever the reason, Paxton, at least for the moment, accepted the pressure of his mouth as if she also had been waiting for this moment to arrive. As if it had been merely a matter of time before this happened, given their attraction to each other.

Possibly she needed an outlet for getting rid of her recent fear. Maybe he kissed her for the same reason, or because of the growing suspicion that his desire for her wasn't normal. This wasn't how strangers behaved. Something else had to be driving them together.

The kiss deepened. He couldn't seem to get enough of her and didn't want to stop. Distant thoughts nagged about being needed elsewhere, but Grant shook those warnings off in favor of exploring his ardent desire to possess Paxton Hall.

In that moment, he felt exactly like the animal he was. As his lips moved over Paxton's, his sense of connection to her doubled. Flames of greed licked at his insides, piling higher and higher with each passing stroke of his palms over the fine bones of her spine. She didn't struggle to be free or pound him with her fists. Her mouth was pliable, plush and accepting. If she had offered any hint of wanting to get away, he would have backed off.

That's what he told himself, anyway.

Enough, his mind cautioned after more seconds slipped by. But he didn't want to listen. He took hold of her shirt, intending to tear it from her body without giving a damn about who might be looking. The sheer force of that thought made him draw back.

Paxton's breath came in rasps. Her face was extremely pale beneath the glare of the café's lights. As their gazes locked and his body continued to harden in all the wrong places, Grant knew for certain he was in real trouble where Paxton Hall was concerned, and that his wolfish impulses were the instigators of those feelings.

She stood there, looking at him.

He wasn't sure what to say.

The quick fix for this problem was to drive away and leave her there, as he should have done in order to regain his wits. But he did have to get her back to the motel. See her safely there.

Taking her hand in his, Grant led her to his truck in what amounted to a race against time. Sooner or later they would come to their senses about this connection and be able to manage the passions accompanying it. He preferred that to be later, because what he intended to do to and with Paxton was going to take some time.

Paxton's curious expression told him she wasn't going to stop this madness, either. Not yet, anyway. Whatever was taking place between them was seriously spiraling out of control. Not just for him, but for both of them.

She climbed into the truck when he opened the door. Grant was already mulling over the added difficulty of getting her out of the jeans she now wore.

All women should wear skirts, he thought. *Black silk, preferably.*

His passenger sat silently as he drove, her focus glued to the windshield. She was all legs—long, slim legs encased in dark blue denim. Her shirt was tight enough to show off curves he wouldn't have anticipated, given the leanness of her overall silhouette.

She didn't know what do with her hands, so they fluttered in much the same way his insides were fluttering, as she tried to rest them in her lap.

Are you pondering what might happen when we reach the motel?

Why didn't she look at him?

Grant's body and mind were at war with each other over those rampant desires. Emotions usually reserved for after a shape-shift were hitting him hard. Each of his fingertips stung as if his claws were going to make an unexpected appearance…all because of his sudden need for the woman across from him.

Back off, Grant said to his inner wolf.

Keep cool.

Neither he nor Paxton said anything, because what was there to say when she was in the dark about so many things? Strangers had a certain level of anonymity where one-night stands were concerned, she might have been thinking. But they'd have to deal with each other tomorrow.

Will you pack up and go away if we hit that bed together, Paxton? Will shame taint our business dealings after a night in the sack?

She might give up, he supposed, and give in, if shame played a part in a day-after scenario.

He had vowed to stay away from her for so many reasons, and look how that had turned out. The last of his willpower was fleeing because of a woman he'd just met.

All right, he wanted to say to Paxton. *You can have it all, and to hell with your dad.*

Of course, there was no way he could let Desperado go. Not now. Not ever. As alpha, he had responsibilities that lay beyond Paxton Hall, responsibilities to his pack and any other werewolf looking for help and direction.

How could he tell Paxton how easy it was for him to read her, or how much he shared her discomfort over this whole ordeal?

Pulling into the motel's parking lot, Grant figured he could change the outcome here. He could drop Paxton off and say good-night. He was close to promising himself to do exactly that, in spite of his urges. Maybe, though, he should walk her to the door. Make sure she got safely inside.

She was out of the truck before he could get around it and coming straight at him. Grant thought she might finally raise a hand and slap him for that kiss. But she didn't.

Stopping a few feet away from him, she stared. Seconds later, as though pulled by forces beyond her control, her body impacted with his.

So much for vows...

She was in his arms and looking up at him. There was only one thing to do in reaction to that.

Their mouths joined in a kiss that was hungry, angry, deep, and a heady surprise in a growing list of surprises. Touching Paxton's hot, damp tongue with his was a torment. She nipped at him like an animal with its desire unleashed, as though her wolf was already partially in control of her actions. As if the longings of man and woman, wolf and she-wolf, had joined up, making lust a priority that could not be ignored.

Her breath, in his mouth, was hot. Her skin felt hotter. Was he supposed to brush this off and leave? Put a stop to it?

Was there actually a way to do that?

They wouldn't get anywhere in the parking lot. Pulling back to catch a breath, Grant again took Paxton's hand and made for the stairs, still vowing not to let the strength of his insatiable ardor take the lead. He didn't kick in the door to her room but waited for her to open it with the key she had taken from a pocket.

Then they were inside. Two consenting adults who weren't quite human, although one of them hadn't realized that yet.

Maybe he could do this. Possibly Paxton's wolf wouldn't respond to his wolf, and it would be all right to indulge in some mind-blowing sex. She'd go away tomorrow and the chains he feared would go with her.

Telling himself that was a lie, of course, and Grant knew it.

He unbuttoned his shirt quickly, studying Paxton for any sign that she was going to change her mind. When she removed her T-shirt, silky blond hair brushed the tops of her shoulders, sending him a drift of that fragrant, woodsy perfume.

She stood by the window in her jeans and a filmy lace bra that would be no barrier whatsoever to the deliciousness beneath it. He could have looked at her like this forever, staring, thankful, ravenous. His body pulsed with longing. His temperature spiked dramatically. His inner wolf, caught up in these new emotions, wanted to get in on the fun.

Without knowing how he got there, he had Paxton on the bed, on her back, and was leaning over her with his hands on the mattress. Her face was serious, sober. She was quiet.

Kissing her again, briefly, teasingly, he drew in her breath and played with her lower lip, backing off seconds later to look into her eyes. The corners of her lips quirked to show him she was on board. Her scent already saturated his face and his skin with she-wolf pheromones that were exotic and intoxicating.

Paxton was gloriously beautiful, and also so very small when pitted against the sheer force of his desire for her. Having her for himself had become necessary. Grant felt truly possessive as he got down to the business of removing her shoes. He then rested a hand on her zipper, testing his willpower by waiting out several harsh breaths, counting each tick of passing time through the strong pulses in his neck.

The zipper hummed a siren's tune as it slid downward. There was still time for Paxton to stop this. Once her jeans came off, it would be too late.

All you have to do is whisper one word, Paxton, and I'll be gone.

That word didn't come.

Fragile lace underwear, a deep midnight black, peeked out from behind the zipper, barely covering a taut belly that stretched between sharp-bladed hip bones. Grant stared at those things as if temporarily transfixed until Paxton made an impatient sound that made him glance up.

"What are you?" she asked when their eyes met.

"Hungry," he replied.

Paxton's amber eyes were bright. She wasn't smiling now. He knew she couldn't possibly have seen the wolf lurking behind the man's facade, because she wasn't yet in a position to recognize it. So he waited for her to back up her question.

"I'm not sure what this means," she said.

She was confessing to being as confused as he was about ending up on this bed with a stranger. Grant supposed she thought men were often more lax about casual sex than women were.

"Does it have to mean anything?" he asked.

"I have a feeling it does."

"Yes," he admitted, while knowing Paxton couldn't possibly understand the intricacies of wolf needs, even though her comment showed that she was trying to find a reason for putting herself in this situation. "I have that same feeling."

Her face was smooth and expressionless. "If I think about it, I won't want this to happen," she confessed.

"Should I go?"

She shook her head. "Don't you dare."

Those were the words Grant wanted to hear. Two tugs over Paxton's sleek thighs, and her jeans hit the floor. The next question Grant faced was whether he would take the time to fully undress, or if his rush to have her would win out. He was hard, aching and barely able to suppress a groan. In spite of the things she'd noted, Paxton was willing.

She sat up gracefully, bare except for the insignificant lingerie. Pushing him away, she got to her feet and backed him toward the wall by the door. With shaky fingers, she unbuckled his belt and slid his zipper downward without taking her gaze from his. In those amber eyes, Grant watched a flicker of wildness grow.

Deep inside him, his wolf moved, stirred by his racing pulse. He'd never felt so large, so strong, raw and powerful as he did right that moment. Hell, yes, he wanted this. Wanted her. What he felt for Paxton Hall, the sheer depth of emotion, was a first for him. He'd been with plenty of women. Hell, he was no saint. But he hadn't felt the need to devour or possess any of them.

As much as he hated to believe it, signs all pointed to that damn word he had managed to avoid for all of his life so far. *Imprint.* Because if that were true, and that's what was happening to the two of them, there really would be no escape clause if and when Paxton's wolf finally emerged.

It was far too late to worry about that now. Paxton's hands were on his zipper. Her fair hair curtained the sides of her face, contributing to that hint of wildness. Contained in the gleam of her golden eyes were flames that might have set his soul on fire.

"To hell with it," he whispered, wrapping his arms around her. "Question time is over."

Paxton's breath whooshed out as he took her back to the bed with the kind of speed she should have questioned. As he stretched out beside her, Grant bristled with pleasure. His wolf silently called to hers, but the moon wasn't full tonight, and that fact was in Grant's favor. Man to woman was how this was going down. Paxton couldn't shift without that moon, given that now was the time for her first transformation to happen. He didn't have to worry about intimacy tonight, though tomorrow would be another matter.

Slipping his hand between her thighs, he skimmed the black lace, seeking the soft feminine folds that lay beneath the filmy scrap of fabric. Paxton made another sound…a surprised, breathy, totally sexy sigh.

He stroked her gently with his fingers, studying each reaction she made. Paxton clutched at the covers and arched her back. The light pressure of his fingers on her sex made her reach for him. In an attempt to hold on to whatever pleasure she was experiencing, she dug into him with her nails.

"Go ahead," Grant whispered to her, his voice hoarse with expectation. "Enjoy this. Hell, your father might have planned for things to happen this way."

Paxton's lips parted as if she might challenge his remark. Grant's mouth again found hers, sealing off any argument she might care to make.

Her hands moved, sliding up his neck and into his hair to tug him closer. He didn't need the extra invitation. His hardness, at the moment still tucked inside his jeans, pressed against her hips. She, in turn, writhed on the bed enticingly, seductively, as if she couldn't wait much longer to accept everything he held back.

But sliding his fingers over her arms made him hesitate. What he found there made him balk. Paxton had a birthmark on her left upper arm, a few inches down from her shoulder. Without having to see it up close, Grant knew exactly what that mark meant. Christ, he had one just like it.

Paxton Hall had a moon mark—a special kind of birthmark that would look exactly like an old bite from a full set of wolf teeth. And moon marks were proof of Were heritage that went way back.

What did she assume that mark was? Wouldn't any-one question something like that?

"Do you know?" he asked her with his lips moving over hers, hoping she was too caught up in the same sensations moving through him to understand what he was getting at. "Do you understand what this is, be-tween us?"

Realizing there was no way for Paxton to make sense of those words, and feeling way too wolfish all of a sud-den, Grant took the fragile ivory skin beneath her right ear between his teeth and bit down lightly, as if teeth were part of the mating game.

He brought his lips back to hers for more kisses, more connection, more fire, tasting Paxton's heat and allowing the flames she gave off to sink in. Her body moved like liquid sin beneath his. Her mouth was a monstrous delight.

The time had gone for adhering to rules governing wolf behavior. These moments were full and incredibly rich. Here she was. Paxton Hall. A she-wolf in human form. And she was waiting for the very thing he wanted most without realizing it could mean they would never again accept any other partners.

The sting of her nails on his back kept Grant's wolf tethered, so the man could have his fill of the woman beneath him without interference. Faint traces of the scent of blood filled the air. Her nails were going to leave welts.

With his hands on her hips, Grant pressed his body against Paxton's, tight to the spot that would soon open and accept him.

She was ready.

He was ready.

To hell, he wanted to shout, *with everything else*.

As he pressed her into the pillows, Paxton made another sound, one that abruptly brought Grant up from the world of dreams and rapidly fading willpower. It came from deep in her throat. Not a moan, a sigh or an argument against what they were about to do.

No.

Not this time.

Paxton growled.

Chapter 9

Her cowboy drew back as if he'd been slapped. Paxton's eyes flew open. What had happened? What was wrong?

Grant had stopped moving. His eyes bored into hers as if searching out a reason for his sudden reluctance to go through with what they both wanted. His hand was wedged between her legs with his fingers splayed. He was hard as a rock inside those jeans he wore.

The suddenness of his restraint was a shock to her searing, blistered senses. The room seemed to whirl.

"What?" she demanded, her tone rough with leftover anticipation.

"It's nothing," he replied in what was obviously a lie, since his body was still and only his gaze continued to probe.

The interruption in whatever raw passion had brought them together was accompanied by a swift return of Paxton's common sense. In that moment, she began to feel foolish and way too exposed. She was on a bed in a motel room, almost completely naked, with Grant Wade's muscled body hovering over hers.

Had she been hypnotized? Mesmerized? She didn't know this man. Grant Wade was nothing more than a hiccup in her plans, and she had almost lost whatever dignity she'd had in their standoff by being caught like this, with his hand between her legs.

Closing her eyes, she considered how she was going to get out of this situation gracefully and quickly realized there wasn't any way to accomplish that. She pondered how to salvage what was left of her rapidly dissipating self-control. Clearly, something had caused the interruption in their plans to tear into each other, so wishing they hadn't been on this bed in the first place was a total waste of time.

Grant had merely come to his senses before she had. Did he expect a medal for that? Would he hold this little slipup over her tomorrow when paperwork crossed his desk? Embarrassment didn't begin to describe what she was feeling as the man she'd been about to get down and dirty with sat back on his heels. She couldn't meet his eyes, so she concentrated instead on the way his pulse beat softly beneath his right ear.

Cool air flowed over her without Grant's incredible body heat to block it. Swallowing the lump in her throat, Paxton finally glared at him.

"You're right," she said. "This was a bad idea. I applaud your self-control."

Grant shook his head. "I wanted this. Wanted you."

Wanted. Past tense.

"I'm flattered. Really. You're…" Paxton let that remark dangle for several seconds. "Well, you are very strong, and I had a scare out there tonight."

She hated how that statement made it sound as though she had been about to use her body to thank him for being there when she needed somebody. Bodyguard sex.

"Fact is, I'm no good for you right now," Grant said in a low-toned, gravelly voice.

Hardly able to speak after a remark like that, she said, "Thanks for the heads-up," and shoved him away.

Rolling sideways, she edged off the bed and stood. Any attempt to cover herself would have been absurd, so she planted her feet near the air conditioner wearing nothing but her fancy lingerie.

Grant Wade stared at her for a long time before reaching for his shirt. There were, Paxton noticed, only a few buttons left.

Having him stand there with his chest exposed and his six-pack visible made her uneasy all over again. This guy was one of the finest specimens of manhood she had ever seen. She had let that go to her head, and promised herself not to let that kind of lapse happen again.

Seeing him tomorrow was going to be a bitch.

Her cowboy turned from her to retrieve his hat, but didn't leave the room. Did he have more to say? Anything to explain the awkwardness of the situation? Because that might have made her feel better.

"That thing you assumed was a bear. How did you happen to see it?" he asked, foregoing any mention of what had nearly transpired here, just several moments ago.

"That's it? All you want to say to me?" she fired back, sure this was strange timing for a complete switch in subject matter. Yet, because Grant seemed serious, she answered his question.

"I was driving along the dirt road I assumed led to Desperado, and the thing came out of nowhere."

"You thought it was a bear—why?"

"You saw the dents it made in the car."

He nodded. "You mentioned that the animal looked at you."

"Through the windshield."

"Then what did it do?"

"It went away."

"You didn't do anything? It just went away?" he asked.

"The thing was there and gone in several very frightening seconds. I'll admit to panicking and maybe forgetting a few details."

"Did it have a shape?" Grant asked.

Paxton shook her head. "The whole thing happened very fast. Seconds. All I saw was a dark blur."

"So you didn't actually see what this thing was?" he pressed.

"I'm not Sherlock Holmes. I had no desire to stick around and find out exactly what that thing might be. Are you suggesting it might not have been a bear?"

"No. Nothing like that. I'd just like to get the word out for folks out that way to be on the lookout."

Again, she found this conversation odd in terms of timing. On the plus side, however, Grant hadn't chastised her for the spying business or alluded to the fact that she might have gotten what she deserved for flaunting his warnings about going to Desperado on her own after dark.

"Look," she said, glancing to the bed. "We made a mistake, like people do from time to time. Hopefully what happened in this room tonight won't hinder our negotiations."

Grant Wade went to the door and paused with his hand on the knob. Over one broad shoulder, he said, "Are you feeling okay, Paxton?"

She considered shouting, *No. Actually, I'm standing here in my underwear, feeling like an idiot. What do you expect?*

She said with effort, "You've helped to ease the fright that thing gave me. So, thanks."

He waited, as if unsure about how to respond to her remark. Then he nodded and left the room, closing the door softly behind him as though nothing had happened, or almost happened, between them that deserved any kind of explanation.

Paxton's legs gave out the second she heard the door snap shut. Holding on to the air conditioner for support, she parted the curtains and looked out.

When Grant reached the parking lot, he looked up at her with a somber expression on his handsome face that caused a reactionary ripple between the thighs the man had nearly been on intimate terms with. Grant Wade was gorgeous, for sure, and had almost made her forget herself. Throughout history, good-looking guys like this one had ruled what happened on motel mattresses.

It just happened that Grant's willpower had won out tonight in the absurd onset of lust between a couple of strangers destined to oppose each other over her father's will.

"Let that be a lesson about future negotiations," she muttered, feeling slightly unnerved.

Stumbling sideways, she face-planted on the bed, listening to her skyrocketing heartbeat begin to slow down before bouncing back up to make sure the door was locked. After that, she was back at the window, expecting to find Grant still out there, perhaps feeling as foolish as she did. She was unable to explain why the fact that he wasn't in that parking lot left her feeling disappointed.

The truck was gone. He had gone. Only his scent lingered in the room, and Paxton closed her eyes as she breathed it in.

"All right. Okay," she said with finality. "What's done is done."

That truck wasn't going to magically reappear because she wished it would. Nor could she replay what had happened and give it a better outcome. So with her dad's will in mind, Paxton turned her thoughts to more serious possibilities for Grant Wade's behavior and his sudden disappearance.

What if it hadn't been willpower that ended their near-miss lust fest? What if he had been messing with her?

Maybe Grant supposed he could chase her away by combining the fine arts of shame and seduction. Maybe he planned to have sex with her and then talk her into caving on her requests. Kiss her into giving him what he wanted. Corner her into pursuing new negotiations by proving himself the better negotiator.

What if he had somehow planted that bear on the road to Desperado, hoping she would turn around and head back to town?

He had, after all, been out there. He had found her on the road.

Then what? He planned to take advantage of the situation and play at being a white knight for a damsel in distress?

Paxton sagged against the wall. If any of those things proved to be true, Grant Wade would be a devil in disguise. A monster.

"Unfair tactics hidden behind such a pretty face?" Paxton grumbled as she stared at the empty space where the blue truck had been parked.

"So you know, Mr. Cowboy, I've always been stubborn, so I will take up this challenge and be here in the morning. Just you wait and see. You can't get rid of me that easily."

If Grant had somehow manipulated the whole second half of this long day for his own benefit—the ride in his truck, the meal at the café, chasing her in the desert in the dark, the kiss and what else had almost happened in this room…

"If that's what you think, then you have another thing coming," she declared. "I might not have known my father well, but I carry something of his strength inside me. Enough to get what I want in the end."

Putting a finger to her mouth, to the residual imprint of Grant's talented lips, Paxton was even fairly sure most of that last statement was true.

Chapter 10

Would she stay? Grant wondered as he drove out of the city for a second time that night.

The story about her encounter with a bear bothered him, since there hadn't been bears in the area for as long as he could remember.

No. Paxton had not seen a bear. And she had been extremely lucky to have survived a run-in with whatever kind of creature she had encountered. He knew it had been a beast scary enough for Paxton to have telepathically broadcast her fear.

As far as clues to Paxton's hidden possibilities went, that kind of broadcasting was a big one and more proof of what lay nestled inside her. The fact that he had heard her without her having transitioned was disconcerting, though, as was the growl she had let escape in the damn motel room.

Had he caused that?

He wanted to flat-out refuse to believe those imprinting chains were being fastened to his own ankle by a stranger. Grant thanked his lucky stars he had left Paxton in the nick of time. The growl had to mean that she was responding to his wolf when she wasn't supposed to. Going to bed with her might have made things worse. He'd had to let her go, had to escape from the exotic feel of the heat in that motel room.

Paxton was…

Well, she was…

Hot. In more ways than one.

"A fine mess," he muttered, slinging his hat on the seat so he could rub his forehead. An ache was building there. Each mile he traveled made that ache worse and took him farther from Paxton. Grant slowed the truck.

He turned his head.

Through the open window came a peculiar scent that raised the hair on his arms. Almost instantly, a different, more familiar scent piggybacked on the first one.

He stopped the truck and got out, leaving the engine running and the headlights on as he scanned the surrounding darkness.

"Ben?" he called to the familiar presence.

"I thought you might come this way." His lanky, thirtysomething packmate stepped into the headlights. "I've been waiting."

Grant looked beyond him. "Our rogue is nearby. I can smell him."

Ben nodded. "I tracked him to this point and then the sucker disappeared as if he'd been swallowed by a black hole. The creep isn't afraid of cars, which speaks to the point that he must either be used to them or he's human at least some of the time."

"Where are the others?" Grant asked.

"Half the pack is at Desperado doing the cleanup you requested. The rest of us are taking a look around out here. Our freak should be in human form tonight, right? If it's a shifter we're after?"

"Paxton said he looked like a bear."

"Paxton?"

Grant explained about Andrew Hall's daughter, leaving out the part about Paxton's wolf and the bed in the motel room. He added, "You assessed the bones found near that campfire, Ben?"

"Yes. They're human, as far as I could tell. Male. Young. No sign of that human being a wolf."

"Hell."

"Probably was hell for whoever that poor guy was," Ben agreed. "The bastard we're chasing gnawed on some of those bones."

Disgusted by that news, Grant swore under his breath. "You found bite marks? Teeth imprints can tell a lot about the animal doing the biting, if I'm not mistaken."

"That's the odd thing," Ben replied. "I couldn't tell anything about what kind of creature made those marks. They were more like scrapes of teeth. Long vertical drag lines."

Grant looked up. "Christ, could it have been a bear?"

Ben shrugged. "Have you ever come across one out here?"

"Not personally."

"Me, either. But I tend to think it couldn't have been a bear because of the width of the drag lines. I'm thinking a bear's teeth would have made larger grooves in the bone or ground up those bones."

Grant sidestepped the headlights. "I wonder what we have, then? What that leaves?"

"The Paxton woman said the thing that jumped on her car was big?" Ben asked.

"I saw the dents it made. Not much exaggeration there."

"Wolf?" Ben suggested, steeping closer to Grant.

"Not possible tonight, since our rogue couldn't have been furred-up."

Ben was serious. "Unless this guy is more like you than like the rest of us?"

That suggestion made Grant uneasy. Ben meant it could have been a Were able to shift without a full moon present, making the rogue not just any werewolf, but a full-blooded Lycan version with a long Were lineage. So far, Grant had never heard of another Were this side of the Mississippi, other than himself, able to perform that trick. The possibility couldn't be ruled out, though. And if that was possible, things would be twice as hazardous for everyone involved, including the neighboring ranchers.

"Bad scene, if true?" Ben noted.

"If this guy is a full-blooded Lycan, he would be far stronger than most of our Weres chasing him, and deadly in a showdown with the neighbors."

However, Grant thought, it also might explain what Paxton had encountered out here. Werewolf. Not just any Were, but one with fancy DNA.

"That kind of ability might explain a lot," Ben went on. "Like how it's able to outrun us and why its scent is hard to define. Also of note is that a Lycan can probably hear everything we're saying, even if we whisper. Am I right?"

"Partially right," Grant had to admit. "If he is within close range, yes, he might hear us talking. Otherwise we'd have to channel our thoughts the way we do when we're furred-up and on the move."

"But perhaps," Ben countered, "if this is a special type of Lycan, he can tune into you, Grant, easily avoiding us each time we make a plan to catch him."

Grant didn't utter the oath that came to mind regarding that possibility. He didn't like the sound of this at all. Worse yet, if the rogue they sought could shift without the moon and tune into Grant's thoughts, that beast might know about Paxton being a she-wolf and about Grant's budding feelings for her. Would that mean something to a rogue Lycan? Could hunger be passed along from one Lycan to another over the same silent channels?

Was a she-wolf fair game to all males of the Were species?

"Grant?" Ben said.

Grant turned his head.

Ben said, "I'll follow this road and see what I can find. You do whatever you have to do."

But could he, Grant wondered, in all good conscience, continue to send the pack out if this intruder turned out to be what they now suspected—an unconscionably strong beast with a taste for blood?

"I'll take care," Ben said, reading the worried look on Grant's face.

Grant couldn't demean Ben by mentioning again his doubts about Ben or the others facing off with a monster like that. He threw up a mental block so he wouldn't communicate his sudden fear about Ben potentially being right about what kind of beast they were chasing.

"Okay," he said. "Connect with the others now that we have a good guess as to what might be out here. Let them know."

He wondered again about how Paxton had escaped with her life. Supposing that her encounter had been with such a monster, why weren't they looking for her bones?

The thought made him sick. He wondered if her eyes and the beast's eyes had connected through that thin sheet of glass, and if the beast, a possible rogue Lycan, had let her go for some other ungodly reason, such as the recognition of another wolf.

Grant glanced warily to the west. Across the distance, he felt Paxton thinking about him. She wasn't scared at the moment. For the time being, she was safe in that motel. He found that something of a comfort.

There had to be a new plan. Given that this beast might indeed be a Lycan with special abilities, Paxton would either have to leave Arizona or be taken to Desperado, where she'd be safely surrounded by his pack. No human in this world could stand against such a beast, especially one with a nose for female pheromones.

"Dangerous rogues, whether of special lineage or not, have never dared to set foot or claw in a place governed by other wolves," he said. "There are strict rules about marked pack territories."

Another thought occurred to Grant. He spoke out loud to hear the idea voiced.

"Since Desperado is notorious among many Were communities, possibly that's the reason this werewolf has come, if it is a Were. So why then hasn't he shown himself?"

"I can't even make an educated guess about that," Ben returned, moving into the darkness before calling back, "See you in a few."

"I'm headed to Desperado now," Grant said.

Yes, he had to get going, but he was still torn. Ahead lay the hideout he had created for werewolves, which was also the home of his pack. Behind him was Paxton, who might be in significant danger if that beast on the loose sought a further connection to her. Paxton's moon mark, that white ring on her arm, could mean she was Lycan bait for more Weres than just Grant.

"Damn it. You shouldn't have come here," he said to the woman who was miles away at the moment, feeling right then as though he might be the only thing standing between Paxton and an unforeseeable doom.

Pack.

His pack came first. Had to come first. Paxton Hall wasn't his responsibility. Others depended on him.

Back in the truck, Grant drove, wishing he could join Ben and the others in their search. For now, though, he needed more than ever to make sure Paxton found nothing out of the ordinary at Desperado in the morning.

As for sending her away for her own safety and away from a raging beast…well, that wasn't a viable option. Even if imprinting chains could be stretched, Paxton might have an unexpected surprise the next night. An agonizing surprise that often killed some Weres going through their first transition. There was a slim possibility that since Paxton hadn't shape-shifted in all this time, when that was long overdue, distance from other wolves might postpone her wolf's appearance for a few more years.

Then what?

Who, in her fancy East Coast cities, would help her?

Hell, she couldn't leave here, especially on the day of a full moon, after showing the first sign of her wolf's awareness by issuing that growl. He had to see that she stayed.

"Holy mother of…" he sputtered, wincing as he glanced out the window at the dark desert tableau.

Instinct promised him that postponing Paxton's fate wasn't going to happen. Somehow he sensed that her wolf was about make its debut. Now. Here.

Tomorrow night.

The truth was that both he and Paxton owed Andrew Hall's ghost a swift kick for keeping some secrets too damn well.

Paxton paced back and forth across the worn carpet. Sleep was a nonissue. She felt antsy, like she had downed too many cups of coffee when she hadn't had one. She kept looking out the window at the parking lot.

At ten in the evening the motel was quiet. There were only two cars in that lot. She supposed the lobby lights would be on all night. With her curtains open, those lights vied with the moon's opalescent glow.

She wanted to go out and also wanted to stay where she was. She thought about telling Grant all of the excuses she had come up with for not staying here after their negotiations were over. Closure was what she needed, damn it. Couldn't Grant empathize with how necessary it was for her to end her association with Arizona? It was just like her father to stick it to her again, this time from the grave.

She'd have to wait for Grant to pick her up in order to get to Desperado, since she had ruined the rented car. It was either that or go back on her pledge to remain here and ask her dad's lawyer to turn everything over to the cowboy without having to see him again. Closure, the easy way, seemed an attractive option for about five seconds before the rapid beating in her chest returned at the mere thought of Grant Wade.

Maybe part of her didn't want to put Arizona behind her.

Possibly a cowboy named Grant was the new sticking point.

But he had not believed her about the bear.

So, okay. She had never been weak, and going home was not going to reinforce that. ER nurses couldn't afford to get weak-kneed when it came to facing trouble, and she'd seen her share in three long years in the ER.

Swear to God, she wanted to shout. *Although I don't live in or anywhere near the Wild West, I'm pretty sure I'd know a bear when I saw one.*

Leaning back again, against the wall by the window, fatigue was a real physical strain. Even that couldn't keep her from glancing out the window again.

Everything beneath the balcony was illuminated by moonbeams so bright it was like a searchlight had been centered on this motel. She had never thought much about the moon, and this one made her uneasy. The thing was too big. Too something.

The glass was cool to her touch, due to the humming air conditioner beneath it. The rest of her felt feverish. She blamed the fever on Grant. His kiss had kindled inner fires that his hasty departure hadn't doused.

"Damn cowboys."

Her forehead hit the glass. Nerves jangled. Out of the corner of her eye, she saw movement in the parking lot. The fact that someone was between the two parked cars shouldn't have been of concern since people were free to come and go as they pleased in motels. Yet the blur of movement down there caused a nerve spike that made her want to hide.

Paxton purposefully regulated her breathing. She was being far too dramatic and allowing her brief encounter with the bear to upset her equilibrium.

I'm better than this. Tougher than this.

Inching sideways, determined to put a stop to her anxiousness, she peered out again. Finding nothing out there didn't make her feel any better. Nerves kept firing. Her fingers were clenched. That damn bear and the fright it had given her had strung out her nervous system.

A sudden crashing sound made her stiffen, though everything in the lot looked the same as it had minutes before. Had someone tried to break into a car? If that were the case, she expected the motel's manager to take a closer look. Those cars weren't parked far from the open lobby door.

Paxton picked up the room phone and hit the key for the main desk. After several unanswered rings, a machine picked up. Without listening to the canned information about the motel, Paxton slammed down the phone and reached for her jeans. She tugged on her shirt and opened the door, hearing nothing now but normal distant traffic sounds. No one was in the lot to investigate the noise she'd heard. She noticed no glint of broken glass on the asphalt from a shattered car window.

She cautiously moved across the balcony, looking, listening, waiting to see if other motel guests had heard anything. As far as she could tell, no one had.

Taking the stairs slowly, Paxton headed across the parking lot and toward the lobby, careful to scan for further signs of trouble. In the doorway, she stopped abruptly with her hands covering her mouth. The place looked like it had been ransacked. Like a storm had blown through. Tables were upturned. Papers littered the floor. The registration desk had been upended and no motel personnel were present.

When she called out, there was no response. She picked up the desk phone and hit the posted three-digit code for Arizona emergencies.

"Need help," she said breathlessly to whoever had picked up.

Chapter 11

Special lanterns burned along the dirt road leading into Desperado, with small flickering lights that would be invisible to anyone not passing over in a low-flying plane.

Dots of lights in some of the windows of a supposedly abandoned ghost town always produced feelings of wariness in Grant, given that the neighbors had no idea anyone was living there, let alone fourteen werewolves. However, a bit of cleanup was necessary, and that called for light in places the moon couldn't reach.

There hadn't been much to do here these past few months. Shirleen had been right about that. It was damn lucky that no newbies had shown up needing to be locked in.

A few more nails on the doors would make Desperado look the way it had when its gates had closed to tourists twenty years before, and Grant saw that things were already well in hand on that score. He also saw the flaw in all of this, as far as Paxton's thinking would be concerned. What good was an abandoned ghost town that brought in no cash? She'd be wondering why he would be stubborn about either selling or buying her out.

"If you only knew," Grant muttered, parking near the old saloon, where he was greeted by Shirleen and two other packmates holding hammers.

"Nearly done," Shirleen announced. "If no one pokes their noses too far into where they don't belong, we should be fine."

Grant nodded, but his mind was distant. The hairs were rising on his arms again. His cell phone was ringing.

"Yeah, Steffan?" he said, answering.

After listening to the local sheriff's brief message, he stared at the truck, already fishing in his pocket for his keys.

"Break-in at the motel. The manager was missing," he explained to the others.

And this, he realized, was too damn close to being a complete farce when it came to the theory of coincidences. He had to get Paxton out of there.

When he looked up from inside the truck, Shirleen was at the window. "I'll come along," she said.

Grant didn't have time to mull over the benefit of having company. The local sheriff had given him a heads-up and was on his way to the motel. Steffan was a loyal pack member and had sensed the possibility of trouble that lay beyond the scope of other law enforcement officials, given the strange events that had been going on recently in this desert. The pack knew it took a werewolf to deal with a werewolf. In this case, however, if that bastard was as big as the dents on Paxton's car, it might take four or five.

Before he could reply to Shirleen, she was in the passenger seat and speaking. "My talents don't include hammers, so I'm not much use here."

He didn't argue. Chances were that Paxton might respond better to the presence of another female if the motel was no longer safe and they had to relocate her.

Was that the case?

He had to wonder how comfortable Paxton would be as his guest for the night at the ranch where she grew up. Just the two of them under one roof, with the added bonus of a couple of Weres coming and going.

"I'm pretty sure Paxton is going to argue her way out of an invitation after what almost happened in that motel room," he said, not stopping to explain to Shirleen about that motel room. "Steffan said she made the call," he added. Which meant she was all right, for now, and that Steffan would be there in minutes after a call like that.

Tires spun in the dirt as he backed the truck up and turned toward the road. Chills were climbing his spine with a sensation similar to the prelude to shape-shifting. One lone claw popped on the steering wheel, which he quickly reabsorbed as he fixed his attention on the dark stretch of road between Desperado and the highway. He couldn't seem to shake off his nervousness and was stuck in a dangerous loop of thoughts.

"She can stay with me," Shirleen said, eyeing his hands.

"With you and Ben getting down and dirty in the next room?"

That was as close as Grant could get in an attempt to

somewhat lighten the mood and ease his own tension, but no one was fooled.

"I see your point," Shirleen said.

Miles flew by. With Steffan the only lawman on duty tonight, there was no one to slow this truck's speed. Still, it took ten minutes of pushing ninety to reach the motel.

He saw Paxton before getting out of the truck. She was standing beside Steffan, looking wan. Other motel guests were there, too. Families. Maybe six people, in all.

Paxton's gaze found him immediately. Her expression made Grant's previous chills seem like child's play. She wasn't swaying or shaking. Two scares in one night, and Paxton Hall stood her ground, showing grit.

"I like her," Shirleen announced as she got out of the truck. "Don't ask me why."

"So do I," Grant muttered, striding toward the lobby. "So the hell do I."

Paxton didn't rush to meet him. She didn't take a single step. All the same, Grant felt the extent of her relief to see him. She was glad he had come back. Her beautiful face lost some of its tightness as he got closer to her. Lips he had kissed parted slightly, as if she was about to speak.

He stared at her mouth, recalling how those kisses had sent them both over the top in terms of temporarily forgetting their differences. He thought about taking her into his arms now.

When their gazes connected, the same thing happened to him that had happened in the café parking lot. Time seemed to stop. They seemed to be the only two beings at this scene. The only two who mattered.

Surprised by the sensations slamming into him,

Grant hesitated. Paxton was assessing him. Her long lashes hid her eyes only briefly before her amber gaze again met his. Heat replaced his chills. He felt his face grew hot, and also his groin. Although the air he breathed in was fiery with expectation, he could not reach for Paxton. He had to maintain a surface calm so that he wouldn't frighten her further or appear to be taking more liberties.

"Steffan." He greeted the sheriff near the doorway to the lobby, running a hand through his hair to keep from touching the woman who didn't really belong to him.

"Grant," the sheriff returned, holding a pad and a pen he'd been using to take notes.

"Do we need to worry about this?" Grant asked, his eyes still leveled on Paxton.

"The lady heard a noise and came down to find the place in disarray," Steffan said. "Looks like a burglary, except for one thing."

"The manager's missing," Paxton said.

Grant shifted his attention to Steffan. "He's still gone?"

Steffan waved the notepad. "AWOL, as far as anyone can tell."

"That's unusual," Grant noted.

"Highly," Steffan agreed. "I can't let you in there until we determine the extent of the damage."

Grant nodded. "Others are on the way?"

"Yep. Had to call them in."

"Can the lady go, or do you need her?"

"There might be more questions, but Ms. Hall is free to leave, as long as she stays in the area," Steffan said with an unspoken warning about what might have been the cause of this latest disruption.

For show, Steffan added, "I believe Ms. Hall is new

in town and on her own. Do you suppose you can help with that? Put her in touch with another place to stay, maybe?"

"I can and will, if Ms. Hall agrees to accept my help," Grant said.

Paxton was looking at Shirleen now. Grant read the tinge of jealousy that crossed her mind, and that made him feel hotter. She had asked about Shirleen in the café and he'd told her there was no liaison, but here Shirleen was. It would have been hard to explain to Paxton about that.

He said, "You remember Shirleen?"

"Yes," Paxton replied. "Help would be appreciated."

"I needed a ride," Shirleen said, explaining to Paxton about her presence. "Still do. We all can fit in the cab of Grant's truck, and he can run me home."

Paxton's amber gaze slid back to Grant.

"Might as well come out to the ranch," he suggested. "It's yours, anyway, according to your father's will. And it's a long way from motel robberies."

"And bears?" she asked.

"I can't promise anything in regards to the intentions of any bear that might be roaming around these parts. What I can promise is that you won't see one at the ranch."

Paxton was quiet before nodding her head. "Will we be alone there?"

"If that's a problem, I can sleep in the bunkhouse," Grant said.

"It's no problem."

"Good."

Shirleen broke in. "I'll go with Miss Hall to her room to get her things."

Paxton nodded again without moving toward the

stairs. Grant got the impression her legs might not be working properly after everything that had happened to her in a single day. She'd hate it if he tried to carry her, so he took her arm and tugged her away from the door she'd been leaning against. He steadied her when she swayed on her feet.

"Shirleen, can you pack up her things?" he asked.

"Done," Shirleen replied.

"Twenty-two. Second floor." Grant glanced at the balcony. "The door is open."

Paxton didn't protest this arrangement. She didn't try to evade his touch. Although she appeared fairly calm, the fact that her arm shook beneath his fingers told Grant a lot.

The sheriff was inside. The motel's other occupants were heading back to their rooms after assurances that the motel would be watched tonight, and safe. That left Grant alone with Paxton in the small space near the lobby door.

"I'm sorry this happened," he said to her.

"It's not your fault." She was looking at his hand on her arm.

"You'll be safe at the ranch."

"I know."

Grant quirked an eyebrow in question.

"I know you mean well," she elaborated. "And I know you have your reasons for holding out on any deal I might want to make."

"We don't need to talk about that tonight. Let's get you to bed."

She looked up at him.

"All by yourself," he clarified. But the thought of Paxton in bed, in a room at the ranch, made him question the interior quakes that came each time he thought anything about her. Just thinking her name increased his core temperature by several degrees.

Yes, at the ranch, she would be safe from anything outside. He just wasn't sure if she would be safe from him.

The hand on her arm was warm. Grant Wade's grip was firm, supportive and distressing. If she jumped into his arms, only the two of them would see it or care. She could ditch all the reasons for her concerns regarding Grant and the transactions facing them, and get on with a night that promised pure tactile bliss.

Why not?

What was stopping them?

With a glance to the motel, she said, "I'm fairly sure no bear did this."

Grant's expression changed when he heard those words. She had let the world back in when they had somehow been temporarily removed from it.

"Seems likely that you're right," he agreed.

His grip on her didn't ease. He didn't do her the courtesy of looking away or allowing her some breathing room. Paxton felt heat rising to her cheeks.

"I've been nothing but trouble for you since I arrived," she said.

He didn't argue with that statement.

"And you have been kind," she added.

His penetrating gaze made Paxton want to look down to make sure she was fully dressed. He had the ability to strip her emotions and her body down to bareness.

"You have returned twice, believing I need help," she said.

"Don't you?" he countered.

"The truth is that I'm not sure. Weird things seem to

be piling up. Is this city usually so creepy? It feels like I've become a magnet for trouble."

"You'll be protected at the ranch," Grant reiterated, his voice filled with an emotion Paxton thought she could almost read. Further truths had to be examined here, she supposed, and part of that was the fact that Grant was far too sexy for her own good. The other part was about her being a fool for not getting a grip on herself.

"Come on." He turned her toward the truck. "Maybe a good night's rest will help."

Paxton could have ignored the sound of Shirleen's little burp of laughter over that last statement if it hadn't been for Paxton's notation of how quickly the woman had returned from packing up her things.

Startled, feeling slightly sick from mounting fatigue, Paxton checked out Grant's face, thinking he also looked concerned.

"I know how you feel," he said seriously. "Let's get you home."

That was the second to last thing Paxton remembered as she felt consciousness slipping away.

The other thing she remembered was a brief final glimpse of Grant's hand, where, in her disappearing awareness, every one of his fingers sported something that resembled a claw.

Chapter 12

Other images came and went as if Paxton were trapped
in a dream sequence. In the dream, she was in the truck,
stuffed between two warm bodies, and those people
were talking about things Paxton didn't fully understand in a language that seemed foreign to her.

The truck jostled and bumped its way over a rough
road. She wondered vaguely if her bear would appear
in the headlights or if they were driving in the wrong
direction to find it.

Then she was out of the truck and being carried up a
short set of stairs. Each breath she took was filled with
scents that brought back bits of memory. Wood. Leather.
Paint. Dust. Sagebrush. Smells belonging to the West
she remembered and that existed nowhere else. Was she
a kid again, being carted to bed after a long day? Had
a hole in time sent her that far backward?

There was a sudden softness beneath her and the

squeak of bedsprings. Her head fell back against a pillow. Whoever had carried her had laid her down on a bed, and that person hadn't gone away.

Grant Wade.

Reaching up, Paxton took hold of his shirt and held on until his two hands covered hers. The heat in those hands was a further jolt to her senses and served to wake her up.

"You're at the ranch after a rough day," he said, looking down at her. "I'll find you something to eat and then you'll feel better."

"The ranch?" Paxton's mind filled in some of the blanks, but not all of them. "What happened?"

"You lost consciousness," Grant said.

"For the whole drive out here?"

Paxton glanced at the hands covering hers. No claws were in sight. This was Grant, not the bear.

"I'm pretty sure you'll be okay," he said.

"You know that? Because I'm not so sure."

Paxton studied the excruciatingly handsome features of the cowboy she'd nearly been on intimate terms with not all that long ago—the perfect chiseled features, wide brow, intelligent eyes and shiny hair. For once, embarrassment about allowing her gaze to linger didn't enter the picture.

This guy was a freaking white knight, willing to come to her rescue over and over. And though she never would have imagined it, and had been independent all her life, Paxton knew she temporarily needed his kind of help. Then again, maybe she just wanted to believe Grant had her best interests at heart in spite of their business dealings. One human being to another.

"I take care of people for a living," she said. "That's my day job. You're good at the same kind of thing."

He nodded, accepting her compliment.

"A blackout like the one I've just had isn't normal," she said.

"It is for some of us," he returned.

"I have never fainted," Paxton insisted.

Her host, who had been sitting on the edge of the bed, got up. "Let's have a drink before I search for food. I know I could use one."

He looked around the space, then spoke again. "I hope you'll be comfortable here. I believe this might have been your old room."

Paxton followed his gaze to a tall dresser beside the open door. On top of that dresser stood several plastic horses in prancing postures. Her horses. The ones she had placed there over twenty years ago. Surprised, Paxton sat up. Her stomach turned over.

"I guess your father kept some of your things," Grant said.

Was he talking about the same man who hadn't spoken to her in all that time? Never once showed his face or the least bit of concern for her well-being? That was the person Grant was referring to?

"There are other things in the closet," he said. "You might want to have a look tomorrow."

Paxton shook her head, ready to deny that her father could have been sentimental in any way and thinking that it was more likely her father hadn't bothered to clear things out.

"He stayed here? Lived here for years?" she asked.

"Your father? Yes, he resided here until a year before his death."

"How long have you been here?" she asked.

"Five years, mostly in the bunkhouse."

"Why did you come? You were a Ranger."

"Somebody had to watch over things around here. Your father was ill and needed help."

That news was yet another surprise. She hadn't known about an illness.

"How did you meet him?" she asked.

"Andrew reached out to my family for help with this place. Our fathers were old friends."

Paxton said, "I didn't realize he was sick."

"Not many people did. Your father was tough and very private."

"I'm well aware of that last part."

Grant's smile made her chest tighten. Though it wasn't a completely light expression, the smile made his eyes seem even brighter.

"This was an opportunity to give back, to help others. I couldn't refuse. That's why I came," he said.

"You're talking about helping the town's ghosts?"

"No. Not the ghosts."

He left her with that, walking away with calm, easy strides. Paxton wanted to call after him that he was wrong if he meant there were no ghosts around here, because she felt like they were lining up to welcome her back.

But what good would taunting Grant do at this point?

Warily, she stood up, tired beyond what was left of her endurance. Her legs wobbled slightly. She felt lightheaded. But she didn't want to be in this bedroom. And she wasn't an invalid.

Walking cautiously into the tile-floored hallway, running her fingertips over the stucco walls, brought more memories of this place back. She knew each dent and ding in those walls, as though she had lived here long past her early years.

The big front room of the house was decorated in a

Western theme. Brown leather couches and chairs sat in a cozy pattern beside the fireplace. Moose antler lamps lit the tables. A thirty-foot ceiling was shored up by rough-hewn log beams. All of this was familiar, too, minus the fact that no artwork hung above the stone fireplace now, and the mantel that had once displayed pricey bronze statues was bare.

Moving toward the front door, Paxton thought briefly about what might have happened to those things and why Grant had kept the same furniture configuration when he could have made the place seem more like his own.

On the porch, she breathed a sigh of relief to be in the open. She welcomed the night's hot, dry breeze and the darkness intensified by the lights at her back. But those same things also brought on more feelings of unease. She no longer belonged here, in this place, on this porch. Her life had taken a different turn.

Grant's blue truck was parked near the steps. In the distance, outbuildings that had once held ranch equipment looked skeletal in the moonlight. She remembered a lot, but not everything. Dark, vague images of the past crowded the outer edges of her memories like the shadows cast by half-forgotten nightmares.

Had problems been highlighted in the moonlight back when she was a kid? She never had figured out what those dark shapes might have been, and trying to pinpoint something so far back in memory was useless.

Another puzzle was the question of how her mother had died and where she was buried. The subject wasn't broached with the couple she had lived with in the East, and had always been taboo.

The top question at this moment, though, was what had trampled the hood of her car.

Her mind was moving too fast for her to catch up, but the ranch did seem darker than she remembered. Probably she was allowing what had happened tonight between her and that damn bear to taint her perceptions. Darkness didn't have to be full of surprises. And although she had assumed her childhood was good while she was experiencing it, running and riding and playing with plastic horses obviously wasn't always indicative of what went on between the people living here.

Grant returned and handed her a glass. "Whiskey," he said. "It could be argued that everyone deserves a drink now and then," he added.

The liquid in the glass sparkled in the light spilling from the windows. Paxton took a sip, relishing the unfamiliar burn as she swallowed.

"Is it as you remembered?" Grant asked, waving at the area beyond the porch.

"Almost, though not entirely," she replied truthfully.

He was waiting for her to explain her remark. Maybe she owed him that for acting as her protector.

"On the surface, things are the same," she elaborated, observing how Grant's lips touched his glass and the way he showed off more bronze skin when he tilted his head back to take a drink.

"How much time did you spend at Desperado as a kid?" he asked.

"Most of my time. When the place was closed to tourists, I imagined it was my town."

He nodded. "Were you ever there after dark?"

"I wasn't allowed out past the barn after dark. Too dangerous for a kid, I suppose."

Grant lifted his glass as if toasting the rightness of that remark.

"Are there horses here?" Paxton turned to look at the barn she had just mentioned.

"No. Not anymore."

"You don't ride?"

"I prefer the speed and comfort of the truck."

Paxton was aware of Grant's attention veering from her. Without his scrutiny, her skin began to cool a few degrees. She was sure she detected a new tenseness in Grant's stance as he checked out something in the distance that she couldn't see. It was obvious he didn't like what he thought he had found.

Call her nuts, but she imagined there was a change in the air. The breeze had grown thicker, cooler. The night, usually filled with the lulling sound of insects, had gone quiet. Listening, staring into the dark, slivers of old nightmares returned to haunt her. Old shapes and shadows. Unusual smells. Warnings by others in the household to stay inside the house after the sun set.

"Maybe you should go inside now," Grant said, as if he had read her mind about those past warnings.

Whatever Grant perceived out there beyond the lights made his voice rumble. Suddenly he was all business and again taking a stance as her protector.

"What is it?" she asked. "What do you see? Could it be the bear?"

Grant stepped in front of her and set his glass on the railing. "I'd really like to keep my promise to you about safety. I can only do that if you're willing to listen."

"What's out there?" Paxton repeated.

"An animal, I think."

All she could think of was the word *bear.*

"Do you have a gun, Grant?"

"I do."

"Is it close by?"

"Close enough," he said.

"If it is the bear, you'll see I was right."

"It can't be allowed to come closer, whatever it is," Grant said to her. Without turning around, he called for Shirleen.

Before Paxton looked over her shoulder, Shirleen was at Grant's side, appearing as suddenly as if the slender young woman had just materialized out of thin air.

"Call Ben," he said. And the woman was gone again.

Paxton blinked slowly, needing to understand what was going on. "You'll go after whatever is out there?"

"Yes, if you'll promise to remain here and stay inside."

"There's no way I'm staying here if you all go after that thing," she protested.

"This is no time to be stubborn, Paxton. An animal like you described could be dangerous."

"Fine. Then you be the one to relent on the issue of me staying put. This is my place, remember? My ranch."

"Are you always this stubborn?" His frustration with her was evident.

"You have no idea," she said soberly.

Grant swore under his breath.

"Ben's on his way," Shirleen announced from the doorway, her cell phone resting on her palm.

"You'll stay with Paxton?" Grant asked, and Shirleen nodded.

So, if Grant had his way, she was to be quarantined on her own ranch with a babysitter. Needless to say, that idea didn't sit so well.

"Maybe you're hard of hearing," she said to Grant.

"And maybe you have a death wish," he returned. "But even if that were the case, I wouldn't want to be responsible."

He backed up, pushing her into the doorway where Shirleen laid a hand on her shoulder. Damn it, she wasn't a kid. If a bear was roaming these parts and scaring the pants off people, she wanted to help find it. She would give that asshole a swift kick for scaring her.

The night sounds had returned, filling her ears with a whoosh and a whisper. Grant's attention hadn't strayed from the barn.

The whisper came again. Paxton heard a voice. But Grant hadn't spoken and neither had Shirleen.

Paxton turned toward the distant hills, struggling to hear past the irregular uptick in her heartbeats. When the voice came again, she heard every word.

"You have returned," said someone who wasn't on the porch with this small group.

Paxton pressed on her ears, trying to discern if she'd made that voice up and if her mind was up to its old tricks.

"Who are you?" she said before realizing that Grant and Shirleen had heard her.

They were both looking at her as if she were one of Desperado's ghosts.

Chapter 13

"Who are you talking to?" Grant asked, confused by Paxton's question.

"No one," she replied soberly. "I sometimes talk to myself."

He didn't press her, but did notice that Paxton had gone a shade or two paler.

"Okay, then." Taking the cell phone from Shirleen, he went to the truck, swung his legs in and slammed the door. Ben was on the line, and Grant didn't want Paxton anywhere near the conversation he anticipated. She was too much of a rebel already.

"Trouble?" he said into the phone before Ben could get in a first word.

"That's a benign way to describe it," Ben said on the other end of the line.

"Where are you?"

"At the gates to the ranch."

"And?"

"That sucker is here somewhere. I'll swear to it," Ben said.

"Yes," Grant agreed. "The wind has changed."

There was, he told himself, no way Paxton could have perceived that subtle change without her wolf in residence. She hadn't yet been able to explore the extra senses that came with being a Were. Hell, she didn't know she was a wolf, so her ashen pallor had nothing to do with sensing the stealthy approach of a rogue.

Ben was quick to respond. "So, maybe you can tell me how it could be here right now, even if this were to be a Lycan we're after? Assuming it's the same creature that hit the motel, miles from here."

"We're only assuming it's Lycan," Grant reminded him.

"And we can also assume it's driving a car?"

Grant didn't like this. If the creature they were chasing was looking for Desperado, why would it have gone to the motel? And why would it have followed them back here to the ranch?

"Doesn't make a whole hell of a lot of sense," Ben said.

Not unless that beast was after another look at Paxton, Grant thought.

"Paxton Hall is here. Shirleen is with her," he said.

Ben's voice lowered. "I can read between the lines of your reasoning, Grant. You're formulating an idea that Paxton has something to do with tonight's revelries?"

Grant tightened his hold on the cell phone and glanced up to make sure Paxton was out of hearing range. She stood on the porch as if anxiously waiting for something. *And when it does appear, you'll get a hell of a surprise*, was what he didn't tell her.

"I can't come up with any other excuse for the sight-ings," he said into the phone, to Ben. "And I can't let this thing come here. I'm on my way." He tossed the phone onto the seat and started the engine.

Paxton watched him leave. His eyes remained glued to the rearview mirror until the house was out of sight.

Cursing every single rut in the road from the ranch house to the distant gates, Grant half expected the neb-ulous creature to jump out at him. He actually hoped it would.

Things were in a tangle. Paxton might not be central to this latest round of hide-and-seek with the beast they were after. Cattle had been disappearing for months before she arrived.

It was possible that she had met that creature on the road tonight by accident. Possibly the break-in at the motel had nothing to do with her or anything else mon-sterish by nature, and was merely coincidence.

When he reached the gate, he saw that Ben stood in the center of the road in a wide stance, a flashlight in his hand. Two other members of the desert pack were with him. All these guys were big, serious and intimi-dating. No one would have wanted to meet these Weres on a dark road, whether in their human forms or not.

Grant got out of the truck.

"Nothing," Ben said, reporting what the others had told him. "A further search has turned up a big fat noth-ing."

"Which is, in itself, suspicious," Grant acknowl-edged, looking from Ben to the other two Weres. "It's here somewhere. I felt the bastard's presence from the front porch."

"Slippery as an eel, is how the saying goes," Ben agreed. "I'm not sure how any Were, if this turns out to be one, could make itself known and then immediately disappear without a trace."

"Not without a trace," Grant corrected, raising his face to sniff the breeze. "He's here, nearby. I can feel it."

"That's just it. We all can," Ben agreed, to nods from the others. "So, do we have a plan to lure that thing into the open?"

Grant didn't like what Ben might have been thinking. That, unknowingly, Paxton could indeed be a key figure in this wicked game of show-and-tell. The image of Paxton, white-faced, in the rearview mirror had stayed with him.

"Not going to involve her," Grant said, putting an end to the unvoiced idea. "She doesn't know what she is and is about to find out the hard way. Piling another shock on top of that could throw her over the edge."

Ben nodded. Every werewolf remembered with horror their first transition to man-wolf.

"Let's call the others and circle the main fence," Grant said. "Leave two or three of the pack at Desperado."

Ben nodded again. Grant was alpha and to be obeyed. As Grant's lieutenant, Ben was already on his phone.

"We circle, then gather to protect the town tonight if the ranch fence is breached," Grant continued. "The ranch house is our priority while Andrew Hall's daughter is in residence."

The other Weres scattered, save for Ben, who closed his phone and had more to say. "You'll stay with her? The Hall girl?"

"Just in case," Grant confirmed.

Ben melted into the night. Alone again, Grant searched the darkness. *"I know you're here,"* he silently sent to the elusive beast. *"We have a good idea about what you are."*

Surprisingly, he got a reply in the form of a thought carried in the now almost nonexistent breeze. Fleeting, distant, but there.

"No," the deep, resonant voice returned. *"You know nothing."*

Grant leaned back against the truck, blown away by the suddenness of the communication, but not much more enlightened than he had been before the bastard decided to speak up. Due to that voice in his mind, however, Grant did know one thing for sure.

That sucker was one of them.

They were chasing a werewolf.

Paxton was rooted to the porch, sensing how much Grant had been worrying about her. She didn't know why, exactly. Grant had told her he had a gun, which would take down a bear if the bear posed a threat to other people in the area. Did he keep the weapon in the truck? He hadn't gone into the house to get it.

"Do you want to go inside?" Shirleen asked.

"No," Paxton replied. "Do you?"

"No," Shirleen admitted.

Turning her head, Paxton took her first good look at the woman standing beside her. Shirleen was exotic. Black hair, long and loose, reached to her waist. She was slender, yet solid, and medium tall. Light brown skin, big brown eyes and the sharp features of some Native Americans made Shirleen a beauty.

Paxton fought off another pesky pang of jealousy. Shirleen was comfortable here, both in and around this ranch, which meant she had known Grant for some time.

"Ben and I live a little farther to the east," Shirleen said. "Ben inherited his father's place."

Paxton nodded, believing she might get a straighter answer from Shirleen than from anyone else.

"Do they think it's a bear out there, Shirleen?"

"Unlikely," Shirleen replied. "Though not entirely out of the realm of reality, I suppose."

"If not a bear, what could it be?"

Shirleen shrugged. "Another kind of animal. Or a man in a bear suit."

Shirleen wasn't smiling when Paxton looked to her again. Paxton considered whether Native American traditions and superstitions might actually make a man dress up in a bear suit. However, she didn't think it prudent to ask questions about Native American religious practices with so much going on.

"He's coming back." After making that announcement, Shirleen focused on a spot in the dark distance.

Paxton moved down one granite step. "How do you know?"

"If you listen carefully, you can hear the truck coming up the road."

Paxton closed her eyes and listened, hoping she wouldn't hear another imaginary voice. Hoping Shirleen was right about the truck.

"Out here, sound carries. There's not much to get in the way," Shirleen explained.

Paxton moved down another step, gazing out with her heart in her throat and realizing that she was anticipating Grant's return far too much. Her anxiousness to see him wasn't merely about information and learning what he might have found out there in the desert. Her need to see him was more than that.

Though she had jokingly called him her bodyguard,

the truth, if she dared to acknowledge it, was that he truly did make her feel safe. She couldn't see anyone besting Grant Wade in a physical fight.

As she waited for him to arrive, she began to sense Shirleen's tension and had to wonder why everyone was on guard.

She had a feeling this ranch and all the people involved with it were embroiled in a mystery that she, as an outsider, wasn't privy to. Years in the ER had sharpened her awareness for puzzling out potential problems, yet she was out of her element here. Did this mystery have to do with her father's will, or Desperado itself? It seemed to her that she wasn't to be trusted with what might be going on.

Grant's truck rumbled into sight at a slower pace than when he had left. Only Paxton's heart sped as Grant parked and got out.

Sober-faced, he spoke first to Shirleen. "Thanks for staying awhile. Ben's expecting you, so I told him I'd send you along."

Only then did Paxton realize how tight her grip on the railing was, and that she had descended all of the steps without noticing.

"No bear?" she heard herself ask.

When Grant's gaze lit on her, the same sense of connection to him she'd experienced before snapped into place. His looks didn't help her ignore the return of the flutter deep inside. Neither did noticing that he moved with the grace of a panther or how corded his tanned forearms were. His shaggy hair was in need of a trim, but somehow suited him. Fact was, she couldn't picture him looking any other way than exactly as he did in that moment.

His expression was one of anger and regret. Though

he hadn't been gone long, he hadn't found the animal he'd gone in search of.

Her heart skipped several beats when his worried state registered. He was avoiding her eyes. Was that because his concern had something to do with her?

She was so tuned in to Grant, and so glad to have him back, she could have sworn she heard him say to the woman beside her, *"Go ahead. You're needed elsewhere,"* though his lips hadn't moved. But that was just her imagination working overtime. She wasn't psychic; she had no special talent for reading things outside of patient symptoms in the hospital where she worked.

When Grant finally turned his attention to her, she almost took a telling step toward him. Shirleen's departure was silent and Paxton barely noticed it. The night had again gone quiet, as if for the second time in a small span of time, someone had punched the mute button.

Grant stood a few feet away from her. The space between them was alive with a kind of palpable friction, each of them wanting to move toward the other without doing so.

To break the silence, Paxton asked, "What happened?"

Grant's eyes were waiting for hers to find them now. His serious expression projected a fierceness that left her pulse pounding.

"Friends are watching for your bear," he replied.

That information would have been mildly pacifying if she hadn't known he was lying. Either lying or not telling her something vital to her peace of mind. After her brief conversation with Shirleen, the word *bear* had lost its shine as the monstrous opponent she'd met on the dark road to Desperado. So, what kind of animal was as large and as heavy as a bear? That question, posed moments ago to Shirleen, still awaited an answer.

"What's really going on?" she managed to ask, feeling a flush heat her cheeks due to the intensity of Grant's blue-eyed observation.

Grant didn't answer her question. Instead, he closed the distance with three long strides to stand close enough to her to make her look up to see his face.

"We've been hearing things about a trespasser for a few months now," he said. "This might be the same one."

"Man or animal?"

"We're not entirely sure," he replied.

"If it turns out to be a person and not an animal that you're searching for, would that person be dangerous?"

"He's already a danger to livestock in the area. By default, and because we're trying to stop the thievery, we can't rule out the possibility of drawing that freak's anger. That's why it's safe to be on the lookout."

She felt better, knowing this. Felt better thinking that it might be a man, rather than a giant animal. Still, having a human trespasser didn't explain why the man standing in front of her right now believed she might be in danger, personally.

"You're not telling me everything," she asserted.

"No. Not everything," he admitted after taking time to think about his response.

"You believe I might be in danger and won't tell me why? Is that fair? What good can come from keeping me in the dark?"

"I don't want to frighten you," Grant said, and his remark rang true.

"It would only upset me if I had something major to fear. Since I don't know anyone here, except for you and Shirleen, what is there to link me to the danger you seem to be expecting?"

"Nothing concrete. And not just you. This concerns everyone around here. My neighbors aren't happy about the missing livestock and are out there with guns."

Paxton tried to break eye contact. Grant's smile, weak, though still dazzling, kept her from turning away. Even with all the mystery and secrets, she wanted him around. She wanted him, period. She couldn't imagine him being hurt by a livestock rustler and didn't want him to leave her again, for any reason.

Who the hell cared about any outside event when Grant was looking at her the way he was? When her first instinct each time she saw him was to jump his bones?

They were adults. There was no danger in this yard that she could see. So it truly seemed as though they had some unfinished business to attend to and get out of the way, so that she could again think clearly and pave a new path for herself in the days ahead.

Sex was the obstacle to more negotiations. Sex had to be taken off the table so they could get on with things. She had to stop thinking about how much pleasure she'd derive from running her tongue over every inch of his unbelievably honed body. And vice versa.

Paxton looked away.

"What now?" she asked breathlessly.

"This." He placed a finger under her chin to tilt her head back.

Holding her captive with no more than one single finger, and proving himself a talented master in the art of seduction, his mouth did exactly what Paxton wanted it to.

Chapter 14

It didn't matter that she had questions Grant couldn't answer or that now wasn't the time to give in to the impulses overwhelming him. Insatiable hunger ruled the moment, and Grant was all for that.

The woman in his arms kissed him back with the fervor of a female with her wild side taking over. She might be demanding on the outside, but her mind no longer seemed to be revolving around the concept of reason.

Unlike him, she had no idea why she was feeling this way—so hot and so very bothered. She could no more have resisted him than he could have stayed away from her. Their attraction was supernatural in scale. Preternatural. Inescapable.

He kissed her long and deeply, curving her spine backward, holding her tightly. Warnings about voices at the gates and monsters on the loose scattered, burned away by the incredible heat of their embrace.

Paxton's lips were pliant. She was desperate for feeling and had come to the right place. Through the deep, drowning kiss, Grant willed her to believe he had her best interests at heart and that he would be there to help when the moon came for its newest Were acquisition.

Then even those thoughts left him.

The kiss was unending, a true devouring and an example of experiencing the sublime. Ruthlessly, they explored with moving hands, their hips rubbing in all the right places. Mindfulness became a thing of the past, overruled by the blistering heat of Paxton's body pressed to his.

But they were in the open and nowhere near a bed. The ground beside them was hard.

Paxton's eyes held a golden glint when he pulled back far enough to meet them. Her cheeks were flushed a becoming shade of pink.

Grant waited for her to argue that this behavior was one of his tactics for avoiding more of her questions, but in truth, she had asked for the kiss.

Smiling, Grant stroked her right cheek with his fingertips. Without returning the smile, she said simply, "Not my room," and turned toward the steps leading to the house.

Grant stared after her, earlier dilemmas returning to haunt him. In order to protect Paxton, he had to rely on an acute awareness of his surroundings and tune in to the Weres guarding the ranch. In spite of that and the possibility of her future anger, Paxton was expecting him to follow through on the invitation she'd just issued.

Not my room...

Grant's gut twisted. He desperately wanted to follow her up those steps. If he did, the damn beast roaming out there somewhere might tune in and take advantage of the situation.

What the hell had that monster said to taunt him?

"You know nothing."

Paxton walked slowly, using the railing to haul herself to the porch. Her jeans molded to her legs, showing off each luscious curve he'd glimpsed once before.

Her spine flexed fluidly as she climbed. Her shiny blond hair fell to her shoulders in tangles. When she reached the porch, she paused to glance at him over her shoulder. *Are you coming?* her eyes seemed to ask.

Hell, he was already moving, consequences be damned. Only in having her, having one intimate moment with her, would he be able to get on with things, even if it meant piling more trouble on top of the trouble already at hand.

She led him through the main room of the house and down the hallway without stopping at any of the rooms or using the stairs to the upper floor. Grant didn't question this. Her words echoed inside his head.

Not my room...

From the kitchen, she exited through the back door. She led him across the fenced backyard and toward the bunkhouse where he had lived before Andrew Hall died. In the doorway of that rustic building she stopped, turned to him and offered a weary smile.

But she had not changed her mind.

Shoulders rippling, chest on fire from withholding the swift rise of an exquisite kind of passion, Grant moved to the doorway where she stood and put a hand to the wall for support. Inches from Paxton, he breathed in her heady scent while watching her expression alternate between acceptance and defiance, her features changing mercurially, second by second. She knew nothing about

Were imprinting, or the factors behind their almost dizzying attraction, but she was game, nonetheless.

The gentlemanly thing for him to do would have been to wait until she landed on one of those emotions so vividly expressed on her beautiful face. A gentleman would have allowed her all the time she needed to realize where she was and what she was suggesting they do…and been offered an out. But being this close to her had its disadvantages in terms of his behavior. With his body calling for action, Grant could hardly keep from taking her right there in the open doorway.

Paxton was the first to end the temporary standoff. Rising on tiptoe, she brushed her mouth over his. No touching or meeting of their bodies this time, just those warm, supple lips, featherlight on his.

Grant pressed closer, sandwiching Paxton between his body and the wall. Moonlight flooded the room beyond the doorway, streaming in from the yard through a series of windows to cast long shadows across the floor. Grant would have felt the moon's presence without having to see it. Though his insides shuddered in recognition of the moon's presence, the light illuminated Paxton with a silver caress.

He liked everything he saw and everything he was going to touch. Paxton had become as addictive for him as the moon was. And, like Madame Moon, the woman whose scent and body he craved had lured him into a dangerous and possibly permanent relationship.

Her fingers breezed over his face as if searching for something she couldn't see. Only Grant would have seen the irony in that.

Their mouths parted. His eyes bored into hers.

"Just for tonight," she said with a whispered breath.

"Tomorrow we're those other people needing different kinds of answers."

And…well…who was he to argue?

Everyone had a weakness. Patience was his. Although Grant would have preferred to take things slowly, appreciating every move and gesture between them, that kind of control wasn't in the cards. Time was a luxury they didn't have.

He tugged Paxton's shirt over her head before kissing her again. The rough wood wall behind her might had been uncomfortable for her with his weight pressing in, but that thought fled as she snaked her arms around his waist.

The damn internal flutters he had been experiencing in her company rushed to meet her hands as she ran them up his back. His skin moved beneath her touch. Desire for her became unconquerable. With a snap of his fingers and a well-balanced move, the woman in his arms became braless. Through his shirt, Grant felt the hard, round tips of her breasts pressed against his chest and the little quakes that shook her.

Slipping his thigh between her legs, he widened her stance. Her hands now slid to his waistband, searching for a way inside.

Grant gracefully swung Paxton inside the bunkhouse and closed the door. One more tug and she was back with him, hip to hip and half naked, her mouth as demanding as his.

They were standing in the middle of the lofty space, surrounded by beds and brown leather chairs. The closest piece of furniture was a long, narrow dining table.

"Good as anywhere," he said, stretching Paxton out on top of that table's dusty surface, leaning over her to soak in the beauty of her bare arms and torso.

"We've gotten this far once before, Paxton."

He vowed not to let anything stop them this time, and hoped she felt the same way. The atmosphere in the bunkhouse buzzed with a sense of urgency he couldn't explain. Paxton was here with him, and willing, but timing had become an internal pressure.

He had experienced this moment once before—his eyes on hers, his fingers on her zipper. That zipper now whispered down its metal track, filling the night with promise, while Paxton remained quiet, on her back, on the damn table.

She never once took her eyes off him.

Grant wished he had the ability to twist minutes and hours to their advantage. He had been hard, aching and erect, since Paxton had turned to him on the front porch steps.

Forgetting about his superhuman strength, Grant tore open his shirt, losing the buttons that remained from earlier that evening. With wolf-gifted hearing, he listened to those buttons hit the floor.

Paxton smiled up at him. She opened her arms wide, giving him an unimpeded view of her perfect breasts and issuing an invitation for him to join her on the table.

As alpha of a Were pack, he was used to being in control, and yet that control was slipping. This small woman was besting him in ways he'd never dreamed of. All she had to do was wet her swollen lips with the tip of a pale pink tongue and let a sigh of impatience slip from between those lips…

He couldn't get to the rest of her fast enough to suit what throbbed beneath his waist. He had to stop kissing her and tasting her mouth if they were to do what they had come here to do. With her mouth this hot, he couldn't imagine what sliding into her soft, feminine folds would be like.

Her shoes were off. He removed her jeans. She let him do all the work. Wildness continued to blossom in her eyes.

One small scrap of black lace remained to cover her—the same nearly transparent dark strip he had encountered earlier at the motel. Black lace, he decided, was even sexier than her black silk skirt. Seeing her like this was a turn-on.

Grant tore the lace panties from Paxton with a simple closing of his fist, eagerly anticipating what would come next. Lying in complete stillness, Paxton's eyes roamed over every inch of his shirtless anatomy, appreciating what she saw. He was happy he could please her.

Her long, silky legs parted, as if he needed to be guided to what lay between them. He snapped his belt open. After discarding his boots and jeans, Grant stood before her completely naked, open to Paxton's inspection. Her eyes were wide and gleaming. Her torso glistened with a light coat of sweat. It had to be ninety degrees in the unused bunkhouse, and it was about to get hotter.

Between Paxton's slim, shapely thighs, a small patch of blond fur beckoned to him. And that was just too much. Grant was with her on the table after one more unsteady breath, on his hands and knees.

As Paxton lay back again, Grant lowered his mouth to one of her rosy-tipped ivory breasts and ran his tongue over the pink nipple. Paxton tossed her head from side to side and bucked. His weight pressed her down.

No time for exploration, his mind warned. *No matter how hungry you are.*

"All right," he said soberly, after sampling the delights of her other straining breast, the light suckling making a direct connection with his groin. "Are you with me, Paxton?"

Eyes closed, she answered in a tone indicative of the same need spiking through him, "Yes. We have to…"

Her remark dangled unfinished. Her breath rushed out as Grant entered her body gently with his rock-hard cock. All the while, he studied her face. Braced on his hands, he moved his hips, inching deeper one small push at a time, relishing the fire of Paxton's moist inferno.

She was far hotter than he had imagined. Molten was exactly how he would have described her. As Paxton began to move, raising her hips to meet his, making way for him to find the spot she wanted him to find, their tongues danced and their lips burned. Hips slapped against hips as Grant built up a rhythm that took him deeper into her plushness. He dipped in and out of her body with a series of plunges, thrusts and withdrawals that drew moans of delight from her.

He stroked her, worked his way deeper and deeper toward what lay nestled at her core. This is where a wolf's soul resided, and by God, he'd have that, too.

When he touched that sultry spot, Paxton closed herself around him. A growl tore through him that he almost couldn't swallow. Grant wanted to howl, throw his head back and put sound to the extremes of the pleasure he was finding, locked between her sleek legs. But the woman beneath him needed him to be a man for a while longer, at least for tonight. Any sign of Grant's wolf would have hindered that.

Pleasure came at him in waves, tilting, churning with incredible speed. The rhythm of his fiery physical assault matched their breathlessness. Grant shut his eyes as his thrusts became faster, harder. She took it all, and all of him, urging him on. As he made love to her, Grant crooned to her with words that lay beyond the realm of his comprehension. Words like *love* and *chains* and *futures*.

Seconds later, he hit the sweet spot he had been seeking. Rigid beneath him, Paxton gasped. The distant drumbeat he'd been aware of for some time got measurably stronger and rushed to meet him there.

He touched that spot a second time, and a third, backing off long enough to make her claw at him for more. Nonsensical sounds bubbled up from Paxton's throat. She started to tremble, her interior quakes indicative of an imminent climax.

She wrapped her legs around him as if fearing he might finish before she could reach the peak marking the culmination of this union. Deep internal pulses inside her drove Grant on. Merging with that rising beat would possibly seal their fates, and at the moment, he didn't care. Paxton's body was issuing demands he had to satisfy. Their mating had to be complete.

His desire to possess all of Paxton Hall, body and soul, woman and wolf, was the impetus for one final thrust, and that triggered an immediate response. Paxton came hard. She cried out, shuddered, writhed beneath him, gripping his shoulders, digging into his flesh. Bodies locked together, they rocked in unison as a tsunami of pure sexual bliss crashed over them. Peaking together, their bodies arched, strained, as they fought to hold on.

And then it was over.

Tangled together on a table in an unused bunkhouse,

and with the possibility of danger outside, Paxton's sexually sated cries faded. Her heartbeats slowed.

When the opportunity arrived for a full breath, Grant looked down at his lover, not sure what would happen when Paxton opened her eyes. They had scaled the heights of pleasure together, but a rocky road lay ahead.

It wasn't hard for Grant to imagine how beautiful Paxton would be once she had shape-shifted. How gracefully she'd move. How it would feel to have her stretched out beneath him, opening to him over and over again. He would have given a lot to start that future right then, and grew hard again just thinking about it.

But a replay of what they had shared here wasn't to be. Not yet. This one session had been dangerous enough. They both had caved to desire.

Tomorrow, he thought, pressing the fair hair back from her face before kissing her forehead, her cheek, her mouth. *In the middle of all this potential danger, we'll see what you are and what will happen next.*

For now, their time together was up. These wonderfully private moments were over.

Someone is heading this way, my beautiful Paxton, and that presence will demand my attention.

Although the real world had been temporarily set aside in favor of touching the sublime, it now returned with a vengeance.

There's a monster to catch and a full moon on its way. There's a pack to protect and a potential new member. That new member is you, little wolf.

As Paxton's lashes opened, Grant whispered out loud, "Welcome back to the Wild West, lover. Only the hardy can make it here, and I'm hoping you are one of them."

Chapter 15

Ignoring the whispers and sounds flowing through her mind, Paxton found Grant Wade studying her when she opened her eyes.

Speech was difficult with white-hot nerve endings zinging. Although she wasn't a beginner when it came to sexual escapades, she had never experienced anything like what had just happened. She had never felt like this. Never been left panting.

Was it merely the incredible sex or was it something else entirely? Because sex like that didn't belong to this plane of existence.

Grant was composed of waves of electricity, and the charge was ongoing. The explosive climax he had given her had been similar to detonating dynamite, and was taking its own sweet time to recede.

He wasn't relaxed or smiling, in spite of the release. Grant's tenseness had returned with a speed she hadn't anticipated, signaling clearly that their time together was over.

Had sex been all Grant Wade wanted from her?

Even so, it had been worth it.

"You okay?" He asked her this as if he actually expected her to answer the question seriously.

"Yeah," she said, since he was waiting to hear her confirm that she was all right. "Fine."

She assumed Grant would get up, take his clothes and leave. If he thanked her, she would give him a good kick. She'd take a cold shower and try to wash off his scent, knowing she would have to put this little indiscretion behind her, like strangers often did after a one-night stand. Because the truly awkward part of all this had arrived.

Grant nodded as if he, too, understood this.

To ease any potential embarrassment either of them might be feeling Paxton said, "This doesn't have to be strange. It happens all the time."

"All the time to you?" he asked, studying her.

His face was close enough for her to feel his breath on her cheek. Her body continued to quake inside, craving more of everything Grant had to offer.

Damned if she'd let him see that.

"I mean random meetings between two people attracted to each other for whatever reason," she clarified.

Instead of responding to that statement, Grant turned his head to look at the door. His broad, bare shoulders rolled in agitation.

Paxton followed his gaze, alerted by the kind of glance he'd settled on that door. "Is someone out there?"

"Yes."

That explained one possible scenario for his sudden nervousness. She was a little bit relieved.

"I didn't hear the knock," she said. Then again, that wasn't really a surprise, since she hadn't been able to pay attention to anything beyond the sensations of their exquisite coupling.

Grant smiled warily. The expression told her he was holding something back. Was there a jealous woman outside, ready to burst in?

Paxton reminded herself that she wasn't part of his life and therefore didn't need to know everything Grant did. But his wary expression bothered her.

"I have to check on something," he said, his gaze swinging back to the door. "And I don't want my departure to seem to you like avoidance or insult."

"Thanks for telling me," Paxton returned drily. "Now I won't think that at all."

It was her turn to stare at the door. "Go," she said, giving him permission to find some distance. "It's all right. I'm all right. I'll get dressed and…"

Her remark was interrupted by a sound she clearly heard, coming from outside. She sat up quickly as Grant got to his feet. His demeanor had changed again. She noticed he had fisted his hands.

In the moonlight streaming through the window, Grant's picture-perfect face suddenly seemed more angular than chiseled, and much more defined. His expression had grown darker and resembled a scowl. He was seriously anxious about what might be out there, beyond the bunkhouse door. Paxton also figured he truly was loath to leave her like this, so quickly, because he didn't rush over to the door.

"Go," she repeated firmly.

Slipping off the table, she hastily gathered up her clothes.

The knock that came soon after startled her, though

Grant appeared to have been expecting it. Without giving a damn about being buck naked, he opened the door and spoke in a low tone to whoever stood there.

"More trouble," she heard the person outside warn.

Grant threw her a worried glance before turning to pick up his jeans. Once he had donned his pants and boots, he came back to her.

"You can't stay here, Paxton."

"I'll go to the house," she said, monitoring his change in attitude. He seemed so much more formidable. Warier. More dangerous.

His head shake was firm. "It's too late for that now. The trespasser I mentioned is sniffing around, so I can't let you out of my sight. Please get dressed. Sorry about the shower you might be anticipating. You'll have to come along."

Pulling on her jeans, she said, "Where are we going?"

"To Desperado."

Paxton stopped moving halfway through the act of getting her shirt over her head, thinking she might not have heard Grant right. After stuffing her arms into the sleeves, "Now?" was the only thing she could come up with to say.

Thing was…

Grant really didn't quite look like himself. Half in and half out of the shadows, he seemed bigger, more muscular and somehow larger than life. Shadows hugged his bare chest, creating valleys of light and dark. His arms were corded with the same kind of tension that made his shoulders ripple.

Was the lack of light making her think those things? Was she imagining things that weren't there?

His tension was contagious.

Her hands shook.

Then she noticed the mark on Grant's left upper arm for the first time—a small silvery circle that could have been a recent tattoo.

She stopped moving with her gaze riveted to that mark, and touched her own arm. She'd been born with a similar circle in the same spot.

Coincidence?

Tossing her hair back from her face, Paxton remembered that there was a hell of a lot she didn't know about her old home and about Grant Wade. Actually, she knew next to nothing about either, and again felt afraid.

She felt sick.

Glancing from the open door to Grant, who stood bathed in moonlight and was visibly on edge, Paxton fought off a second wave of nausea. Reaching to the table for support, she closed her eyes, counted to ten and said, "It might be a good idea if you explained a few things first."

"Grant?" Ben said from the doorway, showing respect for his alpha and friend by not mentioning Paxton, Grant's nudity or what so obviously had gone on in the bunkhouse.

Careful to keep a rein on his inner beast, Grant didn't dare go to Paxton. His reaction to Ben's warning had been swift, causing his wolf to slip its tether for a brief partial appearance.

Had Paxton seen it?

More trouble, Ben had said, which left no time for explanations, either the short or the long versions, Paxton was asking for. The monster they'd been seeking had returned to the area, as he'd feared, and was closing in on the ranch.

Damn persistent sucker...

"Later," he said to Paxton, relieved to hear the even tone of his voice when the rest of him was in flux. His skin undulated like the surface of a disturbed pond. Claws, fur and teeth had to be monitored. Now wasn't the time to give Paxton the second fright of her life.

"We'll talk later, I promise," he said to her.

Paxton had backed into a corner with one hand gripping her upper arm. Her fingers covered her moon mark as if it was something foreign. She was unable to hide the fact that she had seen his mark without understanding what the similarity meant. To the human portion of her mind, none of this made sense. Of course, it made sense to every other Were on the planet.

Only pure-blooded Weres bore moon marks and passed them on to their offspring. The fact that Paxton had one was proof, as Grant had thought, that Andrew Hall had to have been a werewolf. Not only that, Andrew's lineage had to have been pure enough and strong enough to pass the wolf and the mark to his daughter. It also meant that both of Paxton's parents had to have been Lycans.

Christ. This was incredible news.

Andrew's daughter was a Lycan.

And, as fate would have it, Grant would be the one to tell Paxton her mommy and daddy had been werewolves, and that Arizona was a magnet for Weres, both good and bad. Once she knew this, Paxton would have to rethink her entire existence and consider the possibility, as Grant had, that her father had sent her away for more reasons than just wanting to be rid of his family.

Grant just wasn't sure what those reasons would have been, since Desperado was a werewolf Mecca and Paxton would have been at home here, among others of her kind.

The whole thing felt off, somehow, now that he thought about it. Still, would having more facts help Paxton come to terms with the long-term loss of her dad?

What would she do when she found out what she was? Would she pass the test all Weres had to go through during their first transformation, not-so-lovingly called The Blackout for good reason?

"There's danger all around us tonight, and we have to head straight toward it," he said to her, hating that she looked so pale. "I'm sorry to involve you. That wouldn't have been my choice."

Paxton didn't appear to be buying this. Stubbornness was often a she-wolf trait; he had learned that from his dealings with Shirleen.

She said, "Someone found the bear?"

Grant shook his head. He kept his hands behind his back in case his claws slipped through. Even now, his body wanted a rematch on that damn table.

"I'm pretty sure there is no bear," he said.

In response to that statement, Paxton's eyes blazed angrily. The hand covering her mark dropped to her side. "Then tell me what that thing out there is, and why you're so concerned."

"No time to explain. We have to go," Grant reiterated. "Now."

She pushed off the wall, a little steadier on her feet than she had been the minute before, and said smartly, "Okay. If you say so."

Damn it. Did everything have to be so difficult?

Nevertheless, Paxton was dressed and standing. Ben was waiting for them outside. They'd take the truck to Desperado and see who turned up looking for a fight.

Surrounded by his pack, Paxton would be safe. Grant would see to that.

Paxton didn't take the hand he offered her. The honeymoon was over as far as she was concerned, when it had been, well…it had been everything he'd ever hoped making love to a woman would be, even considering the time constraints. He sincerely hoped there would be a round two.

Paxton preceded him from the bunkhouse looking disheveled. Her porcelain skin was a shade lighter than it had been. She had pulled her T-shirt on backward. Anyone looking at her right then would have been able to tell what they'd done in that outbuilding, and maybe even how good it had been.

For the record, he wanted to tell her that it had been damn good.

She walked without help, gaining strength from her anger. Yet he would have liked touching her. After being with her intimately, wanting more of her was expected.

"Paxton, this is Ben," he said when she faced his tall, dark-haired packmate.

Ben nodded in acknowledgment of the introduction, then turned toward the house where Shirleen waited for them at the back fence. Ben spoke as if Paxton was one of them and in on what was taking place before Grant could urge caution.

"He breached the fence less than a quarter of a mile to the south," Ben explained.

"A human trespasser?" Paxton asked, drawing a long look from Ben, who continued speaking without addressing her query.

"Nothing about this guy is usual or explainable, Grant. He might be heading here. I can't hear his chatter. Maybe you can?"

"I'm not sure why he'd come to the ranch," Shirleen said. "What's in it for the bastard? There are no cattle or horses here for him to steal. Maybe he wants to chew on something else for a change?"

From two feet away, Grant felt Paxton stiffen. However, it was too late to take back those remarks. Everyone here was angry that their lives had been disrupted.

As they moved through the house to the front yard, Paxton remained quiet. Without a single request for fresh clothes or a bathroom break, she climbed into the truck. Ben and Shirleen slammed the front door and loaded themselves into the truck bed, taking up positions on opposite sides to keep watch as they drove the short distance to Desperado.

In essence, Paxton was getting exactly what she wanted, give or take having a monster on the loose. They were going to Desperado, and she was about to have a very rude awakening as to the town's purpose.

"There is something out there, as I said earlier," he finally explained. "Whatever it is has been killing cattle and causing an uproar with the ranchers. It's dangerous, and so are those ranchers wielding rifles when they give chase."

She gave him a brief sideways glance.

"There's more to the old ghost town than meets the eye," he went on. "It's protected on all sides."

Paxton said, "Protected by what? Fences?"

"Electric fences," Grant replied, keeping the rest of the explanations about the town's protections to himself. No use going there until he had to.

"You believe Desperado is safer than the ranch?" was her next question.

"More of us are gathering there, and there's safety in numbers."

"Why not gather at the ranch?"

"Desperado is the place we've designated as a meeting spot."

"These gathered people are your friends?"

Grant nodded.

"And you will go after this person or thing that has been bothering ranchers in the area?" Paxton asked.

"Not this time. I don't think we'll have to."

"You assume the trespasser might come to you?"

"That's what I expect, and I could be wrong. I'm sorry you're in the thick of things, Paxton. The timing sucks. I'm also sorry about the interruption back there in the bunkhouse. We needed more time to enjoy the company and figure things out."

"I'm pretty sure we covered everything," she said.

Grant took his focus from her when Ben tapped on the back window.

"Someone else thinks they've seen our beast," Ben said through the sliding window. "Listen."

Sure enough, the sound of gunfire was like an explosion of firecrackers in the distance. And maybe, Grant thought, Paxton was starting to believe him about the danger. She slid closer to him as she stared out at the night.

Chapter 16

The sounds Paxton heard in the distance had to be gunfire, making Grant's explanation about ranchers going after trespassers seem real. But she couldn't figure out why they were on their way to meet Grant's friends at Desperado, and what made an old ghost town a better bet for a rendezvous than the ranch, when she would have thought the opposite.

More secrets? These people were feeding her half-assed explanations that didn't actually explain anything. What wasn't Grant telling her?

Images of that old abandoned town from her childhood flashed through her mind, though most of her memories were long gone with time. She remembered the electric fences surrounding the town that had been meant to keep out trespassers even back then.

If given half a chance, determined tourists would have run off with shutters, floorboards and any other pieces of the place they could pry up, she recalled her father telling her. She supposed some things never changed, and that an off-limits ghost town was likely to be an even bigger target for that kind of thing.

Still, if this was one lone trespasser Grant and his neighbors were after, a gathering of the clan seemed a little like overkill.

Just as she remembered, the road leading to Desperado had no streetlights. This far out of the city, the roads were only partially paved. The streets of Desperado itself were dirt, as tourists would have expected from a relic of the Old West. What electricity there had been in the town itself when she was a kid had been minimal, for emergencies, and carefully hidden in a tribute to the full Western experience.

She stared out of the truck's closed window, expecting to see the town's main gatepost any minute, no longer sure how to gauge the distance from the ranch to Desperado. It couldn't be far. At six years old, she had ridden her pony over this same road.

Night in the desert would have been beautiful if things hadn't turned so serious. Moonlight and stars in the clear night sky lit parts of the scenery. Saguaro and other types of cactus cast long shadows over the white, sandy ground. In the distance, a long, low mountain range stretched dark and colorless in the night. Though Paxton had no idea what time it was, she figured it had to be very late. Temperatures had cooled considerably, but she hardly felt the chill with her metabolism revved up by adrenaline and tonight's hot, sweaty sex.

A shower would have been nice. Her skin and clothes were saturated with Grant's scent. She smelled like sex. Like him. The fact that he was a few inches away from her at the moment didn't help her concentration much, either. When Grant wasn't looking, she gave him furtive glances.

The guy looked like himself again…all bronze and brawn. His shirt, open in front due to the missing buttons, showed off his shape. Fair highlights in his auburn hair glinted in the moonlight each time the truck swept around a curve.

Paxton rubbed her eyes and withheld a sigh, believing she had imagined the changes she had seen in Grant at the bunkhouse. However, his anxiety, so like a living thing, permeated the cab.

Uncomfortable with the silence, she spoke. "Those ranchers wouldn't actually shoot a person for trespassing, would they?"

Grant's attention remained on the road. "This idiot has been stealing their animals."

"He dares to come back for more?"

"Seems so."

"What does he do with the cattle?" she asked.

"He kills everything he steals."

Paxton sat back on the seat. "Why would he do that?"

Ignoring Grant's reluctance to answer this line of questioning, Paxton pressed on.

"What did Shirleen mean when she suggested this guy might want to chew on other things for a change?"

Grant's gaze, drifting to her, felt like a tractor beam. Paxton made herself stay put.

"Might as well cough up some real answers," she said. "I'm nothing if not persistent, and I'm not going anywhere, it seems, except into the heartland of a bunch of secrets you don't think I have any right to know."

Paxton met his eyes defiantly.

"You have every right to those secrets," he said. "It's just that, as I said before, the timing sucks. Bad timing means it's unlikely that you will believe anything I say. Until you experience some stuff for yourself, you will remain in the dark."

"That's rather cryptic and pretty damn ominous, Grant."

"Yes, well, the world, it turns out, holds many more secrets than anyone would assume. Most people wouldn't be ready for a close look at those secrets."

"As far as cryptic goes, you're getting worse by the minute," Paxton argued.

"I get that."

"Yet here I am, in this car, on my way to Desperado, and you won't trust me with a close look at whatever it is you're hiding."

"What if you didn't like what you saw?" he asked.

"I believe that's entirely up to me."

"All right. Let's test the concept of sharing, shall we? How about if I start by telling you we believe the guy we're searching for out here isn't human."

"In my book, no one who kills animals for sport can be considered human."

Grant glanced away briefly before looking at her again. "That's not what I mean."

"Okay. What do you mean?"

"Not human, as in this guy is from another species altogether. One you're not yet familiar with."

Paxton shook her head. "This is nowhere near Roswell, New Mexico, and you're suggesting this guy is an alien?"

She was ready to either laugh or jump out of this truck if Grant answered that question positively. It would definitely make her think twice about secretly desiring him on a level that could very well make her do something stupid. Again.

He was curiously tight-lipped now.

"You are going to have to explain. Especially now," Paxton insisted.

Without letting his gaze linger longer, Grant spoke in a voice that took on the aspect of a deep rumble.

"The truth is that we aren't sure what this guy is," he said.

"*What* he is?"

"Signs suggest he might be a werewolf."

Paxton turned on the seat and answered with a not-so-hearty laugh that didn't make her feel any better about what Grant had just told her. In fact, the grim expression on his handsome face let her know that he was deadly serious.

Hell, if Grant believed in werewolves, he had to be out of his mind.

"You wanted in on our secrets," Grant said, noting the way Paxton stared at him.

She had no immediate response to that remark, so he went on.

"Of course, this sucker might not turn out to be a Were. In that case, however, he'd have to be something dreadfully similar."

"Like a bear?" Paxton quipped.

Her lips were as bloodless as her face. Grant had expected that kind of reaction and guessed the time had come for revealing a few more things. If the beast out there showed up at Desperado, Grant wasn't sure how they could keep its existence hidden from Paxton. Sooner or later, she had to have more details about her species.

"This guy is unusual," he said. "Maybe he's not an idiot all of the time, because I've heard him speak."

She said tentatively, "Then you've seen him up close?"

Grant shook his head. "Never up close. I heard him speak to my mind."

Paxton's hands were on the dashboard as if she was bracing herself for more bad news. "So you came up with an alternative to alien and made him the next best thing? A werewolf?"

Her voice reflected her disbelief and also a few new suspicions about his state of mind.

"You're thinking I'm crazy," Grant said.

"Don't you think what you've said warrants that?" she fired back.

"As a matter of fact, I do not, unless you have an explanation for the reason that mark on your arm matches mine."

That was harsher than he had meant to be in breaking the news to Paxton about her hidden heritage, but it was too late to stop now. He had been driving slowly, with Ben and Shirleen in the back of the truck, and yet they would reach Desperado in a few more minutes. Time was short for any kind of believable explanation.

Paxton's voice was hushed. "What does the mark on my arm have to do with you imagining the guy you're after is a werewolf? Come on, Grant. I can't wait to hear what you'll say next."

"It has plenty to do with what I'm trying to tell you. You see, if the guy we're chasing is a Were, and using his abilities is how he has been avoiding capture, it's almost certain he will have a mark like ours, too."

Paxton's tone tightened. "Maybe you'd like to start making sense?"

Grant reached out to touch her arm. "Only full-blooded werewolves have this mark. We're all born with the same one."

Paxton's hand again covered her upper arm, as if doing so might make the mark disappear. Her face had gone paler, and Grant wasn't sure how that was possible.

"It's called a moon mark," he explained, hoping she would listen to him. "The marks resemble the leftover scar of an old wolf bite for a reason. That reason harks back to the first bite a wolf gave to a susceptible human being centuries ago. A human whose genes carried a defect allowing a specific wolf virus to infect them."

She said in a clipped tone, "I've never even seen a wolf up close."

"You not only saw a wolf up close, you inherited some of its traits."

Her hand moved to the door handle as if she'd use it to escape what she had to assume was a conversation comprised of madness.

Grant lowered his voice. "The only bear around here is the fact that you bear that white ring on your arm. You bear it because you are one of us, and a child of the moon."

"Get real, Grant," she snapped, though it was no more than a whisper. "You believe you're a…"

"Yes. And so are you."

Completely speechless, Paxton stared at him with her lips slightly parted for an argument she couldn't quite access.

"We're all werewolves here, Paxton. That's why your father left Desperado to me. He knew Desperado was the perfect place for werewolves to find solace in a world where people would hunt us down for sport if that world became privy to the fact that Homo sapiens aren't the only species on the planet."

All Paxton said was, "You're actually serious."

"Completely," he confirmed.

"You're a werewolf."

Grant nodded.

"And Shirleen? How about the guy with her? Both of them are werewolves, too?"

"They're part of this pack, yes."

"Pack?"

"A tight-knit group of…"

"Don't tell me. *Werewolves?*" she said.

Grant waited for her to go on, sensing she had more to say. Paxton wasn't taking this well, but who would? Who, outside of select insiders, could possibly have believed what he was asking her to believe?

"Don't you suppose I'd know if I was something like that?" she countered adamantly. "I mean, truly, Grant. This is absurd."

"I understand how it sounds, Paxton. And I know you have a hundred questions, which we will eventually get to. Until then, the quick fix to the question you just posed is to say that you obviously weren't told about your background or your family's special inheritance for a reason, and that omission was terribly lax on everyone's part. Unheard-of, actually, if you want the truth. Hell, you're worrying about the kind of inheritance that's written on paper, when there's been something so much more pressing in need of your attention."

She started to argue, then gave up in frustration.

"You haven't shape-shifted yet," Grant continued. "That's ground zero for belief in all of this. Holding your wolf back for so long is highly unusual for someone your age."

"I'm only twenty-six."

Grant nodded. "Most she-wolves transition at or

around the age of sixteen. Earlier, if puberty hits before that."

She muttered, "She-wolf. That's rich."

The conversation was far from over. Actually, it had just started, and wasn't sitting well with Paxton. But they had reached the gate leading to Desperado, and two of his packmates stood beside the entrance.

"I suppose those guys are werewolves, too?" Paxton's tone dripped sarcasm, with a little fear thrown in.

"As a matter of fact…" Grant started to say, but his remark was cut off when the two Weres guarding Desperado's front gate whirled toward something Grant couldn't see from the cab of the truck, and Ben and Shirleen jumped out of the back.

"Damn it." He opened the door, understanding the sudden directional shift, and muttered, "I'm hoping this guy is a werewolf, rather than some other rendition of the word beast," sensing Paxton's frozen reaction to those words.

Paxton sat without moving, fairly sure she had lost the ability to control her limbs. Several choice cuss words passed her lips when Grant left her to join the party at the gates. Not just any party. One for werewolves. A pack of werewolves. And according to Grant, she was one of them.

Yeah. Right.

She had made love to a madman and was trapped in his truck. If the other people in Grant's little circle of friends also believed themselves to be *Weres*—as Grant had called them—she was in the middle of nowhere at the moment with a pack of crazies.

Her next move?

As she saw it, she could either play along and wait

for Grant to take her back to the ranch, or borrow the blue truck and get the hell out of there before the craziness spread to her.

Keys dangled in the ignition.

Through the windshield, she saw that the two new guys by the gate were gesturing. Those guys looked like people. There was nothing furry about them. Everyone had turned in the direction they were alluding to with a series of hand gestures, possibly trying to pinpoint the location of some creature straight off the pages of mythology books. According to Grant, the grand-master madman, all of the people present believed they actually were furry on the inside.

Shuddering at the thought, Paxton slid sideways a few inches at a time until she was behind the wheel. Turning the truck around to face the city wasn't going to be easy, and maybe even impossible with Grant so close. Her only real option was to go forward and hope she could locate another way out of Desperado in the dark.

She saw with some relief that the road into the old town was lit by small globes of light supplementing the light of a receding, nearly full moon. The outline of the open gates stood out, easy to see, as well as at least twenty feet of dirt road beyond them.

Five people stood to the side of the gates, not far from the truck. They were ignoring her for the moment, their attention elsewhere. Would she be able to start the engine without those people stopping her from stepping on the gas?

Have to try.

She leaned forward. The keys felt warm to the touch.

She wasn't up for playing at being a goddamn werewolf, no matter how hard Grant tried to convince her.

Now or never...

Foot hovering over the gas pedal, Paxton turned the key in the ignition, thanking God the truck was an automatic. Grant turned his head to look at her with a puzzled expression on his devastatingly handsome face. The others with him glanced her way.

Heart in her throat, hands shaking big-time on the steering wheel, Paxton hit the gas. The truck lurched forward, tires spinning and tossing up clods of dirt and dust. It was a powerful machine and well tuned. She was through the gate and heading for Desperado in seconds, distancing herself from the strangers and their oddball beliefs.

Chapter 17

Staying on the road was easier than Paxton had imagined. The last time she had come this way was on the back of her pony. That time, she also had been trying to distance herself from bad news.

Now, as then, she was running away, seeking solace in the old ghost town. She had loved her father and Desperado…at least, that's the way she remembered things looking back. Now, she was getting away from a man who tried to tell her she was a werewolf.

Desperado's outline appeared a short distance ahead. Paxton's heart was heavy. Part of her had been left there years ago, along with more questions than Grant could possibly have answers for.

She drove at a crawl through the town's main street, surprised to see that the place wasn't empty. Every curse word she had ever heard slipped from her lips in a long stream of syllables as Paxton processed the idea that the people gathered here weren't ghostly apparitions, but quite possibly more of Grant's werewolf cult.

The old town called to her as she passed through, in the way it always had. History and age had been kind to the buildings, and Grant had mentioned making repairs.

She had loved this place once and considered it her personal property. She had been familiar with each empty store and alleyway, and by the looks of things, not much had changed. As fate would have it, Desperado was never to be her personal property, because the town now belonged to someone else.

Shirking the desire to stop and look around, Paxton wished she had arrived in different circumstances that would have allowed her to lay her hands on the old boards of the saloon. Strolling through the mining office and general store would have been like walking into the past. All of that was out of the question now that she was a fugitive for stealing Grant's truck.

The truck garnered stares as she rolled by the people on the street. Grant had been expected here. Seeing someone else at the wheel was a surprise for the onlookers.

"See ya," she whispered, passing the old hotel, unable to resist a quick peek at the place.

No one stepped into her path or tried to hail her as she passed them. She'd have to pick up some speed soon. If Grant was in the kind of shape his body, with all that muscle, indicated, he might possibly be able to catch up with her before she left Desperado behind.

She could add car theft to her list of accomplishments. *But werewolf... Really?*

Arms aching from her tight grip on the wheel, she tried to rationalize that the mark on her arm had been caused by childhood inoculations. Tetanus? Smallpox vaccinations? Maybe she and Grant had experienced the same kind of birth trauma, and the mark was indicative of that.

Who knew why or how such things happened?

Moon mark. Did she really care if birthmarks had a name?

Yes. Damn it. All right. The similarity of those marks was one mystery too many.

Desperado was behind her now and merely a series of dotted lights in the rearview mirror. There were no little light globes on this side of town. Darkness enveloped the truck. An alley of skeletal trees hampered what moonlight there was.

Paxton could no longer see past the headlights, but if memory served, somewhere out here was the electrified fence marking the town's boundary. With people in town tonight, that fence would be turned off. The truck was probably strong enough to barrel through a bunch of wire without too much damage.

No one had chased her down. Grant hadn't shown up. It could be that he was letting her go without a fuss, glad to be rid of Andrew Hall's daughter and her endless queries. Possibly he was as sorry for what had happened in that bunkhouse as she was.

Oh, yes, she was sorry.

Sorry she had liked what they had done on that table. She was regretful over how badly she had instantly wanted more of the same, and that with everything that had happened since then, how suspicious she was of the way her body quaked each time Grant's name crossed her mind.

Thoughts about Grant dissipated suddenly, overpowered by a loud crashing sound. Paxton applied the brakes, nearly missing the tree that had fallen across the narrow, single-track road. Falling trees weren't a rarity in the desert, given the parched state of their roots, but this was a holdup she didn't need.

The truck idled as she sat there, staring out, considering her options in light of this latest hindrance. Going around the tree was bound to be a terrible idea for the truck, given the tough landscape's giant ruts and chasms, invisible in the dark. Without the truck, she'd have to walk, by herself, with no flashlight. Since there was no way she'd make it to the city, miles away, in any case, she'd have to go back to the old ghost town and face the consequences of running off with the truck. Maybe Grant would lock her up in Desperado's jail and throw away the key.

Something else that crossed her mind stopped her from getting out of the vehicle to see if she could budge the damn tree. The word *beast* resonated there, along with Grant's explanation that they did not know for sure what category of beast their trespasser was.

Paxton didn't want a replay of her meeting with the thing she'd thought was a bear. Grant had told her the creature that had jumped on her car might be a werewolf. She didn't believe that was possible, but damn it, was everyone in this part of Arizona insane?

"Go to hell, Grant," she shouted.

As those words echoed in the truck's cab, the sensitive skin on the back of her neck chilled as though someone had dropped an ice cube down the back of her shirt. Red flags of warning began to wave, telling her...

Oh, God...

She wasn't alone.

Grant's chest had tightened as he had lunged for the moving truck, aware that the special speed he possessed wouldn't get him to Paxton in time to stop her from whatever she had in mind by taking the vehicle. Surprise had made him hesitate a beat too long.

Paxton was long gone.

Ben, on his cell phone, barked a quick heads-up to the pack members in town. Shirleen raised an eyebrow when Grant whirled to face her—she was waiting for instructions on how to handle the situation.

"Headstrong," Grant muttered, taking off at a brisk jog toward Desperado.

Too damn headstrong for her own good, he silently added.

"At least she won't get far," Shirleen called after him.

As for the not-getting-far business, Grant wasn't so sure about that, given the possibility of Paxton's memories of the area and how many details a six-year-old kid's brain would retain.

He didn't remember much about his own life prior to his first shape-shift. When a body temporarily closed down for a complete system rewiring, more than just a few nerve cells were fried.

Room had to be carved out for a long list of new senses and abilities that included a wolf's enhanced sight and the power to smell things no other species could. His body had been loaded with new muscle for both protection and the kind of speed he could have used now to chase down stubborn she-wolves who hadn't yet experienced their own physical awakening.

Turning on the heat, Grant raced on, his legs churning on the dirt road. He had to pay attention to his surroundings and was glad moonlight exposed what lay in the shadows on both sides of the road to town. Desperado was only a mile ahead of him. He heard Shirleen, always light on her feet, running behind him, and he swore out loud, fearing that his pack might be in trouble because of the attention needed to handle Paxton's breach.

"Paxton. Stop. Wait for me. Keep out of the dark spaces. I don't understand your need to run."

He sent that silent message on a closed channel reserved for personal things in order to keep other Weres out of his thoughts. Chances were good that she wouldn't hear him, because Paxton retained most of her humanness at the moment, and old human habits were often hard to break.

He glanced up at the moon, well aware that last thought wouldn't be true for much longer. To most of the Earth's population, the moon overhead already appeared to be full. Werewolves knew better. However, now, tonight, the big silver disc tugged on his will to remain in human form. Emotion was ruffling his skin, bringing chills.

In a fully morphed state, he could have reached Desperado faster, arriving seconds after Paxton did in spite of the truck's massive engine. But he didn't want to scare Paxton. In any case, the rutted road they hadn't bothered to repair would help to delay her departure.

"Don't hold back on my account," Shirleen sent to him, reading parts of the thoughts he hadn't purposefully hidden. "All right. Done deal," Grant said aloud, changing his mind about shifting in order to catch Paxton sooner, knowing he'd have to shift back when he did.

Claws popped at his invitation. Layers of muscle began to seize, shimmy and quake. His arms burned beneath the layer of chills. So did his legs. Facial bones began to rearrange. A dusting of fine brown fur sprang from chest pores, and the hair on his head lengthened to brush his neck with what should have been half a year's worth of growth.

With a larger lung capacity, breathing was easier and required less effort. Embracing his true nature brought him an exquisite sense of freedom. He didn't have to ditch the open shirt or his jeans and boots, being in full control of how far he could take this shift.

Running was easier now. Sprinting through the landscape was like experiencing a suspension in time and space. In Were form, he always had the feeling of being pasted onto the world rather than being part of it. Always, when wolfed up, he imagined he could hear, far off in a distant time, his four-legged ancestors howling.

This was what being a werewolf meant, and nothing in polite human society could have covered it.

Without the ability to speak, Grant sent his thoughts winging through the night. *"Paxton. Wait. There are so many things I need to tell you."*

Another shape-shifting perk, aided by his connection to Paxton, was Grant's ability to tap into her emotions. He knew her heart was racing and that she felt lost. Hell, she *was* lost. Paxton had been stranded for far too long in a form that didn't truly explain her. She'd been lost to part of her family and to her heritage, ignorant of what lay ahead for her in less than twenty-four hours, now that she had come home.

"Stop," Grant sent to her again as the town came into view. *"Wait. I'm coming to get you. I can't protect you if you don't listen."*

Shifting to his human form again would be necessary before he reached her. She couldn't see him like this. Not yet, before she believed the things he had told her.

Near the first building on Main Street, he found nine Weres waiting for him. One of them shook his head and pointed north. Grant growled his acceptance of the news that his truck had already passed through town.

Worry set in as his pack gathered around him. All of these Weres were tense. Sharing his emotions made them more anxious.

"She just blew through," one of them said.

"Where are you, Paxton?" Grant silently called before growling again. Her fear had spiked suddenly in a reboot of what had happened earlier that night—her brush with an animal she had assumed was a bear.

He had to find her. Tonight was off the charts in terms of oddness, and Grant had a terrible feeling that Paxton really might be the focus of this latest series of close calls and mishaps.

He wasn't sure why he thought so, though the sour taste in his mouth meant trouble awaited him around the next corner. There was a new pressure in the atmosphere and a needling sensation on the back of his neck. His discomfort sang to him, urging him to find Paxton, pressing home the point that she might be in peril.

"I'm coming," he repeated for the tenth time, heading in the direction she had taken.

Chapter 18

Paxton stood beside the truck, gauging the viability of finding an exit from Desperado's vast acreage in the dark after so many years. She had grown rigid, sure she was being watched. Nerves were prickling.

Her body quakes had returned in full force. She called out, "I know you're there, so you might as well show yourself," hoping in this instance she might be wrong about having unwelcome company.

"Actually, I insist," she added, whirling around every time there was a noise in the brush.

No one met her challenge. No intruder appeared in the truck's headlight beams. Yet she sensed a presence. Inching sideways, toward the truck's open door, Paxton tried to calm herself down. But when a different kind of awareness came that was more like a feeling than a series of spoken words, she imagined a voice say, *"I'm coming."* And *"Hold on."*

The sensation the tone gave her was one of familiarity, leading her to believe it was Grant's voice.

With her back pressed to the truck's warm metal, Paxton glared at the nearly invisible landscape, searching for this other presence.

"You're scaring me." She spoke, not to the distant idea of a familiar voice, but to the closer presence she sensed hovering in the dark. "What do you want? Are you one of Grant's friends? Can you help me move this tree off the road?"

She suppressed a gasp when she heard the snap of a twig, followed by the shuffling sounds of someone or something moving just beyond her field of vision.

"Show yourself," she insisted, not liking the way her voice wavered.

The next sound that reached her was one an animal might make—deep, guttural and very much like a growl. Rather than adding to her discomfort, the thought of this visitor being nothing more than an animal came as a relief. *Wolf, then*, she thought. Real wolf, since Grant had nixed the idea of a bear. And yet that growl resonated in the night, too loud and too deep to have come from a wolf.

Turning swiftly, Paxton climbed back into the truck. More chills came. More icy waves. Her head felt light. Movement out of the corner of her eye made her swivel, wishing she had taken the time to close all the windows. With shaky hands, she felt along the inner surface of the door beside her, looking for a button that would seal her inside.

When the screech of something scraping against metal came, her fear escalated to nearly overwhelming proportions, freezing her on the seat with one hand on the steering wheel. Pulse exploding, she watched the dark blur of a moving body pass by the open window too swiftly to match it to an image.

Scared out of her mind, and unable to deal with the latest state of fright, Paxton screamed.

Grant heard Paxton. She was in danger, scared.

Doubling his effort to reach her, he flung silent curses that did nothing to alleviate his own budding fear over what might be happening to her.

He felt responsible.

If he hadn't picked her up at the airport like an inquisitive ass, and had let her find her own lodging and make her own way, maybe these feelings of extreme connection to Paxton Hall could have been avoided and she would be safe. Certainly, she'd be nowhere near Desperado right now. He had brought her here, where a trespassing son of a bitch, whatever this rogue bastard turned out to be, could get a peek at her.

Imagining Paxton was the key to solving the latest version of this mystery was probably absurd, and yet he couldn't shake the idea. That beast had shown itself to Paxton and hadn't harmed her. Something had been at the motel where she had checked in, and Grant had a bad feeling about that, too.

"How could you know about the motel?" he asked across silent Were connections. *"You spoke to me once, so why be silent now?"*

He didn't actually expect a response and wasn't surprised when none came. And he was an idiot for trying to reason with an unknown entity responsible for doing plenty of damage in the area. But, really, all he and his pack needed was one pertinent clue as to this sucker's location.

There was light ahead that had to be from the truck's

headlights. Changing from his werewolf shape to a more user-friendly appearance, Grant raced on through the slap and sting of yet another downshift in too short a time.

His face reverted to its human semblance with a swift recall of power. The sting he felt was due to his fur being sucked back inside his skin. His shirt flapped in the wind created by his sprint. Claws were the last detail to go. His human shape would be best for Paxton, and worse, in theory, for facing whatever had frightened her.

He saw the truck. Found Paxton inside. His relief over finding her unharmed was monstrous. She didn't turn her head when he came up alongside. Nor did she acknowledge him at all. Paxton was ashen-faced, stiff and staring into the distance with glazed eyes.

When he spoke to her, all remnants of his wolf had gone. This was the voice Paxton would know. This was the guy, at least on the surface, she had made love to.

"You could have been hurt," he said softly, yanking the door open, waiting until she looked at him.

She spoke in a voice weakened by what had made her heart thunder. "No bear. Not even close."

Grant searched the dark, more concerned for Paxton than anything else. He sensed no one. Nothing jumped out at them. Paxton appeared to be alone. The only obvious details out of place were the tree blocking the road and the new two-foot-long scratch running the length of the truck's left rear panel.

Had Paxton gotten too close to the brush in her rush to beat him to an exit out of town? Grant didn't think that would explain this kind of damage. The scratch was deep and looked to have been created by a very sharp object.

In even more of a hurry now, Grant climbed into the

truck, gently shoving Paxton aside. Throwing the truck into reverse, he drove backward, his eyes on the road through the rear window. The last spot wide enough to turn the truck around was some way back, and he was determined to reach that spot as soon as possible.

His next uttered curse, whispered vehemently through clenched teeth, drew Paxton's glassy gaze.

"What was it?" he asked her. "What did you see?"

The tires kicked up dirt and other desert debris, but Grant knew where he was headed. He was familiar with every inch of land surrounding Desperado, as well as most of the territory in and around the distant city. Weres often roamed far and wide, driven by the wildness inside them, before returning to their homes. *Sort of like you, Paxton, moving to the other side of the country before returning to the land of your ancestors.*

"Okay. No bear," he said aloud. "So, what did you see?"

In a slightly stronger voice, Paxton said, "I'm not sure."

She was telling the truth, which in this case might not have been such an odd response, since no one around here seemed to know exactly what they were chasing. Even the word *Lycan* covered a lot of ground.

"Describe what you saw," he said.

"It was the same damn thing."

He nodded. "The thing that jumped on the other car?"

"Yes." Paxton's eyes were huge, her pupils partially dilated. He saw no evidence on her face of her earlier stubborn streak.

"And?" Grant prompted.

"And, as crazy as it sounds, I think it might have been expecting me. I think whoever is out there put that tree in my path to keep me from leaving."

Grant slowed the truck mid-turn and faced Paxton, anxious about her reply. "What was it?" he repeated.

"I swear I don't know. I didn't see it. Not clearly."

"But you did see something?"

She nodded. "Something."

Her pallor told him Paxton had reached the end of her ability to describe what she'd witnessed and that it would be useless to keep pressing her. However, she wasn't quite finished, and the next words she spoke pierced Grant's soul.

"It wasn't human," she whispered breathlessly. "And if this is your trespasser, we're screwed."

Chapter 19

Paxton expected the man sitting beside her to blanch at what she had just said. At the very least, he should have questioned her judgment and current mental state. Grant Wade did neither of those things, which led her to assume he was one step ahead of her.

"You believe me." She watched Grant for any hint of a reaction.

He nodded.

"Damn it, Grant. Has the world come unglued, or are there things I'm obviously missing? When did the word *inhuman* become shock-resistant?"

His sideways glance, there and gone, might have been an example of avoidance. He had the truck turned around and was heading back toward Desperado.

"Maybe I should be the one asking the toughest questions," she suggested. "Like what the hell is going on around here?"

After a deep breath, she continued the interrogation.

"Why do I imagine I can hear you speaking to me at times, when you're not close to me? Am I nuts, or is there a reason I think this?"

He seemed to be concentrating on the road, and that wasn't going to do it for her.

"You could do me the honor of an honest reply, since it appears I'm not going anywhere, anytime soon, and that rescuing me is your current MO."

He threw her another sideways glance that showed no expression of anger or gave her a clue about what he was thinking. He gave no indication of believing he might be dealing with a madwoman. And that, Paxton decided, spoke volumes about his belief systems.

When he spoke, it was in a low tone reserved for passing along a secret he wanted no one else to hear, even though no one else was present. "We believe this trespasser is unique."

"That's putting things mildly," she snapped, bristling with a desperate need to understand the things presently eluding her. Fear tickled her nerve endings. Her stomach again turned over.

"So how about telling me what else you know, Grant?"

"I'm not sure you're ready to hear what I have to say," he returned. "Especially since you didn't believe the last few things I've mentioned."

"Try me."

"At the moment, I'm acting as your guardian and attempting to keep you safe."

"I didn't ask for you to watch over me, only that you deal with my father's goddamn will."

"You're absolutely right, Paxton. And you're safe

now, so you can calm down. I'm not going anywhere and I will answer your questions one at a time."

Paxton sat back. Telling her to calm down after everything that had happened so far in Arizona was like telling a child not to cry when it fell down. Nevertheless, she managed to steady her voice, and gathered her thoughts together in spite of how fast her pulse was racing.

"What do you mean by unique?" she asked, attacking that comment first. "You said you think the thing out there is unique, and also that it's a werewolf. If you're a werewolf and your pals are werewolves, what would make that thing out there different?"

Desperado's lights were twinkling. They would reach the center of town in minutes, and then what? With other people around, Grant might postpone the explanations she was waiting for.

"I was born here," she added tonelessly and out of context, her voice exhibiting the weariness she felt.

"Yes, this was once your home," Grant conceded calmly. "And now it is home to a few others who need this place as much as you're about to."

"Nostalgia has no place in dealing with my father's will," she countered. "Presently, I can take this town or leave it. What good did it do, in the end? I loved the place and it was taken away. I had forgotten about it, and yet here I am again, reliving pain that goes way back."

"Pain?" he said.

Paxton hadn't planned on confessing any of this to anyone. Some things were too private to see the light of day. But now that she had begun, she said, "Everything I loved was here at one time, Wade."

The man beside her stopped the truck at the edge of town and let it idle. Turning to her, he spoke slowly in a tender tone incongruous with the situation that was like a brush of silk over her tired, sensitive skin.

He might have been crazy, but Grant Wade, in that moment, was more gorgeous than anyone else on this planet.

"There are things in the world that are kept apart from it for a reason, and out of necessity," he said. "Some of the old barriers between worlds have been broken, and yet as time passes it becomes more and more difficult to maintain the few remaining secrets. Those of us living in this town need a sanctuary just as much as anyone else does. Maybe more. People in this world are not kind or sympathetic to those unlike themselves."

"Any minute now, you'll start making actual sense," Paxton said, repeating an earlier sentiment.

Grant hesitated before speaking again, as if trying to think of the right words to say.

"There are over a dozen beings living in this town at the moment and calling the old ghost town home. More come and go on a regular basis."

Paxton wasn't about to let such a cryptic statement get past her and jumped in. "What do you mean by *beings*? Are you talking about people? People with problems? People with a past in need of someplace to go? Homeless people who would otherwise live on the streets of the city? Are you saying you don't want to sell Desperado so that those people won't be displaced? Oh, and please tell me we aren't circling back to the werewolf theory."

Grant rubbed a crease from his forehead.

Paxton went on. "Which is it, Grant? Pick an answer for one of the questions I've just asked."

He ran his right hand over the back of the seat and

touched her neck lightly with warm fingers that had pleasured her less than an hour ago. Paxton wasn't immune to how that touch made her feel. She hadn't forgotten how much they both had wanted that session in the bunkhouse. It was, however, a pity that Grant couldn't come through with a viable way to explain any of the strange things that had happened since she stepped off the plane, other than to make up a few fantasies.

"Here's what you're missing and what you think you want to hear," he said, feathering his fingertips across the bare base of her neck, which, for Paxton, was a toss-up for the second most sensitive place on her body.

"I'm all ears, Grant."

She had to close her eyes. The electrical jolt that hit her each time Grant laid a hand on her threatened to send her right back into his arms. Problems or not, being in the same space with Grant Wade was erotic. Breathing in his scent made her chills scatter.

His voice broke the spell.

"The beings living in this town aren't *people* in the strictest sense of the word. The beast we're chasing is a threat to more than just the neighboring cattle, because if Desperado's neighbors were to catch that beast before we do, this town's secrets would be out. Desperado would be exposed for what it has become, and would likely be razed to the ground."

Paxton looked straight at Grant, expecting the half-truths to become real explanations requiring no stretch of the imagination, and thinking he might need an extra push in that direction.

"What secrets stand to be exposed?" she asked. "That you're werewolves and a pack, and that you hide out here to maintain some distance from everyone who isn't a werewolf?"

Ignoring those questions, he chose to relay other information she had asked for. "I wasn't lying, Paxton. Chances are better than good that the animal you encountered tonight is a wolf of some kind."

He held up a hand to stop her from interrupting when she was about to do just that. "Not just any wolf. One with the special designation of Lycan," he said.

What he said was so absurd, Paxton laughed to offset a sharp stab of panic. Grant's face, his expression, his eyes, showed no sign that this was a joke, when it had to be. Clearly, he wasn't going to let up on the werewolf thing.

"Lycan," she echoed, not liking the turn this conversation had taken any more than she liked the direction the truck was facing. Grant's friends were on hand tonight. Maybe insanity was contagious.

In the silence that followed his little dissertation, Paxton groped for a connection between reality and the extraordinary words Grant had offered her. *Werewolf. Lycan.* Thinking back, she recalled the loud thump on the roof of the rental car and the dark blur on the hood. She pictured the big scary eyes that had peered at her through the windshield, relived the hallucinatory awareness of feeling a strange presence at the motel. Moments ago, she'd had the same kind of eerie awareness on the road out of Desperado. And then there was the dark blur she'd seen out of the corner of her eye.

Long tentacles of fright returned. In spite of that, Paxton went over the thoughts again, freeze-framing the moment when she'd thought she heard voices whispering to her in her mind. Grant had mentioned the same thing. He'd told her the beast had spoken, not in person, but in his thoughts.

"Werewolf," she repeated, tasting the word, finding it sour and completely unacceptable as an answer to her dilemma. She couldn't fathom what would make Grant assume she'd believe what he was telling her.

Was this a ploy to throw her off-balance? Grant trying to gain some advantage in their negotiations over the property her father had left them?

He'd go so far as to suggest that Desperado was haunted by, not ghosts, but half-man, half-wolf creatures out of legend?

Quite obvious to her, when Grant spoke again, was the fact that he favored continuing with this game.

"The beings living in your father's town are werewolves," Grant said. "Although tonight you'd never know it, never believe it. They can only shift their shapes to become something else on the night of a full moon."

Paxton felt sick, not for the first time since arriving in Arizona. She felt sicker as she stared at the handsome, enigmatic man sitting beside her. It was so blatantly apparent that something was wrong with him mentally, something not so obvious because of his spectacular looks.

Then again, her mind nagged…

Hadn't she imagined subtle changes in Grant in the doorway of the bunkhouse? The longer physical frame and more angular features?

What about that?

She said, "I think you might be in need of meds," in a voice that hardly carried over the sound of the truck's idling engine.

Grant shook his head. "There's more."

"I can't wait."

"It involves you, Paxton."

"You've already told me that I'm a werewolf. Could there conceivably be any other incredible information about me to divulge?"

At this point, there was no laughter in her, regardless of the absurdity of the situation. As she saw it, the immediate problem facing her was how to get out of the truck without Grant chasing her.

Any way she viewed things, she was trapped. Grant's captive. One possible direction would be, as she had figured while en route to Desperado, to let Grant go on with this ruse. Pretend to believe him about werewolves until another opportunity came to get away. Could she do that? Make it work and keep a straight face?

God. If she had been to bed with this man, and had loved it, what did that make her?

What did it say about her that she had loved everything they had done and had to work hard now to forget the fever caused by Grant's talented mouth on hers? She had to breathe shallowly to dispel the memory of having his warm breath in her lungs. Crossing her legs wouldn't have stopped the tingling sensations that came from remembering how his hand had pleasured what lay between them.

And now he was betraying her trust.

Grant Wade was showing his true colors.

He had more to say, and she had no option but to listen.

"Sometimes, reality is a bitch, Paxton," he began. "At times, life can read more like science fiction. I get that, because I'm living on the bridge that joins both worlds."

"The human world and the world of the werewolf,"

she said to clarify his meaning as she moved toward the door to get away from Grant's touch.

"Your father left Desperado to me in order to protect the Weres living here and those in need of assistance regarding how to deal with what they've become. Desperado is a safe haven for the werewolf species. The only one I know of in the West. Your father knew about us. Leaving Desperado to me was no fluke, and no purposeful slight to you."

Paxton met Grant's eyes. "You said *us*. So I'm truly a werewolf?"

"Yes," he replied.

"And my father believed this? He might have thought so, too?"

"Completely, just as you soon will."

"Sorry. I'm afraid that would take a miracle," Paxton said.

"Then we'll have to show you one," Grant returned.

Defiance took over her ability to speak as calmly as he did about issues so nonsensical. Crossing her arms, Paxton uttered a challenge. "Okay. Go ahead. Show me that miracle."

Grant's focus was intense. His eyes were luminous in the moonlight coming through the window as he pointed at the moon. "Tomorrow, when the moon is full, everyone here will change shape, including you."

Paxton shoved aside the return of the chills threatening to bring on more quakes. "I've seen the movies. Nevertheless, if what you say is true, and we all require a full moon to do its particular brand of voodoo, why didn't the thing I saw tonight look like the rest of us do right now?"

I have you there, Grant Wade. Try to explain that.

While Paxton waited for him to try, it was easy to

note how that line of enquiry bothered Grant. She wondered what kind of sordid, fantastical tale he'd invent next to cover his ass. As her stomach roiled and her hands fisted, she dreaded hearing what he would come up with.

"Some of us are different," he finally said.

"That's all you've got? Really, I expected so much more."

"Did you?"

She glared at him.

"As far as we can guess, the beast out there can shape-shift without the moon's help," Grant said. "Few Weres possess that trick, and that's what makes this guy so unique."

He was looking at her strangely, perhaps beginning to understand that she wasn't going to fall for any part of his explanation.

"I understand this is hard to process, and even harder to believe," he admitted.

"Next to impossible," Paxton agreed. "And let me state again for the record that if I was a werewolf, I'd know it."

He said, "I might have thought the same thing if my parents hadn't schooled me about it early on."

Grant's expression hadn't strayed from being completely serious. "You'd know about your status unless both parents decided not to tell you about it."

Opening her mouth to protest, Paxton closed it again when the crazy conversation was interrupted by an eerie sound that echoed through the car. It was a horrible, haunting, gut-wrenching howl, and very much like the sound a goddamn werewolf might make.

The truck rocked into motion so quickly, Paxton was thrown backward. The only thing she could offer before they had reached the center of Desperado's main street was one word.

"Impossible."

But there truly was more, as Grant had predicted. None of it good.

One sideways glance told her that Grant Wade was no longer there. When that distant howl began to fade, Grant had simply melted into someone else.

Something else.

The shock of witnessing a real shape-shift tipped Paxton over the edge of reason and into a horror story.

God help them all...

Grant Wade had been telling the truth.

Chapter 20

It was a hell of a time to prove to Paxton the hard way that he had not been lying. Ready to jump out of her skin before his shift, she was now as white as a sheet.

And although Grant felt for her about learning of her heritage in this manner, he had other things to worry about—the damn Lycan interloper being foremost on that list.

That roar hadn't come from far off, which meant the slippery beast had penetrated Desperado's perimeter, somehow managing to slither past Ben and two of their best guards, or else finding another route inside. Moreover, it had to have been close to Paxton again, near that downed tree.

Anger crowded his thoughts.

His vision darkened.

The pack was already on the move. No one could afford to ignore that son of a bitch's challenging howl. By now, every Were here would know this sucker might be related to their species, if not exactly like them.

His desert pack was made up of strong, confident Weres who would protect their secrets with their lives if they had to. Grant hoped none of them would be pushed that far. This confrontation was going to end up being one lone rogue against another Lycan and fourteen desert Weres used to dealing with half-crazed newcomers. Surely the sucker out there would calculate the odds and either give up or go away.

Paxton was dead silent as she stared at him, and he had no way to appease her. No voice with which to comfort her. It was sink or swim time for Andrew Hall's daughter, and not in any way Grant would have planned for her big awakening.

When they got to Desperado, he jumped from the truck to join the others massing in the street. Everyone was concerned, keyed up and ready to rumble. But as he had explained to Paxton, without the presence of a full moon, his packmates were stuck in human form.

Although they all possessed superhuman strength, these Weres didn't have the extra punch of power embedded into Grant's DNA that allowed the full extent of his abilities to be at his beck and call. Tonight, in a standoff with a creature with similar abilities, he'd have to be the front man. Everyone here was aware of this.

"Bring it on, you filthy bastard."

Shirleen took his place in the truck as the temporary guardian for the female frozen there. Ben, still at the gate, would get the message and respond if he hadn't heard the cheeky trespasser's yowl.

The rest of the pack was scattering to take their places. One or two of them would search along the fence near where he had found Paxton. If the bastard had been there, the atmosphere would still be disturbed in a way that would be easy for other Weres to pick up on. Grant hadn't had the chance to investigate, since getting Paxton away from danger had been a priority at the time.

Two or three packmates would position themselves near the end of the main street, while others had designated areas to watch over. Moonlight, though unhelpful to these Weres tonight in other ways, lit the street with an iridescent glow.

Grant stood in the center of the main street waiting for all hell to break loose, certain it would before long. In the months leading up to now, the rogue hadn't ventured close enough to breathe down Grant's neck, but something had changed that.

He glanced at the truck, refusing to believe the creep they had been chasing could have anything to do with Andrew Hall's daughter. The theory he'd been hatching seemed to be a wild one, given that Paxton had only arrived that day. Yet the damn beast had tracked her twice after their initial meeting and was hanging around here now. Doing what? Biding his time? Looking for a way to get past the pack?

"What do you want?" Grant sent, figuring only two things might send a werewolf into tracking mode in spite of the potential danger involved. Those two things were piqued interest in a potential mate and a desire to challenge the alpha of a pack for that title.

"Which one of those things are you after?"

Of course, the answer to that question didn't really matter. He wasn't going to allow any other Were with big ideas to get near Paxton. Nor was he about to turn the guardianship of this pack over to a butcher.

When Paxton left the truck and approached, her closeness wafted over him like a hot August breeze.

He had to look at her. Couldn't help himself. She was so damn beautiful, and so very pale.

She stopped several feet away, speechless. He wanted more than anything to go to her, hold her, make love to her, chase away the demons he had helped to set in place. A firm hold on his resolve was what it took to keep from doing any of those things.

He morphed back into a more familiar shape and said in his human voice, "I'm needed elsewhere. I'm sorry."

Explaining Paxton's presence in the street, Shirleen said, "Can't keep a good woman down, it seems."

Grant stifled a human-sized growl. His wolf was still close to the surface, wanting to be freed. His pulse was pounding dangerously, but not because of the rogue he needed to find. With chaos all around, Paxton was the larger draw. She stood motionless. Her tousled hair shone in the moonlight like spun gold. Delicate features were set in a grim expression, but no longer frozen in disbelief.

He took that for progress.

As her emotions settled over him, he knew that fear made up only a portion of what Paxton was feeling. Curiosity tangled with other emotions that weren't so easy to read, and Grant was heartened that one of those elusive emotions wasn't disgust.

"It's true," she said softly without budging. "All of it."

Sink or swim, Grant repeated to himself, raising both hands to display leftover claws that had never looked as lethal as they did right then. Nerves burned across taut interior wires while he awaited Paxton's reaction to the only part of him at the moment that hinted of wolf.

"And I..." she started to say, without finishing the remark. Paxton was thinking over the fact that she had screwed a werewolf. She was considering the possible ramifications of that.

There was so much he needed to say to her and tons of information to impart, when none of that would have appeased her. Seeing him shift shape in close quarters had been step one in her introduction to the moon's cult.

There was no time to commiserate on the fluctuations of reality. Seconds were ticking away and he had a job to do. Paxton wasn't the only treasure he had to protect. His pack depended on him to help set things straight.

Would Paxton have understood any of that if he had explained?

Each cell in his body protested when he backed away from her. He faltered when she stumbled forward as if she'd been caught in his wake, and Shirleen put out a hand to stop her. Side by side the two females watched him tear off what was left of his shirt.

He dislodged his human countenance for the fifth time that night with a twitch and a series of shudders. When his spine began to lengthen and his bones snapped, Paxton whispered, "No." She said, "God, no," as his muscles bunched and began to mound with the sound of raw meat being slapped on a counter.

"Welcome to my world, little wolf. Our world," he sent to her as their eyes met.

He watched Paxton stagger and raise a hand to her head, possibly to feel for an injury responsible for making her see things. With his shift complete, Grant filled his lungs with night scents, searching for the one smell among them he needed to find…the scent of an entity that was taking him away from Paxton because that rogue quite possibly coveted things that belonged to someone else.

"Impossible," Paxton repeated, as stone-faced as a statue.

It was too late now for cover-ups and illusions. Wildness was calling. He'd found the scent he needed, and it was too close to ignore. Grant turned from Paxton, who just might have been the love of his life if they had met some other time, whether or not imprinting chained them together.

He looked back at her only once to view the stunned, shocked expression he expected to find frozen on her face. Again, he found that he was wrong. Stunned? Yes. She was registering that. Strangely enough, though, Paxton didn't sway, faint or run the other way. Her expression had turned thoughtful, as if she might have been thinking back and piecing together the events that had taken place since her arrival in Arizona, through the lead-up to this moment.

He let her have those thoughts.

Her big eyes never left him. Her attention was focused and extremely hot. But he could not turn back. Didn't dare. The beast out there was tampering with his pack and this beautiful, as yet undeclared she-wolf, and he was the only barrier standing between them.

Don't you see that, my lover?

Power soared through him. Impatience flared. Feeling strong, fed up, angry over having to leave Paxton and his friends, perhaps at the expense of one or both of those things, Grant let loose a fierce, feral growl that rolled like an aftershock through the dirt beneath his feet.

Then he was off and running, sensing the beast nearby, determined to end this game of hide-and-seek once and for all.

"Impossible."

The word didn't begin to describe what Paxton had witnessed, but she kept repeating it anyway, needing to expel the shock icing her limbs.

Grant Wade really was a werewolf…which led to the possibility of other things he had told her being true. The beast. Desperado. And what about her?

She might have believed she was dreaming if it hadn't been for the pressure of a hand on her arm—a real pressure that helped to keep her grounded and belonged to a werewolf named Shirleen.

God…

Managing a slight turn of her head, Paxton found an expression of empathy on Shirleen's pretty face. Gathering words together, Paxton asked, "What is this place?"

"Our sanctuary," Shirleen replied.

"Whose sanctuary?"

"Beings like us. Like him."

"Werewolves." Paxton had a hard time saying the word out loud.

"Yes. Werewolves."

"And you?" Paxton asked.

"Not exactly like him, but a close enough rendition to be here with the rest."

"How does this happen, Shirleen? How could it possibly be real?"

"It's a long story, Paxton. Centuries old."

"Then maybe you can start that story now."

"I'll let Grant do the honors," Shirleen said. "Filling you in is the alpha's place."

Alpha.

Hell.

"Where did he go? Where did they all go?" she asked.

"I believe you had a run-in with the wolf they've gone after. Did Grant tell you about this guy?"

"He tried to tell me what that trespasser might be. *Rogue* was the word Grant used. Killing cattle, he said."

She couldn't remember much else with her mind issuing warnings about getting out of there in spite of how dangerous they all seemed to think this rogue was.

"Rogue. Yes." Shirleen waved to the closest building. "It would be best to get off the street now."

The woman who had just admitted to being a werewolf kept one hand clamped to Paxton's arm, so that running anywhere was not an option, though Grant's truck wasn't far from where they were standing. Besides, where would she go if she could run away this time? As far as she knew, and after what had happened to her with the downed tree, the roads in and out of Desperado would probably now be guarded.

Look where trying to escape had landed her. Inside a den of wolves.

The motel in the city now seemed like a stupid place to retreat to, and the airport was too damn far, especially when somewhere between here and there a mad werewolf lurked.

Werewolf.

True.

Several small globes of light winked along the sides of the street. Moonlight on the tips of her shoes made Paxton want to cringe. In all the movies she'd seen, moonlight was the catalyst for werewolf transformation, but the moon wasn't full tonight, so the woman beside her still looked like Shirleen.

Grant had told her about that, too.

This wasn't how she remembered Desperado. As a kid, she had explored every corner of this town without even once coming across a goddamn werewolf. As far as she knew.

"Twenty years," Shirleen said, as if reading her mind. "That's when Desperado first opened its gates to the likes of us."

"That's right after I left it," Paxton mused, briefly closing her eyes to try to assimilate that news.

When Shirleen urged her to move with a strong tug on her arm, Paxton accompanied her to the old general store, where the windows were boarded up and nailed tight. In the past, she had pretended to be the proprietor of this store. When tourists came, she had handed out candy to other kids. Now the tourists were long gone and the town had been taken over by a species of beings that turned furry in the moonlight.

This was hard to believe. Impossible to believe.

She was one of them? Could Grant be right about that one little detail?

They stopped on the store's threshold. The space inside was dark, but not completely. Paxton saw that it wasn't only the missing seasonal residents that had changed Desperado over the years. Where there had once been a counter, a woodstove and some chairs, there was nothing but the gleam of cold steel bars.

It took a minute more for Paxton to understand what she was seeing. Those bars were on cages. The kind of cages that contained wild animals at the zoo. There were two cages, each of them large enough to house a small elephant. On the walls beside them, thick ropes of silver chain hung. Closed metal boxes were stacked near the door.

"It's not pretty, but sometimes necessary," Shirleen said.

Paxton didn't ask the question screaming for an answer in her mind. *Necessary for what?*

Because, deep in her soul, she already knew.

Aiding werewolves going through a tough transition is what Grant had said. But the place looked like a torture chamber, and viewing it made her feel ill all over again.

Chapter 21

Grant followed the scent of wet fur across the rise just north of Desperado. It wasn't usual for werewolves to carry an odor when furred-up. Then again, this one ate cows and, on at least one occasion, while nestling in a dank cave, gnawed on human bones.

Grant grimaced at the thought. He'd never heard of such a thing, yet he knew that bad-guy Weres with grudges against humans existed. He had forgotten to check with Ben about asking the sheriff for a list of missing hikers, and that seemed more important than ever.

Walking at a swift, purposeful pace, he noted how quiet the night was, and that the sky was filled with stars. Desert heat seeped through the soles of his boots. Too bad there was no time to stop and enjoy any of those things.

His packmates guarded the fence line. Grant nodded

to them as he passed. Those Weres were silent, diligent, watchful and used to seeing him in his current form. In a fight, he could count on any of these Weres to have his back. They trusted him to eventually find the crazy rogue who was twice as dangerous as anything they had encountered to date.

Near the section of fence where Paxton had encountered her second fright of the day, Grant halted. Ben had been there and gone, but the place reeked of another, more feral presence.

That elusive sucker hadn't disappeared after all. He was still here.

"Come out," Grant sent.

A response came in the form of a deep, guttural growl, reminiscent of a wolf's stern warning to back off.

"Can't do that," Grant said. *"Since you've been hanging around for a while, you know why."*

The next growl was louder and more menacing than the first one, and raised the hair on the back of Grant's neck.

"Come in and set things right," Grant sent. *"You're causing too many problems that can't be overlooked. Half of the residents in the area are looking for you. We both understand why they can't actually be allowed to find what they seek."*

Sounds came to him of something heavy being dragged over the sandy soil. Christ, had the bastard tagged more cattle?

Waves of chills met with Grant's elevated body temperature. He swore inwardly and turned in a tight circle for a good look around.

"Show yourself. It's not as if I haven't seen the likes of you before."

The voice that responded to his invitation echoed in

his mind with the muffled clang of a rusty bell. The surprise for Grant was how old and weary it sounded.

"You believe that, wolf, about having seen the likes of me?"

Contact.

Grant ran a clawed finger across his left thigh, slicing through his jeans in a show of anger as he spoke.

"I'm guessing you're more like me than I'd care to admit, though I'm leery of your fetish for thievery and teething on things that don't belong to you."

"Then, as I said earlier, you know nothing," was the reply.

"I know this can't go on," Grant warned.

"Who is going to stop me? You?"

"I'm here now for just that reason."

Another growl came from the bushes beside Grant. His muscles tensed, readying for whatever this guy was going to do. Another round of chills rapidly melted behind the heat of his revved up metabolism.

"In a fair fight between us you would lose," the invisible bastard taunted.

"Why don't we test that theory?" Grant raised his hands to prove his willingness to try.

"You have never been my target. If you had been, you would not be here now to defend your little pack of wolves," the trespasser said.

"All the same, you're bringing unwanted attention that none of us can afford."

"Shall I take my hunger elsewhere, then? Bother someone else?" the cheeky bastard said.

"Wouldn't the consequences be the same wherever you went, if stealing animals is your MO?" Grant suggested. *"Not to mention your nasty habit of pouncing on the occasional human. That was you, I assume?"*

Silence fell for several long minutes before the beast spoke again.

"You know about that kill and still believe we're alike?"

"I can smell the power in you," Grant said. *"But I claim no kinship. Your actions sicken me."*

"All wolves once hunted in the wild."

"Until some of us evolved," Grant countered.

More silence, then the rogue said, *"The difference is that you try to fit into a world that would kill you as soon as they found out what you are."*

"Yes." Grant nodded. *"So I'm curious about how you've existed this long, given that you don't seem to give a damn about how anyone might react to your actions."*

"My actions aren't completely selfish, I assure you."

"Prove it. Show yourself. Come in and accept our help."

"I can't do that."

"Then, with so much at stake, it will have to be a fight," Grant challenged.

"Perhaps some other time," the beast said.

Grant shook his head. *"After you've satisfied your need to bring more trouble down on us? Do you even know what we do here?"*

"I know what you do," the beast in the bushes conceded.

"We help our kind deal. We give Weres a place to land when they spin out. Why do you think we can't help you?" Grant asked.

"Because," a human voice said, as if the beast had shape-shifted in seconds to press home the idea of how much power he truly did possess, and to get these last words in, *"no one can help me now."*

The scent of this newcomer dissipated along with his words, as if the sucker had simply blown away on a stiff breeze. After a minute, nothing of its presence remained.

For Grant, this newest disappearing act was not going to cut it. He moved several paces north, then south and west, inhaling deeply, striving to gain an awareness of where the rogue had gone. He felt like the being he chased wasn't as insane as he'd imagined. In fact, that Lycan had seemed lucid and in control of his faculties.

Grant couldn't fathom why the creature had not wanted to fight. There had been no challenge for the leadership of the desert pack, when if that beast had won, a new alpha could have walked into town that night. The creature he still thought of as a monster hadn't harmed Paxton near the fence, either, which made the tally three for three in benign Paxton sightings.

"What the hell do you want?" he sent far and wide in frustration.

Perplexed, unsatisfied with this meeting, Grant went after the other Lycan. He swept through the area looking for anything that might lead him to the rogue's whereabouts. Eventually, his search paid off. Kneeling down, he ran a claw over the thin red trail that had appeared almost out of nowhere and ended several feet ahead. The blood trail was puzzling, but didn't offer up any real clue as to the Lycan's actual direction.

"Who the hell are you? Houdini?"

Standing, scanning, barely breathing, Grant let out a howl of irritation that was answered by every coyote between where he stood and the ghost town behind him. The blood on the ground didn't belong to any missing steer. Not this time. So what poor, unsuspecting human being had lost it?

* * *

Paxton shrank back with a shoulder to the doorjamb. The room, and what it contained, was scary. What were the cages for? What was going on here? Worse still, in terms of causing a hair-raising adrenaline rush, was the way Shirleen suddenly bolted for the door, nearly knocking Paxton over in her hurry to get outside.

Loath to be alone with those ominous cages, Paxton followed Shirleen, supposing the woman was tuning in to a sound Paxton couldn't hear. Two others joined them in the street. People? Weres who hadn't shape-shifted tonight? They were large guys, tall, relatively young, very well built—and examples of a world that had gone mad.

All three of her new companions were facing west, so Paxton whirled to stare in that direction, fighting the desire to duck in case more bad news was coming.

"He found something," Shirleen announced, and the men beside her backed into the shadows hugging the buildings.

Anxious, Paxton said, "Grant?"

Shirleen nodded, then turned again toward the entrance to town, visibly tensing. "Shit," she whispered.

If Shirleen's body language hadn't caused Paxton's nervousness, that one word would have done the trick. It didn't take a psychic to understand trouble was in the air and headed their way, although Paxton had no idea what kind of trouble everyone here was expecting.

By the time she began to consider this, strange feelings began to take her over. She couldn't have described them. In spite of the fact that she couldn't see anything past the old saloon, she somehow knew...yes, she *knew* Grant was returning.

His nearness brought unexpected heat. A spot deep

inside her began to quiver, as if Grant would again soon touch her there. Limbs began to quake, as they had when wrapped around Grant's waist. Her stance wobbled. Her head hurt. Grant was coming back and she wanted to run out to meet him, but couldn't.

Grant wasn't a man in the strictest sense of that word. He was something else.

Beside her, Shirleen spoke. "Now isn't the time to distract him."

Paxton had seen Grant go from man to werewolf and still hadn't been able to grasp the full meaning of that. She had seen the claws and the face that, though changed, still had the same baby-blue eyes. Not a mindless monster's eyes, but eyes glowing with an intelligent gleam.

He appeared at the end of the street now, as if she had conjured him. As Grant walked, he began to change back to the man she recognized. But truthfully, his alter ego wasn't so far removed from the human persona's glorious package. It was somehow more of the same.

As he headed toward her, Paxton's knees weakened. Her heart slammed against her ribs. Grant was coming for her and something had upset him. He was broadcasting concern in ways she easily understood.

"Paxton."

She was sure she heard him say her name.

"Yes?" She inched forward.

And then she was in Grant's arms, tight against that marvelous muscle, enfolded in his incredible heat. All the while, her mind urged her to be careful and to stop the madness. Warnings came to break away because Grant wasn't normal. He wasn't even human.

Breathing was difficult. With her head pressed to his chest and her resolve on hiatus, Paxton heard him speak in thoughts to Shirleen. His words and sentences were like whispers from a far-off place.

"Dangerous," he said. *"More than we thought. So far beyond what we had imagined."*

Grant had found the trespasser he was hunting. Possibly that trespasser and the creature she had, early on, believed to be a bear were one and the same.

Concern wasn't the only thing Grant was telegraphing to her through their closeness. He wanted to protect her, save her from having to face what he had found. That goal was paramount in his short list of objectives. Save her. Save his friends. Save Desperado and whatever he did here with those awful steel cages.

Nerves that ran along the wires under Grant's skin seemed to fire hers up in an invasion of blistering heat. The hardness of his body and the realization of how much she noticed it became another insurmountable obstacle to regaining her wits.

Thinking seriously about pulling back, and about reexamining her mental state, Paxton knew that yelling for help was completely out of the realm of possibility. Who would hear her and come to her aid when this man was their leader? Which of these werewolves would challenge or defy him?

She felt him begin to shake. She felt his heat spike to a degree well beyond impossible range. And, still, she did not run.

When Grant tilted her head back to look into her face, there was no claw on his index finger. When he forced her to meet his eyes by whispering her name seductively, Paxton obeyed.

Their bodies were pressed tightly together, and Grant didn't seem to mind that there were others present. Holding her hostage with an apologetic gaze and an unspoken promise, it was a man's lips that rested on hers lightly, briefly. Except that the kiss didn't feel light or brief to Paxton. It felt like goodbye.

When Paxton opened her eyes, she found herself being lifted into Grant's strong arms. "I'm not a baby," she protested. "And I'm perfectly able to take care of myself."

Swear to God, she would have said more if Grant's hungry mouth had allowed her to. His lips kept returning to hers, sampling, tasting, as if he couldn't get enough.

She was in Grant's arms and they were moving off the street. Light disappeared when they went inside the old general store. She wondered if he was going to take her there, on the floor. If the kisses didn't stop, she might even allow that, in spite of what he was.

After several more steps his mouth finally withdrew from hers, but Grant continued to hold her.

Finally, he set her down.

Their eyes met again. His were filled with regret. Was this the goodbye she had anticipated, felt, sensed? Would he head back out to continue his search for the bad guy, maybe without hope of returning?

Grant backed away from her slowly and spoke to her for the first time since his return to town minutes ago. "I'm sorry for this. It is necessary. You will have to trust me on that."

"What do you mean?" Her voice was raspy with hunger for Grant Wade, whatever the hell he was.

The sound of metal clanging on metal filled the space. Following that came the sound of a bolt sliding into place. Still, it took more time for Paxton to comprehend what had just happened, and by then Grant had moved out of sight.

Dread struck. Panic hit with sheets of ice that replaced the former heat of her internal furnace. *Had he? No. He couldn't have.*

Shoving both of her hands forward, Paxton took hold of the steel bars keeping her from accompanying Grant's departure. They were the cold steel bars of one of the cages she had seen.

Her head swam with the uncertainty of the situation. Her mind protested over and over again. Hell, had she been wrong? That kiss, hot, insatiable, had not been meant as a sad temporary goodbye or been evidence of the pleasure of a blissful reunion between lovers.

It had been a distraction.

A lie.

And a trap.

Chapter 22

Grant's heart hurt. But his reasons for caging Paxton had been sound. She would be safe until the time came for an all-clear. That stubborn streak of hers could get her into trouble, when trouble is exactly what they didn't need more of.

His body continued to ache from too many shape-shifts in the span of a day. Even Lycan bones and tissues had their limits. Part of his discomfort also stemmed from another source, however, and that was from having to leave Paxton like this.

She didn't call out to him, scream or shout obsceni-ties. Silence accompanied his exit from the building. An absolute absence of sound. Bless her, Paxton might actually be trusting him. Either that or she was too stunned to react.

He wanted to go back in there and explain why she needed to be out of the picture for a while. He'd tell her that cage was as much for her protection as it was for everyone else's, and that the rogue out there had more on his mind than waylaying hikers or cattle. The bastard hadn't been able to hide from another Lycan the emotions driving him toward Desperado.

That wicked creature was interested in Paxton. Too interested. While the beast's brief conversation hadn't resulted in an explanation of what that rogue wanted, his mind had offered up the first real clue.

Paxton was the unspoken name that had filled the creature's mind.

Since there had been ample opportunity in the past few months for the rogue to have headed into the old ghost town and he hadn't, Grant might have done them all a disservice by bringing Paxton here. Actually, it turned out that he had ended up using Paxton as bait to corner a madman.

There was no way he could he have told Paxton this, frightening her more than he already had by shifting in her presence. No. She had to remain ignorant of this new turn of events.

"Paxton, I'm sorry," he said, knowing she wouldn't hear that or the sincerity of his apology.

One good thing was in their favor. His fair-haired lover was stronger than she looked and had wolf blood in her veins. They had mated, man to woman, forming a bond that went beyond anything in the human world, and no good-for-nothing Lycan with foul habits and evil tendencies was going to set foot here or have face time with her again.

I promise you this, Paxton. He will not get to you.

"Was that necessary?" Shirleen asked, coming up behind him. Shirleen had confessed to liking Paxton, so she would be wondering why he had locked Paxton in that cage.

"She is the draw," Grant replied. "He wants to come for her."

"Strange how you all seem to think so," Shirleen said thoughtfully.

"Yes, well, you're already taken, so what kind of extraordinary she-wolf does that leave?" Grant teased.

"You think he will come here for her?" Shirleen pressed. "In spite of how many of us there are?"

"I think he might."

"To do what? Why her?"

"Lycan," Grant said, uttering the one word that possibly explained what that rogue wanted.

Shirleen's eyes widened. "Andrew Hall's daughter is Lycan?"

"Afraid so."

Shirleen let that go. "It isn't that rogue's blood I smell on you. Whose blood is it?"

"He left a trail to throw me off the scent. It worked. I lost him."

Shirleen looked past him, toward the building housing the cages. "How long will she be in there?"

"As long as it takes to get to the bottom of this creepy escapade."

She blocked his path when he began to walk. "Full moon tomorrow. Paxton might actually need that cage then."

Grant shut his eyes to ride out the sensation of falling through space without a parachute. Shirleen was right about Paxton. Who could predict what would happen when that full moon rolled around and how it might affect the woman he'd started to think of as his mate?

He'd have to be watchful on two fronts if that thing—

that mad beast out there—caught a whiff of Paxton in the middle of her first shape-shift and decided to do something about it. Even worse would be for the rogue to come after her tonight.

Shirleen spoke again with the kind of logic she always displayed. "If he waits until tomorrow night to confront us, it will be better for us all. Half the wolf power this pack will have under the full moon would surely be sufficient to contain one Lycan."

Grant had to agree. But he felt nervous about how much damage a rogue Lycan could do, whether or not his friends were furred-up and ferocious.

He said, "Don't you suppose he will have considered that scenario?"

"Then if he has any plans to come here, he would implement that plan tonight when we're more vulnerable. Right?"

And that, Grant thought, was the reason for his anxiousness and the impetus for caging Paxton. The bastard out there could shift without the full moon, and that trick could cost this pack dearly.

He glanced to the end of the street, aware of the positioning of each member of his pack. With his eyes shut, his abilities allowed him to locate Ben and the others at the fence. Given that the beast out there had similar abilities, the rogue would also know those things.

It wasn't safe to think about Paxton. It wasn't safe to feel anything for her. He had to close down all channels that led to her and hope the sudden silence would be sufficient to keep a monster out.

That was the plan.

Such was his intention.

Until Paxton, just twenty feet behind him and enclosed by a metal cage meant to withhold the strength of a male Were in the throes of a life-changing event, touched his mind with a call that was a plea for help. A call he couldn't refuse in spite of the obstacles facing this pack because they were so completely connected.

Holy hell!

His mind reeled. She wasn't just a she-wolf in the disguise of an unsuspecting human. Nothing so simple as that.

Paxton was much, much more. And tonight, after all these years, without a full moon in attendance and in a scene complicated by the added bonus of having a mad wolf knocking at their door... Paxton Hall was coming into her heritage one damn claw at a time.

Sickness twisted Paxton's stomach with a grip so tight, breathing was nearly impossible. Thinking was out of the question. Standing up was no longer an option.

Sinking to her knees, blinded by the onset of pain so sudden and intense she wondered if she had been shot, Paxton cried out. The onslaught of agony was all-encompassing and not focused in any one spot. Her head was being crushed in a vice. Strength left her limbs. Her heartbeat fluttered weakly and she couldn't lift her head. She felt as though she were dying, one desperate, insufficient breath at a time.

Vision tunneled, blotting out the small globe of light that had been her lifeline. But moonlight flooded the space, cutting through the dark to reach her from the open doorway and creating a dappled pattern on the front of her thighs. With it came a wave of cold almost as terrible as the initial strike of pain that had driven her to the floor.

She had to be dying. But why?

"Grant!"

Had she said his name out loud when breathing was a stretch?

"Grant…"

He had promised to protect her. Or had she imagined that?

"It's killing me," she whispered, doubling over without any real idea about what *it* was.

Moonlight touched her face now with a cold caress. She shrank back from the only light left in the dark, having nowhere to go and no way to escape her steel prison.

Inhaling the moonlight brought up bile that made her choke. Paxton felt her pulse take a dive. As a nurse, Paxton understood what those symptoms meant. She was going into shock and had never felt so sick and so completely alone.

"Grant. Please."

Why did she think Grant Wade might swoop in to help her when he had put her in this cage and left her here? If someone was to blame for her current state, it was Grant.

Not true…

She had wanted to come here. To Desperado. All along, she had pushed toward the events that had befallen her.

There was no energy left to raise a shout. Her blood pressure had plummeted. The first convulsion arrived swiftly with a nasty body wave that pressed her against the steel bars for support. Paxton's forehead slammed against metal highlighted by a beam of silvery lunar particles, and she hardly noticed the impact. Her back arched dramatically. Bones crackled. Inside her, more trouble was brewing. Something deep in her gut was clawing its way upward from her stomach to her chest, wreaking havoc along the way.

The second convulsion sent her to the floor, curled up in a fetal position. She shook so violently, the hard surface she laid on scratched through her clothes, bruising tender, stinging skin. She was sinking beneath a wave of darkness streaked with those damn light particles.

And then, as though someone had flipped a switch, the remaining light went out.

Eyes shut, pulse faint, Paxton thought she heard shouts in the distance. Her mind buzzed with static. She breathed fresh rounds of pain, shook with pain, absorbed each wicked example of extreme physical torture by curling up tighter and trying desperately to hold on to the remaining vestiges of life.

"I don't want to die here," were the last words she got out before that darkness became nearly total.

But she wasn't gone yet. Thoughts still blinked in and out, though the breaths she groped for were inadequate. Only one tactile sensation remained—the icy burn of the steel bar her fingers were clamped to.

Refuse to give in.

Refuse to give up.

Sharp screeching sounds rang in her mind…unfamiliar noises of no particular concern when she faced pain so encompassing.

Was someone approaching?

Maybe she imagined that.

Wait. Yes. Someone was there. Her fingers were being pried from the steel bar, and she didn't want to let go. If she did, all sensation would be lost.

"Paxton," a deep voice crooned. "It's okay, I'm here."

Grant's voice. He had returned after leaving her there.

You put me here, you bastard. She could not say this out loud.

The stronger voice overrode her unspoken thought. "This was for your own good. I left you here to keep you safe. Please believe me. I had no idea this would happen now."

Bastard.

A set of instructions followed that she had to consider.

"Don't let your mind slip away. It's important that you hang on to what makes you *you*. That might sound strange, but I'm sure you know what I mean. Can you open your eyes, Paxton? Open your eyes and look at me?"

Hurt. She couldn't have said that out loud, either, because her lips were numb. Fear of seeing a face that might no longer resemble Grant was what kept her eyes tightly shut.

"I know you hurt," he sympathized. "I understand what that pain is like. However, you must do as I ask. Open your eyes. Trust me. Take a chance and open them now."

Her lashes flapped once, twice. She couldn't communicate the fact that she lacked the strength to do what was asked of her.

Can't.

"You can," he directed, as if he had heard her reply. "You bear the mark that indicates a strength you might not yet comprehend. Remember? There's a mark on your arm like mine. It's there for a reason. Only those of us from a long-lived family line of survivors possess that mark. When you open your eyes, you'll see that."

More cold rushed in. Shaking ensued, along with more convulsions. Paxton again had the sensation of being about to leave her body, and she picked up the inward chant that had become her mantra.

Refuse to let go.

Refuse to give in.

"Yes. That's it," the deep voice applauded. "Fight, Paxton. I've seen that fight in you. The pain is temporary. Rise above it and become what you're meant to be. There's no going back or holding back the tide once it has begun, so you must stay with me, little wolf. It's time for you to understand who and what you are."

Don't like what you're suggesting, she protested in silence, unable to argue. Was she supposed to place her trust in a man who hadn't been honest with her from the start? A man who wasn't actually a man at all, but a creature straight out of late-night TV?

Grant was here with her. Who else would know about the mark on her upper arm? His voice had the ability to move her.

Excitement jump-started her heartbeat, and yet Paxton still felt half in and half out of the world, as if she floated somewhere in between two places. *A bridge between two worlds*, Grant had said.

She feared one more quake might do her in.

"Paxton."

Grant's authoritative tone served to gather up her rapidly fraying attention.

"It's a good life," he said. "You'll see. You have to want it badly enough to get through this phase. Most of us with the mark can. You can. There is no acceptable alternative. Now open your eyes and see the world as it really is."

Having no idea where the energy came from to do as Grant asked, Paxton opened her eyes. The light hadn't gone. Grant Wade's broad shoulders were blocking it. He was beside her on the floor, looking completely human and cradling her against a bare chest that supplied enough warmth to burn through her tremors.

The icy fear began to melt. Her body's tightness eased slightly. Paxton blinked up at Grant, wanting to thank him for coming back, but unable to do so because his human semblance was a disguise that hid the secrets beneath his bronzed skin.

Not a man...

Still, God, his heat was soothing and necessary. Paxton wanted desperately to curl into him and hear Grant tell her there was nothing inside her that didn't belong there, and that the sickness rolling through her wasn't related to him and what he was. She needed him to confirm this was a dream from which she'd soon wake up.

But he called her a "little wolf," and the words rang in her ears with a discordant sound. Those words were a mistake. Grant was the wolf. Werewolf. She was Paxton, and that was all. Next up would be to get out of there the minute she could move her legs.

"This is just the beginning," Grant said slowly, as if trying to soften bad news. "There's just a little more. The next flash of pain will be worse. You might want to die. But you will withstand that pain, Paxton. You must not leave me. Handle what she will throw your way, my beautiful lover."

"She?"

When she asked that question, Paxton heard Grant's reactive sigh of relief.

"The moon," he said. "To me, the moon is female. For you, it might be different."

She felt Grant lifting her. He was rescuing her after putting her here in the first place. Before her next breath, she was in his arms and they were moving toward the doorway, toward the light shining there.

That light wasn't the final white glare that sick and dying people mentioned in hushed voices, because she had not died in the cell. Already, she could breathe easier and move her arms. Fresh air filled her oxygen-starved lungs.

More of the terrible tunneling darkness receded as Grant carried her onto the covered porch outside the building. Moonlight lit the street, slanting in from a position low over the top of the nearby mountain range. Though the light was weaker now, it was in a perfect position to have reached her inside the room behind them through the open doorway.

Grant carried her into the empty street, holding her tightly, probably realizing she couldn't have stood on her own. Whereas she had always been fiercely independent, Paxton now felt like a child.

"If this has already started, moonlight might aid the transition, might make things easier. Are you ready to see?" he whispered with his face close to hers.

Grant's face. No mistake. Big eyes. Chiseled cheekbones. Expression of concern.

"And may fortune be in our favor, Paxton, so that the damn beast sniffing around won't get wind of this before it's done."

Paxton had no idea what he was going on about. Concentration hadn't caught up after sliding into a caged abyss. Her face and lips tingled, coming alive after being numb. Her body felt brittle and way too rigid.

The way Grant held her suggested that he thought she might break if he set her down. Maybe he thought she'd pass out. His energy buzzed through her as if he could, by some kind of fancy transference, shore up her energy with some of his own.

It was, of course, too late for anyone to help her. When Grant leaned back and moonlight touched her again, the thing nestled inside her soared to the surface.

Chapter 23

In his arms, Paxton shuddered once more.

Grant shored up his grip on her.

Her head was thrown back, exposing a smooth expanse of pale ivory neck he wanted to nuzzle. Her legs, clad in dirt-speckled jeans, dangled over his arms. Paxton felt so very light; he feared there would be no room for her small-boned frame to graduate to the next phase of her first shape-shift.

But her body was trying to do just that.

He wasn't going to let her go or let her die. Silently, he sent her one message of encouragement after another, backing up those messages with a push of his own personal power. She didn't scratch at him or fight. Her hands covered her face because the light was hurting her eyes. On her upper arm, below her short T-shirt sleeve, sat the ring of silvery tissue that looked like his.

Who the hell knows where your moon mark comes

from or how Andrew kept it a secret? he mused, not wanting to mention Paxton's father's name. Andrew Hall had never set foot in Desperado since Grant took over as caretaker and alpha of the desert pack. Though Grant had bunked in the guesthouse, Andrew had seldom been in residence, preferring another, undisclosed location for his long-term illness.

They had never crossed paths or spoken face-to-face. After word of his death arrived, Andrew's will had been the only remaining link to a legacy directed at werewolves…from a man with knowledge of the species who, for some reason, cared enough to help.

Paxton had to be that reason, Grant surmised. Her father had brought her here and had sent her straight into Grant's arms. He hadn't been wrong about Paxton's wolf blood—it had to have come from family. There was no way to copy a mark like hers. Although he didn't have proof of her father's heritage, and Andrew Hall had certainly never admitted to being part of the species he protected, the man had to have been a pure-blooded werewolf.

If Andrew had been a Were, it explained *her*. This. Now. What it failed to address was how Paxton had held off her wolf for so long and how she could be going through the change without a full moon present. Those things would suggest she was Lycan, and also that he had been an insensitive idiot for not picking up on it when sensing Weres was his business.

Damn it, he was anxious for Paxton, who was in the dark in so many ways. If offered the choice, he would gladly have changed places in order to take on her pain. At the moment, with her shirt torn open and what remained of her flimsy lingerie exposed, the belief that she could be a Were seemed ludicrous.

He wished they'd had more time in that damn bunk-house and that he could have explained to her what to expect. She wouldn't have believed him, of course. Not many people could have, in her place.

Grant's heart skidded in anticipation of what would happen next. Paxton would be enough like him to be able to stay with him if she chose to. She would be free to love him if that's the way her heart ran after just one day together.

One frigging day that felt like years.

Imprinting was a hell of a thing to have taken hold of him so quickly. Taken hold of both of them, it now seemed to him.

New shudders rocked Paxton, punctuated by her muffled groans of surprise and pain, before her body went limp in his arms. Grant anxiously waited for movement that didn't come. For her big break from human status to manifest. Paxton didn't open her eyes or acknowledge where she was. Her breathing again was shallow. So far, other than a few good quakes, there had been no real hints of a big reveal.

But he wasn't wrong about what she was going through. Any werewolf could have recognized the signs.

As if his last thought had nudged a reaction, Paxton suddenly kicked out with both legs. She squirmed and began to fight his tight hold. Her head came up with a snap. She opened her eyes.

Their gazes met and held long enough for Grant to see a reflection of the moonlight in those amber irises seconds before the golden color began to darken.

Next clue. The flash of gold all Lycans possessed.

The time for ignorance and denial was over.

Paxton's face began to alter like soft sand sifting into a new shape. Slowly, and with the moon granting his plea for leniency on Paxton's behalf, her pale cheeks sharpened without making her scream. Deep hollows formed, and the angles made her thin face seem twice as delicate.

Moonlight melted on her skin. Her face and bare neck shone with a silvery luminescence, as if she had swallowed moonlight and it shone through her pores. Because breathing was difficult for her, she panted, taking in air through her mouth. As her chin began to elongate, her moan of discomfort was a barely perceptible sound.

"Yes," he said to her. "Let it out."

She had larger eyes now, and a longer neck. She had taken on an otherworldly look that was ethereal, yet backed by steel. Her arms were defined. Long blond hair flowed down her back.

Paxton was shifting in his arms and hadn't cried out or doubled over to retch her guts out. Her overall size hadn't changed. Some of her features hadn't yet rearranged because she had paused part of the way through her transition. And though Paxton no longer looked quite like any human on Earth, and didn't resemble Shirleen or any other she-wolf he had ever known or seen, she was a Were in her very soul. Different. Beautiful. Unique.

Lycan.

Grant stared at the result of the moon's purposeful early caress with his heart thundering. The wolf in him begged to respond to Paxton's wolfishness. She was the wolf of his dreams. His wishes for a mate had been answered.

"You are beautiful," he said to her, slightly in awe, meaning every word.

But the face-altering business was only a moment of

calm before the storm. After another racking shudder, Paxton again went rigid. The familiar crack of bone on bone came as her spine snapped to a new alignment. Soon after that, her struggle to get free intensified.

Though Grant wasn't so sure about obliging that request for freedom, or what she would do if left on her own after the shock of this new identity, he loosened his hold.

"What if you get away? What if you run?" he said. "Danger lies beyond these walls, Paxton. Tonight, if the beast out there has his way, everything might come tumbling down around us."

She couldn't speak. Her body had changed in this second wave of shifting, but not tremendously, and she was still breathing.

Paxton Hall, she-wolf, was breathtaking. This close to her, Grant's wolf was not to be caged. His claws, face, chest and spine, morphed in seconds as he continued to hold Paxton close. The look on her new face when she witnessed this was priceless, but she couldn't protest, argue or feign disbelief. There were two werewolves here. Paxton's inner self, long in captivity, had finally been set free.

"Damn!" Shirleen's tone was one of surprise. "What the hell?"

Fully shifted, Grant's senses strengthened. While he wanted to deal with Paxton, something else dared to vie for his attention. He looked west with sudden interest. Silently, swiftly, Grant set Paxton down, ruing the need for a few inches of distance when he wanted to go at her in animal-to-animal fashion and solidify their bond. His need to possess her was so strong, he backed up a few more steps to keep from touching Paxton again, afraid he'd never let go if he did.

Paxton didn't run away. She sank to a crouch, attempting to deal with new parameters for balance. Her eyes were damp when they again met his, and reddened by the pain she had not yet put behind her.

"Welcome to my world," he sent to her. *"To our world."*

Soft growls of protest escaped from her throat.

"The beast comes," he sent to her. *"Can you hear me? Can you feel his presence out there, somewhere close?"*

In spite of her quakes, Paxton stared back.

Bless her, she was on board. Paxton was Lycan, another term for strong and fierce. However, there was much more to come, just as he had promised her.

His first instinct was a primal one—an urge to throw her on the ground and possess her. They could imprint their brains out if he showed Paxton everything a Were could do with a mate, twice over.

The ache he carried inside for finding a real partner had intensified a thousand times, and at the moment there was nothing he could do about it. Whatever he and Paxton had to work out had to be postponed. His terrible, gnawing need for her had to be ignored.

"It will be okay," he promised.

But could he keep that promise? She might be stronger as a werewolf, yet she remained a fledgling, without the knowledge of how to access and wield the new power she possessed. Christ, she couldn't even stand up.

Paxton was vulnerable, sick, and he had to leave her. Had to. He was alpha. Helping Weres come into their own was his gig and what he had signed on for, but they were all stuck in the middle of a mystery only partially solved by Paxton's arrival and late transformation.

What happened to you all these years, to keep you from this? How have you postponed what your heritage demanded?

* * *

Big freaking surprise.

By fornicating with Grant the werewolf, she had caught his disease, and she could have killed him for that—if she didn't want to ravage his body first.

The only sound Paxton could dig up was a growl— the kind of sound wild animals made when angry, threatened and in distress. That was appropriate as hell, she supposed, since it seemed like she *was* an animal.

The world had tilted off its axis, and she was hanging on by her claws. She had somehow been treated to an unwelcome physical software upgrade that had tripped her system into uncharted territory, and she didn't know what to do or how to react.

The shock was not only staggering, it was slowing her defenses and leaving her afraid to even try to comprehend what she had become. Her skin was on fire. Nerves were frying with each upward degree of core body temperature. Her legs felt like someone else's legs. She didn't recognize her trembling hands.

But Grant was on the move, and she could not lose him. He had the answers to this riddle. If he had given her this disease, perhaps he knew how to reverse it.

Without knowing how, she found herself shadowing him, somehow able to walk, quickly finding her balance, if not her sanity. He didn't like having a shadow and growled a warning for her to stay back. Without him, though, she was in limbo. Fear clenched her insides. Desperado's buildings seemed darker, more sinister, when she had long ago loved this place.

Was she going mad?

Grant strode toward the end of town, halting twice more to issue sounds of displeasure when she ignored his warnings about being left behind. Paxton prayed he soon would wake her up.

"Help me."

His shoulders tensed as if he heard her thought, yet he kept moving toward the darker places beyond the old wood walls.

Paxton's shock was making way for a litany of strange new sensations. The warm breeze ruffling her hair was unusually sensual. Desert heat slid down her body to slip inside her jeans, leaving her thighs tingling. She wanted to tear off her clothes and run naked through the dark, cool off and mate with Grant on blistering desert soil, rutting like animals.

Off came her shirt, tossed aside. The mark on her upper arm felt like it had been made by the kind of hot iron brand ranchers used to mark their animals, and it seemed larger, deeper, more visible. Scarier still, it did look like leftover damage from a large animal bite.

Moon mark was what Grant had called it. Bearing the mark was proof she was like him, he had said. If that were true, it had taken having a sexual liaison with Grant to find out she was something unimaginable. Something inhuman.

Stumbling twice before getting her stride down smoothly, Paxton refused to slow until she reached the edge of town, near the old mining office. Grant had stopped there and was looking at her over his shoulder. His expression was one of regret. It took her a few seconds to register that he had shifted again, so fast she hadn't had time to notice. The human face he presented to her was a camouflage, as was his hunky cowboy body.

"Not a lie," he said soberly, in response to her thought. "This is the face I was born with. It's the one

I present to the world most of the time so that we can all get along."

Paxton shook her head, but was sorry she did. The piercing pain behind her eyes was excruciating. The inability to speak brought more panic. *"Not the real you, Grant."*

"Both faces are me," he corrected. "I'm the same guy who picked you up at the airport and…"

He was hearing her thoughts, however absurd that idea was, and he wanted her to understand what was going on without having the time to tell her exactly what that was.

"Show me the other one," she said to him in her mind. *"Change again for me."*

"I have to stop a beast from getting here, Paxton. He is too damn close, and though you're a Lycan, you are new at it and much too vulnerable to help in this fight. You'll have to stay here and keep back. A stint in that damn cage truly was meant for your protection."

Paxton's hands stung so badly, she growled in terror. Hearing the sound made her want to cry. As she stared at the sharp little claws working their way through the tips of her fingers, she vowed not to faint.

Never been weak…

This is only a dream.

She ventured another silent question. *"Does that beast have something to do with this place? Does it have anything to do with me, since I've encountered it twice?"*

"Damned if I know what it wants here," Grant replied. "Nor do I really want to find out after everything I've learned about this creature. But I have to find him. You do understand that, after what I've told you?

You do see how necessary it is to keep Desperado off human radar?"

He wasn't telling her the truth. Paxton leaned forward. The inferno inside her was taking its toll, driving her crazy, making her twitch. The wolf in her was outrageously issuing X-rated demands in spite of the appalling situation she found herself in—this unshakable dream that seemed so real.

And Grant was withholding secrets that pertained to her.

She saw the same level of lust she was feeling reflected in Grant's blue eyes, but it seemed that his ability to control it was a hell of a lot better than hers. Fear, lust and greed were like a sudden heat wave coloring the space between them.

Grant was upset, nervous and preoccupied. When he turned to sniff the air, the scent he was after hit her like a flying brick. In that breeze was a smell she recognized.

Paxton dropped to a predatory crouch. With one hand in the dirt and the other on the mark on her arm that burned like a sharp-tipped arrow had been embedded in her flesh, she glanced up in time to see Grant shape-shift again in a fast ruffling of time and rippling flesh.

Screaming was not an option. Arguing took a back seat to the sheer amazement of what she was seeing for the third time. In this form, the intimacy of their connection blossomed. She had a new appreciation for the large, formidable werewolf whose face exposed the anger he was feeling and whose skin undulated continuously as though unsure of which form to take.

"I know that scent," she sent to him, and he nodded without asking more details.

The creature Grant was expecting was none other than her bear…the bear that wasn't a bear at all, but something everyone here expected to be far worse. Hell, her instincts shouted, what could be worse than a god-damn werewolf?

Still, now, as she inhaled the scent of the stranger out there beyond Desperado's walls, bits of memory, sharp as broken glass shards, came crashing back. Memories tied up with that same scent in a not-so-pretty red bow, suggesting that Desperado had always been strange, and she had just been too young to notice.

Grant ran, skimming the ground with a burst of speed.

In his mind, he had connected with Paxton's vision of what this intruder was, and that picture left a bitter taste in his mouth. This creature she had mistaken for a bear was a werewolf, all right. He'd pegged that early on. What he had not foreseen was the immensity of power connected to that wolf and the sheer force of the creature's oncoming presence.

Grant felt as though he'd been hit with a battering ram square in the chest as Paxton's haunting howl rang from the town behind him. She was in need of help, but she hadn't followed him. Paxton hadn't moved from the spot where she crouched to duck the fear coming at her from an awareness of that unseen creature's approach.

The air again was filled with the odor of damp fur, nearly missed because Paxton's sweet scent still filled his lungs, taking his mind off business.

Sour odors grew stronger near the fence. Ben was there, watching, waiting, with another pack member, equally alert. Neither of those Weres would be tuned in to this. Their wolves were tucked away and buried deep for one more day.

Lycan to Lycan was how this would happen, with Paxton included in that scenario. She had noticed the scent. She bore the mark of her Lycan lineage, however unfortunate that might have turned out to be. Her transformation without a full moon kept the puzzle of her existence foremost in his mind.

Ben nodded a silent greeting. As soon as Grant cleared the gates, he took off running.

When he reached the small rise of earth and sand he had stood on the month before, Grant stopped. The foreign pressure was growing stronger by the minute. Edgy, and with his nerves charged, Grant's silent internal alarms tripped. How much harm was this beast hoping to inflict? It was here again, so soon.

"This gets tedious. Where the hell are you, beast?"

The desert was the same unusual quiet that didn't bode well in terms of surprises. Claws ready, Grant dragged in a raw, ragged breath and widened his stance. Time seemed suspended as he flexed his muscles and rolled his shoulders.

From a pool of darkness no longer blessed by moonlight, the damn beast finally showed up in the flesh.

Chapter 24

Paxton was a kid again and reliving the past.

She had never been afraid of the ghost town that had been her special place, at least in secret. Back then, each moment spent on her own in the town had been stolen and short-lived. Just her and her pony, breaking rules.

Rarely had she been allowed here after dusk, even with others around. Never alone. Never when it was dark. That rule had been at the top of her father's long list and set in stone. Her father's rules were to be obeyed.

But she had always been a rebel, even at an early age.

Now, a certain familiar scent had triggered an uncanny resonance with the past. The buildings around her began to shift the way Grant had, growing, darkening, wavering, until their shadows stretched to find her…as if reaching out to the shirtless freak with a new face whose hands were decorated, not with rings, but with the markings of an animal.

Paxton shook off a bout of lightheadedness and concentrated hard, realizing that something unusual had been here then, too…breathing, hiding, watching. Kid senses had perceived the anomaly and filed it away because to a six-year-old, not much in the gray area registered as either good or bad.

Desperado was the gray area, she now knew, and always had been.

More shards came, sharper, slightly out of reach, as Paxton thought back.

There had been sounds in the afternoons beyond her pony's hoofbeats on the packed dirt road. Whispers. Chatter that mimicked the wind passing through cracks in the old boards. She was bothered by a similar kind of chatter now, in the present, and this anomaly served to temporarily link both time frames.

Her ability to stay in the past was disturbed by Grant calling to her in his thoughts. He hadn't really told her what he wanted from her. There hadn't been time. What, then, would happen if she pursued her objective to sell off this town, now that she was one of the creatures Desperado housed?

Impossible had become her key word of the day.

In the span of a few hours, everything had changed. She had changed, literally. Desperado not only held Grant's secrets, it held some of hers, if she could only find them.

Grant was regretting his hasty departure and needed her to know that. But other whispers returned to tug at her thoughts with more remembrances of older days, as though those old secrets were just out of reach. Inside those memories, it seemed to her now, someone other than Grant had spoken her name with determination—not out loud, but as a thought sent directly to her mind, similar to the way Grant sometimes communicated with her.

Those two worlds Grant had spoken of were merging with a dizzying display of overlapping sights and noises. Underneath it all, the ringing in her ears signaled a possible imminent loss of consciousness that she wasn't going to allow. *Not now. No way.*

"Paxton?" a voice called out.

She couldn't decide if this voice was real or imagined. In the present or from her past.

"Paxton, can you hear me? I think you can. It's Shirleen. We've got to move out of the street. Take cover."

Shirleen was interrupting her search for the missing part of her past Paxton was determined to find. She had to know what had been hiding here back then and what she hadn't seen.

"Can you change back, the way he does?" Shirleen asked, strain evident in her tone.

Paxton had no idea if that was possible.

"The rest of us are strong and mostly human tonight. In Grant's absence, we're charged with your safety and the safety of this town," Shirleen said. "You, like this, standing in the middle of the street, doesn't help the cause."

Paxton got that with the force of a sucker punch to the gut. Desperado was being threatened and Grant supposed she was part of that.

Four-letter curses stuck in her throat. Her palms were bleeding from fisting her claws. Without Grant there, the agony of her shape-shift felt far worse, and she had to survive when that, too, seemed impossible.

Her father had set a strange series of events into motion with that damn will. She wished she could give him a piece of her mind right now.

Shirleen stood ramrod straight, waiting with the patience of a saint for Paxton to move. Paxton wasn't sure she *could* move. Grant's pull on her wasn't only physical. Despite his warnings, every fiber of Paxton's being clamored to go after him, as if he had taken part of her with him.

The street scene was clearer now that her vision had sharpened. Incredibly, every board and nail stood out on Desperado's exterior walls. She noted that the dirt road she stood on had a waffled appearance from too many shoes recently trampling it down, and that the old wood on the buildings had a decadently aged odor that threatened to again toss her back in time.

Shirleen wasn't going to allow that. "It's important," she warned.

Thawing from their former numbness, Paxton's arms felt heavy and foreign. Her legs ached. Yet she was sure she could have run faster than she ever had, if given the chance.

Any minute now, I will wake up.

In the event this wasn't a nightmare, she had to deal.

"Can't leave," she sent to Shirleen.

"It isn't safe in the open, Paxton."

"A memory is here that I have to find."

"Can't you find it later?"

It was too late to find out anything from the past. The elusive whispers had gone, chased away by Shirleen's insistence that they get going.

Paxton offered Shirleen a dangerous glance that resulted in silence. But that silence lasted mere seconds before Shirleen jerked to attention and two more strangers came running.

"You have found me."

The beast, trespasser, Lycan rogue, stepped into

Grant's sightline in human form, dressed in dark clothes and a hood that hid his face. He was so tall, his presence alone made him formidable.

Grant fielded a thought about whether to shift back so he could speak, and whether that might put him at a higher risk. He decided to wait.

"Don't bother," the other Lycan agreed, attuned to Grant's dilemma. "I can hear you perfectly well, either way."

"Why have you returned? Have you changed your mind about coming in?"

"I have no intention of submitting myself to closer scrutiny. Surely you know this by now?"

"You're a wanted beast."

"And you're lucky I'm here."

Grant failed to appreciate that remark.

"Anxiousness is an emotional state that broadcasts over quite a distance. Yours is particularly strong," the Lycan warned.

"Where do you come from and what do you want here?" Grant tossed back, hoping to get a glimpse of the Were's face.

"I want what you want," the Lycan said.

"Is that a joke?"

"Like you and the others you watch over, I need to be free. I must not be caught. That is imperative for all of us. You must stop looking."

"It's too late for anonymity. If not us, the ranchers will find you."

"They won't find me, no matter how hard or long they try."

"We know about the cave," Grant said.

Silence, then "Yes. There is a cave. Several of them actually."

Grant refrained from taking a harsh breath as he adjusted to that news.

"Who are you?" he repeated sternly.

"Need to know basis only," the Lycan replied.

"What do you want with Desperado? Why come here now?" Grant asked.

"The town contains something dear to me."

Grant rolled his shoulders. *"Dear to you? What could that possibly be if you have never set boot or claw there?"*

The Lycan facing him didn't bother to answer that question.

"I believe you said I was missing something, earlier tonight," Grant said. *"Maybe you can explain now that we're face-to-face."*

"What I meant was that there is danger all around, wolf, and it's not what you're expecting."

"That's supposed to be a surprise, when you're central to that danger?"

"I was right. You know nothing."

Grant sensed the frustration mounting in this creature. The air had changed again, thickening more, carrying the scent of anger and another hint of blood.

The Lycan had turned, so that only his silhouette was visible. He was looking to the west, as if he also smelled the blood.

"Perhaps you can enlighten me," Grant suggested. *"After leading us a merry chase, I'm assuming you wanted me to find you tonight for a reason. Am I supposed to be your next meal? Is that what you're thinking? Get rid of the competition, knowing I'll use all resources at my disposal to find you?"*

"Honestly, I'm not thinking anything of the sort. I

came to warn you about what's coming, and that's the only reason for allowing this conversation."

"What is coming? More of your wicked antics?"

The Lycan brushed that remark off with a wave of his hand. "What's coming is the worst thing you can imagine. Maybe even worse than that."

"Presently, you hold that honor."

"If I did, you and your pack would have been dead long ago. As you know, none of you are."

That, Grant thought, was an odd thing for a challenger to admit. As taunts went, it was pretty benign and a complete mystery. He was having a hard time wrapping his mind around the possibility of this creature not wanting to harm the pack. Honestly, he still wasn't sure what was going on. This meeting with the Lycan wasn't going the way he had anticipated it might. There had been no attack or move in Grant's direction.

"Besides you, what else is coming?" Grant asked, expecting another cryptic remark that wouldn't lead anywhere. Strangely though, the Lycan answered.

"Old enemies have come back, multiplying too fast for me to keep up or stay hidden."

"Are you talking about humans?" Grant asked.

"Not humans," the Lycan replied in a thoughtful, civilized manner that went against the rogue cattle rustler image Grant had pictured. Also, the scent of the blood he had detected couldn't have been due to anything this sucker had done, since the Lycan was in his presence at the moment.

What wasn't he getting?

Perhaps the bastard was trying to throw him off-balance.

When another rustle came from the bushes, Grant readied his claws in case the Lycan had an accomplice.

That could have been the terrible thing this guy was alluding to. Not one rogue, but two. Three. A dozen.

"What's left if you're not talking about humans?" Grant demanded. *"If you know about the nearby pack and have no bad intentions toward us, what have you got to lose by accompanying me back there?"*

"Maybe I would prefer to be my own master."

"What is coming?"

"Old enemies," the Lycan repeated, turning his head, interested in whatever he had perceived in the wind.

"How much longer do you think you can avoid those rifles and search parties? This desert isn't as large as you might think. Both ranchers and a wolf pack are on the hunt, and they'll find you eventually. You've been a wild card inflicting too much damage, bringing too much notoriety."

"Yes, I've inflicted some damage, as you say, though I doubt if it's the kind of damage you're assigning to me."

"Cattle. Maybe a hiker or two. Bones in a cave. Months of hide-and-seek. I can smell the blood now, Lycan," Grant said with an edge to his tone.

He could have been wrong, had to be wrong, but Grant thought he detected the same kind of weariness in the hooded Lycan's voice that he had heard earlier.

"Blood is the key, the direction," the creature said. "If you follow the trail, you won't find me as the cause."

With that bit of questionable insight, Grant sensed he had again been left alone and that the mysterious Lycan, with all his cryptic secrets, had gone.

Grant charged into the brush after the rogue. Pulse racing, he searched for footprints and scents, utilizing the full scope of his supernatural senses.

He turned into the wind to soak up the iron-rich odor he had perceived. *Blood is the key.*

The key to what? To where to find that sucker? Follow the scent and this rogue will be waiting? The rogue whose voice had not reflected the complete derangement everyone had expected?

What could be worse than an intelligent opponent?

More sounds filled in the quiet. Among them, Grant picked out the faint swish of boots in the sand. Growling, he glanced behind him, where the lights of Desperado's gates held a welcoming glow and Paxton Hall's wolf called to him in a language he understood on so many levels.

But he had to see this through. A man had placed his trust and property in Grant's hands for the sole purpose of keeping Desperado and its inhabitants safe. His pack trusted his decisions. A new she-wolf needed him. And now there were two anomalies to face. Paxton was one of them. The other was a Lycan he had to continue to hunt. He had to either bring this rogue in, or take him down. *"I'm sorry,"* he sent to Paxton. *"Hang on, lover. I don't know what I'd do if you..."*

Unable to finish that sentiment, and with the nebulous warning the Lycan had given him about what was coming ringing in his ears, Grant took off, doing exactly what that Lycan had suggested by allowing the scent of blood to guide him toward whatever awaited him in the dark.

Chapter 25

Paxton smelled what the others had caught a whiff of. That scent permeated the air.

Her strength returned with a rush of adrenaline as she took a step toward the darkness beyond Desperado's buildings. Aware of Shirleen and two others behind her, Paxton swiped at the air with her claws to warn them back.

Claws.

Blood was rushing through her arteries, ramping up her blood pressure, skyrocketing her pulse. Her heartbeat echoed loudly inside her head, leaving scant chance of hearing much else. But the onset of an enhanced sense of smell was another matter altogether, and Paxton was familiar with the iron tang of blood, just as every nurse was. The blood wasn't hers and had not originated from the Weres behind her. So, whose blood was it?

Grant's?

Although she was already filled with dread, another persistent idea needled. She knew Grant's scent, so this couldn't be his blood she smelled.

When she closed her eyes, she could almost see an image of him, upright, half wolf, perfectly all right. It seemed to her that some of her racing heartbeats stemmed from their strangely attuned connection and had to do with Grant's current state of agitation.

There was no way to call him. Trying to further their unique and uncanny bond might distract him from his objective of seeking out a madman. Shirleen had warned her against being a distraction.

Shirleen and the two other Desperado inhabitants were maintaining several feet of separation from the new werewolf in town. Their wariness over what was happening to her tonight, without that damn full moon, radiated off them.

Paxton swallowed the urge to scream.

According to Grant, everyone here was a werewolf, and this was his pack, so she couldn't help wondering where that left her. Her world had radically changed with a terrifying turn of direction. If this wasn't a dream—or, hell, if it was—she could fall down and whimper over the hand she had been dealt or get on with it. If she was dreaming, she would eventually wake up. If she was dreaming, she couldn't really be hurt by anything she did.

With a cursory glance at the others, Paxton strode forward, as Grant had done, getting better at balance with each step as she headed out of town. Once Desperado was behind her and darkness filled the empty spaces, she willed her new body to run.

That wasn't so easy with new muscle and sinew.

Stumbling often at first, Paxton shored up her determination to find Grant and get the hang of her new body, a feat made more difficult by the way her eyes processed the dark. Even without extra light, she easily saw where she was going. Everything around her took on a dull red outline, like something in the infrared spectrum. There was also a subtle layering of scent, vision and awareness that told her exactly which path Grant had taken.

Utilizing those resources, Paxton ran. Her nerve endings sparked, squeezed by muscle that seemed to have been replaced by thin sheets of steel. Her hair, longer, darker in color than usual, flew in her face as she moved.

She didn't dare look at her hands.

The pain of her shape-shift hadn't disappeared. Her head ached. So did her chest. Both legs burned like they had been dowsed in fire, and all ten fingers stung. In spite of that, Paxton kept moving, desperate to find Grant, the creature who held all the answers she needed now, more than ever.

When she detected him some way ahead of her—a wavering mirage of joining senses—she saw that Grant repeatedly looked over his shoulder, toward Desperado. Toward her. Her mind told her that he was keen on getting back to her and that he had feared she would come after him.

How right he was.

Their astoundingly intimate connection was a heady reminder of the moments they had shared in the bunkhouse. Their insatiable passion for each other hadn't been tapped out by multiple explosive orgasms, but strengthened by the keenness of their fervor.

She still felt him inside her, penetrating deep, sending her soul to new heights. And in the process, he had unleashed a wolf. Her wolf.

Werewolf.

She felt feverish, new, different…and also the same. She felt stronger, fierce, feral and angry. Hell, yes, she was furious over being caught up in someone else's nightmare. Grant's nightmare. Because it was obvious Grant had instigated all of this.

Running churned up clouds of dust that got stuck in her mouth. Leftover desert heat brought moisture that dripped like falling tears down her cheeks. She was fast now, incredibly fleet as she covered ground on two long legs like a heat-seeking missile. Possibly all she had to do was call to Grant with her mind and he would hear her.

She didn't make that call.

He was on a mission, and she wanted to know what and who the beast was as much as Grant did. She didn't want to meet that beast again, but being left alone with a bunch of strangers in the ghost town she had once considered to be her safe haven wasn't a comforting thought, either. Neither was staying in this new shape for much longer.

This could be a dream.

In a dream, she'd be free to experience all that life had to offer without repercussions. She could again run without fear of being found by her father's minions. No longer a kid, she got to decide how she spent her time and who she climbed into bed with, even if that person wasn't actually human.

"Grant."

The thought slipped into existence before Paxton could withdraw it, and the red mirage in the distance halted as if Grant Wade had run into a solid brick wall.

* * *

Some said that curiosity killed the cat, and that, Grant thought, might be expanded to include she-wolves too suspicious for their own good.

Paxton on the loose was adding significantly to the problems at hand, and he couldn't leave her on her own out here with a rogue Lycan on the loose. Taking her along on his search could lead her directly into harm's way.

Paxton's imminent arrival also put him at odds with his vow to figure things out, and no muttered curse he could think of was good enough to describe how he felt about being at this crossroads.

He turned toward her without backtracking. They were less than a half mile from Desperado's gates, following the dry, sandy wash that ran east to west toward the outskirts of the city. Cactus silhouettes stood like prickly soldiers on all sides of him. All but the rim of the moon had sunk behind the mountain range. Daybreak wasn't too far off. In the time between now and then, the night could potentially hold more surprises.

"Okay, Paxton. All right."

She was going to be burning with anger. He had put her in the cage, and that hadn't worked for either of them. Making love to her might have helped to catapult her wolf into existence, but couldn't have been helped, given their attraction to each other.

"In my defense, I couldn't help myself. You are so very alluring. How was I supposed to resist?"

"Wait," she sent back. *"The others don't understand. Can't possibly understand."*

Grant knew what she was saying. Paxton's past had been tied up with Desperado in ways she had never guessed, and in a few hours she had learned a lot. More than anyone would have cared to learn. She might now know firsthand about the existence of werewolves, yet had only an inkling about what was going on. And he was no better at piecing together this puzzle.

The intelligent rogue's warnings had been steeped in mystery, and he was here somewhere. Grant could feel him. Paxton had fled Desperado hoping to find answers of her own without realizing she might be doing exactly what that rogue wanted.

They were treading on treacherous ground.

Life was about to get real.

She ran toward him, easily covering the distance, already at one with her new physical form. Confusion ruled her thoughts and emotions, though. He was her focus. If she assumed he could offer her complete enlightenment, she'd be grossly mistaken.

Paxton was also counting on this being a dream. The kind of dream where anything goes. He wished that was true and that they would all wake up.

Appearing suddenly, as beautiful as anything he could have imagined, she stopped inches from him. Minus the ability to speak, she slapped him hard on his wolfish face.

Lord help him. In spite of everything, Grant smiled. Ignoring for the moment the night and all its wicked possibilities, he pulled her close to him with a slight tug on one arm.

Paxton shoved him back, then again stepped close. With her chest still covered only by a useless scrap of lace, her heat scorched his bare chest. She looked up with gleaming golden eyes.

"Wolf to wolf, at last, and no time to finish this, little wolf," he said, encircling her with his arms while

damning himself for each second stolen from his reason for being out here.

Standing there, wrapped up in each other, craving each other, they were sitting ducks ripe for plucking. He had never been so lax in regard to issues of safety. And yet, having this she-wolf in his arms and her eyes trained on him were all the proof he needed that they would find no way to outdistance their affections. Paxton would stay in Arizona with him…if they lived long enough.

Now, his body shuddered with a desire for her that he could not express or act on until they were safe and Paxton fully comprehended her new reality.

Her eyes were changing color from amber to gold and back as her desires melded with his. She had temporarily forgotten what shape she was in, with her wolf ruling her emotions. Her wolf sensed kinship, sought her mate, craved contact. That was the way of the wolf.

"Must get you back," he sent.

"No," she responded. *"Tell me how this is possible."*

"There's no time to explain," Grant replied. *"We're too far out here, and I have met the rogue."*

"Show me how to change back."

"Not yet. Not here. I'll help once you're safe. We're faster like this. Stronger."

She tensed. *"We're not alone."*

She was right.

A new scent reached Grant that was foul, fetid and reminiscent of a decomposing animal carcass. Sounds disturbed the quiet, odd noises of something skimming the ground.

Grant's heart began to race as he took Paxton's hand, whirled and encouraged her to run. The rogue had warned of trouble coming. Grant hadn't considered that the Lycan might have been hinting of a return visit to finish what he had started.

That rogue might have seen Paxton all wolfed up, and was coming back for her.

With Paxton in tow and a hold on her hand that would have broken bones if she had been in human form, Grant aimed for Desperado's gates. Jolts of electricity sparked through him each time he glanced at Paxton. He reaffirmed his vow that nothing would happen to her on his watch.

But tables had turned, and the hunters were being hunted. Alone, he would have waited for whatever kind of creature was going to show up. But he wasn't alone.

Flapping sounds, the kind giant birds made, reached him. No clear picture formed in his mind as to what he and Paxton were running from. Although Lycans possessed a lot of talents and special abilities, flight wasn't one of them.

The strange sounds came from several directions, too many for this to be any one person, creature, abomination. Maybe that Lycan actually had accomplices. They could have been waiting for the bastard's signal to attack.

Negating that was the fact that there was no scent of wolf in the air. With more than one Were on the loose, Grant would have read the signs. This scent was new and uncategorized in his databanks, suggesting that after all this time, a new species might have turned up.

Old enemies, the rogue had warned.

For the life of him, Grant didn't know what that meant.

He and Paxton ran like the wind, utilizing the reflexes handed down by their ancient ancestors. Paxton kept up as if she had been born to race, all balance and grace now. They reached Desperado's gates in minutes. Ben and his companions came to meet them.

Grant began his reverse shift as he and Paxton slid to a stop, shaking off the discomfort of realigning bones that had grown worse in the last few hours and now plagued him no matter what shape he took. This reversal left him sweating and out of breath.

"Don't know what's out there," he said to Ben. "Can't tell what it is."

"The Lycan?" Ben asked, anxiously scanning the desert.

"That bastard is as intelligent as he is wily. But he's not alone. Something else is haunting the desert tonight. The Lycan warned me about it."

Ben continued to search the area. "If you don't think this is him, do you have any ideas about who is out there?"

Grant shook his head. Paxton's clawed fingers slipped from his and everyone's attention turned to her, sensing the she-wolf had something to say.

"Not wolf," she sent to him, frustrated with her inability to speak those words out loud.

"What else is there?" Ben was quick to ask.

Grant waited to see if Paxton, so new at this werewolf gig, had the answer to that question when he didn't have a clue.

"Dead," she said.

Red-hot bolts of nerve fire roared through Grant, knocking on his skull, vibrating his ribs, as Paxton repeated the word.

"Dead."

Any queries he had about that remark had to be postponed. Paxton had begun her reversal and sank to her knees in the sand.

Chapter 26

*D*ead.

According to Paxton, the thing or things out there were dead. Grant would have worried about her mental state if it hadn't been for the look of abject horror on her face, added to the rogue Lycan's power of suggestion.

The words *old enemies* bothered him. And anyhow, he couldn't figure out how Paxton might know things he didn't or how she had come up with a word that united the sounds and smells pervading the night so eerily.

Paxton couldn't say more. Reversals were new to her system and this one was taking longer. Doubled over, she sucked in breath after breath of air as if each of those breaths might be her last. In this state, she wouldn't have heard his assurances that she would be all right.

He wasn't sure what *dead* meant in this case. Maybe Paxton had come up with the word because the scent of blood had intensified. The flapping sounds had vanished, and yet the air around them seemed heavier, as if the area had become crowded with things none of them could see.

This was downright spooky. Grant's skin prickled with warnings to get out of there fast. Tucking an arm around Paxton's waist, he hauled her up and stood her on her feet. Supporting her with his body, he pressed the hair back from her face and cupped her chin with his palm.

"Can you run?"

Golden lashes fluttered over closed eyes when he spoke to her. Paxton's face had regained its human characteristics and worrisome lack of color. Spine bones popped and snapped as each of her vertebrae found its groove, most of those sounds bringing a groan.

As he waited for her to acknowledge him, the wind picked up, blowing sand in their faces. Enough of his senses were working to tell him this wasn't good. With an arm protectively around Paxton, ashen-faced and weak from her recent ordeal, Grant whirled to face the expanse of darkened desert beyond the gates. Ben and the other two packmates joined him, wielding clubs that resembled baseball bats.

What was out there?

He kept his attention on Paxton's white face. "What do you mean by *dead*?"

In answer to that question, a deep, familiar, unwelcome voice filled Grant's mind. *"The dead rise again,"* the rogue Lycan warned, his voice an unwelcome whisper, as if the bastard stood right next to Grant, understanding everything that was going on by the gates.

Grant felt the blood drain from his face. Paxton had heard that warning also. He had to pull her tightly to him to strengthen his support. As the Lycan's voice in his mind retreated, Grant's brain shuffled random details into a pattern he hoped to be able to access.

Blood.

Slaughtered animals.

Human bones in a cave, scratched by tooth marks Ben couldn't identify.

Words the rogue had spoken earlier that night came back to him: *What's coming is the worst thing you can imagine. Maybe even worse than that.*

And finally, *The dead rise again.*

With a snap of insight, centuries of data began to add up, and the image that data presented made Grant blanch. "We have to get the hell out of the open," he said. "Right now."

"What?" Ben asked nervously. "What is it?"

When Grant could speak again, he turned to Ben. In a harsh, gravelly voice, he said the word that would have made anyone who heard it wish they never had.

"Vampires."

Paxton's ears rang with the word Grant had spoken.

There wasn't one place on her body that wasn't plagued by pain, and on top of the skin-tearing horror of her own shape-shift, a new terror had been introduced.

"Vampire," Ben said. "You've got to be kidding." His expression conveyed that he was waiting for Grant to renege on that statement.

It was a ghastly idea but, given that werewolves were real, why not fang-bearing dead people who drank blood?

Grant hustled her through Desperado's gates with an arm still wrapped around her. "No dream," he said.

"Should I wait?" Ben shouted after them. "Shouldn't someone wait to see if it's true?"

"Hell, no," Grant replied sharply. "Come in. Get them all inside. I can almost guarantee that Lycan was onto something."

"What if he comes back?"

"Let him," Grant muttered. "Let him come."

Somehow, Paxton kept up on unsteady legs. Back in her human form, her real shape, she felt heavier, awkward. Grant's unhealthy buzz of fear had become hers, but could vampires actually exist?

"Can't take a chance," Grant said to her as they trotted toward the lights in the distance.

"He could be lying," Ben said, following behind. "That rogue could be pulling one over on us."

"Yes," Grant returned. "There's always that possibility."

"The bastard eats cows," Ben said, pointing out the mental imbalance of anyone who could do that.

"Suddenly, I'm not so sure he does," Grant argued.

"What can…a vampire…do?" Paxton asked in disjointed syllables as they reached the first light globe leading into town. "Out here?"

"I'm not sure," Grant admitted. "My knowledge of bloodsuckers is next to useless."

"Do we have to worry, then?" Ben called out. "Because the wolf out there said so?"

Really, none of this was making sense to Paxton. Ben was right to question Grant's enthusiasm for trusting the wolf they had been after. No one could imagine why Grant might believe anything like that.

Was that rogue the thing that had jumped on her car? Grant was letting some information slip through his carefully monitored net. She saw the rogue's outline in his thoughts—the size of their opponent and the hood that covered his face.

"I think we have to believe it," Grant said, reading her thoughts clearly. "Just don't ask me why that Lycan seems willing to help us out on this occasion."

They were halfway to town when another harrowing howl stopped everyone in their tracks. It had come from behind them, near the gates. Not too far away.

Paxton faltered when Grant tugged her ahead, before catching herself. Fear overwhelmed her. Her stomach turned over as the sound the beast had made rang in her mind.

Not just a sound. *No.*

God...

Was she the only one here who knew the damn beast's howl had been meant for her and her alone? And that inside that awful sound, curled up in a wolfish disguise, the beast had called her name?

She sent her mind outward, reaching, searching for the thread tying her to that beast. When she felt that thread snap tight, Paxton leaned forward to reel it in, imagining her hands rolling up that thread, willing herself to find what connected with her on the other end.

When another, sharper image came, it rocked her backward. Paxton stumbled with a hand over her mouth. The connection she had searched for was with the creature that had dented her car, the thing that had looked at her through the windshield with unblinking eyes. She saw that thing now in her mind—big, dark, furry and ferocious. She relived the fright of seeing it in person.

Grant's beastly Lycan—it had to be the same—had just made contact with her on a personal level. She had never been so afraid. She was petrified.

"We can't stay here," Grant warned. "Paxton, are you all right?"

Hell, no, she wasn't all right. She was as far from all right as was humanly possible, because she wasn't human and neither was anyone else around her. Out there in the desert was a beast that had her number. Knew her name. Knew how to disrupt things so utterly and completely by flooding her mind with a memory so clear she could have touched it.

Paxton was so white and dazed, Grant shook her gently to regain her focus, determined to carry her back to town, if necessary.

There was a faraway look in her eyes that he didn't like. She swayed slightly on her feet. Paxton had turned inward.

He wondered if fear caused her glassy-eyed state, or if it was due to the shock of her first shape-shift. She had retreated, and all he could do was try to make her understand the danger they might be in if they dallied too long in the open.

"Talk to me," he said to her.

"Grant," Ben warned. "Pressure is building out there."

"Go on," Grant directed. "Get to town."

"Not without you," Ben said.

With a firm hold of Paxton's shoulders, Grant said, "Damn it, Paxton. Where have you gone? Tell me what you see."

Her large amber eyes didn't meet his or show any indication that she'd heard him. Shifting again in order to carry Paxton the rest of the way to Desperado at a sprint wasn't a trick he'd like to perform with his body already quaking from the inside out, but he was game to attempt that if he had to. Still, saving strength was necessary, and he figured he had only one more good shift in him tonight before his body gave out.

"I can take Paxton," Ben said.

The jealousy Ben's offer induced was vastly out of proportion with the situation they found themselves in. Grant couldn't stand the thought of anyone else laying hands on his she-wolf. He wasn't going to allow that. Could not allow it.

"No one will touch you," he sent to her, adding aloud, "You were right when you said that no one could possibly understand what you're going through. You didn't know. No one told you what to expect."

Her skin would be supersensitive and feverish. She would feel like she had been through hell and back. Paxton's insides would feel like they had turned to jelly, and he could see she was having trouble regulating her breathing, due to the extreme distress of the shock to her system. Grant had a feeling Paxton was also fighting something unrelated to that shift, and as new to the game as she was, had found a way to cordon that other thing off from him.

"Grant," Ben said in a low tone meant to get them moving.

"Yes," Grant returned with his gaze steady on Paxton. "Time to go."

But, by then, it was already too late.

Chapter 27

The night began to roll toward them. That was the only way Grant could have described the sensation of being trapped inside a moving pressure cooker.

Ben and the other Weres beside him circled their alpha and the newest she-wolf, hands raised, wooden clubs ready to do some damage to whatever was using the darkness for cover. They didn't wait long before their belief that this was a lone rogue attack was shot down. This was no wolf attack, and *vampire* was a term no one wanted to accept.

Sections of the landscape around them grew darker with a black mist that blotted out scenery beyond their small circle. From the mist came high-pitched chattering, the kind of sounds made by old telephone wires. The strangeness of those sounds brought a terror that Grant quickly shook off.

"Who are you and what do you want here?" he called

out, realizing that any attempt to run back to Desperado now would be futile.

Bracing himself, Grant gathered Paxton closer, feeling the warmth and temporary comfort of having her body pressed to his. He withheld the impulse to shift, waiting for the right moment when his strength would be needed most.

Everyone with him understood that this new dilemma facing them was evil and were at a loss to conceptualize it. When a white face appeared like a glow light in the middle of the traveling black mist, they all took an involuntary step back.

Gaunt to the point of being skeletal, with red-rimmed black eyes in deep sockets and malice in its emaciated expression, the white-faced creature that appeared before them brought a whole new meaning to the word monster. *Freak* was the description Grant's mind dug up. Combined with the term *death*, the existence of vampires became a terrible reality.

There was to be no discourse. Grant supposed the abomination facing them couldn't talk. He had no idea what animated the dead or the kinds of characteristics vampires possessed. But he could sense the thing's raging, insatiable need for blood.

As the black mist floated closer, more faces appeared. Two. Three. The pressure these walking corpses caused on Grant's system was outrageous, squeezing his lungs, compressing the rest of him. Tight against his side, Paxton chose that moment to move. She shivered and tensed as if only then becoming aware of where she was.

She looked up at him with beguiling amber eyes, and he could not comfort her or tell her things were all right. He couldn't allow himself to think of her at all when the situation was grim and his promise to protect her was about to be tested.

The black tide swept forward. Those awful chattering noises filled Grant's ears until he wanted to cover them with his hands.

"That's right. Come and get us," he snapped. "Try."

Beside him, wooden clubs swung at the creeping blackness with powerful strokes. Grant heard Ben swear. Someone else groaned as the clubs, singing their own kind of violent song, connected with an enemy's arm or shoulder. The time had come for him to jump in, but in order to fight he'd have to let go of Paxton, which was his worst fear.

In the end, she instigated the separation by stepping back. Her shaking turned convulsive. Her mind buzzed with jolts of wayward electricity that Grant felt as if they were his own. There was a sudden rise of temperature in air that had gone icy. Grant fought the cold front facing him by merging with the heat of his wolf.

Yes. Let's get this over with, freaks!

The vampires arrived too fast to track their movements, the first appallingly ugly face inches away from Grant before he could blink. Its mouth opened to show off a pair of sharp yellow fangs. Its breath was beyond fetid.

Swathed in black, the rest of this creature's body was difficult to see, even for a Were with exceptional abilities. Grant willed his wolf into existence with the human equivalent of a growl and a snap of mounding muscles. The energy accessed for this latest transition from man to werewolf threw off enough heat to prevent the vampire from immediately traversing the rest of those inches.

Duly noted. You don't like heat.

Grant filed that fact away as he raised claws sharper than the vamp's treacherous teeth and planted his feet in preparation for this meeting. Roaring a dangerous warning to the fanged aggressors, he opened his arms wide in invitation.

Undeterred, the vampires circled the Were party, snapping their fangs, seeming to float like the mist that had at first hidden them.

I have no time for games.

Tired of waiting, Grant sprang toward one pasty-faced freak with his own fangs bared. Their bodies met with a thud. The damn vampire's body felt like ice. As bony as the freak was, Grant's lunge hadn't sent it stumbling in the opposite direction.

Ben and the others were silent now, which added to the eerie sensation of having been swallowed by the dark.

With terrible insight, Grant realized his packmates wouldn't be able to fight off these vampires, and that he, being the only Lycan here and able to fight at full strength, would have to take the brunt of this attack.

"Hang tight," he sent to his pack as the tips of two razor-sharp fangs grazed first his arm, then his left shoulder, in a blur of movement.

Anger rising, Grant narrowed his focus and tuned in. With wolf energy flowing through him, he again met the white-faced freak. One good shove, followed by a fast misdirection, and Grant had a hand around the vampire's neck. The creature fought like a madman, with hatred in its dull black eyes. Hatred for the living. For warmth. For werewolves, who were the epitome of warm-blooded life.

Grant had never met a creature like this one, or knew anyone who had. Except for that rogue Lycan, who seemed to know a lot of things no one else did.

The vampire got free, ducked and parried with a series of actions almost too fast to see. Darting in and back, sideways and forward in an endless battering, the creature seemed frighteningly tireless. Grant fought the bloodsucker with an as-yet untested skill set, whirling, lunging to keep the fangs away from his neck. Those fangs would have sliced through the hide of a steer with no effort at all, and nearly reached Grant's jugular more times than Grant cared to count.

In what had to look like a bizarre danse macabre, Grant renewed his efforts. At last, by calling upon every last bit of his strength, he managed to get his claws into the speedy abomination's ragged clothes and spin it around.

Should have tried this naked, freak.

A sharp keening wail came from the throat of the vampire. The sound was magnified by the other vampires moving inside scattering mist. Two more wails echoed that one, which meant that Ben and the others truly hadn't taken any vampires down.

It was at that moment, as Grant looked into the creature's sallow face, that he saw who the damn vampire's focus was actually trained on and who that vampire wanted to get to so badly. The surprise nearly made him loosen his hold on the creature. His anger went red-hot and felt like a living thing. Paxton stood where he had left her, and the vampire's gaze was riveted to her.

As the bloodsucker struggled and worked its canines, Grant realized with horror that the vampires might not have come to face off with the Weres at all.

It seemed that everybody wanted a piece of Paxton Hall.

The only real question now was why.

With a volcanic heat overtaking her, Paxton watched the fight as if separated from it by a mile. The edges of her thoughts were blurring, just like the landscape was.

Deep, murky blackness cloaked the remnants of the memory that had been shoved aside by events taking place around her. But the epiphany had been to remember she had seen werewolves before, long ago. And she had seen vampires. What she couldn't recall were the specifics.

Paxton closed her eyes. Desperado held the key to all of this—the attack tonight, the rogue on the loose in the area and her father's wish to close the ghost town the same year he had sent her away.

How many times had she gone over this, searching for reasons for that separation? The questions had become fixtures in her nightmares. Why had she been sent away? Why had her dad never made contact with her? Why had Andrew Hall recruited an alpha wolf of Grant Wade's stature to protect the place? Because, in bringing Grant here, her father had to have known about werewolves, just as Grant had told her. And if he was up on werewolves, her dad must also have known she was one of them.

She had a sense of pieces starting to fall into place too slowly, and that everyone here had to live long enough to help her with that.

Desperado. What other secrets do you hold for me?

Paxton reopened her eyes with a start. Spectral forms were attacking and regrouping with astonishing dexterity. Only the white faces of these attackers were visible. Their death masks. She was awake enough to see them now, and that the Weres were holding them off.

As the cold these monsters brought with them met with the fire of her anger, sparks of energy imploded inside her, waking her beast, kicking into motion another shape-shift. Paxton dropped to the dirt, dizzy with a fresh rush of adrenaline. Hands in the sand, she gasped for air and rode out what she knew was the second birthing of her wolf.

It didn't take long this time, from start to finish. In less than a minute she was on her feet. She didn't run the other way to save herself, wasn't about to let others fight to protect what was rightfully hers. The town. The ranch. Her heritage. That's the way Grant had put it. *Heritage.* She had been slow to realize he hadn't been talking about anything tangible. Grant had been alluding to her species and how she had come to be one of them.

She was not going to allow Grant or anyone else to be harmed because of her. Losing Grant Wade would be the worst thing since she had long ago lost everything else.

For several seconds more, she watched him fight. Grant the werewolf was fast and fluid. His muscles were spectacularly sculpted. His back was a thing of real beauty. He moved as if he was a principal dancer in a choreographed routine, darting here and there to keep his hold on the monster captured in his claws. In silhouette, Grant's chiseled man-wolf profile gave him the look of a pagan god.

He was fighting for Desperado. He was fighting to protect Ben, Shirleen and the others in his desert pack. And he was fighting for her.

God, how she loved him for that.

When the vampire's eyes moved to her—those terrible, empty, red-rimmed eyes—Paxton's fear levels did not escalate. Instead, she experienced a thrilling sense of rightness and of being in the right place at the right time to discover another clue to this mystery. Suddenly she felt incredibly strong. The power sparking inside

her made her willing to use her new strength to stop
those ghastly eyes from turning her way.

One step was all it took to channel her anger about
this attack on her lover and his friends. Without thinking twice, she rushed in to join Grant. He tossed her
a worried look, but her wolf ruled her actions now.
Whirling, she undercut the vampire's spindly legs with
her own. The monster was too wily to go down, so she
jumped on its back, going for its face with both clawed
hands.

Someone pulled her off. Paxton growled as she
was lifted by the waist and tossed off-balance, but she
jumped back to Grant to help with the sucker in his
grasp.

She was too late. Another furred-up werewolf had
replaced her efforts—this one far larger, much stronger, with superior fighting skills.

Grant had told her very few werewolves had the ability to shape-shift without the presence of a full moon,
so who was this? Which one of his pack members also
possessed this trick?

Night overlapped night. Frenzied activity created
clouds of dirt. Grant's packmates were fighting for their
lives now, and though she was tired, she wasn't helpless.

Paxton moved back in again with the fury of a lion-
ess whose cubs had been taken away. She couldn't allow
Grant to be hurt, to be harmed, not only because he was
needed here, but because he was hers.

He was hers body and soul.

And both of them knew it.

Thawed by the energy she radiated, and not particularly adept at fighting, Paxton clawed and kicked
her way back into the deadly skirmish. White faces,
gaunt faces, spun inside their black camouflage until the

sound of a muted explosion reached her, and the vampire that had been wrestling with Grant disintegrated in a freaky shower of dark gray ash.

Terrible shrieking wails rent the night before the white-faced fang bearers receded back into the hovering mist and the mist retreated suddenly, as if blown away by an invisible wind, taking the horror and reality of the vampire attack with it.

The night again went quiet. No one moved. Paxton's heart beat as hard and as steady as any of theirs.

Ben and the other two Weres had been left standing and were looking at each other in disbelief. A fine layer of falling gray ash coated their shoulders. More of it swirled in the air like a drift of discolored snow.

"Grant?"

No reply to her call came, and Paxton saw why. Grant stood a good distance to her left in his werewolf form, his eyes and attention fixed on a large male werewolf she didn't recognize.

He was a big sucker with a lethally powerful appearance. He had dark brown hair and mounds of muscle similar to Grant's, but was both taller and broader. Nothing else, either in his looks or his demeanor, resembled her lover. Paxton's first impression was that this Were had been a werewolf much longer than anyone else present and was far more experienced.

The newcomer must have been the Were who had pulled her off the vampire. In helping to fight off the vampires, this guy had turned the tide.

Neither of the large males spoke through their thoughts, as far as Paxton could tell. Grant didn't appear to be pleased to see this guy. He was tense, antsy. His claws dug into the sides of his jeans.

The two Weres faced each other like this was some

kind of new showdown, without a ripple of movement from either of them. Then the larger Were's eyes drifted to her, pinning Paxton with the bright intensity of their interest and sending her stomach into free fall.

Chapter 28

Grant gritted his teeth as the rogue faced him—the elusive Lycan, in the flesh, larger than life, intimidating as hell and covered with scars that should have healed the way most wounds did for their kind.

Streaks of gray-peppered hair hung past a pair of massive shoulders. He wore no shirt, and Grant supposed no human-made shirt would have fit this guy all wolfed-up like he was now. They had chased this Lycan for months, and here he stood, dangerously powerful and open to their inspection.

The idea of the Were they had called a beast and a monster coming to aid this pack was curious, as was the warning the Were had given about their attention needing to be turned elsewhere. Putting two and two together, it was obvious the big wolf had known about the vampires. More of a heads-up would have been nice.

The big wolf had pale eyes that shone like lanterns in

an unrecognizable face stretched to an abnormal length by his transformation from man to his wolfish state. As those eyes landed on Paxton, Grant strained against the urge to grab that wolf by the throat if he so much as inched in Paxton's direction. Luckily, that didn't happen, and the big wolf's disconcertingly rapt attention returned to Grant.

"Those creatures are gone, and yet you remain," Grant sent. *"No running away. No hiding this time. Could it be you're waiting for something else to happen? Maybe you think those fanged bastards will return."*

Taking a chance backed by intuition, Grant tucked his wolf back inside. The pain accompanying this latest shape-shift was staggering in scope, hinting that it would do him in if he tried another one anytime soon. More beats of time passed before he got his human act together. His voice wavered when he spoke.

"The cryptic warnings didn't begin to describe this. You might have been more specific."

Expecting a response was ludicrous, Grant decided. After all this time eluding capture, the Lycan facing him wasn't apt to give anything away.

"We acknowledge your help, offer our thanks and will repeat the offer to accompany you to town. If you accept our hospitality, it will come with questions and a possible quarantine," Grant added.

The Lycan didn't nod or return the favor of changing into human form. Instead, he turned casually, without a sound, and disappeared into what was left of the longest night that Grant could recall.

Instantly, Grant was at Paxton's side. Controlling the need to touch her, in case she was already hurting, he said, "It's not safe here. We have to go."

The sun hadn't yet risen, but dawn wasn't far off.

Grant felt this in his bones. Glancing past Paxton, he wondered if novels were right about vampires being unable to move around in daylight, and if the so-called children of the night spent their daylight hours snoozing in dark, dank places, like…*caves*.

"Shit," Ben muttered from someplace behind him, having come to a similar conclusion. "This might explain a lot. It also leads me to wonder if this big guy wasn't the one killing cattle, and those fanged freaks were responsible."

Grant was in complete agreement with Ben's analysis. Problem was, given the new light just shed on what kind of other creatures currently called the desert home, plus the swift disappearance of the rogue, there was no way to classify that lone wolf now as either ally or just an enemy with benefits.

There was no justification for a rogue werewolf helping them if he was the one causing trouble.

And what was his interest, and the vamps' interest, in Paxton, whose attention was fixed on the spot where the big Were had stood? Grant had no idea what Paxton was thinking. Either she had again found a way to hide her thoughts from him or her mind was blank.

"Come on," he said to her, waving to include Ben and the others. "The sun isn't actually up, so who knows what those fang-bearing bastards might do next?"

He did know one thing, though. Paxton had chosen the word *dead* to describe what had been coming, and she had been right. While he didn't want to press her after what she had already been through, who wouldn't have had a whole bunch of questions on that score?

Paxton appeared to be assimilating her transition from human to Were. She was in pain and dealing with it. In her wolf form, she was just as untrusting as she had been as a human, and she growled when he got close.

Grant saw how tired she was. He felt the burn of the deep-seated anger that flushed her skin. Too many secrets had been revealed to her tonight. Any lesser, more fragile female would not have been able to cope. But Paxton Hall was special.

"It would be enough to drive a weaker person insane," Grant cajoled with a calmness he didn't really feel. Her pain added to his own. He could tell Paxton wanted to bend, yet stood tall.

If I could touch you...

He couldn't lay a hand on her because Paxton wasn't going to allow it.

The air near the gates remained as odorous as if vampires had tainted it and left their mark on the night. It stank of decomposed bodies and the damn gray ash they became after being dealt a final death blow.

Grant figured they had sent at least one vampire to its final resting place—wherever the hell that was. He contemplated whether the other vampires would be angry to lose one of their number and seek revenge. Heaven only knew if the undead had brains or feelings outside of the hunger that ruled them.

There was an hour at most before a new day arrived. For Grant, sunrise could not come too soon.

"Don't think about anything now, except getting to Desperado," he said to Paxton, losing precious minutes by giving her the time to recover. "You need shelter, a comfortable bed and a hot meal."

He would have given all ten claws to be able to crawl into bed beside her and sink his hard length into her lush, waiting depths. He ached to waken her each morning with a kiss, and had never wished for anything so badly. But he wasn't sure any of that would happen now that she knew about werewolves. About herself, and about him.

"Paxton, let's move," he said, nodding to the others, butting up against his she-wolf with his hip and one bare shoulder.

When she took a step, he could have kissed her right then and there. She had heard him. She was going to comply and would be all right once they reached shelter.

"I am not to blame for this," he whispered to her. "Please believe me."

Urged into action by his silent additions to the things he voiced aloud, Paxton began to walk. He saw no evidence of her fatigue in the way she carried herself. Paxton the she-wolf was the epitome of grace and courage, in spite of being new to the gig.

There was a lot more than shape-shifting in her future, Grant wanted to tell her. Chief among those things was the fact that they had imprinted. She might not want him to touch her at the moment, but she wouldn't be able to leave him, any more than he could abandon her. The first meeting of their eyes had sealed their fate as lovers and mates. Making love so blissfully had finalized the deal.

Thinking about hot, sweaty sex with Paxton, now that she knew nearly everything, made Grant hard all over. Made him ache in places that weren't already aching. Ahead of him on the road, Paxton growled again, and what he heard in that sound was, *"Over my dead body."*

Uneasy, sick and tired beyond belief, Paxton turned toward Desperado. She had kissed her old self goodbye and there was nothing she could do about it.

There was no going back.

So, all right. There were now three Lycans in the area, and she was one of them, according to Grant and her ability to shift shape without a full moon's help. The wolf they called a rogue was the third Lycan to show up, and when his eyes had found her, a strange emotion had stirred her insides. Those pale eyes seemed familiar. Then again, for all she knew, all wolf-to-wolf contact might feel that way.

She looked back at a desert that would have appeared normal to most people, and in reality was anything but. In her mind, behind the clash of leftover pain and the wish that none of this was real, the rogue Lycan's eyes continued to haunt her.

Grant was silent now. So were the others. Night birds and bugs had resumed their songs to herald a dawn that would soon light the mountain range.

And yet…

She knew the rogue was out there, and that he was watching her just like the invisible eyes she'd felt as a kid. Here, in real time, the idea was as vague as it was frightening. Older now, and wiser, she wasn't about to let that memory go, because after meeting the rogue, memories and ideas in a world full of questions suddenly began to connect. Perceptions marched into focus.

Yes, damn it. She had met werewolves before. There was no doubt about it, or the fact that she had first encountered them here in Arizona.

The surprise of that realization made her hesitate. In following the path of that memory, surely the presence of werewolves in and around Desperado was part of the reason she'd been sent away.

Beside her, Grant had stopped and was eyeing her curiously. She had forgotten about his ability to share her thoughts and hadn't protected them. Grant, however, had not been here when she was young, and therefore hadn't been privy to all the years of self-doubt between then and now. The years of believing she'd been unwanted, unloved and dispensed with by the father she had, since then, continued to yearn for in secret.

Now, Grant's shining allure was like a welcoming beacon backed by a promise of danger. She would find comfort, of a sort, in his arms and should have allowed that to happen. But those other eyes, the rogue Lycan's eyes, kept her turning to Grant.

She was learning too fast, feeling too much, when she had only begun this unbelievable journey. Her world was never going to be the same. Not even remotely close.

Shut up and deal, she told herself.

The back of her neck ached. Her stomach was in knots. So far, her reasoning seemed right, but didn't address the reasons for a rogue Lycan's presence disturbing her.

"Don't go there," Grant whispered to her, concern weighing heavily on his princely features. "Now isn't the time to consider what is or isn't. Safety comes first."

Grant's right cheek was bloody. His shoulders were crisscrossed with red scratch marks beginning to welt. Her werewolf lover had fought to protect her, was continuing to do so, and what she was about to do might appear ungrateful.

She spoke to Grant from her heart. "Forgive me, but I have to."

Spinning in place, Paxton uttered a growl that got stuck in her throat...and took off for the desert behind them, hoping this time Grant couldn't catch her.

Chapter 29

"Bloody hell!"

Grant's packmates were equally surprised by Paxton's sudden, incredibly dangerous and ill-timed rebelliousness. Grant was actually afraid of what might happen next.

"Go on ahead," he barked to the others as he started after Paxton. "Warn them about the vampires," he added over his shoulder.

He ran as if he was in possession of all of his strength and he cursed the night for taking so long to end. With the weak wind in his face and his connection to Paxton foremost in his mind, Grant raced back to the wash where he had met with the rogue Lycan.

Paxton wasn't there. There was no sign of vampires or rogues in the area.

He dared to call, "Please wait," listening to how those words fell flat. His mind rushed ahead of him at a frantic pace to test the wind, the ground and various theories as to why Paxton would believe this was a good idea.

Each avenue he mentally tried led to a dead end. He just did not get it. Frustrated, Grant ran as fast as he could, skimming the ground on human feet he willed to take him where he wanted to go without faltering.

"You're smarter than this," he muttered to Paxton, silently adding to himself, *At least I would have thought so.*

The only thing he could come up with as an excuse for her behavior was that somehow, and in some way, the rogue Lycan had issued an invitation Paxton couldn't refuse. She was going after him. The other werewolf. If being scared for her wasn't enough, jealousy was like a huge dark mouth that threatened to swallow him whole.

Once he'd have been sure Paxton would have no feelings for the bastard out here after hearing about the things that rogue had done. But Grant no longer believed the Lycan had done any of the deeds attributed to him. Vampires had stolen that honor.

So, if the big Lycan was cleared of the atrocities formerly assigned to him, Grant had to find out who that guy was. For the hundredth time, there remained the unanswered question of what he wanted here.

Any time now, you'll start to make sense, Paxton had said to him early on.

"How wrong you were," he grumbled.

As if he had demanded that Paxton's scent take a form he could see, Grant suddenly became aware of the imprint on the atmosphere she had created. Her image wavered, going in and out of focus before solidifying into the visible shape of a she-wolf slowing her pace.

His relief was instantaneous and temporary. Paxton

was there, all right, and surrounded by the same black mist they had encountered less than half an hour before.

The same damn mist that also clung to the vampires.

"I have to," she had said to the man she ached for. "Forgive me," she had whispered to him when the sentiments behind her hasty exit had seemed valid. Now, foolishness was going to be her downfall.

The black mist encased her as if she was trapped in an ice-cold pool of water. Already she was shivering and trying to think of a way to get out of the mess she had gotten herself into, but she couldn't see how that was possible.

Nightmarish faces appeared. Mentally Paxton took a count. Only two fang-bearing creatures snapped at her after hissing through the wide gaps in their hazardous teeth. Perhaps they were tentative about facing a werewolf after the last encounter, because neither of those creatures came close enough for her to spit in their ugly, undead faces.

She raised her hands, brandished her claws and widened her stance. Fighting these vampires was the only option left to her. If she was going to be cursed for her stupidity in leaving Grant and the pack, she'd make it difficult for these pricks to get at her.

Growls bubbled up from deep in her chest as one of the vamps floated toward her with a crooked grin hinting that dinnertime had arrived.

Her second wave of growls was louder, braver and like no other sound Paxton had ever heard. But a vampire had closed in and was inches away from the claws she had no real idea how to use.

She swiped at the air between herself and the freak in warning, and the vampire didn't care. It was already dead, she remembered, so the danger she represented was probably small by comparison to the initial loss of their lives. Also against her was the fact that she hadn't gotten a clear look at how Grant and the other Lycan had dispatched this guy's friend.

Once, so long ago, she had seen this. She had been here, surrounded by fanged freaks in the middle of nowhere, all by herself.

That realization inspired another memory. She had been ringed by gaunt faces with snapping fangs while her pony lay lifeless at her feet.

Another memory...

Her pony had gotten loose from its tether at the gate and had trotted off without her, frightened by something Paxton's young eyes hadn't been able to see. She had gone after him. Her father was going to be mad that she had trespassed beyond the boundaries of their ranch at all, let alone without a chaperone and so close to sunset. Riding into the desert had been forbidden. Riding into the desert near or during the time of a full moon would have been punishable by grounding if her father had caught her.

Still, in all those times she had ignored his warnings, he never had caught her, and she had been emboldened by her forbidden freedom. Until that one dusk, when her pony had become a feast for vampires, and she had watched, horrified, as sharp canines tore into her beloved animal before Paxton was rescued by...

Yes. She had it now. Everything came back in one quick vision, as if a movie played in her mind.

She had been rescued by one of the watchers she had sensed in Desperado. Not just any watcher, Paxton's mind now told her. The terrified little girl who had tried desperately to keep the snapping fangs away from her pony's carcass with every means she could think of, had been saved by another creature. A werewolf.

Pale eyes in a wolfish face.

Big as a bear.

A fierce fighter that had come, not to harm her, but to help her escape her pony's fate.

That werewolf had killed the freaks, picked her up, and taken her home, depositing her near the ranch, where everyone pretended nothing had happened and her father sent her away to make sure things like that never happened again.

Banished. Gone from Arizona and from her father after losing her mother mere months before. End of story. The rebel troublemaker got what was coming to her, and after months of promises from a child psychiatrist that she'd imagined the experience, the little girl had started to believe it.

Looking up and into the face of the vampire, Paxton's anger burned with the fire of a shooting star. In her mind, the dead pony lay at her feet once again. She saw it there. Smelled its death. Now, she had run off again and was on her own, facing two freaks in need of their next meal.

But this time, I'm not that same helpless girl.

Now, gathering herself, energized by the discovery of a truth long hidden from her, Paxton charged at the vampire that was attacking her. The bloodsucker was fast, but so was she. Kicking out, her left foot connected with the moving bag of bones and it stumbled back before coming on again. She fought like a madwoman, slashing at the creep with her claws like an angry creature with nothing more to lose.

Though she did have something to lose, her mind argued. Grant Wade.

As if dragged in by mist, Grant was suddenly beside her. Her guardian angel was as fierce as any vampire as he fought beside her in human form.

One vampire went down beneath the fury of two beings at war with the epitome of Evil. Minutes later, the second vampire succumbed to its final death when its neck was broken. But Paxton hadn't killed that one, and neither had Grant.

Big as a bear, and with its unusual eyes on her, the Lycan rogue waited until the last of the funnel of gray vampire ash had settled. She finally got a good look at him.

Struck again by how unlike Grant this rogue was, she stared. This larger version of a werewolf seemed to be from another species altogether. Nothing in his appearance, other than his eyes, hinted at anything human or what he might look like as a man.

When he raised a clawed hand, Grant took a protective step closer to Paxton. But the rogue pointed at the mountain range beside them, where the sun would soon make its case against marauding vampires. The rumble in his chest sounded like the beat of a drum. Hearing it, Paxton began to feel stranger than she was already feeling.

If this guy butchered cattle, she couldn't picture it. Scary, yes, but he had helped to save her ass twice. No maniac did things like that.

Paxton owed the rogue a round of thanks and had no way to say it. Instead, she sent a thought not fully realized until the sentiment came out. *"I'm not afraid of you."*

The pale eyes blinked. The rogue's elongated head tilted slightly, as though the Lycan might have been thinking about her little speech. There was no response from the beast. Not so much as a growl. Paxton waited for the big Lycan's next move, and that move was to turn and disappear so quickly, Paxton was left wondering if he had been there in the first place.

"No," Paxton growled stubbornly. *"Not this time."*

She was after that Lycan in a flash, sensing the big Were hadn't gone far. Fast on her feet, she seemed to fly over the ground, no longer bothered by fatigue.

She would have caught up with the Lycan if Grant hadn't stopped her. With strength more than double her own, her protector dragged her to a stop before they had reached the rocks at the base of the mountain range and spun her around so abruptly, she fell onto her back.

Straddling her on his knees, with his hands on her shoulders, he looked down at her with his handsome human face, the face she loved and needed to see because of the beauty of the humanness in it.

Grant was panting, his bare chest rising and falling with effort. His magnificently sculpted abs rippled as he bent low over her. The shaggy auburn hair she wanted to run her fingers through stuck to the sides of his face.

"Paxton," he said with his mouth inches from hers and as their gazes locked. "Change back."

She didn't fight. In truth, there wasn't much fight left in her. So she did what Grant asked and willed herself to be the person she had always believed she was. And when she lay beneath Grant, with the sand at her back and his body's warmth inviting her to relax, Paxton nodded her head, took a deep breath and began to cry.

Chapter 30

Watching tears track down Paxton's cheeks drove a nail through Grant's heart. He was sure that heart would break.

His lover was going through something he wasn't able to follow. She was experiencing an emotion hidden from him, and he had a good idea what that might be. Paxton's world had changed forever. Her future was murky and vague. Her new life experience would be positive, if he could help her see it that way.

But first he had news to share that he dreaded. Not concrete news. Not yet. It was just a feeling in his soul, the little spark of an idea that had come to him while he watched Paxton fight. *Later*, Grant told himself. *Wait for the right time.*

He ran a gentle thumb over her cheek to capture a tear and looked deeply into her eyes.

"You'll do," he said.

Such a simple statement for the immensity of his feelings for her. For sure, he was no damn poet.

She blinked back more tears and refocused on him before wiping her cheeks with an open palm. After studying her hand, she spoke. "Because we're two of a kind?"

Grant shook his head. "Because you are here in answer to my prayers."

Her eyes widened. "You don't know me."

"Don't I?" Grant countered. "Tell me, do you know me? Do you know my secret, my objectives and why your father left Desperado to me? Haven't you had your hands on my body, felt my breath in your mouth and experienced the same kind of pleasure I did in that bunkhouse?"

Trapped by his body, she made only one half-hearted attempt to move. That alone spoke volumes about her intrinsic need for this conversation.

"Yes," she said. "I know that much."

Grant nodded with satisfaction. "And do you feel anything for me, after such a ridiculously short time together? Answer truthfully."

She bit her lower lip with tiny white human teeth before replying reluctantly, "I'm sure plenty of females would answer that question in the affirmative."

"How about this one?" he pressed.

She blinked again, slower this time.

"How about you?" Grant asked.

"Will you let me go if I answer?"

"No. Not until you promise not to go after the other Lycan."

"Then, yes. Okay, I won't go after the other one. And in answer to your question, I might have a crush on you. But there are more pressing issues on the table."

To hell with the other issues, he thought. "Crush, is it? After what we've shared?"

Her expression was guarded as she said, "I'm not sure what else you might call this kind of attraction."

"I'd call it fate. Two beings meant to find each other. Although that would make your father a master designer, wouldn't it, since he brought both of us here?"

He watched her think over his remark. Once she had, her amber gaze again met his.

"What is it you see when you look back at the past? Who is there?" he asked.

The question was difficult for her, but she said slowly, "Werewolves."

That answer surprised Grant. He had to wonder how far back in memory she had gone. Bypassing the desire to probe that revelation, he said, "Is that all?"

"Vampires. The vampires were there," Paxton replied with her hands on her face.

Grant lowered his voice to gentle his tone. "The memories are from when you were a kid."

"Yes." The word resembled a hiss.

"Werewolves and vampires."

Her eyes didn't stray from his. "Yes."

"So you knew about this all along. About us and about those fanged freaks."

"I didn't remember until minutes ago. I…" Her remark trailed off, incomplete.

"What, Paxton?" Grant asked. "Tell me what you are reluctant to say."

The amber eyes narrowed as she said, "They didn't believe me. Told me I had made it up. I had to trust them in order to survive. In order to tame the nightmares."

"Nightmares starring vampires and furred-up beasts?"

The look on Paxton's face put another nail in his heart. Her pallor was as white as the monsters that, by her admission, had haunted her early on. Someone had lied to her when she was a kid, without realizing that other species existed. Those nightmares had returned tonight, and she was personally involved. Hell, if Paxton wasn't a Were, and a tough one, he might have feared for her ability to take a next breath.

But she was a Were, and more. Paxton was a Lycan. She was his Lycan.

"What else?" Grant asked. "I can see there's more."

Paxton turned her head to break eye contact, her gaze sliding to the desert beyond them. Grant felt the first breath of dawn on his back and rolled his shoulders to absorb the relief he felt.

Possibly Paxton sensed dawn coming the same way he did and also was relieved that any minute now they'd be free of vampires and fights and big scary rogue were-wolves for a while. Back at the ranch, where he'd take her, Paxton could safely rest in his arms. He would whisper softly to her about their future together and pray that she agreed.

They would make love and satisfy the cravings so easy to read in Paxton's face amid the horror of everything else. Perhaps it would take days, weeks, for their passion to allow a slower exploration of what their bodies were capable of. At that moment, however, as Paxton tore her gaze away, Grant realized there was a little way to go before his dreams came true. Paxton had to trust him first. She had to believe in him. And, along with everything else, they had to find the truth about her mother and her father.

Getting to his feet, he held out a hand to Paxton, trying not to look too long at the way her beautiful body glowed with the fine layer of perspiration left over from her efforts. With the special gift of sight he had been given, he was able to clearly see every detail of her slender, nearly bare torso and the small quakes running through her.

If she accepted his offer and took his hand, whether or not she needed to, it would signal a positive first step toward the future he had mentally outlined.

She was still looking at him when she sat up. Even after all the fighting and shifting, the filmy lace thing covering her breasts was intact. He had to marvel at that. Her jeans, cut low enough to expose a portion of her flat, toned belly, were dirty, and her shoelaces were untied. Blond hair, lighter in color than Paxton's she-wolf version, hung in matted strands over both of her shoulders.

All of this was so damn hard for him to resist, and at the same time it was heartbreaking. Paxton lacked the knowledge he'd had about what he was. Her heritage had been sprung on her without any sort of advance notice.

She didn't torture him by showing further hints of the rebellious streak he had witnessed tonight.

She took his hand.

Her fingers were long and delicate. Grant felt the throb of her pulse in her soft palm. As he pulled Paxton to her feet, she said one more thing.

"I take it back."

The remark could have meant anything, but Grant sincerely hoped it dealt with her earlier comment about him not taking her to bed again. The *Over my dead body* remark she had thrown at him. Because vampire dust had to be put behind them for the night, and the rogue

Lycan would be impossible to track after sunrise. That left just one more thing to fill his mind.

Paxton, in his arms.

Rest.

Comfort.

Safety for the time being.

And the chance to be together.

With her hand in his, Paxton stood upright, considering how long it would take Grant to figure out that the rebellious streak he was thinking about hadn't gone away. Rather, it was rising like an internal storm to impel her to take action.

She had to find that rogue Lycan with or without Grant's assistance, and in spite of what she had said. What was left of her sanity depended on it. Everything she had been told not to believe hinged on locating him. And though she desperately wanted to go with Grant and find a temporary respite from the night's bizarre events, she would never have a moment's peace unless she put the ideas she was forming to the test.

Only by seeing that Lycan in human form would she be able to understand the familiarity she felt in his presence. That familiarity had a taste, a smell and an uncertain texture that came at her in a jumble without translating into anything tangible.

She thanked the stars still twinkling overhead that Grant didn't fold her into his arms the way they both wanted him to. She'd be an idiot if she didn't want closer contact with something so fine. She longed for his mouth on hers and to hear his whispered assurances.

Yet accepting pleasure from her lover would postpone what had to be done. Finding that damn Lycan felt like a necessity. If Grant loved anything about her, he'd have to let her solve the mystery of Desperado.

And there were plenty of mysteries to go around. Chief among them was the ambiguity of that all-powerful fate Grant had mentioned, and how her father could have planned all of this down to the minutest detail. She had heard Grant's thoughts on this.

"You are adept at hiding things from me," Grant said as she pondered those things.

She knew, because he did not hide the thought from her, that he wanted to brush the sand from her back, but refrained.

"You asked if I knew you after our short time together," she began. "It's weird that feel as if I do. Physical intimacy aside, if werewolves can read the minds and thoughts of other werewolves, every one of them is deeply exposed to everyone else. I guess this makes werewolves closer to each other than any group of humans could ever be."

She hadn't included herself in that statement, using *them*, instead of *us*, as if she had not fully accepted her own situation.

She went on. "Thoughts and emotions become intimate, possibly speeding up the process in a..."

"Relationship," Grant finished for her.

His eyes were luminous. She was a sucker for looking into them.

"That barely scratches the surface of what we feel—what I feel," he explained. "I can't hide that from you. So you are the question mark here. And our close bond tells me you're planning something."

"Then I suppose I'm not hiding things very well," Paxton said.

"I can't just let you go after that rogue, Paxton. What

kind of partner would I be if I believed danger wasn't an issue?"

"Don't you mean alpha? What kind of alpha would you be?"

"Partner," he reiterated with a crisp head shake. "You won't find anything out here in the daylight. I can promise you that."

"Then I'll wait."

He shook his head again. "There's going to be a full moon tonight that complicates things."

Paxton felt the dawning of a new day without searching for the sunrise. She felt the last of the stars disappear. "Will you lock me up in that cage again, or try to?" she asked with the tone of a dare.

"What I will do is ask that you include me in whatever you have in mind to do, so you're not doing it alone."

"And if you don't approve?"

"We're way past that, I think," Grant said. "Aren't we?"

He was right, of course. They were past having arguments over secrets both of them wanted exposed. Grant couldn't hide from her his wish to find out who the rogue was. He wanted that nearly as badly as she did.

"We've been chasing that Lycan for four months. What makes you think you would be able to find him?" he asked.

"His eyes."

In silence, Grant waited out the time it took for her to explain the remark. She knew he was hoping she'd bring up real feelings. True feelings. But how was she to talk about a secret that had been buried so deep inside her, and for so long, that it had taken on the aspects of any other dream?

"I've seen the big Lycan before," she confessed, hating the wobble in her voice, loving Grant even more for not arguing about how impossible her statement was.

Paxton doubled back over the automatic, uncensored, term she had used for her feelings for Grant. *Love.* Was it possible to fall in love in one incredibly long, seemingly endless day? Surely people recognized the difference between love and lust and animal magnetism. Because who would believe in love at first sight, especially with all the wolf issues attached to it?

Maybe what she felt had to do with jealousy. Envy for a man who'd had the pleasure of remaining in the West and who had carved out a life for himself here. A man with a family. A pack.

Her own guardians, substitutes for her missing parents, had died several years back, leaving her stranded without emotional ties of any kind.

Grant seemed to understand her vulnerabilities when he really knew nothing concrete about her life. She hadn't shared any of it. Strong arms waited to encircle her. All she had to do was take one step. And he knew nothing.

Paxton had never loved his face as much as she did right then. Grant's liquid blue gaze contained the power and the voodoo to chase away pain and nearly everything else. Looking into those blue depths distanced the mystery of the rogue and made jumping into Grant's arms doable.

Animal magnetism.

Yes.

Love?

"Soon," he whispered to her. "After we rest we can talk it all over and formulate a plan."

"Before the next moon rises," she said.

His nod caused a lock of his hair to fall becomingly across his forehead. And yet this gloriously capable, sublimely sexy creature who was picture-perfect in all ways, if no one held the werewolf part against him, would always be dangerous. Being in his world meant chaos might rain down each time the damn moon got near to showing her freaking face.

"We rest first, Paxton. Do we have a deal?"

What Grant was saying made sense. Rest. Food. Daylight for decisions. It made all the sense in the world. Besides the God-awful aches, she was bone tired, trembling and didn't remember the last meal she'd had.

"Fries." Grant supplied the answer to her unspoken thought with a smile so dazzling, so inviting after the night they'd had, Paxton wanted to forego real food and eat *him* up.

Chase away the bad thoughts…

Replace mystery with the warmth of Grant's arms.

Damn it. Damn all of this.

Paxton took a step toward him, almost ignoring the rustle in the brush beside them.

Chapter 31

Instead of slipping his arms around Paxton, Grant spun her behind him and took a fighting stance. *He* was there? Maybe the damn rogue had returned after all, with dawn on the doorstep.

No. Maybe not. There was no scent. No feel of Were presence. This was something else.

The sky was pink with a yellow glow. Mountains rising above them cast long shadows over the wash in a last mingling of dark and light. Grant's skin chilled as he faced the rustle of nearby brush. His muscles corded in anticipation.

"You are an idiot. More of one than I had previously presumed," he said, in case he was wrong about the rogue and Paxton's delicious scent was overpowering the rest of his senses.

Behind him, Paxton was shaking with fatigue, and he couldn't help her with that. It appeared that he had been wrong about finding nothing out here in the daylight. Even with the sun not fully up, their sandy surroundings would now have been visible to anyone.

The next surprise was a shock that made his nerves sing. Out of the shadows, a woman appeared. *Almost* a woman, Grant's senses immediately corrected, because the filmy apparition hovered over the sand as if slightly suspended from it.

Of course, a voice in the back of Grant's mind warned, that assessment couldn't be right. This wasn't a wolf and couldn't be vampire this close to daylight unless stories about bloodsuckers had gotten the facts wrong.

"Stay back," he warned, tired enough to hear the wariness in his voice, worried that any opponent would pick up on that, too.

The woman didn't speak. Grant didn't actually see a mouth from where he stood. He felt her eyes on him without seeing them, either. The closer he looked, the more he strained to fill in the features of a diaphanous face, the harder it was to make out anything at all… which made him wonder if he was finally losing it.

There was no real contact with this being. Without acknowledging that she actually saw either Paxton or him, the creature turned away. After gliding several feet from them, she stopped again. Grant took this as an invitation to follow her, whoever and whatever she was.

Paxton seemed to understand this better than he did. Possibly he had grown too cautious in his alpha job because he could not fathom what kind of opponent was left after rogue werewolves and vampires.

"Follow her," Paxton said. "Please."

Obviously Paxton saw the creature, too.

"Please," she repeated, leaning against him with her hands on his shoulders. Her hands were cold.

"Do you know what it is?" he dared to ask her.

"Another mystery," she replied.

"One too damn many," he muttered.

He took Paxton's hand. "Stay back. Behind me."

For once, she did as he asked.

They walked forward. As they did, the filmy creature moved again, adding more distance. Each time they tried to get close, she created more distance, until they were out of the wash and had reached the pile of rocks marking the way to the old Desperado mine.

Grant stopped. "Too dangerous."

Paxton said, "She wants to show us something."

"Could be a trap, and more than likely is," Grant argued, not liking this at all and ready to turn back toward town.

Paxton was adamant. "I'm going."

"It's not a good idea," he insisted, scenting strong Were presence that made his claws slide into place.

From somewhere nearby a deep voice said, "Not a good idea? When did Paxton Hall ever let that stop her?"

Paxton refused to let her knees buckle. Recognizing the tone of that remark was another piece of the puzzle. And, well, she'd never had the patience for puzzles.

She stepped clear of Grant's protective stance with her hands on her hips and said, "Time is up. Who are you?"

"You don't yet know?" The Were in the shadow of the mine's entrance turned.

"I'm curiously blank."

"We both know that's not true."

"What I'm thinking right now is impossible," she said.

"Who the fuck are you?" Grant demanded, looking back and forth from her to the boarded-up mine.

It was a hell of a time for the memory to return. Young Paxton had been struggling to follow a small group of ranch hands to their trucks. The people were hatless to show respect to someone who had died. Her mother was that person.

Her father was there to lead the group. Tall, broad, wide-shouldered, he towered over everyone by at least a head, wearing a long black coat that made the dirt at his feet swirl. On the pocket of that coat had been an embroidered crest. Paxton saw this as clearly as if she stood there now. Recognition of that crest made it a toss-up between laughing and crying.

"Wolf," she said, raising her face to the shadows. "Our brand was a wolf."

Beside her, Grant stirred. She was on a roll and couldn't afford to look at him.

"Isn't that interesting?" she observed, searching the shadows for the rogue she knew was watching her.

Eyes watching...

Someone waiting behind old wood walls...

Those things had haunted her.

"Especially since someone eventually turned Desperado over to a pack of wolves," she said.

Grant's anxiety underscored her fear, but also made her braver. She was close to figuring out this mystery. So close.

Voices boomed inside her head. Directions. Demands.

I forbid you to go there again, Paxton.

Your mother is no longer here to keep you in line.

Your wild spirit will get you into trouble here, so you will have to go.

She would have to go...

In memory, pale eyes glowed in the dark. In the distance, came the roar of a man who mourned the loss of the love of his life. But, Paxton wanted to shout as the fog continued to share its secrets, she had lost her mother. And then her dad.

"No." Grant's one-word protest could have brought her around if she paid too much attention to the offer of safety in her lover's voice. There was no way to block her thoughts.

Back down the hole...

Her pony had lain dead at her feet, covered in blood. And she had been sent away for disobeying her father's rules about riding out alone after dark.

Vampires had been there, in her memory, just as she had recalled earlier, and had chewed the life from her beloved pony. Someone had found her, had fought off the bloodsuckers. That someone had fought like a demon to protect her.

Wolf logo.

Werewolf.

Pale eyes.

Big as a bear.

Paxton closed her eyes as the memories faded. When she opened them again, she said wearily, "Hello, Dad. We thought you were dead."

Chapter 32

What the...?

Grant pressed himself against Paxton's side, fearing she had gone off the deep end. She believed Andrew Hall was alive. Not only that, she believed Hall was the rogue they had been chasing before knowing about vampires in the area.

"Paxton," he said, not ready to go along with her dramatic perceptions.

The Lycan came forward in the shadows as if he were part of them. And, Christ, he had been part of them, since the rogue had been so damn hard to find. This time, however, the Lycan faced them, still partially in the shade and looking more like a modern-day wizard than a werewolf clothed in a man's flesh.

"You can't be Andrew Hall," Grant said, trying hard to accept that this could be the same man who had pledged his land in order to protect the future of the werewolf species in this part of Arizona. Paxton's father. And that Paxton could be right.

"This is a joke," Grant added.

"Sorry, son," the big man said without revealing his face. "It was best to remain on the sidelines."

Paxton, silent now, was free of any hint of warm and cuddly feelings for the man in the hood. Her posture was rigid. Her hands were balled. Grant wasn't certain she actually believed this, either.

He would have whisked her away to a safe place where vampires and trouble couldn't find her, but she'd have had none of that. And, in this case, trouble was looking them straight in the eyes.

"Why aren't you dead?" she asked the hooded man.

Grant didn't actually expect the Lycan to answer that question and was surprised when he did.

"It was time to pass the torch," he replied.

"What does that mean?" Paxton demanded in a softer voice.

"I could no longer help the way I wanted to," the Lycan said.

"Why not?"

"I wouldn't have been accepted by my own species."

Uneasy with the Lycan's confession, Grant watched Paxton flinch at Hall's use of the word *species*. Tough as nails, and showing more grit, she confronted the big Were again.

"What made you think that?"

The Lycan replied, "I'm no longer one of them. Not completely."

Grant interrupted. "You're either Were or not. There is no middle ground."

When the eyes behind the hood turned his way, Grant felt heat without having to see those eyes.

"Ah, so we all think until the impossible happens. In this case, it happened to me," the Lycan said.

Paxton inched forward with her head tilted to one side, as if sniffing for the truth. "What is the middle ground you speak of?"

"I wouldn't be telling you now if it wasn't so important," the Lycan answered. "And if it wouldn't save lives."

"Go on," Grant said.

The Lycan gestured to the boarded-up mine. "They found this place and made it their nest. No one else knew this, or that I had found them. By that time, it was too late."

"Nest." Grant absorbed another chill. "You're talking about vampires?"

The Lycan nodded. "They came slowly, at first, and in small numbers. Those numbers quickly grew."

Grant glanced to Paxton. She was holding in her mind an image of a dead pony and had told him she had seen vampires before. Putting those things together caused more interest in what this Lycan, who might or might not have been Andrew Hall, had to say.

"I fought those suckers at night without telling anyone else, thinking I could take care of the problem. As the alpha here, that was my province."

Grant nodded for him to go on.

"Eventually their numbers were out of control. I had to recruit the pack, and together we came calling. The wily bloodsucking bastards separated me from the others as easily as culling sheep. My wolves were slaughtered, almost to the man, and I…"

Grant waited without breathing for the Lycan to finish his statement, already fearing what he might say. At his side, Paxton looked to have been carved from stone.

"Well, I was strong enough, different enough, to live through that massacre. I was strong enough to get my affairs in order and to send Paxton away."

Paxton spoke in a small voice. "You sent me away for my protection?"

The hood bobbed when the Lycan nodded. "Always the rebel. That was my Paxton. Never listening. Always bending or breaking the rules I hoped would keep you from a similar fate."

A punch of emotion rocked Paxton back on her feet as she recalled the werewolf who had come to her rescue. That werewolf now had a name. That werewolf had been her father.

It *was* Andrew Hall facing them.

Paxton took two more steps, feeling weightless now and only starting to process what was taking place as all three Lycans faced off.

It wasn't really a face-off, though. Even as a man, her father outweighed Grant by at least forty pounds. The hood he wore did nothing to disguise his size and bulk.

Something so bad had happened to her father that he had faked his own death. He had torn apart every emotion she'd had since she was a kid with his confession of the reason he had sent her away, but that didn't address his continued silence. She, out of everyone, could have kept his secret, whatever that secret was.

"Yes," he said, listening to her thoughts. "You might have kept those secrets if I had been willing to tell them to you."

"It was you who downed the tree," Paxton said.

"Yes. To keep you inside the fence."

"And it was you on the hood of my car."

"Hoping to keep you from venturing out in the dark."

Paxton tried hard to assimilate this news and could barely breathe beneath the weight of it.

"Middle ground," Grant said, stepping up to meet her. "What does that mean? What could be so bad that you'd fake your death and hide out here, without your pack, your daughter or other company?"

"Oh, I have company. It's just not the sort you'd expect. They keep me busy. And now, they have their eyes on… Paxton."

Grant said, "What are you talking about?"

"To get to me, their archnemesis, they will go after my daughter, knowing she is my only weak spot."

"Who will do this?" Paxton asked.

"Then why did you arrange to bring her here?" Grant demanded before her father could reply.

"Who will come after me?" Paxton repeated.

"Are you talking about vampires?" Grant asked.

Shadows had receded near the entrance to the mine, and the hooded Lycan, her father, backed into them. He didn't leave her there with her questions, but seemed to need those shadows the way she needed light.

"She was buried here, you know," her father said. "A portion of the mine caved in while she was inside."

More emotion struck, tying Paxton's stomach in knots. "My mother?" She was not sure how much more of this she could take.

Her father nodded. "You were…"

"Young," she said. "And not allowed to see her. Not allowed to visit her grave because I was told there wasn't a grave."

"You couldn't be allowed to come here, though I think you tried, sensing her soul was here somewhere. Am I right, Paxton?"

"Yes."

"And you were almost killed."

"They ate my pony," she said. "So you sent me away."

Her father lifted a hand. "You would have returned here time and time again, until one day I might have lost sight of you, and you would have suffered the same fate your pony did. That outcome would have killed me if they hadn't."

Paxton was aware of Grant's energy sparking inside him. She put out a hand to stop him from advancing on her father.

Would have killed me if they hadn't. Those words rang in her ears with a discordant sound.

"What happened to you?" she asked again, willing her father to answer the question that had become the heart of this mystery. She sent him that message over and over, bombarding his mind with her Lycan voice. "You said it's important that we know now, so please tell us the rest."

Grant, impatient beside her, said, "The vampires you hunted got to you?"

Her father nodded.

"Yet you're here now," Paxton protested. "You survived."

"I survived, but at great cost. I lost everything."

Her voice took on a plaintive quality. "You had me. Could have had me."

"No," her father said flatly, as if he had thought of the possibility so many times since he had sent her away that it no longer had the power over him it once might have. "Not you. Not like this."

"But I'm here. You brought me here."

"I'm dying, Paxton. My wolf blood wears thin. I arranged for you to come here for two reasons."

"Those reasons are?" Grant was quick to ask.

Ignoring the interruption, her father said, "Grant had to know about the danger facing the area in order to protect not only the pack, but our neighbors."

"Vampires," Grant said.

"And also because it was time for you, daughter, to come into your heritage. You needed to be here, among your kind. It was time for you to come home."

Paxton felt a tear slide down her cheek. More tears pooled in her eyes. "How did you know it was my time?"

She thought she heard a lightness in her father's tone when he said, "It was the same with your mother's line, twenty-six being the year of her wolf's birth."

"But how...?" Her question failed.

"And because in getting close to me, your wolf would respond to mine," Grant said to her. "Like calling to like, with a little thing we call *imprinting* calling the shots. Once you were here it was only a matter of time before we connected. Isn't that right, Andrew?"

Her father nodded.

Paxton turned to face her father again. "Grant was chosen to be a possible mate?"

"Grant Wade exemplifies the best in us," her father replied. "Nothing was too good for my daughter."

So there it was. Mystery solved. Paxton's head swam. She felt faint. But instead of feeling angry with her father, she suddenly felt grateful and almost euphoric. Instead of feeling lost and alone, she had found her father alive, and he had sent her into the arms of a potential mate. Grant. Cowboy. Alpha. Werewolf. Her father's chosen successor.

She wasn't sure she liked anyone choosing a partner for her. Then again...

"All right," she said to her father, almost afraid she

would collapse from fatigue before hearing more. "Now tell us the rest. Tell us about you."

Grant strode toward Andrew Hall holding tightly to Paxton's hand. The elder Lycan waited as they approached without making any move to disappear. This was what Andrew Hall wanted. He had specifically expressed to them how important this reunion with Paxton was.

"Maybe you can remove the hood, Andrew, and finish this tale, so that we can understand it," Grant suggested.

Andrew was silent for several beats before raising his hands. Long fingers grasped the edges of his black hood. As it was drawn back, Grant stared at what that covering had hidden. He tightened his grip on Paxton's hand when she swayed in reaction to what they were seeing.

Andrew Hall's face was unrecognizable as either human or Were. His features were marred by rows of white scars. Eyelids were fused to the skin above them. His mouth was pulled up on one side in a permanent sneer. The rest of his skin was mottled and as pale as his eyes. No color left. Nothing recognizable as human skin.

The big Lycan looked like an embattled ghost.

Long gray hair hung down his back. On his neck were rows of black dots, in pairs. There were so many dots, seeing them made Grant sick to his stomach. Something nasty had been attacking Andrew Hall for some time, and Grant knew what that something nasty was. Vampires.

"So you see now why I can't fit in," Andrew said sadly.

"You're Lycan, no matter what," Grant objected. "Someone could have helped you. We can find help now."

Andrew Hall shook his head. "Who would have guarded this place and other places like it, if I had left my post? Which member of your pack could have lived through what I have lived through, for as long as I have? Only you might have taken up my role while unprepared for it, Grant, and then my daughter would truly have been alone."

"Lycan," Paxton intoned.

"Yes," her father said. "Lycan, once upon a time. With so much vampire poison in my veins I'm not sure what I have become, and the fear is that I can't hold out much longer."

Grant closed his eyes. Andrew Hall had taken it upon himself to be Desperado's protector. Their guardian angel. In the background, he battled bloodsucking parasites with no one to help him, so that Weres in this part of the desert could thrive.

It wasn't a necessary sacrifice, Grant told himself, when so many Weres would have come to his aid. But the big Lycan had his own demons, and those demons had driven him.

Perhaps his presence here at the mine where his wife had died was due to his need to keep vampires from finding her remains. But that was a question Grant would never ask. What was done, was done. The rogue had been found.

He stopped processing that information when he remembered the woman who had led them here. His entire body chilled with the thought of who that woman might have been, and what she was. Andrew's wife, maybe. Paxton's mother. It seemed to him that there were two ghosts here at this old mine, and many more layers to this earthly existence than he had thought possible. It also seemed to Grant that some of those things should be left alone.

Paxton slid her hand from his and pulled away. She was next to her father before Grant blinked, and looking into Andrew Hall's marred face.

"How did you know who I was?" Andrew Hall asked her.

"It was the eyes," she replied. "I remembered my father's eyes."

Andrew Hall had wanted to see his daughter again, and had held out against all that vampire venom in his system in order to do so. He was handing Grant the torch...so that the desert pack would take over the fight against vampires when Andrew was gone.

The Lycan was a hero, of sorts, Grant decided, and would be honored among the pack whether or not Andrew showed his face there.

Giving in to emotion, Paxton put her arms around her father, burying her head against his broad chest.

Grant watched this with a lump in his throat.

Although her father did not immediately return his daughter's gesture of comfort and reunion, there was no doubt in Grant's mind that Andrew Hall wanted to, but had simply forgotten how.

Chapter 33

Sunlight slanted through an opening in the curtains. Long, thin fingers of yellow luminescence left stripes on the bed and on Grant's lover's naked body.

She had talked in her sleep, as she had nearly every night since that dark one at the mine, tossing and turning until he quieted her with a kiss on the nape of her neck. That wonderfully tender place beneath her cascade of silky blond hair was the spot he had grown to love almost as much as the woman it belonged to.

He had done this same thing every night for a month.

Paxton had not mentioned going back to the East in the weeks that had passed, showing no desire to retrieve her things. She didn't seem to care about anything except being one of the pack, strolling through Desperado and going out to meet her father each evening when he came as far as the edge of town.

And, well, she also liked Grant Wade, and *this*.

Gliding his palm over her taut belly made her stir. Slipping his fingers between her thighs made her growl in a sleepy way.

Daylight had become Paxton's friend. She rested easier after the sun came up, and who could blame her? Still, her body, in his bed, was warm and fragrant, and much too delectable for Grant to ignore his craving for her or the hardness of his erection.

Yes, they knew each other. Absolutely. He understood that she'd make him work a little harder at seducing her before she let on that she'd been waiting for him to do so. His she-wolf was sometimes adept at hiding her thoughts, but never thoughts dealing with her feelings for him. Each morning, he made love to her. Each day she told him she loved him.

The feeling was mutual.

The place his fingers found nestled between her legs was soft and lightly furred. When he dared to insert the tip of one finger into the tender folds beneath all that softness, Paxton sighed and arched her back.

"Wolf," he whispered with his mouth close to her ear.

"Bastard," she responded teasingly, leaving her lush lips slightly open in invitation.

It was always like this, Grant thought to himself. And always would be. Although they sometimes took an hour to satisfy their craving for each other, taking the time to explore each angle and curve, holding himself back was never easy. Paxton Hall was just too damn sexy. And she was his.

Gently, he rolled over to lay his body against hers. His lover didn't open her eyes. But she smiled and opened her legs.

"What? Again?" Grant asked.

Fair lashes fluttered before her eyes finally opened and she said in her best bedroom voice, "If you think an alpha can handle it."

It was his turn to smile. "I'm pretty sure I can, since you insist."

"Of course, if you'd rather not…" she began, the jest fading as he entered her with a smooth thrust that made her fingers curl.

Her eyes never left him after that, and Grant wouldn't have had it any other way. As their bodies rode out the storm that took them over with each renewed thrust, each give and take, plunge and withdrawal, Grant finally sealed his lips to hers. He drank in her groans of pleasure as if every sound were a special kind of sustenance for him.

And when he reached her core, that place where their souls met and collided amid the pulsating inferno, his lover's hard-beating orgasm spun him into his own divine ecstasy.

It was like coming back to Earth after a journey in space when Grant's mind could function properly again. He was a little out of breath and his lips were on Paxton's. Her hands were on his bare backside, frozen there as she came down from the same kind of blissful journey.

"Will that do, little wolf?" he whispered, drawing back far enough to seek the answer in her amber gaze.

"Not quite, I'm sorry to say," she huskily replied. "I expected far more from a Lycan."

So, what the hell? Grant thought, smiling widely, knowingly, happily. He was damn sure he was up for the next round, as well as the one after that…and was ready to prove it.

He had a job to do, a pack to protect and a beautiful

she-wolf in his bed. Maybe, just maybe, his mind had been changed, and being an alpha wasn't turning out to be so bad after all.

And, in the end, he had Desperado's ghosts to thank for that.

* * * * *

Linda O. Johnston loves to write. While honing her writing skills, she worked in advertising and public relations, then became a lawyer...and enjoyed writing contracts. Linda's first published fiction appeared in *Ellery Queen's Mystery Magazine* and won a Robert L. Fish Memorial Award for Best First Mystery Short Story of the Year. Linda now spends most of her time creating memorable tales of paranormal romance, romantic suspense and mystery. Visit her on the web at www.lindaojohnston.com.

Books by Linda O. Johnston

Harlequin Romantic Suspense

Undercover Soldier
Covert Attraction

Harlequin Nocturne

Alpha Force Series

Alpha Wolf
Alaskan Wolf
Guardian Wolf
Undercover Wolf
Loyal Wolf
Canadian Wolf
Back to Life

Visit the Author Profile page
at Harlequin.com for more titles.

PROTECTOR WOLF
Linda O. Johnston

Protector Wolf is dedicated to wolves of all kinds as well as people who love and protect wildlife. And like my other Alpha Force Nocturnes, *Protector Wolf* is also dedicated to shape-shifters and the readers who love them.

Plus, despite this being repetitious, my special thanks to my wonderful agent, Paige Wheeler of Creative Media Agency, and to my delightful Harlequin editor, Allison Lyons. They're so great in helping to keep the stories of Alpha Force an ongoing miniseries. *Protector Wolf* is number eight!

And, as always, thanks to my amazing husband, Fred, whom I acknowledge in each of my books because he inspires me. My hero!

Chapter 1

Lieutenant Ryan Blaiddinger strode quickly down the sidewalk.

Beside him were his dog, Rocky, and his aide, Staff Sergeant Piers Janus. The two soldiers were dressed in civilian clothing—nice slacks and button-down shirts. They were here in Fritts Corner, Washington, undercover.

According to the map on Piers's phone, the park they sought was only a block away. Ryan scoped out the whole street—fairly narrow, considering it was the quaint town's main avenue. Some of the buildings appeared to have been constructed more than a century ago, with spires, decorative windows and wide porches that led into restaurants and other retail establishments.

"We're almost there," Piers said, staring at the phone in his hand. Piers was short and a bit stocky, and despite his being in his early twenties his blondish hair had begun to thin. But he was a damned good helper—in many respects.

Piers held Rocky's leash, and the dog bounded along with him.

The dog with thick brown-and-black fur who resembled a wolf.

A wolf who looked a lot like Ryan…when he was in shifted form.

The air was brisk but dry on this Thursday afternoon in September. Cars drove by in both directions, with no hint of any traffic jam in this small town. People passed by as well, and a few headed in the same direction they did.

Interesting that on the day of their arrival a public meeting was scheduled about the very topic they'd come to check out.

But maybe it wasn't too surprising. After all, though there had been sightings of wild wolves for years in various areas of Washington State, even identification of some small packs, the latest new sightings had been right around here, in this area southeast of Tacoma.

And when Ryan, sounding as offhand as he could, mentioned wolf sightings to their hotel's receptionist a short while ago when they checked in, she had immediately perked up and told him that a naturalist had just come to town and was going to talk on that very topic in less than an hour.

That was really interesting since wolves previously hadn't been spotted around here much for a long time, the receptionist had acknowledged. Lots of people in town were fascinated by the situation…though some weren't too happy about it.

There. The open-air park, mostly green, rolling lawn with a few trees, was finally off to their right. A large crowd stood on the grass facing a raised podium that appeared old and worn, perhaps even constructed around the same time as the rest of the town.

On it stood a tall and slender woman. A screen behind her contained a photo of a wolf, projected there by some modern equipment that clearly wasn't as antique as the town.

"The pictures I've shown you are from other areas in Washington," she was saying into a microphone so her deep, energetic voice projected around the area. "It's so exciting that wild wolves have been returning to this state. Of course WHaM has been keeping up with the Washington Department of Fish and Wildlife's postings online, as well as US Fish and Wildlife, which has jurisdiction for their protection around here. We're thrilled—and tracking them, too, taking a census including the official estimate of nineteen packs in the state. Plus, we encourage the media to let the public know. Any media people here?" A few hands were raised. "Great!"

WHaM. That was Wildlife Habitat Monitoring, Ryan knew. He needed to talk to this woman after her presentation, and using his cover of being with the US Fish and Wildlife Service—not the state's—should make it easy for him to find out everything WHaM knew about the latest wolf sightings.

Of course their agenda was far different from his. Wolf sightings to them would be just that—evidence of the continuing but slow return of wild wolves to increasing locations in this state, fewer here than in the eastern part. And some had already been destroyed after attacking livestock, though not in this area.

Ryan was here on his first lead assignment representing Alpha Force. Rocky and Piers had come along as his backups. He was the only commissioned officer present—and the only member here of that covert military unit of shapeshifters who was actually a shifter himself.

For the moment, he eased his way through the large group of onlookers, men, women and children of all ages, knowing that Piers would follow with Rocky. Rocky might garner some attention since he looked so much like a wolf, but that was because he was Ryan's cover dog. He had been chosen because of his resemblance to Ryan in shifted form. That way, in case anyone noticed him while shifted, they'd be told it was Ryan's dog they'd seen. Him as a shapeshifter? What a laugh.

Or so went the cover story he'd been provided by Alpha Force.

He finally reached the front of the crowd after excusing himself and smiling and looking apologetic to lots of people along the way.

What did they all think of the slow influx of wolves around here?

Were any of them shapeshifters, too?

Ryan would find that out while he was here. Quickly. It was a major part of his assignment.

And if there were other shifters? Well, he'd determine, once he'd found and spoken with them, exactly what that might mean with respect to their lives here… and, potentially, to Alpha Force.

Right now, though, he moved over to give Piers and Rocky room to stand beside him. The woman was still talking, speaking with such excitement that it appeared contagious. Lots of folks in his area were cheering and clapping.

Which meant he'd better take time to listen.

"Wolves are such wonderful creatures," she was saying—and that warmed his insides immediately. This close he could see how attractive she was, with a curvaceous body and a face pretty enough to put her onstage for something other than a wildlife proponent rally. "They're smart, loyal to their packs, loving to their families and more. They're—" She had been scanning the crowd with her gaze as she spoke, sometimes waving her slender arm beneath its black WHaM T-shirt up toward the screen behind her, where the pictures of wolves had now turned into a rotation. But now she stopped.

She was looking down toward Ryan, which gave him immediate pause—until he realized she was instead staring at Rocky.

"Is that a wolf among us?" she asked, this time looking right into Ryan's eyes, or so it appeared from this distance.

He smiled and called out, "No, he's my pet, a shepherd-husky mix for the most part, I think. But I wouldn't be surprised if there's some wolf ancestry in there, too."

"Me, neither," she said. But cocking her head so her long, pale brown hair slipped to the side, she held the microphone back up to her mouth. "Okay, folks, you'll need to see that adorable dog before you leave here this afternoon, especially if you've never seen a wolf before. But one thing I should mention is that wolves are wild animals and should stay that way." She paused, and again stared right into Ryan's face so intensely he felt as if she was almost touching him. Maybe slapping him. But she looked away again before she said, "Everyone, never, ever, try to turn a wild animal into a pet…especially wolves."

Maya Everton wanted to jump right off that stage and confront that guy. No, what she really wanted was to meet that wolf-dog face-to-face, hug it, feel its soft fur.

And then let it loose, as wolves should be. Only she realized that, even if that canine had once been wild, as a pup or older, it could probably not survive in the wild now.

Maybe she could talk to his owner later, find out the dog's background, so she could hopefully feel content that she was wrong, that this truly was a canine with dog genes that had never actually been a wild wolf.

"Okay," she was saying despite her thoughts twisting in so many ways. "Has anyone here seen any of the wolves that have visited this area?"

A woman way toward the back of the generous crowd waved her hand. Maya was thrilled that so many people had shown up to see her, to hear her talk about WHaM and its excellent work keeping track of wild animal sightings—wolves and more. But the latest influx of wolves was a big deal here. Newsworthy, and they needed to be protected. WHaM maintained a comprehensive file on all the wolves sighted recently in this state—more in the eastern areas than here, though that might be changing. Her organization had been in close touch often with the Washington Department of Fish and Wildlife, and had a good relationship with them.

Like other wildlife, wolves weren't appreciated in all areas of the state, especially those where some had apparently attacked local farm animals. But around here, they had a fresh start.

She called for the woman to come up to the microphone and describe her experience. While Maya waited for that lady to make her way through the crowd, she looked again toward that wolf-dog. Gorgeous.

His owner wasn't bad-looking, either—as long as Maya could regard him without anger. Well, for now she'd give him the benefit of the doubt.

The woman soon joined Maya onstage. She introduced herself as Ivy. Ivy appeared in her fifties, with a lined face and a huge smile. "I live near here," she said, "but a distance out of town. It was so amazing. I heard some howling in the dead of night and looked outside, only to see a couple of wolves jump over my fence, run through the yard and then out again. It was light enough under the full moon that it didn't matter that I'd forgotten to turn on my porch lamps."

"Really? That's so exciting!" Maya really was impressed, wishing something similar had happened to her. She'd had to seek out every wild animal she'd seen herself without any miraculously appearing. "And did you let anyone know officially?" She thought she recalled a report on the Washington Department of Fish and Wildlife site, or WDFW, that could have been a description of what had happened to this woman but she wasn't sure.

"Absolutely. I researched online what to do and filed a report there with Washington's fish and wildlife department. Only—"

She stopped, and her face seemed to age visibly.

"Only what?" Maya prodded gently.

"Only the one thing I forgot was to grab my camera." Tears rose in her eyes.

Maya couldn't let her leave the stage feeling bad, so she said, "But you took a picture in your own mind, I'll bet. Will you ever forget what they looked like?"

"No, never." The lady smiled, and Maya gave her a brief hug, encouraging her to rejoin the rest of the audience.

Her presentation was pretty much over—at least for this day. "Thank you all so much for coming," Maya said. "And just remember some of the takeaways I suggested to you. First, you should all be proud, as Washington residents, that wolves are returning to your state and this area, and should continue to as long as you treat them well. And second—keep up with what we're doing at WHaM in our tracking of wildlife and otherwise. Provide reports to us, too, and photos if you happen to take any. But be sure to report, as Ivy did, to the Washington Department of Fish and Wildlife, and maybe the federal fish and wildlife department, as well. And if you care to make a contribution to help us keep WHaM going, that would be more than welcome. Just visit our website that's on our flyers. I've got a boxful right here on the stage."

"There's something else you should all remember," yelled a voice from the audience. Maya's gaze lit first on the guy with the wolf-dog but he was scowling in concern. He hadn't been the speaker.

"What's that?" she asked, feeling as if she was setting herself up for some kind of bad situation.

She proved to be right. A couple of men and a woman separated themselves from the middle of the crowd and made their way onto the stage beside her. She felt her brows go up and a slight smile make its way to her lips, even as she continued to figure this wasn't likely to be anything good.

One of the men, maybe her age of late twenties, wore a plaid shirt and a huge, snide grin. He put his hand out for the microphone. Reluctantly, she handed it to him.

"You all know me," the guy said to the audience. He turned back to Maya. "But you don't. My name's Carlo Silling. I've lived in Fritts Corner all my life. This is my town, and those wolves getting close aren't a sign of wonderful things to come, no matter what you and your wham-bammers seem to think. You don't live here.

You're not subject to the danger that wild wolves can present to people, as well as any livestock they raise. They're just that—wild animals. And I'd suggest you leave this stage, leave this town and let us take care of our own bad luck."

Ryan felt himself freeze with tension as his hands curled into fists at his sides.

He'd been staring at that guy Silling as he'd come onstage, as well as the others who'd accompanied him. The malicious, menacing way they regarded the naturalist whose name he'd learned was Maya Everton made him want to rub those expressions right off their faces.

"I agree with Carlo," the woman yelled to the crowd. "I'm Vinnie Fritts—and this is my husband, Morton." She nodded toward the man in a yellow shirt beside her. "You all know us and how long we've been around Fritts Corner—Morton's family especially. Who needs wild animals here to hurt people and ruin our wonderful town's reputation?"

Ryan stood then and, grabbing Rocky's leash from Piers, maneuvered from the front of the crowd and onto the stage.

Time to express their cover story.

"You're all certainly entitled to your opinion," Maya was saying. She had somehow retrieved her microphone and was glaring at the three interlopers. "But the reality is that if you stay away from wildlife, particularly wolves, they're likely to stay away from you, too. You do need to be careful on behalf of your pets, though, since they can often resemble prey. And—"

The guy Carlo reached out and grabbed the microphone again, even as Maya attempted to hold on to it.

"Yeah? Well, what if that lady Ivy happened to be in her backyard that night she saw those wolves? Or—"

This time, Ryan was the one to grab the microphone, even as the other guy, Morton, started to stride toward him.

That was when Rocky growled—and the guy stopped.

"See what I'm saying?" Carlo yelled out to the crowd.

Ryan smiled as he spoke into the microphone, not pleased to see those who'd admitted to be with the media continuing to take pictures. Oh, well. His cover was solid. "This is my dog, Rocky," he said, "who only resembles a wolf. He's well trained in many ways, including my protection. Threaten me, and he threatens back. But look, everyone. The appearances of wolves in this area clearly started months ago, even longer. I'm unaware of any farms or dairies around here. Have any people been hurt?"

That wolves had been seen, per Ivy's story, around a month ago under the light of a full moon, intrigued him—but he'd check more into that later.

Maya strode up to him. She was as tall as she had appeared from below, though she wasn't close to his height of six-two. He'd noted the fear and dismay on her face as he'd gotten close to the stage, but now she'd recovered all her aplomb as well as a huge smile that she leveled on him. "Thank you, sir," she said. "And thank you, pup." She turned toward Rocky, standing beside Ryan, who nuzzled her hand and wagged his tail just like any well-trained, friendly dog.

"That's his way of saying you're welcome," he told her unnecessarily, loud enough that the audience should be able to hear. He was gratified to hear a bit of laughter.

"So, as this gentleman asked," Maya continued, "has anyone been hurt since the wolf sightings started?"

Apparently not, since no one responded in the affirmative even though the low roar of the crowd's voices grew louder.

"Great. Anyway, please keep in mind what I said before. And thanks to all of you for coming."

"You're welcome," shouted a female voice. "Thank *you* for coming. And I totally agree with you."

"Me, too," chorused other voices in the audience.

"That's so wonderful," Maya called back. "You're totally in the right."

"So are you, and WHaM," yelled a skinny guy in the front row, doing a fist pump.

"Thanks," Maya returned, smiling down at him for a second before turning away.

Ryan was amused that Maya ignored the others onstage as she approached the table where her computer equipment rested. He joined her there, Rocky at his side.

"I'm Ryan Blaiddinger, with the US Fish and Wildlife Service," he told her. "Count me with those who liked your presentation. And I want to hear more."

"That's great, Ryan," she said. "Glad to meet you. You can join us." She once more picked up the microphone from the table and spoke into it. "Hey, everyone," she called to the now-disbanding audience. "I just got an idea. Can anyone suggest a bar in town where we all can meet?"

A bunch of people spoke out once more, this time making suggestions. The decision was to go to Berry's Bar, a nearby establishment that sounded fairly large and accommodating.

"See you there?" Maya said, turning back to Ryan.

"You can bet on it. In fact, Rocky and I would enjoy walking there with you now."

"Of course, though I need to drop some of my things

off at my car. I want to learn more about your wonderful wolf-dog." Her tone had turned soft and loving as she gazed down at Rocky—making Ryan wish for a moment that she'd been speaking about him instead. Which was ridiculous. She was a potential information resource for him, and that was all. And of course Rocky was one special dog.

"Good. Ready to go now?" Ryan glanced toward Piers, who stood near them. His assistant nodded briefly. He was ready to go—and to have Ryan's back, if needed. Maybe Maya's, too, since for now, at least, their goals seemed aligned.

"Just a minute while I gather up my stuff and turn this area back to the park personnel," Maya told him. "Then I can join you."

The idea of her joining him for any reason sounded much too good.

He was going to have to be careful in this lovely wildlife lover's presence.

Chapter 2

Maya had encountered controversy before. She thought about that even more as she moved about the stage, first watching the local park attendants pick up their gear, then packing up her notebook and tablet computers, printed files, WHaM brochures and other items she'd brought.

The crowd below dissipated noisily, leaving the grass they'd been standing on bare, but she didn't hear any arguments among them. Maybe the pro-wolf people and anti-wolf people had gone their separate ways. Good. She hoped to meet with a lot of the pros shortly. Maybe some of the media, too.

But as much as she disliked it, controversy was sometimes part of her job. Despite the growing numbers of outspoken people who liked wildlife, those who despised it—or wanted to kill it, whether or not using the protection of livestock or humans as their supposed rationale—never seemed to get smaller. That was why she not only took census but also spoke before groups, partly to make sure the pro-wildlife faction recognized that the other mind-set existed and knew they had to oppose it.

Usually, her talks and that knowledge helped to make those on her side a lot more outspoken right along with her. They often contributed donations to WHaM, too, which helped the nonprofit.

Finishing her organizing and packing, she glanced toward the steps off the stage and saw that the nice, helpful—and great-looking—guy Ryan stood there with Rocky, waiting for her. She couldn't help smiling. Now, there was a man with proof right beside him of his position on this important subject.

It was almost time to head to the bar. She'd intended to stay in Fritts Corner for only a few days, but now she might hang out longer. Of course, that depended at least in part on who showed up at the bar this afternoon and how they acted.

Maya intended to get to know some of the people around here, particularly the few locals who had already been generous with donations. This wasn't the way she'd hoped to get them together, but it should work.

Now, she walked toward the steps, following the park guys whose hands were full of the town's electronic equipment they had collected. Her arms were full, too, and she stopped at the top of the steps to rearrange what she carried so she wouldn't fall.

She shouldn't have been pleased to have Ryan reach up to steady her—but she was.

"Thanks," she told him as he held her arm.

He didn't immediately let go, either, as she reached the last step. She made herself pull gently away, not wanting to encourage him to think she had any interest in him except as an animal advocate.

Although…did she want him to be interested in her in any other way?

No. Of course not.

"My car is parked just past the bar," she told Ryan. He was watching her with very deep brown eyes. She hadn't looked at him this closely before but couldn't help appreciating how good-looking he was, with angular planes on his face and dark brown hair cut short. She turned slightly to try to prevent his recognizing that she'd been studying him. "You can just go to the bar, and I'll meet you there after I put some of this stuff in my trunk."

He reached toward her and lifted one of her tote bags and a few other things she held, lightening her load tremendously. "I'll carry these. You lead the way."

She couldn't help looking at him again then—continuing to appreciate his tantalizing appearance as well as his gentlemanliness.

Still holding a few things she wanted to carry with her, including her tablet computer, she headed across the grass to the sidewalk, and then in the direction of the bar and where she had parked her car. Both Ryan and Rocky stayed beside her. The three of them pretty much took up the whole sidewalk, but other people didn't seem upset about stepping aside to let them pass. Maya shot each of them smiles—and they smiled back at her as they seemed to enjoy Rocky.

"Nice town," Ryan said. He was watching the people, too, so his reference to the town seemed to mean its inhabitants. At this angle, she was glad to look around nearly everywhere but toward him.

"It sure is. I like the people—most of those I've met anyway—and this area is definitely charming."

She'd enjoyed sightseeing before, on her way to the park. She just hoped the town maintained its charm by continuing to be supportive of the return of the wolves.

For right now, talking in generalities about this area seemed pleasant enough as they walked. They soon reached her car, after passing Berry's Bar on the way. It looked crowded inside despite the time being early afternoon. Were these all people from her talk wanting to discuss wildlife some more? She hoped so.

She opened the trunk of the sedan she had rented and Ryan put his armloads of her stuff into it. She did the same with what she was carrying.

Ryan closed the trunk. "I'll be interested in how things go at the bar this afternoon. And I enjoyed your talk before. But I wanted to say something before we're with the crowd." He stood in front of her, Rocky still at his side, and frowned, which removed some of the allure from his good looks.

"What's that?" She felt sure she wouldn't like whatever he had to say.

She was right.

"I know about your organization, and I like what WHaM stands for. I've heard about how you go talk to groups like this while you confirm and count sightings of endangered animals. But—do all the talks wind up with results similar to yours? I mean, not only did you get people there who are excited about the prospect of a new influx of wildlife, but those who are against it. Outspokenly against it. Doesn't that harm your position and your organization?"

"No," she said flatly. She turned away, starting to walk toward the bar, and Ryan and Rocky joined her. "Well...maybe." She didn't look at them. "Controversy sometimes stirs up people who didn't even know they had an opinion. So far I think that's been helpful."

"Maybe," Ryan said. "But it can also cause problems both for your group and for the animals—potentially risky for both of you. I'd suggest you back off a bit, though I'd like to know more about your intentions. Let's talk about it another time."

They'd reached the crowded sidewalk in front of Berry's Bar. "Sure," Maya said, realizing that the idea of getting together with the gorgeous, sexy man to talk appealed more than a little. But…could it be risky? She hoped not. Should she back off? That wasn't her.

What they would talk about might only rev up the controversy she knew was there.

Ryan saw Piers as soon as he entered behind Maya, with Rocky at his side. He'd told his aide to get here ahead of him and save some seats.

Were dogs allowed in here? If questioned, he would just claim that Rocky was his service dog. He even had paperwork in his pocket that would confirm that—if the person asking didn't dig too deeply.

Inhaling the strong, predictable scent of alcohol, he waved, and Piers waved back, gesturing for him to join the group sitting on stools at the bar. Ryan therefore maneuvered through the crowd—and away from Maya.

Which in some ways he hated to do.

The woman was beautiful and sassy and loved wild animals. What wasn't there to like about her?

The fact that she might be putting herself—and his role here—in danger?

Could be. That was why he had asked her to back off.

Sure, there was likely to be attention regarding each new wolf sighting around here, especially if they continued and grew in numbers. But he needed a bit of quiet in his own search regarding the inherent nature of those incoming wolves, not people talking and arguing, or worse.

And he didn't get the sense Maya would pay any attention to him.

"What's wrong?" Piers asked quietly as he reached the bar.

"Nothing, I hope." But his aide knew him well. "We'll talk later," he amended.

"Fine."

Ryan ordered a dark beer, which was also what Piers had in front of him. He decided to confront the situation of Rocky right off and requested that the bartender, a sizable fellow with a full head of hair and a beard, bring a bowl of water.

"Sure thing," the bartender said. "Nice-looking dog. Is he yours?"

More or less, Ryan thought. He certainly treated his cover dog as his own. "Yep," he said. "Rocky is one really good boy."

"I bet." When the bartender brought a metal bowl half-filled with water to the customer side of the bar and laid it at Ryan's feet—next to several pairs of feet belonging to other patrons—the guy asked, "Have you ever been to Fritts Corner before?"

"No, though I really like this place." He was laying it on a bit thick, but what the heck? "I'm here because of the latest wolf sightings. I work for US Fish and Wildlife."

"Really?" The bartender's whole, round face lit up. "Were you at the talk at the park before? I was here working, but I heard about it."

"I sure was." Why not go for broke—maybe lay into

some of Maya's contentious ground? "There were some arguments. Not everyone is glad there are wolf sightings around here. How about you?"

"I'm definitely for them," the guy said with no hesitation. He held out his hand to Ryan to shake. "I'm Buck Lesterman. My family recently bought Berry's Bar, and I'm happy with everything to do with wildlife."

Which was what Ryan had been looking for. Was this guy a shifter? Were any members of his family?

Or was Ryan just hoping too hard to find some evidence of shifters in this area?

Could be that all the recent wolf sightings were just that—sightings of actual wolves. Well, he would know more tonight.

"Glad to meet you, Buck. I'm Ryan, and this is my friend Piers." They shook hands, too, then Ryan continued, "Not sure how long I'll be in town, but I'm glad I've found this place."

"Hey, bartender!" called a guy nearby.

"'Scuse me," Buck said. "Got to get back to work."

That was when Ryan heard voices raised behind him, and he turned.

Maya sat at a table, hands on her hips. Across from her were the three people who'd come onstage to give her a hard time, and they didn't appear any friendlier.

Time for Piers and him—and Rocky, too—to join her.

As they moved in her direction, so did a few other people Ryan believed he recognized as having been at her talk.

Were they for, or against, her position?

This discussion was getting out of control. Too bad Maya couldn't have just invited the people from her talk that she wanted to come here.

Fortunately, some of the people who'd been on her side were in the crowd, too. In fact, the tall, skinny fellow who'd been at the front and called out something favorable had made his way through the people who were giving her a hard time. Now, standing beside her table, he waved at her and asked, "Can I buy you a snack to go with your drink?" His brown eyes were open wide beneath shaggy blond brows, and his huge smile looked hopeful.

"Thanks," she said, facing him and using the opportunity to look away from the others, "but I'm good." She appreciated that he'd been on her side, yet she felt a bit uncomfortable under his happy stare—even though it was way preferable to the potential argument that had just started.

"You certainly are," he said. He held out his hand. "I'm Trevor Garlona. Trev. And I want to know all about you and WHaM."

"Thanks," she said. "But—"

"Hey, I'm talking to you." The voice across from her sounded familiar—the woman who'd just challenged her. "Don't you ignore me. And why are you even still in town?"

Maya turned again in her seat just a little. She had already recognized the woman who had confronted her after her talk. That woman now stood at the opposite end of the table from where Maya sat with a glass of wine in front of her. Some other people who'd been at her presentation had just gone up to the bar to order their drinks.

That guy who'd introduced himself as Trev moved in the direction she now faced, although other people, including that woman, didn't get out of his way. He squeezed in and looked at her, though, from behind them and raised his glass of beer as if toasting her.

She didn't toast him back, but neither did she try to get away. Not yet, at least.

She felt a little relieved to notice that Ryan had joined her, too, and stood at her side. She wished he'd come here sooner. Despite his attitude before against how she worked, she wanted to spend more time with the great-looking guy. Talk to him more about wildlife.

Especially now, while she was being confronted again. What was this woman's name? Vinnie? Vinnie Fritts, wife of a man who had the same name as this town and whose family had apparently lived here a long time, had maybe even founded it.

She wasn't that old, though—maybe midforties. Her hair was a wavy mass of brown that appeared cut and styled to remain exactly so on her head. She wore bright pink lipstick and dark-rimmed glasses. Surprisingly, the whole package went well together.

Now, if she only had a sense of consideration of others and their opinions...

"Do you have any pets at home?" Maya countered, focusing on Vinnie. "Or small children?" She took a sip of her dry white wine in an attempt to bolster her floundering courage but it didn't help. At least she didn't think she was projecting any nervousness in her tone of voice.

"No. Our kids are in college, and no way would we have animals in our house."

That figured.

"Well, I appreciate your coming to my presentation," Maya lied. "And everyone is entitled to their own opinions. But since you don't have pets or young family members at home, I doubt that you have to worry about anyone being attacked by the wolves—assuming these wolves run away from confrontations with non-prey creatures, as most do. And—"

"And you're trying to convince us that you're not only entitled to your opinion…" said the man in the pale yellow shirt just beyond her who hadn't spoken before. It was Morton, Vinnie's husband whom she'd introduced at the talk. "…but that you know everything, and everyone who lives around here should support your ridiculous position? Now look, lady. This is my town. My family's town, and I intend to protect it. Understand?"

"No," Maya said quietly. "I don't." She noticed then that most conversations in the bar had ceased. It was a lot quieter than when she'd entered. She didn't see any of the people who'd admitted to being with the media there, though.

"We don't want any damned predatory creatures around here." The man spoke through gritted teeth. He appeared older than his wife, maybe in his fifties. His hair was thin, his brows gray and curved over his angry brown eyes. His arms were crossed over a chest that appeared sunken—but his fragility did nothing to ease Maya's fear of him.

She figured that this man hated wildlife—or, worse, wanted to wipe it out. She might not like the idea, but there were laws protecting some species in specified areas, and requirements of licenses before hunting those that were more plentiful and might actually need to have their numbers limited for the good of the rest of the species. She wasn't a vegetarian, and she could understand hunting for one's dinner.

But she had a sense that this guy just despised animals enough to kill for sport. And if that was true, she would despise *him*.

Right now, though, she did not want to continue this confrontation.

"Look," she said, "I recognize that we have very different positions on this."

"Ya think?" Morton asked sarcastically, his hands now on his hips. "Hey, here's what I think. I'll be the one to change my mind, suddenly love wolves. Want to hug them all." He glanced toward Ryan, who stood with Rocky beside him. Morton moved then, approaching the dog with his hand out. "Well, aren't you just the greatest creature on earth?" He reached out and shoved Rocky's muzzle.

The dog didn't even growl, which made Maya very happy. But the man's gesture didn't.

"Don't you hurt him." She hissed between her clenched teeth, "He's a lot nicer than you are."

"That's for sure." Ryan placed himself between his dog and the jerk of a man who'd touched him. Ryan's friend Piers also stood at the dog's side and faced down Morton as well as Vinnie and Carlo, who'd joined him.

"What a great dog that is," said a male voice from behind Maya, and she realized that Trev had moved again.

"He sure is," said someone else, a woman this time.

"Leave him alone," came another voice. When Maya turned to see who was there she was both glad and surprised to see at least half a dozen people behind her, apparently backing her up. She recognized some, maybe all of them, from her talk.

"Back off," said yet another one.

"This isn't over," Morton said, sidling away from Rocky and all the people now confronting him. "Not unless you leave and stop trying to get people to love those damned wolves. They're nasty and vicious and don't belong around here."

"Sounds like you're describing yourself," Maya couldn't help saying in return.

She caught Ryan's eye, then recalled that he had suggested she was endangering herself by her attitude in standing up to these people who didn't see things her way.

But instead of scowling or looking angry, he had a half smile on his sexy face and shook his head slowly as if amused by her.

That made her want to run over and hug the handsome guy—but she stayed still.

Instead, it was Morton Fritts and his gang who stomped out of the bar.

Chapter 3

Good. They were gone.

Ryan continued to stand near Maya, with Piers and Rocky at his sides—and all those nice people behind her who'd spoken up in support of her.

Bartender Buck Lesterman had joined them, too. Interesting.

This group seemed to be filled with wildlife advocates who appreciated what Maya said and stood for, which was a good thing in Ryan's estimation.

But were any of them shifters? All of them?

There'd been hints of an influx here thanks to the wolf sightings, and Alpha Force members had heard those rumors.

If some or all of these folks were shifters, then Maya had helped Ryan start to meet his goal. He owed her for that.

But for right now...

He regarded the group across from them, then strode forward, hand outstretched, purposely avoiding the guy who'd spoken with Maya and offered her a snack, apparently flirting with her. For some reason, that irritated Ryan, even if the guy turned out to be a wildlife advocate.

"Hi," he said to the first of them. "I'm Ryan Blaiddinger, with the US Fish and Wildlife Service. Thanks to all of you for your support of conservation of the latest arrival of wolves around here." He felt Maya stir behind him and figured she wasn't thrilled that he'd taken over the position she probably intended to fulfill.

"Good to meet you, Ryan," said a petite woman with long and fluffy light brown hair streaked with deeper color. Hair that resembled a wolf's?

Ryan knew he was reaching a bit in an attempt to convince himself things were as he hoped.

But he might not be wrong…

"I'm Kathie Sharan," the woman continued. "This is my husband, Burt. We just recently moved here and bought the Corner Grocery Store down the street. We used to live in Montana, and there are wolves there, too. We've no problem with some showing up in this neighborhood. It's kind of cool, in fact."

Could that actually be why they'd moved here?

"Hi, Ryan." Burt, tall and thin with deep brown hair and a hint of a beard, edged next to his wife and held out his hand. His grip was firm as he shook Ryan's. "I hope you'll come visit our store while you're in town. You, too, Maya." He turned toward where she stood and held out his hand to her, as well.

A couple of other people near them also issued greetings that Ryan returned. Maya, too, and also Piers when Ryan introduced him as another employee of the federal fish and wildlife organization. And all of them made a fuss over a clearly pleased Rocky.

Even bartender Buck did so, as did the guy who'd been flirting with Maya—Trev Garlona. He'd introduced himself, as well.

So at least some of these wolf advocates had recently moved here and purchased businesses, intending to stay.

Of course Ryan could be completely wrong. They might have had different agendas when they decided to settle in Fritts Corner, nothing at all to do with wolves—or shifting.

But he had a feeling he would get to know some or all of them a lot better.

Maybe starting tonight.

For now, though, he needed to prepare, perhaps even to rest. He soon said goodbye to the gang of wolf supporters who'd joined them, and they all headed back to their seats—after Buck promised to refresh their drinks. The place remained busy, and the sound of conversations picked up once more. Other bartenders had remained active, so Ryan also inhaled the scent of different kinds of alcohol.

All seemed well again.

Even so, he asked Maya, who had also turned to go, "Where are you off to now?"

The people who'd given her a hard time were no longer in the bar. They surely wouldn't be waiting outside to give her a hard time—would they?

He'd rather be there for her, though, just in case.

"I'm heading back to my hotel," she said. "I may even take a nap. It's stressful to give a talk, and to act happy and energetic and all…anyway, I'm glad how things have turned out so far and really appreciate your support."

"You're very welcome," he said, knowing his face mirrored her large smile. "How about if we walk with you?"

"Which hotel are you staying at?" Piers asked. He was now at Ryan's side and had taken Rocky's leash.

"The Washington Inn," she said, unsurprisingly naming the largest one in town.

"So are we," Piers said.

"Great," Ryan said. "Let's get on our way."

Maya saw Trev waving goodbye as she prepared to leave, and she briefly aimed a wave back at him. But her mind was on something else altogether.

Ryan, Rocky and Piers were all staying in the same hotel as she was.

How close was Ryan's room to hers? That question kept intruding into Maya's mind as they walked out.

No matter. They could be next door to each other and still be worlds apart.

They had to be. Sure, he was a great-looking guy. A nice guy who clearly wanted to walk with her to protect her in case those nasty folks who'd confronted her were still around. He didn't have to say so for her to know that.

But other than their love of wildlife, they most likely had nothing in common. Even if they did—well, she'd been involved with a guy not long ago who'd professed to love wild animals but acted like a jerk when it came to maintaining a relationship with a human being. He'd even publicly slammed WHaM.

She didn't need anything like that—especially since she'd soon go home to Denver and figured a guy with the US government would return to the DC area, far from her.

"I don't see your buddies out here," Ryan said. "Guess they decided not to harass you again."

"I sure hope so," she said. "Maybe they can start picking on each other instead." She admired the few buildings they passed. "This is such a cute town. Where do you live? Is it anything like this?"

"We live near Washington, DC, not Washington State," Ryan responded. Near it? Not in it? That made Maya wonder where, but before she could ask he got in his own question. "And you? Where are you from? Colorado? Isn't that where WHaM is headquartered?"

She acknowledged that it was, and they talked a bit more about her organization as they continued down the block, with Piers behind them.

Rocky trotted between Ryan and her, and she got a truly warm and fuzzy feeling about this short walk and the males near her, including the dog. In a minute they had reached her car and said goodbye.

And because she didn't have far to drive, she arrived at the Washington Inn about the same time as the two men and the dog did. Or maybe, driving slowly, she had unconsciously planned it that way.

The inn, like so many other buildings in town, was quaint, with multipaned windows and circular turrets. The concrete exterior looked substantial, though, and Maya figured it was either a much newer structure than it appeared, or it had been remodeled recently.

She parked in the lot beside it and walked quickly to the front—just as the others arrived, too. She joined them.

"Hi again," she said, waiting while Ryan stopped at the grassy area near the front with Rocky. "So where are your rooms?" she asked Ryan casually, as Piers preceded them inside.

"First floor, toward the back. It's a good spot to take Rocky into the yard if he needs to go. How about you?"

"Third floor," she said, "around there." She pointed toward the right, glad that the windows there indicated multiple rooms so she didn't exactly tell him which was hers.

They proceeded up the walkway to the steps and, crossing the porch, entered the quaint-looking lobby. There were only a few people there, mostly in line at the reception desk. Piers stood nearby reading a newspaper. He joined them.

Ryan lifted his arm with the loop of the dog leash over it and Piers slipped it off him. "You can put him in my room," he told Piers. "I'll be right there." He then said to Maya, "I'll walk you to your room, just in case."

In case her new enemies were around, she assumed. She hadn't seen any sign of them on the road and didn't really need Ryan accompanying her—she hoped—and yet she didn't object.

They soon were in her room, which was as charming as the rest of the inn. He even went inside, glancing around, walking past the bed with a fluffy, lace-trimmed coverlet.

She had a momentary urge to ask him to stay. Just to talk a little longer, of course. About wolves and other wildlife.

Not about a wild life. The guy was one delicious-looking man and had started to get her internal juices flowing when they were together. But he was mostly just a nice guy with similar interests to hers. And he'd given no indication he thought of her in any sexual or other way—a good thing.

That meant she didn't have to worry about any interest on her part that could lead to disaster, as her recent relationship had.

Even so, she found herself asking, "So do you have any plans for this evening?"

She couldn't quite read the odd look that quickly passed over his face, replaced by a smile that almost appeared pleased. "Sleeping," he said. "I intend to order in pizza later for Piers and me. I brought food for Rocky. I'm already a bit tired and may do some hiking tomorrow, so I'll go to bed early." He looked her over. "No offense intended, but you appear a little sleepy, too. Maybe you should do the same thing."

That had been what she was considering…unless they worked out a dinner date, which would undoubtedly be a bad idea.

She noticed that he didn't suggest that she join them for pizza, either.

"I just might do that," she said. As he walked to the door of her room she added, "Have a good evening. And thanks again for all your help."

Rocky was well trained, but even so he wasn't staying alone in Ryan's room that night.

No, right now Piers drove all three of them, in the sedan they had rented at the Sea-Tac International Airport, along the remote, twisty roads outside Fritts Corner, beyond the park and beneath the forest's overhanging trees to a clearing they had previously scouted out.

Near an area where wolves had been spotted over the past months.

The ride was bumpy, and Ryan was conscious of every jolt. It was getting close to twilight now.

It was nearly time.

And since this was the night of a full moon, Ryan would be shifting.

But thanks to that wonderful elixir that had been formulated and modified over time by Major Drew Connell, the founder of Alpha Force, and other members, Ryan would not only have some limited choice as to when the shifting started and a lot of choice about when he shifted back, but he would additionally retain his human cognition.

Unlike the other shifters he anticipated meeting on this night.

"Here we are," Piers said, stopping the car. Rocky, in the backseat, let out a small woof, as if he understood where they were and what was about to happen.

This wasn't his first time, after all, to be around when Ryan shifted—and it wouldn't be his last.

Piers parked, and Ryan immediately exited the car. There was hardly any light in the sky, and the clearing was vast enough that Ryan knew the full moon would soon appear.

There were plenty of times in his past when that would have caused him to shift into a feral wolf as soon as darkness fell. But now—

Now, he couldn't have been more delighted that Alpha Force had found and recruited him into its amazing military unit. He was starting to give back, including by being here. And he loved it.

If he was correct about the nature of at least some of the people here, he might even be able to give back more to his cherished organization by recruiting others who, in turn, could add to its very special mission.

He'd already done some of that while being trained and working directly with other shifters located by senior Alpha Force officers.

Piers pulled the large backpack out of the trunk and approached across the hard dirt of the clearing to the area several feet from the car where Ryan had stopped. Ryan began to remove his clothing, even as Piers extracted the cooler in the backpack and from it one of the vials of elixir that they had brought. He also pulled out the light that, turned on, resembled the light of the full moon, although, since it would not be necessary tonight, he returned it to the backpack.

"You doing okay?" Ryan's efficient assistant now stood there with the vial in one of his large hands, assessing his superior officer.

"I'm fine, Piers. And how are you?" Ryan kept his tone light, even though he knew exactly what he was about to go through.

The elixir helped shifters in so many ways—but nothing could totally eliminate the discomfort of a shift from human to animal form—and back again.

"Okay, buddy. The moon's a-rising. Let's get this thing started, okay?" The stocky young guy grinned as if he couldn't wait for his superior officer's shift to start. And maybe he couldn't.

Ryan was now nude. He felt the pulsing sensations inside him that presaged a natural shift.

It was definitely time for the elixir.

"Bring it on," he told Piers, reaching out for the vial.

His initial shift was over. He was standing again, this time on four canine legs, the discomfort behind him.

Just in time, he thought—since he heard a howl in the distance. Followed by another, and some barks. They all sounded far away, but he would have heard them even without his enhanced hearing.

Shifters? Most likely. Natural wolves might howl and bark like that, of course. But why would they do so tonight? And not just one or two now, but several of them.

Ryan could tell—thanks to that enhanced hearing—

not only the direction from which the sounds came, but he had a sense of distance, too.

The others were likely in the hillsides here, beneath the trees, farther from town, perhaps farther along the road where Piers had driven them only a short while earlier.

Rocky remained in the car. Piers had returned to it to sleep, to wait for Ryan's return early in the morning, when he would naturally shift back on this night of the full moon.

He also had some choice about when to change back, even under the full moon. But if he did not choose when, it would occur once the sun started to rise.

Another set of excited howls. They caused more excitement in Ryan, as well.

Time for him to run through these woods, let his wolfen side loose. Revel in his very special gift, his talent, the other, only partly human feature of his life.

His shifting ability.

He felt his mouth move as he allowed himself to express his emotion in what would have been a smile had he not been shifted.

He aimed one glance toward the car where his companions now sat and waited for him.

And then he ran into the woods.

Maya hadn't been sleeping deeply, though she had been in bed for a while, reading at first, then nodding off.

But her mind had been tossing around all that had happened to her that day.

Her talk. The confrontations with those wild animal–haters.

The support she had received from Ryan, backed up by some of the other people in this small town near which wolves had begun to appear again.

And—

Hey. What was that? Was she imagining things because she was thinking about the local sightings of wolves?

Maybe, but she thought she'd heard not only some canine barking but also a howl. Yes! She had. It was followed by another.

And now there were even more of them, somewhere way in the distance. But close enough to be heard here, right in the downtown area of Fritts Corner.

She froze. If she heard them, so did those wolf-haters. She wasn't in any kind of law enforcement. She had no weapons.

But might the US Fish and Wildlife Service be able to help?

She hadn't gotten Ryan's phone number, not even his room number, but she felt stressed enough to use the hotel's phone to try to call his room even now, in the middle of the night. She did reach a hotel operator—after waiting several minutes. And then, when she was connected to his room, no one answered.

She tried the same with his friend Piers, but again no answer.

He'd said he was going to bed early—but maybe the sounds had awakened him, and now she couldn't join up with him to check things out.

Heck. Maybe there was nothing she could do. Maybe the wolves wouldn't really be in danger.

But if nothing else, she could bring her camera—just in case.

She'd already risen from her bed.

Now, she threw her clothes on, grabbed her purse and camera, and rushed out the door.

Chapter 4

He loved it, reveled in it, this unleashed, unfettered ability to run on four powerful legs, beyond the park, up hillsides and within woods that were entirely new to him, in darkness lit only by the full moon.

To chase in the direction where he would soon see others who were like him in one way or the other: wolves that were born as canines, or that were humans in shifted form.

Those whose howls he still heard—

But he nearly stopped running as he heard something else. Voices that weren't wolfen but human.

Male and female voices in the distance, low but audible to him, with his highly enhanced keen hearing while in wolf form.

And that wasn't all. He knew who was talking. He slowed his pace and inhaled and smelled, from the same direction, those humans with scents he had first sensed *that day but not as intense as he could inhale now, as a wolf.*

The smells included those of the two people named Fritts. And more. Another human scent emanated from that same area.

But they weren't the only ones.

A different scent, but no sound, came from near them, as well. An aroma that was entirely familiar— now—to the wolf who was Ryan.

The scent belonging to Maya.

None of the humans should be here, not with wolves of any origin around, here in the woods in near darkness—except for that brilliant moon.

Most especially not Maya.

Was she not aware of the potential danger from the wolves she also revered and wanted to protect? She had sounded so wise, so knowledgeable before, when she had spoken to an audience and talked with individuals. But did she ignore her own wisdom when wolves were around?

And if they were shifters, without having access to his special Alpha Force elixir they would not have human cognition. They could be just as dangerous as wild wolves to mere people.

And what about those other people? Would they present a danger to the wolves—and, perhaps, to Maya, too? Or were they themselves in danger?

He turned to move more purposefully in the direction from which he scented Maya.

If Maya wasn't cautious, he would have to be so on her behalf.

He wanted to protect them all, the wolves and the woman, and perhaps the other people, as well. If the wolves harmed them, then other humans might hurt those wolves.

But there was only one of him. And if he had to choose who to protect, he knew which it had to be.

Maya had arrived at the edge of the woods, and now debated what to do.

She had known from the moment she had heard the distant howls and barks, while still inside the hotel, the direction in which she had to go, and she had hurriedly driven that way. When she parked her car and got onto the sidewalk at the park where she had given her presentation, she'd stopped to listen even more.

The sounds now came from somewhere to her right, in the woods beyond the park. She had hurried in that direction.

At the time, she had felt somewhat surprised to find herself alone here. Surely other people heard the sounds and could figure out where they came from. And some of the people who'd attended her talk had seemed fascinated, too, by the reappearance of wolves in this area.

Plus some had claimed to be part of the media. Were they interested in wolves or not?

Was she the only one who hoped to actually see them? Or was everyone afraid?

Well, no matter. Although…well, she wouldn't have minded some company.

Too bad she hadn't reached Ryan. She couldn't help assuming he was already outside, also trying to get a glimpse of the wolves. If so, they could have joined up, banded together, safety in numbers. And being with him in the middle of the night would be practical, nothing to do with the fact she found the man attractive.

No matter. For now, all she really hoped for was to see those wolves herself.

The air was cool, and the intermittent sound of the soft wind, plus occasional cars in the distance, were the only sounds she heard at this moment as she stood there.

Still at the edge of the park, she looked beyond the streetlights behind her into the near darkness of what lay ahead. The only light came from above, the brilliance of the full moon.

She carried a special flashlight that she could make as bright or dim as she wanted, as well as a state-of-the-art small camera that took still photos and videos. Mostly what she wanted was to observe and film the wolves from a distance, without them getting too interested in her.

Another howl sounded, followed by some yips and a couple of additional howls. How many wolves were out there?

She would have to be very cautious. Those wolves would sense her before she could get close. And there was no way she could communicate to them that she loved wildlife, only wanted to see and photograph them.

This was probably a bad idea—but it might be her best opportunity to see them.

Here, at the end of the park, the grass gave way to low foliage at first that soon rose to become mountainous woodlands, with trees relatively close together and dry underbrush below. The area was fairly dark, since the treetops erased the light from the moon above.

Maya gave herself one more chance to stop, to back off. But only for a minute. Then, she pulled her flashlight out of her purse, set it for its dimmest setting and started out.

And heard another wolf howl.

She smiled and carefully started forward. She heard her own footsteps on the dried underbrush but not much more. Was she still heading in the right direction?

At least she went in a straight line, so she would be able to find her way back. Even run back, if she had to…

She reached a clearing. Was that a human voice she heard somewhere ahead, off to the side?

Maybe she should go back…

But that was when she heard the crackling sound of dried growth being stomped on by feet—canine feet?

Was she really going to get to see a wolf? Yes!

And in fact, there one was. She upped the intensity of her flashlight as she aimed her camera at it, just as another wolf joined it.

They were both running toward her. Still filming, she looked around. Fortunately, she stood beside a nice, wide tree trunk. Maybe she should get behind it—

But the wolf at the front growled, ran even faster toward her.

Was it going to attack?

"I just wanted to see you," she cried aloud, knowing how ridiculous that was. As if the creature could understand she was on its side, doing her job, learning about it. Quickly, she moved so the tree was between the wolf and her. But where was the other one?

She heard some barks then that sounded angry. Feral growls, just as another wolf emerged from the woods and attacked the wolf that approached her. The third wolf, behind that one, leaped into the fray, as well.

"No. Please. Don't hurt each other," Maya cried out, but she wasn't stupid. Not entirely, she thought. She used the opportunity to light her flashlight beam to the fullest and run back through the woods in the direction from which she'd come.

She glanced back once, though. The fight had wound down, at least somewhat. One wolf—the attacker?—was facing the other two, crouched as if ready to leap onto them again and growling deeply.

The others stood warily but did not appear as if they were ready to attack again.

Which made Maya smile, at least a little, as she turned again and hurried toward the edge of the park.

Yes, she'd been foolish. But she'd seen wolves. Three wolves. And she'd gotten videos of them.

She wasn't hurt, and the canines appeared to be okay, too.

This was definitely a memorable night.

He remained in a crouch, growling and teaching the others he faced who was alpha, at least for now.

Their scents were strong, and not entirely wolfen.

Then they, too, were shifters. That didn't make them less feral, less likely to attack him.

And it wouldn't have prevented them from attacking that foolish human woman.

But at least he had been able to save her from harm.

And soon, tomorrow, when he had shifted back and was in human form, he would find an opportunity to chide her, and more.

To warn her never to put herself in such a situation again.

He was unlikely to be there the next time.

The other wolves had apparently had enough. They both issued loud warning growls back to him, then turned and loped back into the darkness of the forest behind them.

Good. He, too, returned to the darkness but in a different direction.

He wanted to get a better sense of these surroundings and where the wolves by blood might be—and whether these shifters might be in any danger.

Only later, when morning started to arrive, would he shift back.

She was out of the woods, so to speak, and onto the lawn constituting the park. Maya smiled, stopped walking and turned to look back at the dark woodlands she had just left.

The wolves were still there, somewhere. Hopefully, none of them had been injured by the others.

She had seen them, photographed them, and she was fine. More than fine.

Too bad she had no way of rewarding that one wolf who'd confronted the others and allowed her to get away. He surely had an agenda of his own that had nothing to do with her, but she still appreciated it.

With a sigh, she turned and started walking briskly back to where she'd parked. Good night, wolves, she thought as she got into her car.

There were some other cars on the road now. She even saw a few people exit a bar on the far side of the street, though not the one she'd visited before.

Had anyone else heard the wolves?

Did anyone else in this town really care?

Surely the answer was yes, at least those who'd come to her presentation or commented on it afterward, like that bartender she had met. What was his name? Lesterman?

Or maybe the other people who'd been there, the Sharans, and that lady, Ivy, who had seen a couple of wolves. They'd at least seemed interested.

And her new *buddy* Trev. He'd at least expressed

some interest in wildlife at her talk. Had he heard the wolves from wherever he was? Did he give a damn?

Then there had been Ryan, and his friend Piers. They'd surely have been interested.

She'd thought she heard some human voices. Could it have been theirs? Were they also out here checking out those howls?

If so they'd surely left Rocky in one of their rooms. The dog might have been particularly at risk when wolves were around.

She parked behind the hotel and went inside.

She felt so happy and excited that she wished she could shout about her amazing evening to the world.

Or at least to people who might give a damn.

But it was way too late to call Ryan in case she had guessed wrong and he was in bed at this late hour. Nor could she call any of her colleagues at WHaM, since this area was on Pacific time and everyone else would be an hour or more later.

With a sigh, Maya made her way through the empty, dimly lit lobby and headed up to her room for the night.

And figured she wouldn't sleep at all.

But she did sleep, though not at first.

Once she'd gotten into the antique-style bed in her hotel room, Maya had visualized those wolves once more. All three of them.

Were there more in the area? The return of wolves to various parts of the state of Washington had been slow and sparse, especially around here. Even so…

How many? Despite her duty to take census, she didn't intentionally begin to count wolves, like sheep, but she knew there were more than three.

Finally, smiling to herself, she actually relaxed. And slept.

Still, when she woke, the same visions and questions captivated her mind.

Well, somehow she would find a way to use it all, to continue to inform locals who were otherwise unaware that wolves had returned to the area—and how wonderful it was. First thing, she would check her video to see how it looked, since she would show her results to as many people as she could.

And expound even more about wildlife—probably without revealing she'd put herself in danger.

But wouldn't it be fun to let the world know she'd been saved by one of those wolves? Sure, but then she'd have to let everyone know that she'd felt threatened by the others.

Somehow, she finished showering and dressing and prepared to visit the local world again today.

She looked at her video, thrilled at what she'd captured, yet a bit uneasy that it did show the wild and potentially dangerous nature of those feral canines. But, heck, that was who and what they were. People could admire them as wildlife, stressing the *wild* part. She certainly did.

She didn't exactly have a plan, but first thing would be to find somewhere to grab breakfast, hopefully someplace busy. Maybe she could start expounding on her latest lesson about the visiting wolves there.

She pulled on a nice blue shirt over jeans, then looked out her hotel room window. Sun shone between an irregular blanket of clouds. She looked down through the partial brightness toward the street, trying to recall what restaurants she'd seen in the area—and noticed that Ryan and Piers were out there walking Rocky on the Washington Inn's narrow lawn next to the sidewalk.

Hey, no matter that she hadn't reached them before. Now, they would be good targets for starting to tell her story about the night before. They'd at least be interested.

She put her camera into her purse and headed out the door. Not wanting to wait for the elevator, she walked the couple of flights of stairs down to the decorative lobby and hurried through it to the door, then outside and down the walkway to the sidewalk. She looked around and saw the men and dog still on the lawn but near the end of the block. She headed briskly in their direction, noting that a few other people milled around outside the charming structure, probably additional tourists who were staying there.

Now wasn't a good time to stop and be friendly and talk up wildlife to strangers, she realized—despite how strongly the urge shoved at her.

Before she could get to Ryan, though, Trev exited a car parked at the curb and hurried up to her. "Good morning," he said. "How are you today?" He aimed his geeky grin at her again, and she briefly smiled back at him. He was dressed in a white button-down shirt tucked into blue jeans.

"Okay," she said. "Have a good day." She turned away, ready to hurry off toward her goal.

"You, too. You know, I heard about your organization WHaM before. I saw online, on the WHaM website, that you were going to give a talk here, and that's why I came to town."

She stopped for a moment. "Then you don't live in Fritts Corner?"

"No, but I wanted to hear you."

"That's very nice," she said, meaning it. She'd have to tell her coworkers that the small mention they'd put up on the website was achieving what they wanted, at least a little—attracting people to learn more about them, and wildlife. "Then you care about wildlife?"

"I think about wildlife a lot," he said.

"And did you hear the wolf howls last night?"

"I did, from my hotel room. They must have been pretty close to town."

"You could say that," she said.

"Hey, would you join me for breakfast?" He looked so eager that she considered saying yes to this wild-life aficionado who'd come here because of WHaM. But that wasn't how she wanted to spend her morning.

"Sorry, I can't. I have other plans." And she did, even if they didn't work out the way she hoped. "I hope to see you later, though." Maybe. Especially if she had an opportunity to give another talk on behalf of WHaM.

For now, she said goodbye to the guy, who appeared disappointed. She felt bad, at least a little, as she strode away. But if he truly was flirting with her, and not just because he liked WHaM, she didn't want to encourage him.

And right now she wanted to find out if Ryan and Piers had heard the wolves, too. They were the ones who'd been defending her and cheering on the return of those canines to this area. And if they had heard the wolves—well, she would enjoy the opportunity to describe her own adventure last night to them.

Should she tell others, too? Maybe. What she could do, after she reached Ryan and his crew, was to talk loudly enough that people around them could eavesdrop and hear it all.

Before she reached them, Ryan looked toward her.

She couldn't quite interpret his smile, though. Oh, yes, there was a smile on that really great-looking face of his, and yet it didn't look exactly humorous or welcoming or glad to see her, the way she expected. Well, hoped, at least.

Instead…she couldn't quite interpret that smile, but the first thing she thought it conveyed was irritation, maybe. Scolding? Wry, certainly.

"Good morning," she called out, feeling somewhat annoyed herself. Why should she have to interpret this man's expressions?

"Good morning, Maya," Piers said. The smile on the shorter, heavier guy's face looked a whole lot more friendly. "Did you have a good night's sleep?"

"Yes, I did. But not before——"

"Have you had breakfast yet?" Ryan interrupted. "If not, why don't you join us?"

Somehow his words, and his now-challenging expression, definitely turned Maya into the one who was irritated. Maybe she should tell him she already had plans and go find Trev again.

But she really wanted to tell them about her night and at least find out if they'd heard the wolves.

She first hurried toward Rocky. "Good morning, boy." She greeted the friendly wolflike dog by patting his head and scratching behind his alert ears. "And, no." She turned to face the men. "I haven't had breakfast yet. I'll be glad to join you. I had a very interesting evening and would love to tell you about it."

"And we'd love to hear about it," Ryan said. The expression on his face didn't change.

"How about Andy and Family's?" Piers gave the name of a restaurant Maya had noticed a couple of blocks from the hotel, the opposite direction from the park.

"Sounds great to me." Maya strolled around Ryan to stand beside Piers. She'd walk beside him, and hopefully Rocky, too, till they got there. Her conversation with Piers was likely to be a lot friendlier than if she spent the time with Ryan. Although she'd like to understand why. "Let's go!"

Chapter 5

As he walked along the sidewalk behind his three companions toward his upcoming breakfast, Ryan wondered if this was a good idea.

Oh, yes.

What he'd really wanted to do, upon first seeing the lovely, upbeat—and foolish—woman was to grab her by the shoulders and shake her and tell her she could have been killed.

But he would give too much away by doing that. No, he'd have to be a whole lot more subtle, yet still find a way to get that chastisement across to her.

The sky was somewhat overcast this September day, the air a little brisk, although it would warm up later. He felt warm enough now, though, partly because of his suppressed anger—and concern.

What would have happened if she'd been attacked by the wolves? Those wolves would have undoubtedly been considered feral and dangerous and possibly hunted and killed.

And would Maya have survived such an attack? To his surprise, that mattered as much to him as—maybe more than—whether the wolves who might be fellow shifters would have gotten out of the situation okay.

They reached the restaurant. Unsurprisingly, Andy and Family's was family style, and on this Friday morning it was crowded.

"Hey, there are a lot of people here," Piers said unnecessarily. He'd turned to look back at Ryan, clearly giving him the opportunity to decide to go elsewhere.

"The food must be okay." Ryan gave a brief nod to his aide. He was fine with staying here to eat.

"Probably." Piers glanced toward Maya, who was still beside him, but instead of giving her the opportunity to say no Ryan moved past her to the glass front door.

Sure, they'd have to wait even to tell the people seating customers how many of them there were. But at the moment, having a lot of people around to eavesdrop on, after last night and the full moon and those howls and barks, could be pretty interesting.

And maybe he and Piers would be able to determine what to do next, who else to get chummy with, to confirm that at least some of those wolves were shifters.

They needed to go chat with the people they'd suspected were shifters anyway. If they had more ammunition, all the better.

But he believed he had a good idea of the wolves' human identities thanks to their scents while he—and they—were shifted.

Would the Sharans be here for breakfast today, for example? It didn't matter. Ryan had believed it was their scents he'd smelled last night. But he wouldn't confront them here anyway.

He'd also had Piers check online to learn if there'd been any indication that the media—those who'd claimed to be members yesterday at Maya's talk or others—had mentioned Maya, or last night's wolves, in any paper or blog or broadcast somewhere but he had found nothing. Not yet, at least.

"What's the wait time?" Maya asked the middle-aged lady holding menus who'd come by to check on how many people there were in each party.

"We're pretty fast," the lady said. "Probably no more than five minutes. You can wait right here and we've got an area on the back patio where we can seat you with your dog."

Five minutes up here, in the crowd, with lots of gabbing people even before they took their seats. That could work in their favor, Ryan figured.

"Let's wait," he said, looking first at Piers. He turned to Maya and asked, "Are you okay with that?"

"Sure," she said, then repeated, "Let's wait."

Standing behind the rest of her group in the waiting area line leading up to the rows of tables, Maya couldn't help looking around at this crowd. The place resembled nearly every other busy family style restaurant she'd ever eaten at, with servers in the aisles and tables filled with people of all ages, some dressed as if they were heading to work on this Friday morning, and others as casual as she was in her shirt and jeans.

No, not all ages, she contradicted herself. The kids were fairly young. Their older counterparts might already be at school for the day.

But the conversations created a low-key roar, and

she also heard the clink of silverware on plates and the clunk of glasses on tables.

Hey, if she didn't know better, she'd wonder if her visit with wolves had elevated her own senses the way theirs were—like her hearing. But she had no doubt they'd enjoy the aromas around here more.

In fact, she looked toward Rocky. Sure enough, his canine nose was elevated and sniffing and—

She glanced up to find that Ryan was smiling at her, and this time it seemed genuine. Surely he couldn't read her mind…could he?

"You hungry?" he asked. "I am."

Apparently he couldn't—although his question was definitely pertinent here. And her answer, partly thanks to the low-level aromas she could inhale, was, "Me, too. This is a good place to be hungry. But what about Rocky? Will he also eat here?"

"He had his breakfast back at the inn," Ryan said, "but I won't be surprised if he talks one or more of us into giving him some of what we're eating, too."

"Bet on it." Piers was also smiling but his gaze drifted around the busy dining area as if he hoped to glom on to a table they could request. Which would have been unlikely even if they didn't have Rocky along, since, although a few more people had been seated since their arrival, there were still a couple more groups ahead of them.

Maya made herself tear her gaze away from Ryan's great-looking, angular face with just a hint of beard shadow, as if he hadn't fully shaved that morning. Though those dark brown eyes looked a little tired, they seemed to be studying hers. Why? Hadn't he slept well—and had he been out looking for wolves? And now, was he trying to figure out if she was telling the truth, that she really was hungry?

Absurd. And yet she thought she sensed some kind of question, or message, in his expression.

Her mind began churning around possible ways to lead into a conversation with him, get him to reveal what he'd done last night and what he was thinking. But before she got very far the restaurant hostess invited the last groups ahead of them in line to follow her.

They should be next to get a table—at least assuming the patio area designated as appropriate for Rocky to join them had a vacancy.

Rocky. He'd been sitting, examining the air around them and behaving like a well-trained dog, despite his resemblance to wild wolves. But something, maybe the movement of the people ahead of them, apparently got his attention, and he stood.

Ryan immediately tautened the leash attached to his collar, drawing closer to the dog. "Easy, boy," he said.

Maya noticed then the people hurrying toward them from between the nearest tables, people who'd been at the bar yesterday and indicated their support of what WHaM stood for. The Sharans. Kathie and Burt, right?

Kathie was ahead of Burt and she looked first at Rocky, then at the people with him.

"Hi," the short, attractive woman said as she reached them, smiling toward Maya. "So you brought that adorable dog who resembles the wolves you talk about to breakfast with you?" She moved her hand slowly in Rocky's direction as if making sure he knew she was friendly.

Rocky started to rear up on his hind legs, but Ryan, pulling the leash gently and also pushing him with his other hand, got him to settle back down. "Sit, boy," Ryan said, and the dog obeyed, though he began sniff-

ing the air even more than Maya had noticed him doing
before. Interesting. She didn't smell even a hint of a difference in the food aromas around them and wondered
what Rocky smelled.

He pulled sideways again when Burt, a beefy guy
with a short chin and long nose, got close and put out
his hand, too, as if he also wanted to pat the dog. Rocky
seemed pretty interested in these people. Maybe they
were the reason his sniffing had grown more pro-
nounced, and Maya wondered what they had just eaten.

"I'm delighted to have Rocky's company for breakfast," Maya said. "Oh, and Ryan's and Piers's, too." She
lifted her eyebrows as she passed her gaze over the two
men, waiting for their reaction.

Surprisingly, neither was looking at her. Ryan had
one hand on Rocky and was watching him, and Piers
was regarding the couple who'd just joined them here
as they'd been leaving the restaurant.

Maya sensed something going on that she didn't follow, but no matter. She'd ask about it later.

For now, she wanted to say something nice to these
friendly folks who appeared to love wildlife. "You said
before that you own a grocery store, right?"

Kathie nodded. "Yes, we do. We sell pet food there,
too." She grinned as she looked toward Ryan, obviously
knowing who was in charge of Rocky.

"We brought enough for a while," Ryan responded,
"but we'll still check out what you've got."

"Well, I'm sure I'll need some snacks while I'm
here," Maya said. "I'll definitely come to visit your
store." And buy something there, in support of these
people who seemed truly in favor of the idea that wolves
had returned to this area.

The hostess returned then. "We've got a table for

you on the patio, where your dog is welcome," she said, menus still plentiful in her arms.

"We'll let you go now," Kathie said. "We've got to get back to the store anyway."

"See you there later," Maya said, earning another smile from Kathie.

But before Kathie and Burt had taken more than a few steps, another woman stepped in front of them, blocking them—Vinnie Fritts.

Rocky, still under Ryan's control, remained standing—and growled, not a good thing, Maya thought.

But Maya considered growling herself, and more, when Vinnie began talking. "How dare you bring that damn dog here!" she spat toward Ryan. "And how dare any of you say that it's a good thing that wolves are back in this area? What happened last night is at least partly your fault, damn you."

Maya didn't really want to ask but said anyway, "What happened last night?"

"Those damned wolves. Did you hear them howling? My husband did, and he decided to go check them out, make sure the town was safe. And it wasn't. *He* wasn't."

Maya had a sinking sensation that she knew what was coming, but she had to ask again, "What happened?"

"Morton was attacked. Mauled. Fortunately, he's going to be okay, no thanks to you. But those horrible creatures don't belong here. One way or another, they have to go."

Ryan couldn't help it. His first reaction, rather than sympathy—feigned or otherwise—was to glance at the Sharans. They were blocked from leaving by Vinnie but now faced her back as she looked furiously toward Maya.

He felt fairly certain that the Sharans were the wolves he'd confronted last night to protect Maya, shifters with no human cognition or control. He couldn't recognize their scent for sure while he, and they, were in human form, but he did sense that they weren't ordinary humans— and Rocky's reaction to them also suggested a different aroma from a regular person's. The dog hadn't acted that way when they'd been around the Sharans before, but he might sense now that they had recently shifted. Did all cover dogs have that ability? Ryan wasn't sure.

The Sharans' reaction was what his should have been. Both maneuvered around Vinnie so she could see them. They began expressing how sorry they were to hear of Morton's injuries. No admission that they'd had any part in them, of course. But they acted like concerned fellow townsfolk.

Even if they were the cause of the man's injuries, they might not even know it, since they wouldn't have had human awareness—but might they have recalled their attack anyway?

Ryan recalled a lot of what he'd done while shifted before he had joined Alpha Force and learned about the elixir—mostly visualizing, not consciously thinking about what he'd done, or analyzing it.

But would the Sharans? Assuming it had been them. There were probably some truly feral wolves in the area, too—and possibly more shifters.

"Thanks," Vinnie muttered at their sympathetic words, but she still kept her focus on Maya.

Heck, Maya was the last one here who should get any blame for a wolf attack. Ryan moved around this group so Rocky was behind him. He whispered to Piers, as he passed, to take the dog to the table the hostess had found for them. "We'll catch up."

Then he joined Maya at her side. Her expression appeared stricken. Horrified. And remorseful.

"I'm so sorry," she finally managed to say to Vinnie. "But—well, I did remind people that wolves are wild. I gather that poor Morton was outside, and—"

"Like I said, he went out when he heard those howls last night. He wanted to make sure that those damned wolves, wherever they were, were not about to hurt anyone. I don't know exactly how it happened. Maybe he was protecting another person. Maybe he just happened to cross the wolves' path at the wrong time. But fortunately he yelled and ran and somehow got away from them. I'd been worried about him so I called Carlo Silling and he picked me up in his car and tried to follow where the howls were, too. When we heard Morton yell we went after him and got him to the hospital."

"Is he going to be all right?" Maya asked.

"Yeah, we think so. No thanks to you."

At Maya's cringe, Ryan stepped between Vinnie and her. "That's enough. We're all sorry that your husband was injured, but Maya's right. She did warn people that wild wolves are…well, wild. She didn't encourage anyone to face them."

But with herself…? He looked down at her then, attempting to put a chiding expression on his face, but only for a moment.

For now.

"Yeah, they are," Vinnie said. "They're dangerous. They don't belong here. And if they stay around here, near Fritts Corner, well, yeah, they're supposedly protected under the law. But I know we can get around that if we figure out which ones attacked my husband. And if that kind of thing happens again you can be certain we'll do everything possible to make sure none ever gets near this town again."

She pivoted and nearly knocked over some people

in line behind them who weren't hiding the fact they were eavesdropping.

"That's such a shame," Kathie Sharan said. "No one likes to hear that, especially not those of us who care about wildlife." She looked at Maya, and Ryan thought he saw tears in her eyes. In both women's eyes, in fact.

"But she shouldn't threaten any protected species," Burt Sharan interjected, putting his arm around his wife.

"No, she shouldn't," Maya said, "though I can certainly understand her position." Her head drooped—and Ryan found himself beside her, his arm around her the way Burt had done with Kathie.

He felt something amazing, something indescribable, when Maya turned and put her head on his shoulder. He faced her, held her even closer, wanting to comfort her—and more. His whole body was reacting to her closeness. And it didn't hurt knowing that this woman was someone who gave a damn about wolves.

But Ryan's shoulders stiffened at that thought. She cared about wolves, sure—but what would she think about people who turned into wolves, and back again?

Most regular humans, unless they'd had contact with shifters, didn't believe in them. And once they had something like that, which they considered weird and paranormal and scary, happen within their consciousness, they backed away.

Might even become particularly fearful of those creatures, real or shifted.

Even so, for now, he didn't loosen his grip.

But he couldn't help wondering how Maya would react knowing that the wolves who'd nearly attacked her last night were likely shifters.

Or that he was a shifter, too.

Chapter 6

How could she be so very aware of this man's nearness? His arms around her.

His lower parts hard as he pressed against her.

Absurd to even think about it. He was simply being nice. Kind. Sympathetic.

She shouldn't need sympathy. Morton Fritts did. She felt just terrible about what had happened to him, as if it was her fault.

But she hadn't brought the wolves here. She was merely an advocate, excited that a wonderful protected and endangered species appeared to be making a resurgence here.

Enough of a resurgence that she, perhaps acting foolish in her delight, had nearly been attacked, too.

If anyone should have been mauled, it was her.

"Thanks," she finally said in as decisive a voice as she could muster. She pulled back, immediately feeling somewhat bereft as Ryan no longer held her, no longer touched her. But it was better this way. "Let's go find our table—although I'm not very hungry now."

"Don't let any of this get to you." Ryan's tone sounded like an order, and she looked up into his face. His brows were knitted, but there was something in his expression that suggested caring. She started to smile, though a bit weakly she figured—but then he added, "Of course I gather you also did something as foolish as Morton Fritts, but you're just lucky you weren't hurt, too."

She took a step back, bumping into someone standing there in line. She excused herself but didn't take her gaze off Ryan.

How did he know that? She hadn't left a message when she'd tried calling him at the hotel. And all she'd really said on the subject this morning was that she'd had an interesting night.

Still, under the circumstances—the howls and barks in the distance and her obvious love of wolves—he could certainly have guessed what she'd done.

And since he apparently hadn't been in his room when she called last night, maybe he had done the same thing. And maybe he had seen her, though she hadn't seen him.

She needed some answers. "Yes," she said, "I'm lucky, and maybe you are, too. Did you do anything after you heard those howls last night?"

When he frowned and opened his mouth to reply, she shook her head. "Let's go sit down and order breakfast—and we can each tell our reactions to those sounds and what we did about them."

Okay, so he'd gone a little too far in his initial chastisement of Maya. So what?

He didn't have to get into specifics.

As they made their way between tables, with him in front, Ryan spotted Piers sitting at a table outside just beyond the glass door. He couldn't see Rocky at first but figured the dog had been there long enough to relax and lie down on the patio.

"There they are," he said and finished leading Maya to the table.

Rocky stood up, and Ryan couldn't help smiling at the way Maya immediately went over and petted him before taking her seat facing Piers. That was a good thing, since one of the remaining chairs had its back to the far patio wall, and if Ryan sat there he'd be able to keep an eye on the crowd.

Ears, too—although he hoped he didn't regret too much that he was there as a human, with limited ability to eavesdrop. But if someone happened to mention the word *wolf* he was sure he would hear it.

Piers picked up the menus near him on the tabletop. Ryan noticed he'd already gotten a cup of coffee. As he handed a menu to Ryan, Piers looked at him quizzically, as if asking what he'd missed.

But he'd heard the worst of it before heading to the table: Morton Fritts had apparently been attacked by a wolf.

Ryan didn't want to bring that up now. There was nothing they could do over breakfast to research which type of wolf had attacked the man, let alone fix that situation.

As a result, he just gave a brief shrug and opened his menu. "Great! They have a good selection, and I'm hungry." Which he actually was, after his busy night on the hillside.

Not to mention the energy used for shifting. That burned a lot of calories.

As he read the menu, he did hear the word *wolf* and several times with his heightened hearing. He allowed himself to glance in those directions. Other seated diners, both here and inside, seemed to be discussing the events of last night—at least the howls, since he heard that word a few times, too.

He also heard the word *attack* at least once...

News had apparently spread about Morton Fritts. Not that it was likely to be hushed up for any reason—not even by shifters, if they were the source of the problem. They could discuss it while in human form, but would they know who did it—shifters or not? And if shifters, which ones were involved?

But with all the various conversations, many of which seemed to be on that subject, and the fact that there was a curious woman at his side so he couldn't simply sit there listening, Ryan gave up on the possibility of learning much that was useful right away.

Nor did he get any sense, via scent or conversation, that anyone here was a shifter—not that his belief was conclusive.

He decided to order eggs with sausage and toast. Good thing he figured that out fairly quickly since their server, a thirtysomething woman who looked like she'd been at this for a while, came right over to their table for their orders.

Maya asked for only toast and decaf. When the server was gone, she looked toward Ryan. "Did you go outside, too, after you heard the howls?"

Ryan knew he had to be cautious about how he responded. But he'd already hinted that he was aware she hadn't stayed in her room.

Not that she'd recognized him. Sure, he had chased

the other wolves away from her, but he didn't think she had a clue that any of them were shifters.

Before he responded, though, he glanced toward Piers and grinned, knowing his aide would take his cue and keep any answers on his part consistent with Ryan's.

"Yes, we did hear those howls and all and went out for a little while," Ryan said. "As representatives of US Fish and Wildlife, we wanted to gather as much information as we could. We wanted to listen, to try to determine how many animals, presumably wolves, were howling and from what direction. We left Rocky in our car since he wouldn't necessarily follow a safety protocol and stay with us rather than pulling away to chase whatever was making those sounds." He glanced down at the dog, who once more was lying on the patio.

Ryan then shot a glance toward Maya, just as the server came with her decaf and his high-octane coffee. She also refilled Piers's cup. "Your food will be up shortly," she said, then left.

"Did you hear any more when you were out there?" Maya asked. "See anything?"

"A few more distant howls and barks, but that was all—and we didn't see any wolves or other wildlife." He didn't need to tell the truth, of course. In fact, nearly everything he said was a lie. He happened to be one of those wolves. "How about you? Did you go outside to check things out, too?"

He needed to tread somewhat lightly here, but he'd already suggested he knew that answer.

"Yes," she said. "I wanted to see the wolves, so I followed the sounds as best I could."

"I gathered they were on the hillsides beyond the park. Was that what you determined?"

"Yes," Maya said. She sucked in her lips slightly as if in worry, and if Ryan read her expression correctly she was recalling all that had happened.

"And did you see any?" Her response would be what determined how he followed up.

"Yes," she said almost curtly. He gathered she didn't want to continue after that.

But Piers, great aide that he was, was the one to ask, "Really? What did you see?"

Her eyes narrowed, and then she looked down at the table. "They were beautiful," she said almost reverently.

Ryan shouldn't feel so happy to hear her words, her attitude. Maya might be one gorgeous woman with a laudable attitude toward wolves—but she had no idea who and what he was, along with the probability that there were at least a few others in this area.

She might not be so pleased about the proximity of wolves if she did.

"How many wolves did you see?" Piers continued. "Where were they? I assume you didn't get near any of them, right?"

Piers hadn't been close enough to see the encounter among Ryan and the two other wolves he believed to be shifters, but Ryan had filled him in once he had shifted back to human form—including how he had kept the wolves from attacking the lovely and foolish human who'd tracked them down.

"Well…" Maya looked toward Ryan as if attempting to judge how much he knew. He'd already suggested that she might have done something as foolish as Morton Fritts and was therefore lucky she'd not been hurt.

But he wasn't about to tell her why he believed that to be true.

He looked straight back into her soft hazel eyes. "Why don't you tell us what you did and what you saw?"

"Because I'm both happy and embarrassed about it."

Their food arrived then, and Maya looked pleased at the interruption. But a short while later, when they'd all taken their first bites of food—and Ryan had given Rocky a taste of his sausage—he said, "Okay, tell us about your night."

She took a deep breath and raised her light brown eyebrows as if she actually did feel discomfited about her anticipated response. But she described having followed the howls and other canine sounds into the woods, using her flashlight and camera—and being confronted by a couple of wolves.

"But then there was a third one," she said, "who distracted the two that seemed as if they might attack me. I ran away then."

"I hope you sent thoughts of thanks to the wolf that helped you," Piers said, taking another sip of his coffee before glancing toward Ryan.

Ryan couldn't help a small smile although he aimed it at his own cup rather than toward his aide.

"I definitely did," Maya said. "He might have saved me from…from being mauled like Morton Fritts."

"Quite possibly," Ryan agreed. "You need to be careful. In fact, once we find out the details of the attack on Fritts, I'd suggest you give another presentation on behalf of WHaM, or just in general if that's better for you. You should emphasize to people to stay far, far away from wild animals, because they are wild. They don't know even to stay away and not hurt wonderful people like you who give a damn about them." Unless they happen to be shifters with access to the Alpha

Force elixir, he thought, but of course he wasn't going to mention that.

"That sounds like a good idea." She looked him straight in the eyes again.

Damn, but she was one beautiful woman. He was attracted to her. Very attracted. Would like to do more, a lot more, than just have breakfast with her...and save her from other wolves.

But any thoughts beyond encouraging her to be a wildlife proponent were inappropriate.

And so, after exchanging gazes with her, he gave a goofy grin and dug back into his breakfast.

Oh, that look on Ryan's face. It was as if he forgave her foolishness in seeking out the wolves—yet he cared about her, was glad she was okay.

Or was she reading too much into it?

Maya reached over and picked up her last piece of toast, slathering a little apricot jam on it. That gave her an excuse not to look directly at Ryan, at least for this moment.

But she remained fully aware of his closeness. And how she felt glad about that.

But only because the guy also liked wildlife. And maybe he seemed a little attracted to her just because he was glad she was out there promoting the return of wolves to this area and championing all creatures.

"I like the idea, too," said Piers, sort of interrupting the mood, but that was a good thing.

Maya took a decisive bite of her toast. She had no intention of getting interested in any man, let alone one who lived outside Washington, DC.

And just the fact that Ryan appeared to love wildlife,

too, didn't mean they shared anything else in common. Or that the way they cared could coincide.

She had gone through that before with her ex, who'd turned out to be the opposite of what she'd believed. She had even developed what she'd believed to be a relationship with him, a reporter who seemed to support her pro-wildlife position.

But just the opposite. He had turned on her in a number of articles lambasting WHaM for not just documenting and counting an influx of wildlife but acting as advocates, too. She'd been hurt and angry and determined not to get involved with someone like that again.

US Fish and Wildlife undoubtedly had a different agenda from WHaM, despite their few similarities.

And Maya figured she had a different agenda from Ryan—although his suggestion about a modified topic for her next talk actually made sense.

"So how long are you staying in town?" she asked Ryan, turning back to face him again. Maybe he was leaving today and she wouldn't see him again.

That should make her feel relieved, shouldn't it? But it didn't.

"Not sure yet," he replied, which did in fact give her a sense of relief. A small one.

Being in his presence, getting to know him better—would that be a good thing?

Possibly…but only as long as they helped each other in their quest to ensure that wolves remained welcome and safe in this area.

And hopefully didn't attack any more people. But neither of them could guarantee that.

She, though, by giving another talk on staying far away from them might be able to help, at least a bit.

But would she convince herself…?

"How about you?" Piers asked. "How long will you be here?"

"I'd originally thought just a couple of days," she said. "But it sounds as if there is a lot more I can do here, both by informing people and maybe even finding out about the wolves here and how dangerous they might be. If they attack people, that's bad for them as well as for the humans near them. It gives people an excuse—maybe even a good one—to hunt the wolves, even though they're protected in this area."

"I think we're on the same wavelength," Ryan said, his tone decisive and his expression now not particularly warm but highly businesslike—a good thing.

"Then let's work together," she said. "Find out about that attack last night and try to determine the wolves' location. And despite the danger those wolves may present—well, I'm hoping to find a way to make sure they're left alone."

"Sounds good to me," Piers said, nodding, then looking toward Ryan.

"Absolutely," he agreed.

Chapter 7

Maya found the rest of their breakfast quite pleasant—until it ended and she got into a small squabble with Ryan about who was going to pay for her meal. She allowed Ryan to win after he convinced her that the federal agency he worked for might not directly make contributions to WHaM but would be glad to assist it in at least this small way.

On the way out, she noticed that Trev was sitting at a table near the door with another man and a couple of women. Good. Though he'd said he wasn't from this town, he apparently had friends here—and hopefully was putting in a good word with them about WHaM and wildlife.

And those friends included women. Hopefully he was flirting with them, so Maya didn't need to feel so uncomfortable with this nice fellow wildlife lover.

She split up with Ryan and Piers on the sidewalk outside and Maya gave Rocky a goodbye hug. She considered doing the same with the guys—Piers first, although it was really Ryan she wanted to touch again. But she hugged neither man.

"Where are you off to?" Ryan asked. She had wanted to ask him the same question but had decided not to since it might seem too personal.

"Oh, I need a few things so I think I'll head to the grocery store." She left unsaid that she hoped to learn more from the Sharans about the people in town who were happy that wolves were back. Not to mention whether they'd heard more about what had happened to Morton Fritts.

"Sounds good. But are you also going to follow up with our suggestion and arrange to do another talk in the park—one about staying away from wild animals?"

"Yes," she said, "I'll do that later this afternoon. And if you give me your cell phone number, I'll call and let you know how it goes."

All three exchanged numbers, and Maya wished she'd thought of doing that yesterday, after they'd met and learned of their joint appreciation of the wolves' return. Considering all that had happened since then it seemed even more necessary that they keep in touch as long as she remained in Fritts Corner.

The men then led Rocky in the opposite direction from Maya along the fairly empty sidewalk. The street didn't have much traffic, either. But Fritts Corner wasn't a particularly large town. As far as Maya was concerned, its only claim to fame was the proximity of the influx of wolves.

She headed toward the grocery store, figuring she didn't need to drive since she wasn't intending to buy a lot of stuff anyway. Her main goal was to get any information that the store owners could convey.

On her way, she passed what was probably the only

hospital in this area, the Fritts Medical Center. Its appearance was much starker than most of the town's other buildings, six stories high and squared-off red-brick construction.

She wondered if Morton Fritts had been treated for wolf injuries in this facility—and whether he remained there.

How could she find out what happened, where he was attacked and whether the wolves who hurt him could be the same ones who might have harmed her if the other wolf hadn't come along?

Asking him directly, or his wife, didn't seem the best idea, but she'd give it a try if she saw them again.

She walked the few blocks to the Corner Grocery Store fairly quickly. It looked a little larger than other retail establishments like clothing stores that she'd passed. Its design appeared somewhat quaint as well, and the front consisted of long windows that showed off the well-stocked interior.

The place looked relatively crowded, too, with people in all the aisles and lined up at the couple of cash registers near the front. Was that because it had a good supply of healthful produce, reasonably priced food—or simply because it was the only grocery in town? Maya hadn't seen any supermarkets since she'd arrived here.

Was the place too busy for her to approach the owners, who'd seemed so interested in and happy about the nearby wolves? She just wanted a better sense as to whether the townsfolk like the Sharans felt any differently about the situation today, after the sound of howls and more had infiltrated the town last night—and someone had been attacked.

And did the Sharans know the Frittses well? They had expressed concern for Morton at the restaurant, but for the wolves, too.

Was there any media coverage? Maya hadn't seen anything so far on the internet via her cell phone about her talk, or even the attack—although she hadn't spent a lot of time looking. Were there any social media reports that she wouldn't know about?

The thing was, she had a whole lot of questions without any answers—at least not yet. And so she entered the store.

A young man exited as she came in. "Welcome," he said, grinning at her.

Why was he welcoming her? Was he an employee? Related to the owners?

She saw Kathie Sharan as soon as she got inside. The woman chatted with some people near the closest cash register, and Maya approached.

"It's a terrible situation," she heard one of the group say, a senior woman in a loose dress. "And it should have been good for everyone."

"Well, we still don't have much information," Kathie responded. "Maybe Morton was goading those wolves."

Aha. A conversation exactly on the topic Maya wanted to discuss.

"Hi," she said, taking a few strides forward. "Sorry to be eavesdropping, but you won't be surprised to know I've been listening for the word *wolf* a lot these days." She grinned toward Kathie, who smiled back.

"Oh, hello, Maya," she said. "Everyone, this is Maya Everton. She's the very nice lady with WHaM who talked at the park yesterday about the return of wolves to this area."

"Do you know what happened last night?" the older woman asked. "I've always loved animals and was so excited—but maybe having wolves come back is a horrible situation."

"Now, Yola," Kathie said, "as I mentioned, we don't really know what happened. You've lived here a lot longer than I have but I think it's wonderful that even a few wolves have been sighted around here."

"That's right," Maya said. "And of course all of you know a lot more about the area around Fritts Corner than I do, but I realized afterward that maybe I'd given the wrong idea at my talk. I love wildlife, but a lot of it is truly wild. I'm hoping to give another talk to make sure people understand not only to avoid attempting to turn wild animals into pets, but I also want to stress that no one should try to confront any wild animals, especially those that could harm them."

The older woman, Yola, appeared a little mollified. "Morton is a bit...well, egotistical. Maybe he did think he could go find out about those wolves and confront them, maybe even try shooing them away from this area, without their reacting against him."

"And might he have had a weapon?" asked another member of the crowd, a thin guy with shaggy gray hair.

"You're new here, too," Yola said. "Yes, it's entirely possible that our Morton went to check on those wolves carrying something that could hurt them."

"And potentially protect him," Kathie said. "Which would have been fine as long as he just scared the wolves off without injuring—or killing—them."

"Well, however it happened," Maya said, "I'd really like to know how the confrontation went. And I'm terribly sorry Morton got hurt."

"Me, too," Kathie said fervently.

Her husband, Burt, joined the group just then from someplace within the store. "All of us are."

The conversation continued a short while longer—but no one appeared to have any more information than

Maya had. None of them could identify the people at
her talk who'd said they were with the media. According to this group, there weren't, in fact, any local TV
or radio stations, although when things happened here
major networks sometimes sent reporters from Tacoma
or other not too distant towns. Or sometimes they just
showed up here, which might have been the case during Maya's talk—although she wondered if the wolf-
haters invited them.

"I'm not going to be the one to contact any," Burt
said, "but I wouldn't be surprised if those reporters return and start nosing around again."

"Especially if the Frittses notify them about the attack," his wife said, her expression troubled.

Maya's concerns eased, if only a little. Apparently
the Sharans, and hopefully other locals, weren't totally
turned against the wolves by this difficult situation.

And maybe, once the facts—whatever they were—
came to light, the wolves would somehow be exonerated.

Although…well, she had somewhat brought the confrontation she'd had with a couple of them last night
on herself.

She had a sudden urge to return to that area now, in
daylight, to see if she could find evidence of where the
wolves had gone. Would there be paw prints? Other
indications?

But she still needed more information. So, after she
bought a few things to justify her presence at the store,
she just might head to the Fritts Corner Police Department to see what information they were releasing to the
public about what happened last night.

She wondered where Ryan was. Had he already gone
there to learn what he could on behalf of the US Fish
and Wildlife Service?

She'd find that out later, too.

For now, she'd probably just head back to her hotel.

But as she reached the grocery store's door, she saw Trev standing outside talking to one of the women who'd been at breakfast with him.

The fact he had company like that was a good thing. But was it a mere coincidence that they'd wound up at the very place she had headed after her meal?

Drat. She realized that the guy was making her uncomfortable, even though he'd done nothing but be friendly and cheer on WHaM—and her public talk about local wildlife.

She was undoubtedly worrying too much.

But she hoped whatever flirtation he was now carrying on with this lady—a short, slightly plump but definitely pretty girl wearing a bright-colored scarf over her sweater and carrying a huge purse—continued and got Trev to forget about her.

Though not about saying nice things to the world about WHaM.

Was he one of the people now becoming a skeptic thanks to the attack on Morton Fritts? If so, Maya could certainly understand it, even with a person who'd come from somewhere else to learn how WHaM wanted to promote the presence of the newest local wolves.

Maybe she'd have to speak to the guy—or at least be sure he was there if she talked to the public again.

"So what next?" Piers asked Ryan as they walked back toward the hotel from the restaurant.

"I texted a brief description of what happened last night to Major Connell first thing this morning but that's my only communication with him so far since we arrived. I think it's time to give a call to our commanding officer at Alpha Force and give him more detail."

"Good idea," Piers said. "But we need to find someplace more private than our hotel room. I've heard voices in the hallway from my room, so someone might be able to eavesdrop. The old place has some charm to it, but I doubt that soundproofing was topmost in the minds of the people who built it."

Ryan held Rocky's leash, and the wolf-dog stopped to sniff the stonework at the front of a drugstore—possibly where other dogs had lifted their legs. Ryan turned to look at his aide. "I've been trying to come up with a good idea about where to go for it," he admitted.

"How about back to the park?" Piers stopped, probably since they weren't going in that direction. "We can keep walking with Rocky there as we talk and avoid any nosy folks that way. Better yet, maybe we'll find someplace where no one else is hanging out."

"Good idea."

They were soon at one end of the rolling lawn that constituted most of the park till it met the forested hillside. It was distant from the aging podium where Maya had given her talk. Maybe that was a good thing, Ryan thought. He'd have to mention her—not that his mind ever seemed to deviate far from her and her attractiveness both in looks and the way she talked about wolves. But he'd keep his talk about her to a minimum.

As Ryan had predicted, the park wasn't empty, but most people, many with dogs and/or kids, paid them no attention.

Ryan headed for a bench beneath a pine tree and sat down, Piers right behind him. Rocky seemed fine with it, too, lying down on the grass at the end of his leash. If anyone got close, they could walk away.

"You ready to call?" Piers asked.

"Do it," Ryan responded.

His aide pulled a cell phone from his pocket, pushed a few buttons, and Ryan heard it ring. Clearly Piers had put the call on speaker, so they'd have to remain remote and discreet, but that didn't look like it would be a problem, at least for now. The nearest people weren't close, and none came in their direction.

"Hey," Drew Connell said nearly immediately. "I've got Patrick here, too." Lieutenant Patrick Worley was the major's second in command at Alpha Force. "Tell us what's going on."

Briefly, keeping his voice low and continuing to look around to make sure no other person in the park was coming closer, Ryan described what had gone on last night: the full moon, which they of course all knew about. Hearing wolves howl and bark, also no particular surprise but perhaps indicating that Ryan wasn't the only shifter in the area. Describing his own shift with Piers's assistance along with the Alpha Force elixir, with no artificial light under the full moon.

He then told how, while on the prowl, he had seen the woman who'd given a talk to the public the day before in the same park where they now sat—the woman representing the wildlife championing organization WHaM—out and about in the woods beneath the full moon. A couple of wolves had prepared to attack her, and he, in shifted form, had driven them off.

Then, the next morning, he and the rest of this town of Fritts Corner had learned that a local citizen, one not pleased about the influx of wolves, had apparently been attacked.

"We don't know yet if those two wolves I went after were shifters, although their scents indicate the possibility to me. We also don't know if they, or possibly other shifters, attacked Morton Fritts. Shifters or not, apparently we may have a problem here with wolves too prone to attack humans—although we of course don't yet know whether Fritts was doing something to provoke them."

"Better find out soon," replied Drew. "Either way."

"Yeah, we want to talk to Fritts but haven't been able to yet," Ryan said.

"And if they're shifters," Piers said, "we have a month till the next full moon to learn what we need to and ensure nothing like this happens again."

"That's a big if," Patrick broke in over the phone. "First, even if they are shifters, we don't know if they have access to anything like our elixir. We've recruited a few shifters who had done some experimenting, or their families had, and the formulas they came up with sometimes let them shift more at will than just under a full moon—and they had varying degrees of human cognition, just nothing nearly comparable to what we've got with the Alpha Force elixir."

"And even if there are shifters in the area," Drew said, "you still need to figure out if wild wolves conducted that attack and were perhaps provoked enough to do it again—without waiting for a full moon, of course."

"Of course," Ryan agreed. "Well, we'd thought we would only be here for a week or so, but looks like we'll just have to see how long it takes. I assume that's okay, Major Connell?"

"Just call me Drew unless we're in a formal meeting." Ryan heard the smile on his commanding officer's face and grinned slightly himself. "Like I've said before, we've got too much between us in Alpha Force to maintain formality. But we—you—have responsibilities. Keep us informed about what you learn, and be sure to figure out as quickly as possible the details of what happened last night. If you have to stay till the next full moon or even beyond, that's fine, too. But be cautious—and conduct your own shifts whenever you think it's best for tracking any nonshifting wolves in the area to learn what you need to."

"Yes, sir." Ryan's grin grew into a larger smile. "Er, yes, Drew."

"Watch it, Lieutenant," Drew responded. "Er, Ryan. And a couple more things."

"Yes?"

"Keep an eye on that WHaM representative as long as she's there. We won't want someone embracing and promoting the idea of wildlife to be injured by a wolf, no matter whether it's a shifter or not. And as we discussed before, if you do find shifters in the area, be sure to check them out to see if any are worth recruiting into Alpha Force. Our unit, as covert as it is, is strong and growing."

"Will do, with both of them." Of course the idea of keeping an eye on Maya sounded good to Ryan. Too good. He'd have to rein in his inappropriate interest in the lovely woman who liked wolves. Way back. Watch her, yes. Learn from her, sure. But nothing more than that.

"I'll do my part to help him," Piers added. "Rocky will, too."

"Go to it, then," Drew finished—a good thing since some kids tossing a basketball between them headed in the direction of the bench.

"Will do, and we'll keep you informed about anything useful that we learn. Oh, and if you happen to hear any more about shifters in this area—"

"We'll keep you informed," Patrick said.

Chapter 8

Her visit to the local government offices of Fritts Corner had only been partly productive. Maya grumbled internally as she left the lovely, quaint and picturesque set of old-fashioned buildings and stood on the nearly empty sidewalk watching the traffic while deciding where to go next.

At least she had received the okay from the city manager to do another talk in the park. She'd obtained her first authorization from that office as well, but this time she'd had to request a meeting with the manager himself, Perry Fernander.

And Mr. Fernander, politician that he was, had concerns about anyone taking a positive position about the wolves any longer.

He'd sat behind his desk staring grimly at her from beneath shaggy gray brows and shaking his head. "I haven't talked directly to our injured citizen Morton Fritts," he'd said, "but of course the town of Fritts Corner is now concerned about the nearness of those wolves."

"I understand," Maya had told him, and she *had* understood—but without more information she didn't want to hold any wolves, or herself, responsible. "What I want to talk about is staying safe when potentially dangerous wildlife is in the area." A good thing for the people, sure—but also to protect the wolves and their abilities to roam freely.

Fernander had stared at her a moment longer, then nodded. "That could benefit us all. I'll give the city's approval, but you'll need to let me know when you want to give that talk in the park."

"Soon, but I want to check a couple of things." She'd noted his contact information and left.

When did she want to give it? Well, she hoped to confirm a time when Ryan and Piers could be there—perhaps also with Rocky—and lend her at least some moral support. Maybe the Sharans, too, since they still seemed to appreciate the idea of wolves returning to this area. They could also let other pro-wolf people know.

And, okay, sure. She might not want to get extremely friendly with Trev, but he'd been nice to her and expressed his interest in wildlife. He had also apparently been making friends here. Did they have the same affinity to wildlife he did? She hoped so.

Plus, as she'd considered before, she hoped Trev—and lots of locals, too—hadn't changed their minds about the good things resulting from the latest influx of wolves.

She might need to figure out where Trev was staying, since he had indicated he was a visitor like her, and expressly invite him to her next talk. Then, she had to choose a time that he, with his new buddies, could attend, too.

Then there were the Frittses. One thing that had encouraged her when she was in the city hall building was that, while she'd been in the waiting room, she had overheard a receptionist talking on the phone, apparently with a concerned citizen who wanted to stay safe from the wolves.

"Now, I can't tell you for sure," said the thin woman with glasses and a nasal voice, "but what I heard was that Mr. Fritts went up the dirt road at the far end of the park's hills once he heard those howls. He had some kind of large stick with him, I gather, and he was all set to shut those wolves up by pounding at them and scaring them into running away from our area. But when they attacked him—"

She'd shut up then when a couple of uniformed cops walked into the reception area.

Really? What Morton Fritts claimed didn't sound too likely, Maya thought. But what if it was true? And what if instead of his chasing them with his stick they'd felt frightened and attacked the human threatening them?

A stretch, she realized…yet she had an urge to go up that trail now, during the daytime when it was light outside and the wolves might be sleeping. Or if they were hunting they'd surely make noise and she could get out of there.

But what if, after he was attacked, Morton Fritts had dropped his weapon and left it there? It would likely have his fingerprints on it—and Maya could photograph it.

Or maybe there would be other evidence that could show that the wolves only acted for their own protection and weren't the initial aggressors.

It would be an explanation that she—and WHaM—could use to perhaps reduce the animals' bad reputation here…

And it wouldn't hurt to give some proof of the goodness of wolves to the representatives of the US Fish and Wildlife Service who happened to be in town, as well.

That would give her a good excuse to see Ryan again—not that she really needed one beyond the talk she now planned about wolf safety. Oh, and human safety, too.

But for now…

She hurried back to the hotel to change clothes.

As much as Ryan disliked what he'd done, he at least had more information. He had used his power as a representative of the United States government—or at least one of its agencies—to have his contacts in DC get in touch with local authorities to extract what information they had about the attack on Fritts.

Now he mulled it all over again as he walked silently with his cover dog and aide through downtown Fritts Corner.

The story his supposed superiors at US Fish and Wildlife—actually, some members of Alpha Force—had conveyed to the police chief was that they needed all information available to collect statistics. They wouldn't guarantee any reprisal against the wolf or wolves at fault but might allow it locally, the way those that had attacked livestock were being treated elsewhere in the state.

Ryan would need to stay on top of it all and prevent anything similar around here if some other agency or regional authority decided to try to take action against the local wolves. After all, no matter why or how Fritts had been attacked, he had survived it.

If he hadn't, protecting any wolves, especially those involved, would be difficult—no matter what their backgrounds.

Worst-case, if these wolves were wild, Ryan would use some contacts Alpha Force had within US Fish and Wildlife to ensure they were trapped and relocated to a habitat much farther from human habitation.

And if they happened to be shifters—well, things would be handled quite differently.

But the real Fish and Wildlife Service had been informed about this attack. They probably would have been anyway, yet now Ryan felt somewhat responsible for whatever happened to the wolves—shifters or not— who were involved.

Now, he, along with Piers and Rocky, passed through the park that had become so familiar to them. The podium where Maya had given her last talk was in front of them, and just beyond that were the forested hillsides—their destination at the moment.

Was she going to be able to give another talk there— the kind they'd discussed, where humans would be warned to be careful? They should know that anyway.

In any event, Ryan had entered the forest from the other end last night, to prevent being seen by anyone even before his shift began.

He had left the area the same way, after changing back.

He recalled very well the way he had gone after the wolves menacing Maya.

Maya. Where was she now?

He had no doubt she was using her own skills and knowledge to look into the realities of last night and how Morton Fritts had been hurt. She was a lovely, gregarious woman who loved wildlife—very attractive to him.

Not that he, or any member of Alpha Force, could let any interest like that go further. But he appreciated her.

And hoped she was learning something she could share with him. Something to protect wolves, despite the glitch caused by the attack on Fritts.

But for now… "You ready?" He looked at Piers, who'd been equally silent on their trek from the hotel and held Rocky's leash.

"Yeah. But do you really think we'll find anything helpful—even you, with your special…abilities?" Piers had lowered his voice along with only hinting at what he was talking about, like Ryan's special, acute senses even when he was in human form since he definitely wasn't shifted now.

"Guess we'll just have to find out."

They started up the nearest dirt path at the end of the park. Ryan inhaled deeply. Would there be any residual odors from those wolves—any that he could pick up while not shifted?

Would there be anything else indicating where Fritts had been attacked…and what kind of wolves had done it?

This probably was useless, but waiting longer made even less sense.

"Yeah," Piers said. "Meantime, now that we're alone here—except for Rocky—tell me what you hear and see and smell, would you?"

Ryan smiled. His aide had told him many times that he'd volunteered to be a nonshifting member of Alpha Force because he found the concept of shapeshifters fascinating. But would he want to be one if he had the ability to choose?

"No way," he'd spat out when Ryan had asked. "I'd never be able to be as good at it as you."

Which had only made Ryan smile all the more.

He looked down at his cover dog now. Rocky was busy doing his dog thing, sniffing the undergrowth and lifting his leg now and then to leave his own canine scent.

What would the wolves think about that? Although, if they had been shifters, they probably wouldn't know anything about it since the likelihood was that they wouldn't shift again for a month.

Of course Ryan, in his human form, inhaled the odors of wildlife and more around here—including the scents that his own dog was leaving, though a whole lot less acute than if he'd looked just like Rocky.

They neared the clearing where Ryan had jumped in last night to prevent Maya from being attacked.

Which was when he smelled it. Smelled *her*. And not just the residual aroma from the night before.

"C'mon," he growled to his aide and cover dog. He pulled quickly ahead and emerged from among the trees around him, right into that clearing.

"Maya," he said. "What are you doing here?"

Maya gasped and jumped sideways.

She'd been keeping her mind open to sounds, had enjoyed hearing many different types of birds and became aware of leaves blowing in the slight breeze.

But she had listened especially for any noise that could be wolves. And not only wolves. She had done her research before her journey to this area. Although they might not be present right here, there were often sightings of other kinds of wild animals in Washington State, including bears, cougars and coyotes, as well as more usual small mammals such as rabbits and raccoons.

Any of them, if present, could create rustles in the dried leaves on the ground or other noises.

But she hadn't been listening for human voices.

"I could ask you the same thing," she shot back, turning to look at the source of that question.

Although she wasn't exactly shocked by the sudden appearance of Ryan or Rocky or Piers. They were, after all, wildlife advocates, like her.

Still…the tall man who was Ryan now stood beside her, almost as if attempting to intimidate her.

Well, that wasn't going to work. In fact, she had a sense that this guy, and maybe his friend and dog, would do their utmost to defend her if a wolf did happen to show up right now.

"We're still trying to collect all the facts about that attack last night," Ryan said. "We learned it might have occurred around this part of the hillside so we decided to check it out. The more we know, the more likely it is that we'll be able to prevent more attacks from happening."

"Hey, we're on the same wavelength," Maya said, a sense of warmth shooting through her.

"Maybe." Ryan's scowl didn't exactly intimidate her—or even turn her off. But she knew he intended to convey something that wasn't being said.

Something like, *stay away from here, got it?*

Although—how had he determined to come to this particular spot? Surely he hadn't eavesdropped on the same people she'd heard talking at city hall?

But if he had learned about it, that meant more information was getting out—whether by gossip or more official channels.

"But look, Maya," Ryan continued. "You told us that you were nearly attacked last night. What's to say that the wolves around you then aren't still in this area? If they were defending what they consider their turf, or maybe they're even breeding now—they could attack again. And the other wolf that challenged them might not be around then, or might even join the attack. What about the talk you're giving to tell people to stay far away from wildlife?"

"I figured I'd do what I wanted till I give that talk," she retorted. "Once I do, I'll have to live with what I said in case someone catches me disobeying myself." She shot him a huge grin.

Although Piers, too, was smiling, Ryan wasn't.

"Well, obey yourself starting now," Ryan said. "If nothing else, hang out with us while we're up here. Otherwise you could get hurt—or worse. Then think about how people around here would react to the new influx of wolves—maybe justifiably so."

He was right. Maybe her own type of research and showing love to wild animals wasn't the wisest way to go just now.

"Okay," she conceded. "I'll stay with you, and we'll leave this area—right?"

"Yes, let's get out of here," Ryan said. He looked at Piers, who also nodded, and, as if he understood, Rocky rose from where he sat, too.

"Let me show you something before we go," Maya said. At the time Ryan had startled her by talking, she'd thought she had seen something at the edge of the forest.

A slight clearing, with leaves somewhat trampled.

And if she wasn't mistaken…

"When you startled me, I'd just seen that. It might mean nothing, but...well, I was looking for any evidence about what happened when Morton was attacked. We've all heard from different sources that this area could be where it happened. It's a large enough hillside, and there are quite a few animals around that are carnivores. Even so—"

As she'd spoken, she had moved back to the area at the edge of this clearing where she had seen some tromped-down leaves...and more.

And pointed now toward a spot on the ground.

A reddish-brown spot.

A spot that could be blood.

Chapter 9

Out of the corner of his eye, Ryan saw Piers glance toward him as if awaiting his confirmation about the composition of the dark spot on the ground.

He had already inhaled almost instinctively. Despite the lessening of his senses in human form, he did catch the scent of what the spot appeared to be: blood.

Not that he could inform Maya of his certainty.

But even though it was blood, she was right. He couldn't be sure it was human blood, and even if it was, that the blood belonged to the man who'd apparently been a victim of an attack last night.

Ryan, while in human form, had met Morton, had inhaled his scent, but that wouldn't tell him what his blood alone smelled like. Even if he shifted and inhaled this aging and foliage-tainted scent, he might have a better idea but wouldn't be sure.

For now, he would just act like a regular human—at least to the extent he could.

"Wow," he said to Maya. "That certainly looks like it could be blood—but you're right. We've no way of knowing if it could be Morton Fritts's. Even so—"

"Even so," Maya repeated, pulling her camera from the bag over her shoulder and filming the spot, then pulling back to take in more of the area. "We can inform the authorities."

Enough time had passed that, even though Ryan believed he also caught a faint aroma of canines in the area, he couldn't be certain. That could simply be his expectation—or imagination.

Either way, he didn't want the blood to be human, and if it was, he didn't want it to be the result of an attack by wolf; shifter or otherwise.

Or an injured, or dead, wolf's blood.

"Yes, we can," he said, "although since Morton apparently survived it would be better if he told the authorities where he was hurt. Maybe he already has. That might not matter now anyway. It's not like a crime scene where one human attacked another." On the other hand, he wasn't about to mention it but identifying which wolf it was, assuming Fritts had been mauled by a canine or two, would be particularly interesting to him—and to the rest of Alpha Force. He again traded glances with Piers, who was undoubtedly thinking the same thing.

Perhaps it was, in an unusual kind of way, a crime scene, after all—one involving another human in a non-human form...

"You're right, I guess the best thing would be just to mention it to the authorities, maybe show them the pictures I took, and let them decide if they want us to show them where this is. It could just be the result of a wolf or other predator catching its nonhuman dinner. And they're allowed to do that."

"Right." He looked at her. She appeared almost fierce as she nodded toward him, clearly willing to do a lot to defend the wildlife she cherished.

"And in any event, even if it happens to be Morton's blood we can't tell whether he acted aggressively first or just protected himself. The authorities might not care either way, but I certainly do."

"Me, too, of course." Ryan shrugged off the sudden desire to pull her into his arms for a hug. To thank her for her attitude. That was all.

Not because that sudden desire meant anything else...

"Okay, then," he continued. "Thanks for pointing that spot out to me. It never hurts to have information, even if it doesn't make sense to use it. Now, let's head back down to the park."

Maya found herself smiling nearly the entire hike down the hill. That was partly because of the company she was with: other wildlife lovers.

But in addition, Piers gave her the handle of Rocky's leash, and she got to be with the wolflike dog nearly the entire walk. She had to be careful, of course. Although Rocky stuck with her, he could topple her over if he ever decided to start running while she held the end of his leash.

But he didn't, good dog that he was. She patted him often.

Rocky and she led the group, and she heard Ryan and Piers behind her, talking. Which in itself was interesting. They discussed what else they would do for the rest of this day.

They also asked again when she intended to give her next talk, about staying away from wild animals for safety. She informed them she had a phone number to call to set it up, and they agreed she should ask for a time tomorrow afternoon.

"I can give a call to work out the time as soon as we're back in the park and I get a better signal," she told them.

She looked forward to her next talk, especially considering all that had happened in Fritts Corner since she'd last happily discussed the resurgence of wolves into this area.

Now, that talk could have become a little controversial, but she was going to do all she could to encourage the incredible excitement of having some previously missing wildlife return—yet stress how people should react for their own safety, as well as the wolves'.

She would also need to make certain somehow that it was well publicized so a lot of people would know about it and, hopefully, show up.

And as many as possible remain pro-wildlife despite the now more obvious need to be careful.

They reached the area at the base of this portion of the hillside, then took time to walk around it into the park.

There, near the podium, Maya handed Piers the end of Rocky's leash and made the call she'd planned on. She reached City Manager Perry Fernander, and he OK'd the following afternoon at one thirty for her next talk.

"All set," she said as she pressed the button to hang up.

"Good deal," Piers said, and even Rocky, standing beside Piers with his leash slack, panted a little in a way that resembled a laugh.

"I take it you'll come," Maya said to Ryan, who also stood beside them.

The tall man's brows went up, although he didn't smile. "Of course not," he said, "despite my insistence on your giving this additional talk and scheduling it as soon as possible, and—"

"I get it," Maya said with a laugh at his sarcasm, and her insides seemed to warm at the idea that he would be there to listen, maybe to help her, or maybe to contradict her if he didn't like her approach.

But somehow she had an urge to impress him—even as they both did their best to help wolves.

For now, though, she called the police department, put the speaker on so the men could hear her conversation and told the dispatcher who answered about having heard about a possible wolf attack last night and seeing something today that could be blood near a path in the middle of a hillside, then described the general area. The woman put them on hold for a minute, and when she returned said the authorities had already been informed by the victim about what had happened and where. She thanked Maya, then hung up.

Which gave Maya some sense of relief. She had done her duty but didn't have to follow up anymore about that unnerving patch of darkened red on the ground.

But she wished she had more information—like where the attack actually had happened and what had provoked it...

And now, their hike was over and so was anything else she needed to do with these men, at least for the moment. It was late afternoon. They were about to split up, probably not see each other again until her talk tomorrow.

That disappointed her. She wanted to hang out with them—and the dog—even longer.

"Hey, you guys care to join me for dinner tonight?"

She noticed that Piers looked at Ryan, as if he'd go along with whatever the other guy said. Too bad, in a way. She would rather have just invited Ryan, but those two seemed always to stick together. Sure, they had a common employer and common goal, but...

Well, in some ways it might be better not to get Ryan alone. She found the guy much too attractive.

"Sure," Ryan said. "There's someplace we need to go first, but we could meet you. Any ideas where?"

"Not really." She pulled her phone from her pocket and looked at the time. "It's about four now. How about if we meet around six, in the hotel lobby? We can ask there for a restaurant recommendation."

"Sounds good," Ryan said.

They walked in the same direction, toward the hotel, for a few blocks, but then the men excused themselves.

"See you later," Ryan said, and Piers reached for Rocky's leash.

Their splitting up then somehow made Maya feel a bit bereft. But she felt really good that she'd see Ryan later.

They could talk more then about what she would say in her presentation tomorrow. Could discuss wolves even more. Spend a little more time together, even with Piers present.

And as they left Maya figuratively kicked herself for even thinking such thoughts. Ryan and she might share a love of wildlife—but nothing else.

"So where are we going?" Piers asked. He had ceded the handle of Rocky's leash to Ryan, who now upped the speed of their walk along the street in a different direction from the way Maya had gone.

"I'm hungry." Ryan resisted the urge to pivot around to determine if he could still see Maya. He would see her later anyway. And how much trouble could she get into while in town? "I need some snacks. How about you?"

"Oh, then we're going to the grocery store to sound the Sharans out about…well, whatever info we can get from them, right?"

"You got it." Ryan turned back to aim a grin at his aide. They'd learned that Maya had visited the grocery store earlier that day and said hi to its owners, but she wouldn't have any idea of Ryan's suspicions about them.

She probably hadn't the slightest idea that shapeshifters even existed except in books, movies and TV, and that was a good thing.

He needed to make sure she stayed safe, didn't create any waves that would give more credence to the claims of the locals who weren't wildlife fans and that was all.

Except for learning what he really needed to know while here…

They'd reached the block containing the Corner Grocery Store. The place was crowded this late afternoon. Not good, Ryan thought.

Its owners might have less time to talk if they were busy handling customers.

On the other hand, he had some ideas of what to hint about that could get their attention—fast.

"It would be best if you wait outside with Rocky," he told Piers. "He might not be welcome, and he's also likely to be bumped or have his paws stepped on in that mob."

"Got it. We'll go for a walk. But call if there's anything you need." He accepted the end of Rocky's leash back from Ryan, who then headed inside.

He stopped first near the entrance, close to the few cashiers, then went around them to the heart of the place when he didn't see either of the Sharans.

For such a relatively small grocery, there seemed to be a good selection of all kinds of products, Ryan thought. The aisles were barely wide enough for carts going in opposite directions, and those he glanced at had a lot of stuff in them.

This probably wasn't the best time to buddy up to the owners—and hint strongly that tomorrow afternoon, around one thirty, they ought to be in the park again listening to Maya.

They'd been pro-wolves before, and should be again, but it was also a good thing for them to see their fellow locals' reactions once more, especially when Maya told them to stay away from wildlife around here for their own safety.

That should be something the Sharans promoted as well, whether or not they had anything to do with the attack on Fritts.

Or if they were the wolves who'd appeared ready to hurt Maya before he'd come along...

"Hello, can I help you?" A medium-sized guy with narrow shoulders who appeared to be in his early twenties had approached Ryan. Did he work here?

"Oh, I'm fine," Ryan said. "Just deciding what to look for." He paused. "And I had a couple of questions for the owners—the Sharans, right? I met them the other day."

"I'm their son, Pete," the guy said. He did in fact have his mother's light brown hair, not streaked as hers was but with a sheen to it—like a wolf's? His nose was longish, as well.

If he was their son, he was probably a shifter, too, assuming Ryan was correct and both older Sharans were. His scent suggested that as well, along with his physical resemblance to his parents.

Then Pete, too, should hear what Maya—and Ryan—had to say tomorrow.

And what had he done last night, while shifted beneath the full moon? Might he have been the one who'd attacked Morton Fritts?

"Good to meet you, Pete. Are you a champion of the latest presence of wolves in the area like your parents are? I met them at a talk given by a representative of WHaM the other day—Wildlife Habitat Monitoring. I'm Ryan Blaiddinger, and I work for US Fish and Wildlife." He held out his hand while studying Pete's face.

His expression froze for an instant as if he was shocked, or at least uncomfortable, at being approached by a wildlife proponent.

Was that because, as a shifter, too, he tried to keep his opinions to himself to avoid any kind of strife with regular humans?

Ryan didn't get the opportunity to push for an answer, though, since Kathie Sharan walked up and stood close to her son.

"Hi, Ryan," she said with a smile. "Welcome. I'm sure Pete's already asked, but can we help you find anything? As you can see, we've got a lot of stuff here—including people buying it." She blinked at her own joke, and Ryan gave a short laugh, turning his head to once again take in the crowd. He'd already noticed the many aromas of food—as well as the buzz of people talking. There were even scents of sweet, fresh baked goods in the air.

"Yes, I do see that. And I don't want to take up much of your time. Since I'm just visiting and staying in a hotel, I don't need much in the way of groceries except maybe some snacks. Jerky sticks, maybe, roast beef and bread for sandwiches, and some fruit. And I think I'll get some extra dog food for Rocky."

While he was in human form, he felt a lot happier eating produce than while he was shifted—although he rarely had to eat while shifted anyway. But he wasn't about to ask them for beef products that he might love to devour. He couldn't really store and cook in his hotel room. Beef jerky was okay as a snack. So was sliced roast beef. But neither were his favorite food. And he tended to feed Rocky high-quality dog food.

"Sure. Pete, why don't you show Ryan where those are?"

"Thanks," Ryan said. "Oh, and I just started to tell Pete about the next talk Maya is giving in the park tomorrow. I'll be there, too. Since we heard about what happened to Morton Fritts, she's going to be describing how everyone, even wildlife lovers like us, can stay safer—like not getting too near them. And I wonder how close you and your family get to wildlife, and people, at times like last night. Full moon and all, you can certainly see what's out there a bit better than on other nights."

He looked Kathie deeply in her dark brown eyes, reading the shock on her face. Her son must have seen it, too—or maybe he was just reacting to what Ryan said.

"We don't know what you're talking about," he said quickly, planting himself in front of his mother.

"Really? Maybe not." Ryan smiled, then stepped out

of the way as someone pushed a grocery cart a bit too close. "Although your even saying that suggests otherwise to me."

Their conversation, or maybe the way they were all regarding one another, apparently grabbed Burt Sharan's attention, since he was suddenly with them, as well.

"Is something wrong here?" the beefy guy demanded, his arms fisting at his sides.

"I don't think so," Ryan responded, although he knew the question hadn't been directed at him. "Just met your son, and I was telling Kathie and him that Maya plans to give another talk, this time about how to deal with wild wolves now that some are back in the area—hopefully to prevent any more incidents like the one with Morton Fritts. Although there's a possibility that couldn't happen again for about a month anyway."

He kept his expression innocent and calm as he looked straight into Burt's shocked face. "What are you talking about?"

"Just the possibility of different kinds of wolves showing up around here—not just gray wolves, for example, but…well, others, too."

Burt grabbed Ryan's arm in a rough grasp. "Look, if you're insinuating—"

"It's okay, dear," Kathie said. "I don't think Ryan means anything besides letting us know that he's on our side—on the side of everyone who appreciates wildlife, including whatever wolves happen to show up. Right, Ryan?"

He'd already reached down and pried Burt's hand away. "Exactly," he said. "But I really do think it would be a good thing for all of you to come to tomorrow's talk. Can I count on you?"

He looked first into Kathie's face, and though it was pale she had raised her chin and appeared strong. She nodded.

Ryan then glanced at Burt. His face was flushed, but he no longer looked angry. Worried, maybe. Which was probably a good thing.

"Yeah, I'll be there. Pete, too." Burt glanced at his son, who nodded.

Pete's expression was unreadable to Ryan, but that was okay since all three of them might be shifters.

And the talk tomorrow would be to benefit all wolves, no matter what their background.

But Ryan had a pretty good idea what their background was—and hoped to be able to get them to admit it.

Which might only happen when he admitted at least part of his own background, too.

Chapter 10

Maya chatted with the concierge in the lobby of the Washington Inn. His nametag said he was Larry, and he stood behind a tall stand with a computer on top—probably the way he researched things that guests wanted to know for which he didn't have answers. He had little hair to frame his unwavering and respectful smile.

Maya kept sneaking looks toward the stairway. Were Ryan, Piers and Rocky up in their rooms? She'd only arrived downstairs a few minutes ago, just before the time they'd said they would meet, and she didn't even know if they'd returned after their outing this afternoon. She hadn't changed her clothes, but her shirt, jeans and athletic shoes felt appropriate for the casualness of their arrangement.

"I'm not exactly sure what the people I'm going to dinner with will want," she told Larry. "Do you have any kind of restaurant list?"

"Nothing official, but I've got a pretty good sense for what's close by, if you can give me some idea—"

"Oh, I should know shortly." Maya had just spotted Piers and Rocky heading down the stairway. They were followed by Ryan. The men had changed from their climbing outfits but remained dressed as casually as Maya, both in sweatshirts and jeans.

They soon had maneuvered through the fairly empty lobby and joined Maya near the concierge stand.

"What kind of food would you guys like for dinner? And I'm not asking Rocky, since I think I know what he'd say." Maya grinned. Of course a wolf-dog would want some pretty heavy meat.

"How about some kind of steak house?" Ryan asked.

Maya supposed that the dog's owner could share some preferences with his pet but still found that kind of amusing.

"Fine with me." As much as she liked wildlife, she had considered becoming a vegetarian early on but decided against it—although she did limit her meat intake, often preferring more salads to heavy foods like steak.

Larry gave them the name of a nearby dog-friendly place called, appropriately, House of Steak, and handed them a town map, where he circled the location. In a few minutes, they were on their way. There weren't many others walking on the sidewalk, but the weather was fine, a fairly warm evening in September.

Once again, Maya enjoyed being with this group, and not just because Rocky resembled one of the kinds of animals she especially appreciated.

She found she also appreciated being with others who liked wildlife as much as she, but whom she hadn't met through WHaM. And the fact they brought that adorable, wolflike dog along nearly everywhere only added to her appreciation of them.

They were seated on a sparsely occupied patio as soon as they reached the restaurant. Rocky was the only dog present, but there were several other groups of people. Unsurprisingly, both men ordered steaks, which actually sounded good to Maya but she decided that a steak salad instead would be perfect for her. The men both ordered beer but she decided to stick with iced tea. They did, of course, request a bowl of water for Rocky.

When the server, a friendly and knowledgeable fellow, had left, Maya turned to Piers. "Why did you decide to join the US Fish and Wildlife Service? Obviously you care about wildlife, but why make it that official?"

She wanted to know the same from Ryan but thought it would be easier to ask Piers first to lead into the topic.

She caught the men trading glances that looked somehow strange, but only for a second. "My background is in science," Piers said. "I've always liked animals. I started out in the military, then decided to follow up this way."

"Same thing, basically, with me," Ryan said without her even having to ask him. She opened her mouth to ask for more detail but he continued, "And you? Why did you decide to join WHaM?"

This was something she loved to talk about. "The thing is, I'm a statistician by background, as well as a real animal lover. Even before, I loved observing and documenting and forecasting future numbers in different fields. But along the way I met other people as obsessed and adoring of wildlife as I am—so we got together and formed WHaM."

"Then you're one of the founders?" Ryan's tilted head

and smile suggested he was impressed, which made Maya feel even better.

"Yep," she said. "A group of us decided that an organization was needed to document and try to maximize restoration of native wildlife throughout the country. We discuss ideas with each other and, when appropriate, make suggestions to local governments. Of course we recognize the need to make sure that the influx of wildlife occurs as safely as possible for both animals and locals, so my talk tomorrow is entirely appropriate for me—and so was the one I gave yesterday."

"So what brought you here, to Washington?" Ryan asked. "Although I'll bet I can guess."

"I'll bet you can, too," she replied. "We're all so delighted about the return of wolves to this state and wanted to be part of it, though there aren't many yet and even fewer in this area. And some, in other areas, are unfortunately being disposed of for doing what comes naturally to them: hunting prey. But here I am, representing all of WHaM—and maybe all wolves, too!" She shot them both a smile—but noticed they glanced at each other again first. What was going on? She had to ask. "Do you two have some kind of opinion on WHaM or the wolves or whatever that you'd like to share with me? Or some kind of official opinion from Fish and Wildlife?"

"Not really, though of course the more we know about your organization, and the more your organization knows about Fish and Wildlife regulations and standards, the better for all of us—and the wolves here, too." Ryan spoke as if he was a government guy, which he was, and Maya saw Piers's head nodding, as well.

Their food arrived then. Maya wasn't surprised when both men cut pieces of meat from their steak and fed them to the now-sitting and clearly happy, tail-wagging Rocky.

For the rest of the meal, they talked in generalities, sometimes about this town and any sights to see, sometimes about transportation here from Sea-Tac, but never again anything personal about their backgrounds, even though Maya attempted now and then to turn the conversation gently back to that subject.

No matter. She enjoyed her salad—and she enjoyed the company.

She even kind of enjoyed it when Ryan took over the discussion and began telling her what she ought to cover in her talk the next day.

Most of what he said made sense.

But it was her talk. If she chose not to do it his way, too bad.

There was something about this woman that really resonated with Ryan.

Maybe it was her enthusiasm about wildlife—particularly wolves.

Maybe it was her intelligence. Her determination. Her jumping right into a situation that fascinated her and finding a way to share it with the world. The organization she had helped to create was now known by nearly everyone involved with wildlife preservation.

And maybe his appreciation of her was spiced up even more by his attraction to her—physically and otherwise.

For now, though, as they finished their meal, he had already donned his nonexistent cloak of being in command, thanks to his false job with the federal government.

He allowed that once more to be the reason he treated her to this meal—and Piers, too, of course.

"Thanks," Maya said as they stood to leave. "And thanks also for your suggestions about what I should say tomorrow."

The smile on her face, as cute and appealing as it was, seemed false, as if she wasn't overly excited about his ideas on how to give her presentation.

But he didn't mind. He liked the idea of her being her own woman—on behalf of wolves. And he would be there. If she got into anything she shouldn't, whether a topic or approach or anything else, he'd be able to channel her back in the right directions. Even correct her.

And he felt certain that she wouldn't appreciate it.

Their walk back to the hotel was at a nice, leisurely pace, partly because Maya asked to be the one to hold Rocky's leash again. Ryan's cover dog acted as he should, taking his time sniffing out everything and taking care of what he needed to this night before they went to bed.

The air was comfortably cool, and the streets in this small retail area were fairly quiet. In all, it was a very pleasant time.

"Have either of you ever been to Washington State before?" Maya asked as they neared their destination.

"I have, briefly, when I was a kid," Piers said. "My family took a sightseeing trip to the Seattle area. It was fun, but I never really thought about coming back again. Glad I'm here, though."

"This is my first time here," Ryan responded, "but I like it, or at least what I've seen of it so far. I may stick around even longer than I'd first planned."

Like, until the next full moon, thanks to his belief now that there actually were shifters in Fritts Corner.

Or maybe he would leave and come back.

But at the moment, staying as long as Maya did felt best, at least until that next full moon.

When they reached the hotel, Ryan opened the door to the otherwise empty lobby. "Is Rocky staying with you tonight?" he asked Piers—another way of telling his aide that Rocky *was* staying with him that night.

"Sure thing. Good night, you two." Piers took the end of the leash from Maya and tugged gently till Rocky followed him up the stairs—but not before Piers aimed a knowing smile toward Ryan.

A very suggestive smile, but Ryan had no intention of doing anything but acting gentlemanly and seeing Maya to her room.

To the door of her room, and that was all.

They walked up the steps together, side by side. Ryan had an urge to reach over and take her hand—to steady her on the steps—but he knew it would be a bad idea to touch her at all.

He managed to share glances with her now and then on their climb. Was there something in her gaze besides friendliness and appreciation of someone else who liked wolves?

He thought so. And the heat, the interest, he thought he saw there turned him on…no matter how inappropriate that was.

He tried to make his thoughts back off—*tried* being the operative word.

"It's only been a few days since I arrived here," Maya said, her upward pace slow but deliberate, "but it feels as if I've been here much longer." The smile she shot at him was sexy as well as sweet.

"Is that a good or bad thing?" Ryan asked. They reached the hallway to the third floor, where Maya's room was. He again resisted the urge to take her hand. No reason at all to try to steady her.

"Good, I think. And I hadn't planned to stay long, but I may extend it depending on how things go at my new talk tomorrow. If people seem to take the position I do, that wildlife is wonderful but shouldn't be approached for one's own safety, that's great. But I'd still like to know what really happened with Morton Fritts."

"Me, too," Ryan said, really meaning it. Well, he would find out somehow, maybe tomorrow and maybe not, but one way or another he needed to know.

At her doorway, Maya reached into the small purse she carried and extracted her room key—an actual key in this older place. She unlocked her door.

Ryan was about to tell her good-night and suggest they meet for breakfast again tomorrow—when she grabbed his hand and yanked him inside.

In moments, her arms were around him and he couldn't help but reciprocate. Their kiss was hot and long and damn sexy, with her pushing hard against him and teasing him with her tongue.

For a moment, he found himself eager to accompany her across the room to her bed.

But then reality set in. He certainly hadn't brought any protection along, and he wasn't about to make love with this amazingly sexy woman without making sure no offspring resulted.

Although the idea of surprising this wildlife lover with the kind of offspring they'd conceive…

No way!

Reluctantly but with determination he ended the kiss, even as his mouth, and the rest of his body, ached for more.

"Wow," he said, smiling down at her, appreciating

the surprise on her sensual, clearly stimulated face. "Wow," he repeated. "Now that's a great way to say good-night. So, good night, Maya. Let's grab breakfast together in the morning again, okay? Same time as today?"

Before she could respond, he hurried out the door.

And wondered if he would be able to sleep that night—or if his body would be aching for what had been more than hinted about here, but he'd unfortunately had to end.

Chapter 11

The hallway on her floor was empty when Maya finally left her room the next morning to head downstairs and meet her breakfast companions.

She had taken her time getting ready so she was running a little late. She'd even considered calling Ryan to tell him she was going to skip the meal.

Mostly, she wanted to skip seeing him, thanks to her confusion over his reaction to their kiss the previous night. Only…well, the problem was that she did want to see him. Maybe look him straight in those deep brown eyes and attempt to figure out if her attraction to him was wholly one-sided.

She hadn't thought so, but…

Well, it wasn't like her to be so forward, either. Maybe he'd done her a favor.

She walked more briskly down the steps until she

reached the lobby and looked around. Sure enough, the men and dog were waiting for her near the door.

Should she apologize for being late?

No. In a way, it was Ryan's fault—although she couldn't exactly explain it even to him, let alone to Piers.

She made her way through the small lobby crowd till she reached them—and neither man looked at her immediately. They were apparently engaged in conversation, something about what they should be looking for around here.

Here? In the lobby? In town?

Maybe they didn't even realize she wasn't on time. Of course, it was only five minutes past when they'd agreed to meet, which wasn't particularly bad, but still—

"Hi," she said, not looking at either of them but kneeling to give Rocky a big hug. She appreciated the fuzzy, warm feel of the dog, and the way he nuzzled her face. Too bad she couldn't just opt to spend time with him this morning and not the others.

When she stood again and saw both men looking at her, she tried to read the expression on Ryan's face. Maybe she was seeing what she hoped to, but she thought she saw a hint of regret, maybe sadness.

Yeah, and maybe she saw an expression like a scolded dog on his face, too.

"So, you guys ready to eat?" she asked.

"Sure," Piers responded. "Same place as yesterday?"

"Fine with me." Maya pivoted to head out the door. She assumed Ryan would follow.

Instead, he rushed slightly ahead and pushed open the door in front of her. Outside, he positioned himself beside her on the sidewalk as they headed in the direction of the restaurant.

"Good morning," he finally said. "Did you sleep well?"

"Very well, thanks," she responded, inserting a happy lilt into her voice as if their final contact last night had meant nothing to her. "How about you?"

"Well enough," was all he said.

Which was a big, fat lie, Ryan thought as he slowed his pace to stay right beside Maya on the narrow but fortunately nearly empty sidewalk. So what else was new? He was used to lying for all sorts of reasons, especially to regular humans. Why should things be different now?

The thing was, his body told him for a long time into the night that he should have done more with Maya, since she seemed to be interested in him, too.

Yeah, your human body, he kept reminding himself—and also how she was likely to react if she ever learned who and what he really was.

They soon reached the restaurant. Once again there was a bit of a wait, and this morning eavesdropping was not likely to be especially productive. No strangers around here were likely to be discussing howls and wolves. Even so, they were soon seated.

They all ordered food similar to the prior morning's. And once they'd told their server what they wanted, Ryan made a few additional suggestions about how Maya should address her talk that afternoon. Strong suggestions. Dictated it a bit more, whether or not she liked that. Heck, it was for her own benefit.

Not to mention his—and the other wolves around town, natural or shifters.

Once they had coffee and their server had left, Ryan was amused when Maya looked him straight in the eye and said, "I know why you wanted to spend some time with me this morning."

Of course she would after that kiss last night…but that's not what she meant. Her expression was neutral—at least if he ignored what looked like a minor combo of heat and irritation in her lovely hazel eyes. Or was he just reading into them what he expected to see?

"Tell me why." He donned a mask of what he hoped looked like humor without much emotion—despite the inappropriate warmth he felt just being in her presence, especially here, at breakfast, with his aide and cover dog and a whole room full of diners around them.

"You want to try to figure out whether I intend to give the talk you want me to this afternoon. Well, it's my decision—and here's what I'm going to say."

Maya began expounding again on the thrill of having wolves in the area, and speculations about what might have happened the other night—not mentioning her own meet-up with canines, he noticed—and the reports on a person having been injured by a wolf after possibly trying to find the source of the howls.

"After that, I'll get into what WHaM is about again—keeping track of wildlife and appreciating it, and hope-fully getting other people to appreciate it, too. Plus, maintaining as good a census as possible."

She paused as their server reappeared with food and more coffee. Beside Ryan, Rocky stood up and all but put his nose on the table, so both he and Piers gave the beggar a little of their own breakfasts.

As he did so, Ryan said to Maya, "Sounds exactly like what I'd suggest so far, but I assume there's more."

"Of course there's more," Maya asserted. A lot more, she thought—but she'd get into only part of it here. "That's when I'll again stress how wonderful our coun-try is," she continued, "with its wildlife free in a lot of areas to exist and thrive and be there for us, sometimes, to see. But the threatened and endangered animals need to be kept safe. And for that to happen, people who are interested in them have to use their supposedly more intelligent human brains and remember not to get too close. After all, we call them *wild*life for a reason." She gave a sharp nod as she stressed that first syllable. And then she opened her mouth to continue with her approach, what she wanted to say, how she wanted to convince people—

But Ryan interrupted. "I like it all. I know you'll do a great job." His eyes met hers, and despite her mouth still being open and her slight irritation at having been stopped, she felt warm inside. Appreciated.

"Thank you," she said softly, swallowing the rest of her ideas. "And—"

"And we'll be there, of course, to cheer you on," Piers added. Maya dragged her gaze away from Ryan to look at him.

"Thanks," she said again.

"Plus, we may contribute to what you say," Ryan added. "And help keep the audience under control as they cheer you."

Which made Maya feel even warmer. She hoped all would go well that afternoon.

Maybe with Ryan and Piers there, and Rocky, too, it would.

Breakfast was over soon, though the guys hadn't seemed to be in a particular hurry. Even so, after Maya had taken the time to let everyone in the restaurant know about her next upcoming talk, they all soon left. At least this time she didn't have to fight very hard to ensure she could pay her own bill, although they didn't allow her to treat them.

Well, maybe next time.

She felt rather sad when they said goodbye to her outside the door. "We'll see you at your talk this afternoon," Ryan said, and then the men and Rocky started down the sidewalk without asking where she was heading or inviting her to join them.

Oh, well. She had a goal of sorts in mind, although she wasn't sure how to fulfill it.

It wasn't enough just to let this morning's restaurant patrons know about her talk. She had to at least go visit the people in town who'd seemed interested in what she'd said before. Interested in wildlife protection.

Too bad she didn't know where that Trev was staying. She'd like to let him know, too. He'd at least stood up for her and WHaM before.

For the next half hour, she walked the streets of Fritts Corner, stopping in the Corner Grocery Store and other establishments, letting the owners know and inviting them to come to her talk.

When she figured it was almost time to head for the park, she saw Trev across the street, alone this time and not with the girl she'd seen him with the other day.

She waited till the street was empty of moving cars, then crossed.

"Hey, Trev," she called but didn't really have to since he had apparently seen her, too, and was waiting for her. Today his button-down shirt was blue, his light, short hair was messy, and he grinned geekily at her once more. "I hope you have some time this afternoon," she told him, and quickly explained why.

"Keeping the audience under control will be the big thing," Ryan said to Piers later as they stood beside the aging podium. Maya was already at it, getting her presentation together and preparing to show slides again on the screen behind her.

Right now, that part of the park was filling up with a lot of people, and Ryan recognized quite a few.

Any media folks? He wasn't sure but didn't think he saw any who'd admitted to it at Maya's last presentation, and no one appeared to be preparing to take notes and pictures.

Some of those present had been in the restaurant that morning, though. He'd been somewhat amused when, after they'd finished eating, Maya had insisted on circling the tables and inviting the patrons to come hear a talk this afternoon all about the wonders of wildlife— and how to protect oneself, too.

In fact, Piers and he had joined in, and Rocky's presence had garnered a lot of attention that indicated the people they spoke with actually had an interest in attending.

Some had mentioned coming back since they enjoyed Maya's last presentation.

But when they were done, Ryan had gotten Piers and Rocky headed back to their hotel. He'd have liked to stay with Maya but they had some Alpha Force business to attend to.

And he'd known he would see her soon. Here. In the park.

In fact, they'd already met up with her, right where they expected she would be.

"Wow!" she said. "There are a lot of people here already and I don't start for another ten minutes."

Ryan looked up at the podium to see that Maya had stopped fussing with the materials in front of her and began looking at the grounds. Her eyes looked huge, as if she was a bit nervous, but then she smiled.

"Guess I'd better do a good job," she added.

"Guess you'd better." Ryan made his tone sound stern, but when she caught his eye he grinned. "And I'm sure you will."

She seemed to relax a little as she got back to organizing her stuff. And Ryan looked around.

"She's right," Piers said. "And so are you." He stood near Ryan, with Rocky sitting on the lawn beside him looking interested and alert.

"Of course I am," Ryan responded. "You should know that."

He was teasing, of course, but that was a sort of reminder that, in their real life and job, Piers was his aide. Not that Piers ever needed a reminder. He had even taken charge of typing on his computer the list of to-do thoughts Ryan had dictated to him back at their hotel before—mundane stuff in addition to the way he assisted in Ryan's shifts. Now, he just raised his eyebrows at his superior officer, who smiled and looked down toward Rocky.

"Good boy," Ryan said soothingly to his cover dog, who remained still but tense as he sat there. Did Rocky capture the smell of shifters in this group? At least for now, Ryan didn't.

But as he had hoped, the whole Sharan family was there—Burt and Kathie and their son, Pete. At the moment, they all stood off toward the edge of the crowd, with some other folks Ryan recognized from the earlier presentation and otherwise, including bar owner Buck Lesterman. They were too far away from him to catch their scents unless he'd been in wolf form.

There were aromas around him, though: the freshness of the grass, some forest smells from the hills rising beyond them, too many perfumes and aftershaves worn by the growing crowd—and canine scents, since some of those people had also brought their dogs to the park for this talk.

A couple of the larger dogs—maybe a Great Dane mix and a Doberman—seemed interested in getting close to Rocky and tugged at their leashes, but their owners kept them well enough under control that they didn't approach. Rocky was aware of them, though, looking in their direction and keeping his nose working.

Good wolf-dog that he was, he didn't pull at his own leash and remained sitting between the two men who were his pack. Ryan kept his hand gently on Rocky's head to reward him.

As they stood there, Ryan noted that guy who'd been at Maya's last presentation and seemed too interested in her afterward now making his way through the crowd. What was his name? Oh, yeah, Trev. But Ryan didn't want to sound as if he cared if some other fellow flirted with her.

Even though, despite how dumb it was, he did care.

The September day was warm and a little humid but not particularly uncomfortable. It seemed a good day for an outdoor presentation.

And Ryan settled in to listen as Maya started to speak. The microphone worked well, and her voice resonated loudly enough so that Ryan believed everyone here could hear her. It seemed quite loud to his own enhanced hearing, and yet he welcomed it.

Welcomed her, and her attitude, and—

He forced himself to stop that train of thought and listen to the wonderful ideas emanating from her.

He'd already become attracted to her aroma, slightly floral and all woman...

"So who here heard the wolves the other night?" she

was asking. Her arms seemed to hug the podium's stand as she leaned forward against it and scanned the crowd.

Ryan had a sudden recollection of her hugging him last night but shrugged it off as he, too, looked over the small sea of people. A lot had hands raised, including the Sharans and Lesterman and Trev, and a few called out replies like "Me!" and "I did."

"That's so great!" Maya said. She launched into some of the talk she had presented the other day, about how wolves had disappeared from this area ages ago and were only now reappearing in small numbers. They remained particularly rare in this part of Washington, and all were protected under the law.

The audience seemed interested, even though what Maya was saying now wasn't anything new. What she was showing on the screen behind her, though, included some shots of the area Ryan recognized as where she had gone in the middle of the night after hearing the wolves.

And showed first the two wolves that seemed ready to attack her, then joined by a third wolf.

Him.

Ryan attempted not to react. He should have anticipated that, since he'd seen her wielding her camera and knew she had taken video clips. If she knew what she was doing, it was easy enough to pull still shots out. And she clearly knew what she was doing.

As long as she didn't confront any more wolves…

And hopefully she wouldn't. She now began talking about how wonderful it was as an officer of WHaM to be able to potentially see and count wolves around here.

She didn't admit she'd already seen any or where she had gotten those pictures.

"But the thing is, even those of us who are real wildlife advocates have to understand, and remember, that wildlife is wild. I say that often, and I mean it. The animals, especially these wolves, are wonderful, and we all love seeing them, but we nevertheless have to be careful. If we get too close, they don't understand that we appreciate them, want to see them and get to know them better and all. They could get frightened, consider us enemies and attack. That means we should never get too near them. Appreciate them, yes. Approach them, no."

She had the grace to look away from the audience and down toward Ryan, as if looking for his reaction—and approval.

He smiled a bit grimly as a reminder to her that what she was saying worked for her, too, and nodded.

"Okay, then. I'm going to start describing a few scenarios that could happen under present circumstances, where potentially dangerous but oh, so wonderful wildlife is present in an area and what you should do to protect yourselves. First of all, did any of you see those wolves that were howling and barking the other night?"

No one raised their hands, not even the Sharans. Smart to lie about that, though, if they did happen to be shifters.

Or maybe he was all wrong and they weren't, in fact, shifters—although he doubted that. As a shifter himself, even before he had heard of Alpha Force and joined it and gotten access to the elixir, he and his family had been well aware of others, some who mixed with them in the remote area of Wyoming where he had grown up, and others who had stayed to themselves.

The old-timers knew who they were, in any case—even when they had just moved to the area. And Ryan's own parents and grandparents had given him pointers on how to figure that out, such as recognizing the special scents that shifters might give off even when in human form.

It didn't really matter what the Sharans admitted—or didn't. One way or another, whether he remained here or returned, Ryan would be here during the time of the next full moon and hang around them enough to see for himself if they were shifters.

Since sighting of wolves was fairly new to this area, any shifters were newcomers, too. They might already know how to protect themselves, but if Ryan, and Alpha Force, could help them, all the better.

But for now, he would hang around at least long enough to—

Hey. Maya was still talking, asking the audience to respond to various scenarios she was creating in which wolves might become too close to people, but the crowd was parting close to the podium.

Coming closer was someone who had apparently not just been in some fictional scenario, but had actually been attacked.

At the forefront was Morton Fritts, followed by his wife, Vinnie and by their wolf-hating friend, Carlo Silling.

They were stealing attention away from Maya, which wasn't surprising in this crowd that mostly consisted of locals who would know who Morton was—and what had happened to him. And Morton wasn't walking fast but appeared to be limping.

Rocky seemed to sense the tension in the crowd and stood. Piers had a good hold on his leash and looked at Ryan, who shook his head slightly to express his concern but tell his aide to stand down for now.

Maya finally saw what was happening and stopped talking. She seemed to hesitate for a minute, and Ryan quickly weighed whether he could help her better by joining her or staying where he was.

She sort of removed the choice from him when she began talking. "Oh, my goodness. I'm afraid we have an example of what can happen to people who meet a wolf under bad circumstances. Morton, I'm so glad to see you here and hope you're okay."

That was appropriate and sympathetic, yet it sounded sort of like an invitation for him to talk, Ryan figured. And apparently so did Morton.

He reached the far side of the podium from where Ryan stood, and Carlo helped him climb the couple of steps. Ryan got closer to the steps on the other side but didn't go up them—yet.

Morton wore a long-sleeved T-shirt and jeans that hid any of his injuries beneath. But his face was injured, too. The damage could have been bites or claw marks; Ryan wasn't certain.

Maya started talking again into her microphone but Morton grabbed it from her. "What the hell are you doing here again?" he shouted into it, glaring at Maya. "And saying things about how people should be welcoming wolves back to this area? I could have been killed by the one that attacked me. I was just trying to find it, see where one of the animals that was making noise that night was hiding out, and it leaped out at me. And there were more around, too. Wolves back here? That's dangerous. Horrible. And I'm going to do my damnedest to make sure the local laws are changed and we can kill them the way that one tried to kill me."

Chapter 12

"No!" Maya shouted, then took a deep breath as she scrambled to think of what to say next. "No," she repeated, still yelling since she no longer had the microphone. "I'm so sorry about what happened to you. But we need to find ways to get along with the wolves, stay away from them, not kill them. We—"

She was surprised to see a young man who looked familiar join them up on the podium and wrest the mic from Morton, who appeared equally surprised. Staring at Morton, he interrupted her. "Don't the laws of this country mean anything to you, like protection of endangered animals? Don't— Never mind. Why don't you tell everyone here exactly how you supposedly were attacked by that wolf the other night."

Supposedly? From what Maya could see, Morton did look injured. And even though she hated to admit it to herself, his injuries could have been inflicted by a wolf. His middle-aged face had clearly been mauled, and he had been walking slowly enough to indicate that it wasn't only his face that had been hurt.

Even so…

Well, she could have shared a lot with Morton, maybe for the same reasons, if it hadn't been for chance—like that other wolf appearing and shooing the others away.

But she would never have complained about it if she'd survived. She would have realized she had brought it on herself.

And this man? Was he going to do as asked and tell what had happened?

Maya glanced past the others on the podium toward the crowd below. Some people she recognized from the restaurant were there, as were a few of the store-keepers. Trev was there, too. Unsurprisingly, they all seemed to stare toward the two men who now occupied the podium with her. But no one else said anything. Not yet, at least.

Then there were Ryan and Piers. Ryan watched what was going on with a grim but very interested expression.

Piers was working with Rocky who, for the first time since Maya had met the lovely wolf-dog, appeared almost out of control, as if he, too, wanted to join her up here with the quarreling men.

At the moment, the young man was trying to thrust the microphone back into Morton's hands. "Here," he kept saying. "Tell us."

"Yeah, I will," Morton said, finally grabbing the mic. He spoke into it. "I heard those howls and other sounds like everyone else in town. Like all of you, I was curious. Yeah, I'm not a tree hugger or animal freak but figured I should find out what was going on, so I drove as far as I could to where I thought I'd heard the wolves." He turned to point toward the nearby roadway that looped somewhat around the forested hillside behind them. "I parked, got out of my car and went to look for them." He turned to glare at Maya. "And before you ask, I brought a flashlight and a large stick to defend myself. That's all. No gun, which I regret now."

The rest of his story sounded both familiar and somewhat heartrending to Maya. He'd found a pathway, followed it up to a clearing—which could have been the one where they'd found the patch of possible blood just off it. Looked around, saw nothing, then decided to head back down.

"But before I did, I heard noise in the underbrush and suddenly a big, ugly wolf leaped out. Kind of like that thing." He pointed off the podium toward Rocky, who was standing now, and Maya saw that Piers had him restrained close beside him. Now, he hugged Rocky even closer as Morton continued to stare at the dog.

"So didn't you just walk away from him?" the young man asked. "Run away? Go back down the path and leave?"

"Hell, no. Not that I could have. He got close to me, too close, and then, before I could hit him with my stick, he leaped up on me and I wound up on the ground."

"That's not—"

"And then he bit me. My legs. My side. My face." Morton's voice shook and his eyes seemed to stare into the distance.

"But—"

Morton seemed to pull himself together and aim his rage at the other man. "You think it was fun? Or I should just suck it up and forget what happened? Well,

no way. Forget that. I don't want it to happen to anyone
else, and neither should you."

With that, he shoved the microphone back at the
other guy and headed toward the steps at the edge of
the podium. Vinnie and Carlo helped him down the
steps.

The young man looked at the mic in his hand, then
spoke into it. "Er—look, everybody. I'm relatively new
to town, and so's my family. I'm Pete Sharan, and my
parents are right there." He pointed toward the edge of
the crowd where the grocery store owners stood. "I just
don't believe what that man said. I've studied wildlife
for a long time, especially wolves. And unless they're
in protective mode, to take care of themselves or their
families, they mostly just run away when there are humans around. They don't trust humans."

"Right. They don't trust us? Well, we don't trust
them, either." That was Carlo Silling shouting from
where he now stood nearby with the Frittses. "Kill 'em
all. That's what we need to do."

Pete Sharan looked as if he was about to leap down
from the podium and attack the other man, so Maya
drew closer. Arguing here, or, worse, getting into a
physical altercation, wouldn't solve anything.

She reached out and gently pulled the mic from Pete's
hand, at the same time touching his arm as if soothing
him. Or at least easing his temper—hopefully.

"I agree with you," she said into the mic so that others could hear her despite how softly she spoke. "But
we don't know all the circumstances. Despite what
Mr. Fritts said, that wolf could have been in protection mode. Mr. Fritts might just not have seen what
scared the poor animal. It's terrible that he was hurt,
of course, but—"

"But the damn wolves have to go!" That came from someone else in the audience, a person Maya didn't think she'd met.

The call was echoed by others, and Maya felt as if she wanted to cry.

Pete Sharan did cry out. "No! You people just don't understand. They're not—"

Ryan was suddenly on the podium with them. He was the next to take control of the microphone.

"Please listen, everyone. I'm Ryan Blaiddinger of the US Fish and Wildlife Service. What happened to Mr. Fritts is, of course, terrible. I'll report it to my agency. But we need more information, as Mr. Sharan said. We want to prevent anything like this from happening again, and going after any kind of protected animal, like wolves, is not permitted except by obtaining an official exemption under the law. My colleague and I will conduct an investigation while we're here, but in the meantime everyone needs to listen to what Ms. Everton said before. No one is denying that there are wolves around. We all need to stay safe—and that means staying away from them. Now, let's all go to our homes or hotels and get out of here."

Maya wanted to hug Ryan not only for what he said, but also because he glared at the people who'd been arguing to kill the wolves, including Morton Fritts.

She could understand his rage, his desire to do something to the wolf that injured him.

But all wolves?

That man needed to be watched.

Something was going to happen.

Staring down at the crowd, Ryan could sense it—and not as a result of his enhanced natural senses.

But he saw the glares that the Fritts side leveled against the Sharans and other townsfolk who supported Maya and what she said and the return of the wolves.

He saw the equally hostile glares shot back in return.

He felt the anger. The emotions. He thought he understood why, at least from the Sharans' perspective—assuming he was correct in what and who they were.

He assumed that the Frittses' antagonism was partly because of the attack on Morton, yet he felt it was somehow more than that. That faction had been upset by the influx of wolves to the area even before.

Why?

"May I?" He heard Maya's whisper from beside him and looked down. She regarded him quizzically, her head cocked as one hand reached for the microphone. Before he could respond, tell her he had more to say— did he?—she added, "I just want to finish up here." How could he say no? He handed over the mic.

She thanked him with a nod, then said into the device, "Once again, I tell you all to be careful and stay away from any wolves you happen to see or hear—but please let me know about them, or let Ryan know, so WHaM and Fish and Wildlife can follow up. And now, I thank you all and say goodbye. Enjoy the sounds of the wolves—and stay safe."

Then she shut off the mic and placed it back on the stand.

"This is becoming even worse," she said to Ryan. "Dangerous. The two sides are getting even further apart, at least somewhat because of that attack on Fritts. I'm not sure how to handle this, how to protect the wolves. Can you feds do anything to make it better?"

"The wolves are protected here under the law," he

said, staring right into her lovely, troubled eyes. "You know that. Under some circumstances we might capture and relocate them, but not now. And if we started searching for them, we would most likely have to look for the one that attacked Fritts and put it down if we found it. Maybe we should do that anyway, but for now I intend to let it go, as long as that's the end of it. But we all—you and us—want to see how things progress with the wolves now that they've returned to this area. We just need to try to ensure there are no further incidents."

At least the likelihood was that, if the wolf who'd attacked Fritts was a shifter, there'd be nothing else that could happen for a month.

But if it had been a feral wolf?

"I… I understand," Maya said hoarsely, and he wished he could sweep her into his arms and hold her tightly to comfort her. And maybe to comfort himself, as well.

This hadn't been what he had anticipated when Alpha Force had sent him here to investigate the slow influx of wolves and determine if any happened to be shifters. He had thought he would be here simply observing, in whichever form made sense at any particular time.

But now? Now he had an urge to protect. Who? Individuals of many kinds: wolves, and those who cared for them, and people who turned into them. And the wolf who had attacked Fritts? If it was feral and ferocious, was it legal not to put it down? He didn't know, didn't want to find out.

"Okay." He put a dose of strength and encouragement into his voice. "It's time for us to leave. Good presentation, by the way. You handled Morton's interruption well. Now, we'll wait and see what happens."

"Right." She clearly tried to shake off her anxiety, too. She started toward the steps.

And stopped. Ryan saw why immediately. The Fritts group was gathered at the bottom, facing one another and talking. They seemed to block any ability to get by them.

That didn't deter Maya for long. Ryan attempted to place himself in front of her but she walked down the few stairs and said, "Excuse me," edging her way around them.

"No, you are not excused," Vinnie Fritts asserted, planting herself in Maya's path. "Do you want more people hurt by those terrible creatures?"

"I am very sorry about what happened to your husband." Maya's voice sounded exasperated, as if she didn't like repeating what she had already said. "But really, I'm not sure we know the whole story. And even if we do—well, it was a regrettable incident but that doesn't mean anyone who does as I said, and stays far away if they happen to believe a wolf is nearby, will also get hurt."

"You bitch!" Vinnie shouted. "Are you calling my husband a liar?"

"I. Did. Not. Say. That." Ryan admired how Maya spoke slowly and with determination. "I'm sure the circumstances were very difficult for him and may have affected his memory of what happened. But—"

"You'd better watch out!" That was Morton, who'd come around his wife to confront Maya. "I told you what happened and that I was curious, yes, but didn't purposely get near a damned wolf." He was getting too near Maya, though, his fists clenched as if threatening her.

Ryan hurriedly put himself between Maya and the

others. "I think we've gone as far with this as we're going to. We all know the situation. Everyone feels bad about what happened to Morton."

Although it couldn't have happened to a more appropriate person, Ryan thought. He deserved to be whipped by a wolf, shifter or not. But what had happened not only put the influx of wolves into the spotlight, but also potentially endangered them even more.

"But," he continued, "we're through here. Morton is unlikely to identify the wolf, and there's not going to be a change in their protected status because of this incident." Especially since Ryan wasn't convinced that Morton had explained it truthfully in the first place. "We are all sorry, but glad that Morton is recovering." He glared from husband to wife, then turned to Maya, grabbed her hand and began walking to the area at the far side of the podium where Piers stood with Rocky.

This afternoon's event had definitely come to an end. Or had it?

Piers asked Maya some questions about what she was planning to do next on WHaM's behalf, and as she began answering how she would keep her organization informed Ryan looked around. The Sharan group remained at the edge of the park area nearest where the forest began and rose up the hillside.

He focused his attention on them, wishing his hearing was as acute now as when he was shifted. Multiple conversations also made it harder to hear.

But Ryan believed he caught a few words—like *careful*. And *avoid*. And *protect*.

Interesting and appropriate, but inconclusive.

It was time to pay another visit to the Corner Grocery Store. He had more conversations to conduct with the Sharans, and a lot more to learn about them.

* * *

What was going to happen now? Maya wondered as she walked back toward the hotel with the two men and their dog.

She hadn't planned on staying in Fritts Corner for long. All she had intended was to visit on behalf of WHaM and try to rev up all the locals she could about the wonderful situation they had here, while she determined the best way to conduct a census.

Now, she wished she had a way to ensure the wolves' protection.

Could she count on Ryan and Piers and the Fish and Wildlife Service?

She wanted to. She liked Ryan, in particular. A lot.

But his being a sexually attractive guy who also cared about wildlife didn't mean he could work miracles. And ensuring the wolves' survival, their thriving, could wind up requiring a miracle.

"Will you join us for dinner again tonight?"

That was Piers, who walked on her right. The men had been kind enough to let her hold Rocky's leash again, and the dog was on her left.

They followed Ryan, who took the lead. Again. She had the sense the guy was always happy to be in charge.

This time it had been a good idea.

At Piers's invitation, she looked forward toward Ryan. Had he heard? Did he want her with them?

He kept walking at first. But when she hesitated and said, "Well, I'm not sure—" Ryan turned.

"Of course you're sure," he said. "You're joining us. We wolf-lovers need to stick together." The warmth in his gaze suggested that he wanted them to stay in each other's company for more reasons than because they were wildlife aficionados.

Or was she reading too much into it?

In any event, they made plans to meet at six o'clock in the hotel lobby, where they parted now after reaching their inn midafternoon.

Maya headed upstairs, exhausted and needing time devoted to something other than her beloved job. Or did she? She got on her computer a short while after reaching her room and found herself searching the internet for all she could find about the US Fish and Wildlife Service. And when she got onto the site, she tried searching for Ryan Blaiddinger.

She didn't find him, which wasn't a big surprise since many directorships and positions were referenced but seldom those who held them.

But when she Googled him next, she learned something very interesting.

Not that it made any difference, but she decided not to mention it immediately. But it amused her...and made her wonder.

Maya decided she would at least attempt to rest before dinner, but a while after she'd reached her room, as she tried to relax, the hotel room phone rang. She stood from the chair she had planted herself in and picked up the receiver from the small desk next to the TV monitor. "Hello?"

"Hi, Maya? This is Trev. I was at your talk before."

And he hadn't done or said anything helpful in favor of protecting the wolves.

"How did you find me here?" she asked.

"Well—" He sounded rather sheepish. "I... I wanted to talk to you so I kind of followed when you left the park."

She wasn't surprised. "Okay," she said, though she

wasn't particularly pleased. "But why? And why are you calling?"

She half expected him to fumble around but ask her for a date. She felt half-sorry for him. Maybe the other woman he'd been talking to had shown no interest, or had dumped him.

But Maya wasn't about to make him think he had a chance with her.

"Would you mind coming down to the hotel lobby and grabbing some coffee with me? I really want to find out more about WHaM. Maybe I could even come up with some suggestions for dealing with that guy who was mauled by a wolf."

Really? She couldn't imagine how, but she didn't know this guy's background. Maybe he actually could be of some use. After all, he'd said he had come to town to hear her speak about WHaM.

"All right," she said. "I'll be down in a minute."

"So what are your intentions regarding Ms. Everton?" Piers was in Ryan's room along with Rocky, waiting for a call back from Drew. "You seem to be watching and talking with her a lot. Any reason beside her love of wolves?" His eyebrows were raised, and Ryan's aide seemed amused.

"That's the main reason," Ryan said. "And don't start reading anything into it other than I want to make sure she remains safe. Sure, she's hot, but the thing that concerns me is that she's willing to stick her nonwolfen nose into anything that—"

His phone rang, relieving Ryan a bit. Piers was right. Ryan felt much too attracted to Maya, even though he hadn't acted on it. Not yet, at least.

The caller ID identified Drew Connell. "Hi, Drew,"

he said, pressing the button to turn his phone's speaker on. "Just called to give you an update."

And confirm with their commanding officer that they'd be hanging out there, under the circumstances, potentially a lot longer.

"So what did you think of what happened at my presentation?" Maya asked.

She sat across from Trev at a tiny table for two at a coffee shop attached to the hotel. A few of the tables around them were empty, but the shop was fairly busy for being this late in the afternoon.

"I didn't know what to think of it." Trev lifted his cup of frothy latte to his narrow lips and took a sip. His small brown eyes were trained on her face, though, making her feel uncomfortable.

She reached down for her cup of plain black coffee and just held it for now. "Well, I'd heard about Morton Fritts's injuries before," she said. "And I can understand his being upset by it. His family, too. But I gathered from what he said that he wished he had shot that wolf—and maybe that all wolves in this area should now be killed. That's definitely too much. Don't you think? Do you agree with that other guy, Pete, who came up on the podium, too? I do. Despite what Mr. Fritts asserted, we really don't know the full set of circumstances, and no one should rush to conclusions that the wolf was at fault."

Trev at least appeared to be pro-wildlife before. And if he wasn't, why would he have come here just because he had heard Maya was giving a talk on behalf of wildlife for WHaM?

"I sort of understand the Frittses' position," he said plaintively. "Pete's, too, and yours, and that Ryan's. But mostly—well, what is WHaM's position when some-one, a person, is hurt by a protected wolf, or another wild animal that it is in favor of protecting? Or was in favor of protecting before the injury? Do you always assume the animal wasn't just a vicious and danger-ous creature?"

"It depends on the circumstances," Maya stated. "As I've said since I got here, wildlife is wild. People should understand and respect that, and stay out of the animals' way. Allow them to flee if they're scared, rather than challenging them. I still don't completely understand how Morton and that wolf wound up confronting each other, but my assumption is that Morton should simply have recognized that a wolf is a wolf and backed off. Don't you think?"

"So that's WHaM's position?" Trev put down his latte and looked at Maya. His expression was almost accusatory.

Not that she knew the guy at all, but she was a little surprised. He'd seemed to be a wildlife advocate, or so she'd believed. And so far, he'd just seemed like a nice, nerdy guy.

On the other hand, it wouldn't be surprising if he liked people better than the animals and was torn by this kind of situation.

"Yes," she said, "although no one at WHaM is in favor of animals attacking people, or even attacking other animals except as prey for food. But the real-ity is that those kinds of things happen. Even animals recognize that others in or out of their species may be prone to attack or kill in some circumstances. People certainly should recognize it."

Trev leaned back a little, once more lifting his latte to his mouth. He appeared a bit pensive now. "So your position, and WHaM's, is that animals are just that—animals. And they can do what they want, without people having that right, too?"

"In a way, although like other animals, people have the right to protect themselves in dangerous situations. What we don't like is the idea of simply hunting down animals like wolves because they have a reputation of being dangerous sometimes."

Maya wondered what Ryan, as an employee of US Fish and Wildlife, would think of this conversation.

She suddenly wished he was here with her, helping her explain to this guy the best way to react to this kind of situation—or at least the best way from her, and the government department's, position.

She had no doubt that Ryan would back her position.

She also wondered why Trev was asking all this. She asked him. "So what's your position on this? Are you on WHaM's side?"

"Yeah. Sort of. I certainly understand what you're saying. Anyway, how long will you be in town? I'm really glad we got to meet this way."

"Me, too," Maya lied. "And I'm not sure how long I'll be here. I don't have any more talks planned, not now, at least. But I do want to be here long enough to make sure that nothing inappropriate is done to the wolves, despite the attack on Mr. Fritts."

"Me, too," Trev said.

And Maya determined that to be an appropriate end to their conversation.

She also hedged and lied a bit when Trev said how much he'd enjoyed talking with her and hoped they'd get a chance to do it again.

Chapter 13

That night, Ryan pondered whether to go right to bed, or return to the forest and shift and…well, just explore. Wait. Look to see what feral wolves might be hanging out there.

No shifters should be, at least.

He'd said good-night to Maya right after dinner, then done the same with Piers a short while ago. His aide had taken Rocky and headed to his room. Now, Ryan was alone, which should be good for letting him relax and fall asleep.

He was, in fact, in bed, looking up some things about the area on his tablet computer, mostly stuff he had already read. But he hoped to find more on the history of wolves around here.

Also, out of curiosity, he tried looking up that guy he'd met and Maya had mentioned, Trev Garlona.

Maya had said Trev had invited her downstairs for

coffee that afternoon, after her talk. They'd discussed what had occurred in the park, she told Ryan—what Morton Fritts had said and how he'd wanted to kill all wolves, and how Pete Sharan had confronted him about it.

Maya indicated that Trev seemed a bit confused, even though he was a wildlife lover and claimed to have come to Fritts Corner mainly because he'd heard that she, as a representative of WHaM, was coming here to talk about the influx of wolves and how wonderful that was.

Was, perhaps, being the operative word now.

Well, Ryan hadn't been able to find anything about a Trev Garlona, his background, where he'd come from, whether he'd ever done anything to help protected wildlife.

And Ryan realized that he'd looked mainly because he felt irritated that someone, even a wildlife aficionado, would invite Maya out for coffee. A dumb irritation. She was here to talk about wildlife protection, particularly wolves. And of course she'd be thrilled to talk to anyone else who felt the same way. It was her job. It was her passion.

Although…well, no, it was totally wrong to even consider her thinking of Ryan as her passion…

He gave up soon on Garlona, figuring he'd check the name in the morning. Instead, he did some more research to locate any additional posts about wolves in this part of Washington State. He did find a couple of social media posts about the apparent attack on Morton, some anger by people who weren't on the side of protected wildlife, but nothing indicating they intended to do anything about it—a good thing.

Starting to nod off, he shut down the computer, turned out the lights and settled in.

Until—a howl! It interrupted and ended his twilight sleep status. Was it real? Or had he dreamed it?

Another one. He jumped up and reached for his phone to call Piers. They needed to find out where this wolf was. What it was. It had to be feral since the moon wasn't full. And Ryan would need to chase it away before its life was endangered...any more than it already may be.

That meant he had to shift.

But before he pressed in his aide's number, his phone rang. He looked at it.

Maya.

"You heard that howl, right?" he said immediately after pushing the button to answer. "I did, too. Piers and I are going to check it out so you can just stay safely in your room. Got it?"

"But—I want to come with you."

"You'll only slow us down." And no way was he going to allow her to see him shift. "You're slowing me down right now. Promise you'll stay in your room. Now. So I can leave."

"But—"

"Promise."

A silence for a beat, and then she said, "Okay, I promise, if that's the only way—"

"It is. Bye. I'll call you later and let you know what we find. Now, stay in your room. You've promised."

With that he hung up—hoping that the woman would actually do as she'd said.

Then he called Piers—who turned out to be in the hallway outside his room.

And when Ryan opened the door he wasn't surprised

to see that Piers was without Rocky—and wearing his heavy backpack.

"Great," he said to his aide. "Let's go."

Maya stayed in her room for all of a minute, staring at the walls. The windows.

The door.

Sure, she had promised...but had crossed her fingers to take some of the sting out of her lie. She'd had to promise, and she knew that Ryan's heart was in the right place.

He wanted to protect her.

Well, she wanted to protect him, too—but at the moment that wolf was on her mind. If they'd heard the howls, the likelihood was that a lot of other people in this town had, too.

Possibly including the Frittses and their cohorts who wanted to get rid of the newest visitors to Fritts Corner.

The wolf's life was undoubtedly in danger. Also undoubtedly, Ryan, of US Fish and Wildlife, would do all he could to protect and save it.

Well, so would she.

With a sigh, she dressed quickly in dark clothes and athletic shoes, issued a silent apology to Ryan and sneaked her way into the hotel parking lot, which was filled with cars but no other people. She didn't see the rental car Ryan and Piers used. They were undoubtedly already on their way.

Thanks to the direction from which the howls had emanated, she would assume that this latest wolf incursion was around the same location as the last—on the forested slopes beyond the park. The two of them—Ryan and Piers—couldn't cover the entire area, although they had one advantage: Rocky, whose nose could help them find the wolf more easily than people could.

But her advantage was that she thought she knew where the guys would at least start out: the location where they believed Morton Fritts had been attacked, where she'd spotted the stain on the ground that they'd assumed to be blood.

She would head there.

Sure enough, their rental car was parked in the nearest lot to that location. She exited her car and looked around. She didn't see anyone else, though there were a few more cars in the lot. That could be the situation every night, as far as she knew.

She headed toward the path she had taken before in daylight. She hadn't heard any more howls. Did that bode badly for the wolf?

She wished she could run toward her target area, but that would be foolish. First, despite the beam from her flashlight, it was too dark. She might trip and hurt herself—and make herself more vulnerable in the event that wolf truly was ready to chew up some more people.

Second—and probably more critical—she'd most likely make enough noise that not only wolves would be able to hear her. She didn't want Ryan or Piers, or anyone who might be hunting that wolf, to know she was around, even though she might prefer being somewhere near them in case she got into trouble.

And so she moved slowly, frustrated, sure, but this was the safest way to go. She hoped.

Notwithstanding the light she carried, darkness enveloped her among all the tall trees as she trod slowly along the underbrush. She tried to stay alert to all sounds around her, since she would probably hear any wolf before she spotted it in the dark forest.

Any people, too.

The forest at night smelled lightly of pine trees and other plants. Her breathing was heavy, and she thought she smelled a light skunky odor—but nothing nearby.

She'd gone a significant distance, believing the clearing she aimed for was fairly close, without hearing or otherwise getting the sense that any wolf was nearby—and then she heard a sound.

Voices. Soft, yes, but it sounded like one man's voice, followed by another. Off to her right.

Could that be Ryan and Piers?

Or someone out to get the wolf?

Remaining as quiet as she could, she maneuvered in that direction. If it was them, should she let them know she'd lied and come out here this night anyway?

She'd observe them for a while and decide.

A ray of light seemed to emanate off to her left and she headed that way, shutting off her own flashlight.

There. This was a different, smaller clearing. The two men she assumed would be there were, in fact, there.

But what were they doing?

Ryan stood there in the nude. In the nude! Under other circumstances Maya would be more than impressed with his amazing muscular physique. Her gaze was drawn below to his even more amazing man parts, large and taut and the sexiest she'd ever seen.

But why was he undressed?

The light she had seen emanated from a large battery-operated lantern that Piers held, aiming it toward Ryan.

Ryan suddenly let out a sound that resembled a cross between a groan and a growl—and then he began to change.

What was going on? This couldn't be real!

The man writhed as his limbs shortened. The rest of his body shortened, too, even as fur began to emerge from his skin.

And his head. His face. It elongated into...

Oh, heavens! Maya had never even considered that the old myths could be true.

In moments, a creature resembling Rocky, whom Maya had not seen here this night, crouched on all fours on the ground.

Even with the information Maya had seen, and laughed about, online, she'd never considered this as a possibility.

Ryan Blaiddinger was a werewolf!

The discomfort and pain of a shift never became easier. And this time there was the additional distraction.

He had drunk the elixir. Piers aimed the light toward him. And then he had heard and scented and become fully aware that they weren't alone.

They had checked the area before. No indication of wolves or those who wished to harm them, or even other humans.

But she had somehow located them. Maya.

She had seen him shift.

He needed to protect her—and himself and Piers. He quickly motioned his head toward his aide, who had shut off the light. He then turned to indicate the direction he would now be going.

In moments, he was in the woods. He slunk toward her as if in submission, hoping she would not feel threatened or scream.

"What are you?" she demanded. She sounded

hoarse, incredulous, frightened, but fortunately kept her voice low.

He made a noise deep in his throat that was not a growl, then nudged her side with his muzzle. At the same time, Piers joined them.

"What are you doing here?" his aide demanded, keeping his voice low.

"I—I wanted to help protect the wolf. I hoped to find you but didn't know you were here. And—" She turned and faced Ryan. "What is going on?" Her voice had risen and Ryan nudged her again.

"Come with me." Piers took her arm. "We'll stay together and talk. This wolf has work to do."

Good. His aide had things under control as much as possible. Ryan loped into the woods.

He listened with his enhanced, wolfen hearing. Yes. He heard human voices in the distance and ran that way.

Then he scented something off to his side. Another scent similar to his and to other wolves'.

He changed his course, heading in that direction.

He spotted the other wolf soon. Heard the sound of his paws on the underbrush.

He was heading in the direction from which the voices had come.

He had to be stopped, and so Ryan accelerated his pace, aiming to place himself in front of the other canine, soon succeeding.

The wolf growled, showed his fangs, acted altogether threatening.

So did Ryan—for the protection of this fellow wolf. This fellow shifter, for his scent seemed somewhat familiar.

Yet another shifter on this night with no full moon? He would need to learn answers...later.

For now, the only language they shared was that of their wolfen sides. And so Ryan growled as well, crouching as if ready to leap, to attack.

He showed his own fangs first, then nodded his head. Closed his mouth as if in submission. Moved forward to bump his counterpart, urge him to run off in the opposite direction.

He sensed confusion in the other wolf. Stubbornness at first, until Ryan pushed him again with his head against the other wolf's side. And again.

The communication worked. With a look toward him first that looked puzzled yet belligerent, the other wolf stopped. Stood still. Then ran off into the woods—going the way Ryan had urged him.

Away from the sound of the voices.

For minutes, Ryan stayed still, listening in an attempt to be sure the other wolf wasn't simply skirting around to return to where he wasn't welcome.

Then Ryan headed stealthily in the direction of those voices.

In the same clearing where blood had been found stood several humans. One was the male Fritts who had allegedly been attacked here. The others were his female, and that Silling human.

They were listening. Talking about wolves and how they would make sure all were disposed of—properly.

Properly in their point of view.

Ryan had an urge to leap into the clearing and dispose of them properly from a wolf's point of view, but that was his wild and wolfen side.

His human side took charge and he listened some more. Smelled the air.

No other wolves were nearby.

Even if these humans had weapons, no other wolf would be harmed that night.

After a while, they began laughing. Said that seeing no wolf here, despite the howls, was fine.

They began walking farther up into the forest.

He walked back toward where he had left the other humans.

When he reached that clearing, he found the two he had left there remained.

But he also caught the scent of the wolf he had chased off from the other location.

He moved around the clearing until he found the other canine, who also simply stood there in the shadow of the nearby trees, staying at the periphery and appearing to listen.

Not seeming in attack mode.

This shifter outside the full moon. Like him.

They looked deeply into each other's eyes, but only for a moment.

And then the other wolf ran off down the hill.

Chapter 14

Maya's stress level rose, making her feel like shouting. After Ryan, the wolf, disappeared into the woods, she had joined Piers in this remote clearing lit only by the dimmed lantern—where that frightening yet amazing event had occurred—and stayed there with him for a couple of reasons. First, because her legs were so shaky that she couldn't have made her way down the pathway to the park without falling, let alone following the wolf that had previously been Ryan, which was what she craved doing.

Second, because she wanted more information. A lot more. A full and credible explanation, if there could be such a thing.

But when she had asked Piers, who'd seemed shocked and unhappy to see her, he had kept dissembling, hinting he was under orders to stay quiet. From whom? Ryan? Not him? Not *only* him? Then who? And wasn't Maya supposed to have stayed in the hotel? Hey, wouldn't she like an energy bar or a bottle of water? As if that would distract her.

So now, she sat on the ground on a towel Piers had removed from his backpack and laid down there for her.

"How long do you plan to stay here?" she asked for the umpteenth time.

Piers, who'd remained standing, repositioned his stocky frame yet again, scanning the trees blocking the view to everywhere rather than meeting Maya's stare. His arms were crossed, and his expression appeared grumpy—or was that anxiety?

If only Maya could read his mind. Hey, she'd assumed mind reading to be a myth, a legend, wholly untrue. But after seeing what Ryan had done, she wondered if there was truth in all the old supernatural fairy tales of the world.

"I take it you're waiting for Ryan to return," she tried again. "Did you both somehow hypnotize me from a distance? Will he come back here looking like he usually does—" handsome, sexy and wholly human "—or is he really some kind of werewolf right now?"

"Don't know for sure," Piers said, this time glancing at her.

But which didn't he know—whether Ryan was a kind of werewolf, or if, when he got back here, he'd still look like a wolf instead of a person?

He clearly wasn't saying.

So Maya continued to sit there and fume and worry—both about Ryan and about her own sanity.

She listened for the howl of a wolf. The one she'd heard back at the hotel couldn't have been Ryan, so at least one more had to be out and about, possibly in this area.

She hoped Ryan would return soon. Maybe he'd actually explain what had happened. Or would he be able to?

Could he talk as a human if he was still a wolf?

Was she insane?

This all seemed so bizarre. As much as she adored wildlife, as much as she loved wolves and learning about them and conducting censuses where they now resided, she had never even considered what had happened here as a possibility.

And now—well, were there more beings like Ryan? Should she plan on taking a census of them?

Ryan would have preferred doing his shift back to human form in Piers's company so his aide could help with the necessary details, like bringing his clothes over and making sure there were no harmful obstacles in the area that could hurt Ryan during the uncomfortable change.

But, once he'd sensed that Maya was now with Piers, he'd done it while he was alone in the forest. Thanks to the elixir he was able to choose the time as well as the place, and he'd done it not far from this area, yet far enough for them not to know he was there.

He even had some ability to choose the time of shifting back under a full moon, thanks to the elixir. But he, and all other shifters, changed under the full moon, though with more control with the elixir.

And now—well, he stood behind a tree just outside the clearing. Nude. He kind of liked that idea, considered strutting through the coolness right into that area to show it all off to Maya. Bad idea.

He hadn't wanted her there when he'd shifted before. Now, to keep control of the situation this night, he didn't want to be naked in front of her again. Though the idea wasn't exactly displeasing. But this wasn't the time or the place.

Some other time, maybe—one of his choosing. And hers. For more than a shifting.

As if that would ever happen...but he recalled again that kiss he'd backed away from, and a critical part of him that had been pretty much at rest started rising to attention.

Damn. He shouldn't react that way. After all, he was angry with her. She had broken her promise to stay at the hotel.

He glanced around again. He didn't see his clothes, and figured that Piers had tucked them away in his bag as usual till they were needed again.

He considered strutting out there once more, just as he was. Ignoring any stare she leveled on him—or staring right back in challenge.

Yeah, he liked that, but figured there were better challenges to be met that night, like convincing Maya that what she had seen needed to be kept to herself.

He did see a towel on the ground—the one Maya sat on. Hell. Enough of this.

"Piers," he called loudly and was pleased to see Maya's eyes widen, her body spasm because he'd startled her. "I'm here. Bring me that towel."

He half expected an argument from Maya, but she merely stood up, still staring in the direction of his voice—though he felt certain she couldn't see him behind this tree.

"Yes, sir—er, be there in a second," Piers shot back. Damn. The "yes, sir" might give away their military status, although maybe they should tell her anyway. Ryan would have to determine whether to obtain permission to do that as they talked—for he felt certain they would be talking about what she'd seen and who he was, and he'd have to be as discreet about Alpha Force as necessary.

Although, with her love of wildlife, maybe honesty would work with her.

Maybe.

Well, he'd rather have his superior officer's okay before revealing anything about their special military unit.

Piers had grabbed the towel and was now at the other side of the tree. "You all right?" he asked Ryan—no "sir" this time.

"Fine. I'll tell you about it." He took the towel and wrapped it around his middle so it hid everything critical. "She handling this okay?"

"She's one nosy woman." Ryan had stepped away from the tree and saw, in the dim light, that Piers's round head was shaking back and forth, as if he was in total bemusement by Maya.

That somehow made Ryan smile. "Not surprising. Now, whatever I decide to tell her, you back me up, okay."

"Yeah," Piers said. "Although I've got a feeling that no matter what you say she's going to dissect it, and you, till she feels comfortable she knows everything."

"That," Ryan said, "is what I'm afraid of. Well, here goes." He walked around Piers and approached Maya, who stood where she'd been seated before, watching them. "Hi," he called to her. "I'm sure you're having an interesting night. I hope it's a good one, too."

Even though nothing personal was showing at the moment, she looked down toward the critical area hidden by the towel and that made him stiffen there even more. "It could be better," she said, her gaze returning to his face. "As soon as you explain to me what's going on, and what I saw."

"Sure," he said, although he didn't mention there were parts of the situation he'd need to keep to himself—and Piers. "Just let me get dressed and we'll talk." Piers had already retrieved his clothes from the backpack and handed them to him. "Excuse me a minute."

"I'm not sure I'll ever excuse you," he heard Maya mutter as he returned behind the tree where he'd been standing before.

This time, Piers stayed with him, handing him items of clothing to put on and taking the towel.

"You doing okay with all this?" Ryan asked his aide.

"Not really. I didn't tell her a damned thing but even when she wasn't pressing me for information I felt pressure flowing from her. She's determined."

"We already knew that about her feeling toward wolves," Ryan reminded him with a smile. "And now we'll just have to find out how she feels about shifting wolves. You ready?"

Piers nodded. "Sure, I'm ready. Are you?"

"Of course," Ryan lied.

He had a feeling that the remainder of this night—and maybe even way beyond that—was going to be made extremely interesting by Maya Everton.

They all started walking down the hillside, along the same path that Maya had scaled to get there, their way lit only by the flashlights they held.

It wasn't always easy, but she stood right beside Ryan, her athletic shoes allowing her some traction on the crunchy dry leaf-covered slope. Piers followed, and she had the sense the guy was relieved that she wasn't urging him to talk any longer.

"So when are you going to explain everything to me?" she asked after Ryan said nothing for a long minute, although he did take her arm to help balance her. A real gentleman.

A wolf in man's clothing—casual, ordinary-looking clothing, right down to his own athletic shoes.

A wolf…

"There's not much to explain," he said. "You saw me. I'm a shapeshifter who changes into a wolf sometimes."

"Then it was real, not some kind of hypnosis or mind control?" Although even if it had been, she'd have no idea why he'd have done it to her.

"No, it was real."

She slipped a little on some leaves beneath her feet, possibly because of the distraction and unease his words caused within her. He caught her, and she was very aware of his touch.

A human's touch.

But still… "So when does it happen? All the old legends say that shifting occurs under a full moon, right? Like the other night. But the moon tonight wasn't full. It's waning." A thought hit her. "If any of that is real, does that mean the wolves I saw a couple of nights ago were shifters, too?"

"At least one of them was," he told her, and she thought she heard some humor in his tone.

The crunching of dried leaves beneath their feet stopped as she stood still for a few seconds and turned to stare at him. "You? You were that third wolf who ran the others off?"

"That's right." She couldn't see him well in the darkness lit only by the flashlights all three of them held, but she knew he was grinning at her. He found this fun.

She found it…well, actually she was fascinated by

it. She'd always been a number cruncher and a scientist, too, with degrees both in statistics and biology. She particularly loved wildlife.

Could she learn to accept the reality of people who changed into wild animals?

Somehow, she thought she could. How weird!

How fun.

"Then why—" she began, but he interrupted.

"Look, this is neither the time nor place for me to answer your questions."

"Why not? We have a few minutes before we—"

"I'm tired. What I do takes energy."

More likely, he simply didn't want to discuss his shifting.

But she wasn't about to give up. Not completely, at least. "Okay, then. Go back to your room and get some sleep. But let's set a time to meet tomorrow to talk about all this."

He didn't respond right away. Was he trying to come up with some excuse why they shouldn't ever talk about it?

Somehow, that possibility nearly made her eyes tear up. Why was she so emotional about this?

About him?

Because she now associated him even more with wolves, the animals she particularly loved?

"Okay," he finally said, and instead of tears she felt a smile on her face. "It'll have to be someplace with total privacy. And not first thing tomorrow. We can meet for breakfast, if you'd like, but I have some things I need to take care of in the morning right afterward so that won't give us enough time. Let's meet in the park later, find an area with just one bench where we can be alone and talk privately. That okay with you?"

They'd reached the bottom of the trail, and the street was nearby, the parking lot just at its other side.

"That sounds fine." At least assuming he meant it.

They walked together to her car, and she pushed the button to unlock it. There were a few lights hanging on poles in the parking lot so she could now actually see him.

Ryan, the man. The handsome, attractive…and strange and mysterious man.

Piers now stood behind him, clearly waiting.

"See you back at the hotel," she told the two men. "Although if you take much time to get there I'll head up to my room."

"In that case," Ryan said, "we'll see you tomorrow."

As she opened her car door, she looked at him again, recalling how she had kissed him the other night—and how he'd seemed uncomfortable because of it.

Well, heck, he'd certainly made her uncomfortable by more than a kiss that night. And though she had no idea at the moment what she thought of this man, and who and what he was, she leaned toward him, grabbed him again and kissed him once more on those sexy lips.

He seemed to react this time as well, but before he could kiss her harder—or pull away—she was the one to back off and hurriedly plant herself in her car.

"See ya," she said, and pulled the door shut.

"I can't wait till later," Maya shot at Ryan first thing the next morning, when he reached the lobby with Piers and Rocky and found her standing not far from the registration desk. "Please—can we talk now?"

"We figured that out last night," he said calmly, hoping to soothe the clearly upset woman. He led her away from the busy area of the hotel where lots of people were

in line to check out or check in. There was an empty
corner nearby, not far from the single elevator. When
Maya was situated there, he looked down again into her
huge-eyed face. "Like we discussed, we'll have breakfast now, then meet up again later at—"

"At the park," she finished, keeping her voice low as
she shook her head. "I know. But I have so many questions and couldn't sleep for the few hours I had left last
night, and—"

He needed to calm and quiet her. This wasn't the
right place or right time, but they were at least temporarily out of the main stream of people.

He glanced toward where he had left Piers and Rocky
and didn't see them, so he figured his aide had taken
his cover dog out for his morning walk while waiting
for Maya and him. Good.

"—and the thing is I'm not sure if—"

Ryan bent down and placed his mouth over Maya's.
That shut her up.

It also got him possibly as stirred up as she was, for
different reasons.

He had a sudden urge, while their kiss deepened and
grew even hotter, to forget about breakfast and what
else he had to do this morning and lead Maya back upstairs to his room.

But what else he had to do this morning was critical.
It might help him fulfill the mission he had been sent
here to Fritts Corner to accomplish.

And so, just as he'd been the one to start this encounter, he was the one to regretfully pull away.

As he did, he looked down and saw that Maya's hazel
eyes regarded him with what appeared to be both lust…
and suspicion.

"Are you trying to distract me?" she asked in a normal tone, as if what they had done meant nothing to her. Except that, as he watched, she took a deep breath, clearly trying to calm herself.

"Yeah," he said. "Am I succeeding?"

She let out a brief snort of laughter. "I guess so. Maybe it's time for breakfast, after all."

She turned and preceded him out of the lobby.

Chapter 15

Surprisingly, their breakfast had worked out well.

They again ate at the popular local restaurant Andy and Family's. They sat in an area of the patio where Rocky was welcome.

They ordered pretty much the same meals as they had before.

And Ryan was relieved that Maya had gotten the message, that he wasn't about to have the conversation she wanted until later that morning.

So, instead of quizzing him about what she had seen, she instead got into a long discussion and Q&A session about wolves and where they were endangered in the United States, and what Fish and Wildlife was doing about it.

Which suggested to him that she'd guessed he actually wasn't employed by that federal department. But she didn't press him—then—to explain what his connection was, or wasn't, to it. Or to anything else.

He felt certain she didn't know about Alpha Force.

When they were done eating, he had insisted on paying the bill, claiming once more that it was on Uncle Sam. In a way it was, though not via US Fish and Wildlife. Alpha Force was, after all, a US military unit—albeit a covert one.

They had parted ways outside the restaurant. He hadn't told Maya where he intended to go, but he'd already requested that Piers and Rocky accompany her back to the hotel.

He didn't know what she might do to occupy her time until their planned eleven-thirty meeting in the park, but being with him was definitely not on the agenda.

He'd walked the other direction—and was just approaching the Corner Grocery Store. He had called in advance, so the Sharans were expecting him.

Whether they wanted to talk with him was another matter. But he would definitely talk to them—and he had also told them he wanted their son, Pete, to be present.

And in fact he was present—in the store. As Ryan walked in, he noticed Pete taking cash at one of the registers, the line extending quite a ways in the busy establishment. Hopefully, someone else would take his place soon.

Otherwise, Ryan would need to insist on it, and he believed that what he was going to approach Pete's parents with would cause them to ensure their son joined their private conversation.

Scanning the crowd, he soon saw Kathie Sharan talking to someone in the produce aisle. She might have been watching for him, since she immediately caught his gaze, then smiled at the customer she'd been talking to and walked in Ryan's direction.

Her smile disappeared. She soon joined him at the front of the place and looked up at him. "Come into our office. I'll get Burt and Pete." Her voice was cool, but her expression appeared troubled.

Kathie was short and wore a lacy white top that extended over the waist of her jeans. Her multishade brown hair appeared rumpled, giving her the appearance of an anxious woman, and perhaps hinting about the possibility of her shifting background.

She easily led Ryan between patrons to a door near the rear corner of the store, opened it and said, "Go on in. We'll be right there." She left the door open as she hurried into the crowd they had just left.

The office was a small, enclosed square with a plain wooden desk in the middle, a few chairs and a file cabinet. A laptop computer sat on the desk, and nothing else. There were no pictures on the pale yellow walls, no other decoration in the room. It was functional, Ryan supposed, and maybe it hadn't had time yet to accumulate extra paperwork or memorabilia since the Sharans were relative newcomers to town and new owners of this store.

In any event, nothing there stood out to prove or disprove Ryan's suspicions of who the Sharans were.

But he knew.

He walked over to look out the small window near the rear corner. It fronted on the building next door—an ice cream shop, Ryan believed, though from the back portion he couldn't view any signage.

He heard a noise and turned back toward the door. All three Sharans had just entered, and Burt closed the door behind him.

"So why are you here?" Burt's voice was sharp and clearly uninviting. His arms were at his sides, hands fisted, and his expression belligerent—not merely a kindly local grocery seller.

Without responding at first, Ryan walked over to the desk chair and sat, assuming they would recognize that he was the alpha at this meeting. Maybe beyond it, as well.

"Why don't you all sit down, too?" he asked, his tone congenial for the moment.

"Why don't you answer me?" Burt countered.

"Tell you what. I'd like you all to sit down first, then take a very deep breath. I'm going to, right now." And he did. In doing so, he inhaled a lot of scents, some emanating from food in the store outside the office, aromas he had smelled here before. But the strongest were right in here, with him.

He'd smelled them before, at different times and each in two different incarnations—as they were here, and otherwise.

They hinted of shifters. True? Ryan believed so, and he hoped to confirm it right now.

And get some of his questions answered...

Maya's face popped into his mind. He'd be meeting with her later, too, and it would be her questions they'd discuss. Would he let her in on anything he learned here?

Meanwhile, he watched the others crammed into this small office with him. Burt just eyed him warily, but he did sit on one of the chairs, and his wife and son took seats, as well. They all tilted their chins upward then, and Ryan watched their heads move and their chests expand as they obeyed and also took deep breaths.

Pete wasn't as beefy as his father, but his nose was

as long, and Ryan allowed his mind to imagine them as wolves right now.

All three stared at him, suspicion on their faces.

"Good," he said. "Now, tell me what you smell."

"Tell me what you think we should smell," countered Pete. His parents looked at him and nodded.

"Here's where this conversation will get interesting," Ryan said. "I could continue to dissemble, address what I'm driving at only tangentially and keep up the mystery. But let me try this another way. I'm going to get all woo-woo as a human here—or maybe not."

"A human?" That was Kathie, whose deep brown eyes were huge.

"That's right. As we all are at this moment. But otherwise?"

"Otherwise what?" That was Pete, and although his tone was sharp, the younger man appeared both wary and nervous.

Good. He was the one on whom Ryan had intended to levy the brunt of his initial inquisition, focusing on last night.

And Ryan's own plentiful questions.

"Otherwise—well, first of all, consider what you smelled as you took that deep breath. Some would be familiar, since you're always around together. But then there's me."

Pete nodded. "Then you're—"

"Wait a second," his father broke in, and Pete grew silent again though the look on his face was pensive.

"Okay," Ryan continued, "let's do a bit of pretending but also make some promises. I'm going to approach some pretty offbeat things, or at least they'd seem offbeat to a regular…human."

"What are you talking about?" Pete demanded. He

looked anxious and curious, and glanced at his father for approval.

Burt nodded, and Pete appeared to relax, but only for a moment—till Ryan began speaking again.

"Oh, let's go back to last night, shall we? Did you happen to be in the woods up behind the park? If so, I saw you there—and I'm going to assume that neither of us looked…human."

Pete's eyes grew huge, and he looked away from Ryan to his father's face once more, then his mother's.

"Don't let him goad you, son," Burt said. "This conversation is weird. Stupid." He turned from Pete to stare at Ryan, and his expression appeared as if he was trying to look skeptical and scornful.

"Maybe so," Ryan said. "But if you show me yours, I'll show you mine." A little, at least. He wasn't about to reveal all. "I happened to see a wolf up in that area last night, and communicated with him. And that wolf also saw me and responded." His wry smile was levied now on Pete. "Right?"

Instead of appearing frantic now, Pete appeared thoughtful. "Right. Then that was you? I mean—well, tell me what you know."

And Ryan did…somewhat.

The rest of the conversation in that office went pretty much as Ryan hoped. The Sharans did admit they had come to Fritts Corner about ten months earlier with some other people like them when things in the part of Idaho where they'd lived became stressful, and they'd heard that wolves were being seen in the area around here. Wild wolves.

And they had something in common with them. They were obviously reluctant, but when Ryan asked again about what they had smelled, and gestured toward himself, they mentioned that what they had in common with those wolves was that they were like them, a bit. Shifters.

When they admitted it, Burt appeared challenging, as if expecting Ryan to back off the position he had taken before and tell them what fools they were.

But he didn't. And when appropriate, he admitted he was a shifter, too.

"Most shifters only change under a full moon, though," he said to Pete. "You were shifted last night. How?"

"I'm a scientist," he asserted defensively, as if expecting an argument. "I've always been interested in what we are and all its angles. I came up with a formula that allows us to shift outside a full moon. It's pretty new and raw right now and I hope to perfect it soon. But what about you?"

"Oh, I have access to a formula that I think is a lot more perfected than yours. I'm not going to get into detail now, but my bosses—not Fish and Wildlife, by the way—are going to want to hear about this conversation and probably want to hold more talks with you. If all goes as I think it might, you at least, Pete, might get access to that formula one of these days."

After all, part of Ryan's assignment was to see not only if there were shifters around here, but also if any could be recruited into Alpha Force. This young, smart, eager shifter might be one excellent addition to the unit.

"Now tell me," Ryan said. "Why did you shift last night? And why weren't you more quiet about it?"

Pete appeared a little sheepish. "I made a small modification to my formula and, with all that's been going on around here lately, I wanted to try it. It didn't really make much difference, though, and I shifted back right after you and I saw each other. But you're right. I shouldn't have been howling—especially since those admitted wolf-haters are around. But I still can't always control myself... Believe me, I'm glad you're the one who showed up—and I'll be more careful next time."

"Good," Ryan said. "Okay now, I think our conversation today is over—but we'll talk again. And just like you'll deny admitting to anything that came out here if things go wrong or the wrong people ask questions, so will I—and one thing I can assure you of is that I do have some pretty official backing, though it's premature to get into any detail now."

"Really?" Pete sounded impressed. "Like, the government? Someone there actually believes in shifters?"

"Like I said, I can't get into detail now, so believe what you want." But Ryan grinned in partial assurance to the young man. "Anyway, I'll let you know when it's time to talk again, but I can tell you it'll be soon."

Their goodbyes, though somewhat wary, were a lot more congenial than when Ryan first came into the office this day.

He felt good that things had gone as well as they had.

He just hoped they would continue to get better.

Maya sat in her room fuming. Hanging around. Playing with her computer.

Looking up shapeshifters.

But it all appeared unreal, legendary, part of the lore from which fiction books and movies were created.

Somehow the reality had escaped general notice. Or real shapeshifters had been able to hide it, make it all appear like fiction.

Real shapeshifters like Ryan.

She wanted the truth. She wanted more. But how could she just wait here—

Her room phone rang. It was unlikely to be Ryan, who now had her cell phone number. Trev?

"Hi, Maya," said that geeky male voice that she recognized. "Could we get coffee together again now? I'd really like to talk to you."

About shapeshifters? Did he know?

"What about?" she asked.

"Did you hear those wolves howling last night?"

"Yes," she said, "I did." But what did he think about them? "Sure," she told him. "I have a few minutes. I'll meet you downstairs right away."

Which she did. His button-down shirt that day was beige, and his small, dark eyes seemed hidden in shadows.

Had he been awake last night? Had he been on the hillside, too?

She shouldn't want, shouldn't need, to protect Ryan—and yet, she felt compelled to learn what Trev knew. Or maybe she simply wasn't ready to talk about it, let alone accept it.

"So how are you doing this morning?" she asked as they exited the Washington Inn lobby into the adjoining coffee shop.

"Okay," he said. "But tired."

They placed their orders—basically the same as last time, a frothy latte for Trev and plain, ordinary coffee for Maya. The place was a bit less crowded than before, and this time they chose a different small table, near one of the front windows.

As soon as they sat down, Maya prompted, "So you heard those wolf howls last night, too?" She watched his face for any indication that he'd not only heard them, but he knew what kind of wolves they came from.

She saw nothing but some wryness there.

"Yes, I heard them. There really are a lot of wolves in this area. A good thing for WHaM, I guess."

WHaM and not werewolf hunters. She supposed that was an indication that he knew nothing. "Yes," she said enthusiastically. "I'm really delighted." She paused. She wasn't sure what she thought about shifters, but she actually was delighted about real wolves. And surely the wolves near Fritts Corner weren't all shifters…right? "Aren't you?"

"Well…it's a good sign that the wildlife protection around here is working."

She wondered at his waffling. "You didn't go out and try to find any wolves, did you?"

"Heck, no," he said immediately. He smiled right into her eyes. "I listened to you. Wildlife is wild, right? I don't want to go find it. I didn't want to go and get attacked like that Morton did."

"That's good."

"You didn't go try to find them, either, did you?" he asked, the expression on his face now anxious.

"No," she lied. If he wasn't out on the hillside, he wouldn't know the truth about what she'd done, where she'd been.

What she'd seen.

"But do you think it's even safe to be in this town with all the wolves we've been hearing and all?"

"I think so," she said. "As long as no one is confronting them." She assumed the same rules would apply to shapeshifters.

At least she hoped to find out in a little while, when she got to talk to Ryan privately.

"Do you know of any other dangerous forms of wild-life that are close by?" he asked, still appearing worried. "And would WHaM try to protect them?"

"I'm only aware of the newest wolves, and I haven't yet conducted any kind of survey, as I'd like to. But I need to be careful like everyone else, no matter what I'd like to accomplish for WHaM."

"Okay," he said, still sounding worried. "We all have to be careful."

"Exactly. And now, I'm afraid, I'd better get moving. I've got some WHaM stuff going on soon."

And more.

It was eleven thirty. She'd ended her coffee with Trev when she'd said she was busy, then Maya had come to the park as Ryan and she agreed.

Though she had kind of liked the distraction of sounding Trev out about his apparently minimal knowledge, what he had heard and assumed, it was time. She wanted to talk to Ryan.

There, in the distance, apparently holding a remote bench for them near where the hillside forest began, sat Piers with Rocky sitting at his feet.

Where was Ryan? Piers had refused to answer any of her questions before and she didn't expect more from him now.

But Ryan had promised they would talk.

She strode over a gravel path along the rolling lawn till she reached that bench, not far from her favorite spot here, the podium.

She was glad she wasn't scheduled to give another talk now. What would she say? That she was having hallucinations about werewolves?

That she couldn't get the view of one of them, especially before he had shifted, out of her mind?

Or what the sight, and memory, of that naked body was doing to her psyche?

She'd reached the bench. Rocky stood up and wagged his tail.

The dog looked so much like Ryan appeared when he was in his wolf form.

Undoubtedly by design. Ryan might have chosen his twin to be his pet, although she figured there was a more strategic reason for it, whatever it was.

Patting Rocky on the head, Maya said, "Hi, Piers. How's your day going?" What she wanted to demand was where Ryan was, and whether he'd sent his friend here to try to divert Maya and her questions.

"Fine." But the stocky guy appeared uneasy. Even so he said, "In case you're wondering, Ryan's on his way."

"Yeah, I was wondering." She paused to sit down, and he joined her on the bench, still holding Rocky's leash. "I don't suppose you have anything to tell me today that you didn't last night."

"No, although I think Ryan will answer at least some of your questions."

"He'd better." Maya scowled, then asked, "And you? You're friends, so I've been wondering if you have the ability to—what's that called? Shapeshift?"

"That's the right name but, no, I'm not a shifter."

"How about Rocky? He looks like Ryan when…when he's—"

"Oh, there he is." The expression on Piers's round face suddenly looked relieved. Maya turned to look in the direction he was facing and saw Ryan striding across the lawn toward them.

Good. Piers was off the hook to talk to her, at least for now.

And, hopefully, she'd get her answers.

She tried to settle down better on the bench, relax so she would appear more in control. She did have some control over the situation, after all. Whatever a shifter was or wasn't, she doubted Ryan would want word to get out about his strange ability.

She could make things difficult for him if she chose—like revealing the truth, as she'd considered, then cast aside, while talking with Trev.

But she also realized Ryan could make things difficult for her. How could she effectively represent her organization and support the existence of wolves if people thought she was insane? Not that she intended to go public. Ryan would undoubtedly deny what she saw, maybe tell the world she was nuts—

Well, she needed to see how things went here, while at the same time thinking about how to protect her reputation and her work with WHaM.

"Hi," Ryan said with a huge smile on his face as he reached them. He looked so ordinary—well, if one considered a guy as sexy and gorgeous as him ordinary. "Sorry I'm a little late. Interesting morning." That comment was leveled at Piers, not her.

She noted in her mind that she needed to find out what that was about. But not right away.

"That's fine," she said. "But now's the time for truth. What did I see last night?"

She noted that, before Ryan sat down, both he and Piers scanned the area where they were as if checking to see if anyone else was around.

There weren't any kids running around or playing ball as there usually were on weekends. A few people in the distance walked their dogs or stared at their cell phones or both, but no one was nearby.

No excuses for Ryan not to talk—unless he believed someone was aiming some kind of super recording device toward them.

Not likely.

"You saw what you saw," he finally said. Great. What was that supposed to tell her? But he continued, "Things are a little muddled regarding my purpose being here, although that appears to be improving. Because of your background and support of wildlife, I'd like to tell you all and hope to soon. But for now...well, you saw me last night and I do owe you an explanation. Yes, some of the old myths that people look at as sci-fi in movies and all—well, they're true. Or at least there are such things as shapeshifters. And I'm one of them."

"Wow." Maya didn't mean to act all awed and amazed, but one word, wow, probably expressed best how she felt.

Of course she'd had hours to think about it and hadn't concluded that she'd been drugged or turned into a nutcase or anything like that, but still...

"Wow," she repeated. "I want to learn all about it. Were you born that way? And the myth says werewolves shift from people form into wolf form under a full moon—unlike last night. Is any of the mythology real? And—I'd better shut up. I don't want to just keep asking questions and not let you answer anything."

He laughed, and she was amazed when he reached over and took her hand and held it on his leg as he looked straight into her eyes.

His deep brown eyes looked so amused, so intense, so sexy. She couldn't help smiling—and trying to hide the shiver that rushed through her body.

How could she feel so turned on by this man who wasn't exactly a man?

"Look, the main reason I wanted to meet you here was so I could tell you what I'm able—although there are reasons I can't tell you everything, at least not right now. But I'll tell you about me, and a bit about shifters in general, and why I'm here, okay?"

"Great," she said, then added, "Oh, and one more thing before you start. I should have known—kind of. Not that I'd have believed it. But I looked you up on the internet. Didn't find anything specifically about you, but I did learn something interesting."

"What's that?" Ryan asked.

"That *blaidd* is the Welsh word for wolf."

Chapter 16

Of course he had to be judicious in what he said, but Ryan didn't hide his pride in who he was as he talked to Maya.

She sat beside him on the bench. Close beside him, which he liked a lot. Her hands were in her lap, and her attention clearly was on him.

Piers and Rocky were on his other side, so he couldn't observe his aide's expression, which was a shame. Piers, as a nonshifting member of Alpha Force, had nevertheless been given the standard instructions of what to reveal to whom, and when. Ryan had no intention of overstepping his boundaries here—not till he had received at least Drew's okay, and perhaps other commanding officers', which he intended to seek considering Maya's background and dedication to wolves. But not yet.

He watched her face, though—lovely, with lips

slightly pursed as if she was ready to say something yet held back. Her hazel eyes were huge and appeared skeptical yet fascinated. Or was he simply reading what he wanted to there?

He wanted Maya to believe and accept him and… well, like him.

Maybe more, no matter how inappropriate that might be.

He'd started way back, about where legends of shape-shifters originated in ancient times because there really were such beings. "But except for families and some rare and remote communities, they were disjointed, no matter where they existed in the world. At least that's how our legends go, since such isolated individuals didn't share a lot, mostly because they couldn't. And they needed to stay quiet about it since superstitious and fearful humans killed any shifters they came to know about. Plus, shifters not only become wolves, but other animals, too—lynxes, hawks and more, which remains the same today. But you're right about the somewhat ironic meaning of my name. Someone way back in the family must have chosen it."

He went on to talk about the first shifters in the United States, arriving also in small groups during the days of early settlers and finding areas to settle, often where wild creatures of the same kind they changed into lived to make it easier to hide in plain sight.

Today, he told her, there were enclaves of shifters all over the country, all over the world, but they mostly kept to themselves without even letting others know they existed or where they lived.

Mostly.

He felt Piers move behind him on the bench and realized his aide was getting a bit concerned about how much Ryan intended to tell Maya.

He needn't have. Ryan was about done with his talk—and he hadn't even hinted at the existence of Alpha Force.

But he hadn't counted on the intelligence of Maya, who deemed herself a statistician and more, to attempt to push him into a further discussion.

"So how do shifters shift?" she asked. "I guess the old legends are wrong about there having to be a full moon."

Ryan hesitated. She had seen him shifted, so this question was logical. He considered how to respond, but he had to be careful. Maya was too smart just to buy into some stupid explanation.

"The old legends were spot-on during their times," he finally said, looking beyond Maya, not wanting to meet her eyes as he continued to ponder the best way to handle this. "Shifters had no control over when they would shift, and it always happened during a full moon." He didn't bother to mention that they had no human cognition then, either.

Only shifters with access to the Alpha Force elixir or some other kind of chemical modification could choose, at least to some extent, when to change—and be able to think like their human counterpart then, too.

"But now?" Maya pushed.

"Oh, there've been experiments over the years and a few shifters—not all of them—have been able to work things out to have a little more control."

"How?" she insisted. "I assume you're one of those with control. And I saw that Piers took some kind of bottle from your hands and shone a light on you when you started to change."

Of course she had noticed. She was too intelligent not to equate what she had seen with what he had done. What could he tell her now?

The barest minimum.

"That's right. I'm among the lucky few with access to a formulated drink that gives us some control."

"That's how you did it last night. Was it the same under the full moon the other night?"

He wanted to grab this woman and shut her up— by kissing those full lips beneath her light, furrowed, puzzled brows.

He also had an urge to tell her the truth, but he couldn't. Not yet at least.

"It was similar," he said. "Because I like the degree of control it provides, I take one of those drinks then, too."

"And the light is supposed to resemble the full moon?"

Damn, but she was intuitive. And if he didn't watch out, she'd ask about the origin of the drink he took, and why Piers, a nonshifter, helped him, and more that he couldn't respond to.

"Kind of. Now, I've pretty much told you what I can. Would you like to join us? I'd like to go get a cup of coffee."

"So werewolves drink coffee like anyone else when they're not shifted. And you seem to eat pretty standard stuff, too. But why can't you tell me anything else?"

Piers was suddenly standing beside them. "Hey, guys, my coffee addiction's calling. Let's go find the nearest coffeehouse and get a quick cup, okay?"

Maya looked toward Ryan and laughed. "Whatever is going on, I think you have your buddy Piers well educated in when to intrude to protect you. That tells me something, although I don't know what. But you can be sure, Mr. Ryan *Blaidd*inger—" she stressed the "blaidd" part "—that I won't rest until I know it all."

Which was exactly as he'd feared—but expected.

"Then you won't rest for a long time," he countered, but he smiled at her, and she smiled back.

"Oh, we'll see about that. We'll talk again, very soon, here or someplace else. I don't mind us being away from everyone else, but I intend to hear everything from you. Count on it."

Which meant he needed to talk to Drew and others within Alpha Force today. He'd already intended to, since he also wanted the okay to reveal the covert unit's existence to the Sharans after getting their promise of secrecy.

Mostly because he wanted to start recruiting Pete.

"Okay," Maya said, standing to face Piers. "I assume you know what's going on even if you can't change into a wolf. But I also assume you're not about to answer all my questions that Ryan hasn't."

"You assume right," Piers said, nodding and grinning.

"How about you?" Maya bent down to look right into Rocky's face, but the dog just leaned forward and licked her cheek. "Sweet, but not what I was after. Okay, guess I won't get it all today." She turned to face Ryan, who'd also stood up. "But I will get it one of these days. And you can be sure I appreciate the bit that you did tell me."

She looked ready to lean forward as Rocky had done, and Ryan assumed it wouldn't be to lick his cheek. He just smiled and said, "I like your challenge, Maya. And just to be clear, I intend to keep as many secrets as I want. Got it?"

"Just wait and see," she said, standing with her hands on her hips as if challenging him even more.

This was amazing!

Well, the explanation wasn't as amazing as what she had seen, Maya thought as she strode alongside Ryan beneath the sunshine—no full moon now—back through the park toward the street. They talked about the town again, how they had each decided to come here to check out the wolves, what the weather was like, what other parts of Washington State they had each visited, all kinds of neutral stuff.

But all the while, Maya's mind was churning.

As she'd told him, she wanted to know more. A lot more than she'd even suggested to that man. That shifter.

How did it feel to be a human one moment and a wolf the next? What did he do as a wolf—the same thing as real wolves did as far as hunting and prowling or whatever?

Was it possible for a person who wasn't a shifter to become one? If so, how?

And…well, she probably shouldn't even be thinking of this, but if they happened to have sex what would it be like? Not that she'd want to get that near him while he was in wolf form. But in his current, all-man form, would it be different from sex with other men?

She believed it would be, no matter what. This part man, part wolf, was one very sexy human male, and she'd seen the sexiest parts of him. Been briefly in his arms and kissed him.

Oh, yeah, what would it be like? And could she get pregnant by him? She certainly wouldn't want to, but if she happened to, what would their offspring be like—her, or him?

This man, or whatever he was, was making her nuts!

She nearly stumbled on the uneven path along the lawn, and, as if she'd planned it that way, Ryan reached over to steady her and held on.

They followed Piers and Rocky, so there was no embarrassment involved in her reaching over to clutch Ryan's hand as he still held her arm. They walked that way for a while, until they reached the sidewalk at the edge of the park. The street nearby wasn't crowded, but cars passed by frequently. Maya quickly released Ryan, and he did the same with her.

She felt suddenly bereft and alone—and maybe even wanting to see this guy shift again. How odd was that?

"So," Ryan said, "it's lunchtime. I know we had breakfast together, but are you interested in joining us again, and not just for coffee?"

Piers, who now stood facing them with Rocky at his feet as usual, moved a little, and Maya had a sense that he was silently conveying his wish that Ryan hadn't asked—and that she wouldn't agree.

Which might mean he'd hurry them through the meal, and she wouldn't want that.

"You know what?" she said. "I think I'd rather get a dinner commitment tonight. Is that okay with you two?" A nice, long dinner, but she didn't say that. At least if that worked out she'd get to see Ryan again—and maybe come up with a new approach to get him talking more. Too bad they were staying in a hotel. If she had her own place here she could cook him dinner... and seduce him with food. To talk, at least.

"Sure," he said quickly, turning back to her. His expression now seemed somewhat relieved, and that made her feel a bit gloomy. He was jumping at a chance to get out of her company more quickly, at least for a little while. Piers must have reminded him of something.

Oh, well. They'd see each other that evening.

And might she be able to convince him to consume whatever he ate or drank and change into a wolf that night? She smiled at the idea.

But her smile immediately evaporated as she saw a crowd of people heading down the sidewalk toward them. They were still a distance away, but the man in front looked like Morton Fritts.

That identity was confirmed as the people got closer. How many were there? They didn't move fast, but Maya thought that the people bringing up the rear were photographing the area and the Frittses.

Why? As they drew closer, Maya saw Trev among them. Some of the others fanned out and seemed to take photos, and maybe videos, of Maya and the people and dog she was with, too.

What was going on?

Piers asked the same thing. "What are those damned animal-haters up to?" he whispered to Ryan.

"I'm afraid we're about to learn."

"Shouldn't we just get out of here?" Piers pulled slightly on Rocky's leash as if preparing the dog to run.

"No. We need to find out…in case we need to deal with it."

Maya wondered if the group was about to say they'd started killing wolves or something horrendous that they wanted photographed so the world would know about it.

But a minute later, Maya wished she had just fled the area.

Things were never simple.

For as soon as the group reached them, Morton Fritts, his face still covered by healing wounds, bellowed, "So we found you back here again, you wolf-lovers. Bad enough that your damned vicious creatures attacked me the other night. But look at this. Look what they did to my Vinnie."

He moved off to the side, and Maya saw that, behind him, his wife was being wheeled in a chair pushed by Carlo Silling.

She was dressed in shorts that revealed bandages up and down both legs.

And her neck was bandaged as if she'd been bitten, her face even more mangled by scratches, or worse, than Morton's had been.

Maya's mood immediately shot from excited and happy and curious to—well, she still was curious. But she was also scared. Not for herself, but for all wolves around, regular and shifters.

Ryan and others.

Surely he hadn't hurt Vinnie. But who had? A truly wild wolf?

Were there other shifters around besides Ryan? She thought he'd hinted at it, but that was one of the things she'd have to somehow wrestle from him.

For now, she stepped forward around Ryan and made herself ask Vinnie, "What happened? I know you're hurt, but will you be okay?"

As she anticipated, the first thing the injured woman did was say, "What do you think happened? Just like my poor, dear husband, I was attacked by one of your damned wolves." She glared at Maya the entire time she talked, and winced a lot between words.

"I'm very sorry." And she was. For Vinnie, yes, although for her to have gotten hurt by a wolf she had to have ignored Maya's talk yesterday and put herself in that wolf's presence.

It was one thing for Maya to ignore herself, knowing the possible dangers and deciding to do what she wanted anyway.

But Vinnie should definitely have known better, especially after her husband had been hurt, too.

"Of course you're sorry," Vinnie hissed, wincing some more and placing her hand on first one cheek, then the other. "Because you know this can't go on. Something has to be done about your horrible wolves."

"And we're going to do it." That was Morton, who'd maneuvered to stand beside his wife. "You can tell your damned WHaM group. And you—" he looked around Maya toward where Ryan still stood "—can let your damned Fish and Wildlife tree huggers know that keeping wolves on a federal protection list anywhere is not acceptable—never mind that this is the western part of Washington. If anything, our state fish and wildlife group should be in charge here, too, not just in the eastern part, but it really doesn't matter. You won't see which, if any of us, disposes of the wolves so you won't be able to arrest us. But you can be sure they're going to disappear."

"Oh, we'll know," Maya spat back. "You're threatening them. We'll protect them." She certainly would do her darnedest and figured that Ryan, who had even more reason to do so, would do all he could, as well. "And if anything happens to them, just guess where we'll start looking for the perpetrator."

But the very idea of anything happening to those wonderful, wild animals made her quiver inside.

They had to do something to make sure they stayed safe. Immediately.

But what?

She turned toward Ryan, knowing she looked hopeless.

He, on the other hand, stood there straight and tall and strong-looking.

"I don't know what your problem is with wolves," he said, "or why you apparently put yourselves into situations where they attack you. But Maya is right. If it's just one wolf and it's particularly dangerous, maybe we can do something about it. But if you're doing this purposely, for some reason of your own—"

"We just want things to go back to the way they were before more damned wolves started showing up here!" Vinnie stood up from her wheelchair and hobbled toward Ryan to face him. "And if the government won't do something about it, we will."

Chapter 17

What provoked Ryan most at the moment were the members of the media who had followed the Frittses here and were taking videos. They started hollering out questions.

"Why are there wolves around here now?"

"What is the government going to do about capturing dangerous animals like that?"

"What is US Fish and Wildlife doing here now? Are you already involved in locating and euthanizing the dangerous wolves?"

Ryan, who now stood beside Maya on the crowded sidewalk to attempt to protect her from this mess, bit his tongue to avoid yelling at this group of humans who didn't have a clue.

The problem was, he didn't, either. Which wolf—which type of wolf—was doing this?

He'd considered the possibility it could have been

Pete Sharan, since he had been shifted last night. Ryan would ask Pete some questions but didn't believe it was that young shifter. The aspects of their meeting, and Ryan's brief viewing of the Frittses, made that very unlikely.

And why had both Frittses been hurt that way? Sure, they'd apparently put themselves into a dangerous situation, confronting agitated wolves of whichever type. But why?

And why were so many media representatives here, in this remote town? There were more than had shown up for Maya's first presentation. Had the Frittses called them, piqued their interest by mentioning the attacks? Maybe they'd have had no interest in just one, but now it was becoming an epidemic, even though both of those who'd been hurt were in the same family.

"Sorry, everyone," Ryan finally said after tamping down his temper. "No comment. But I will be looking into this situation further. We don't want any more incidents in which people are hurt. We don't want any wolves to be hurt, either. Please remember that they are still listed as an endangered species, especially in this part of Washington, and cannot be hunted." And be sure to put that in any articles you write, he thought but didn't say.

Questions still bombarded him as he turned and started walking toward Piers and Rocky, glad that Maya remained beside him. There was more he could have said about what constituted an endangered species—but in fact he didn't have all the answers.

He was a shapeshifter in the military, not really an employee of the Fish and Wildlife Service. He knew a little, but not enough.

That gave him an internal excuse not to answer any

questions, but he was hardly going to admit that rationale.

"What are you going to do?" Maya asked as they hurried away. "I think we need more information about where the Frittses have found the wolves and gotten so close and—well, do you think they're endangering themselves on purpose?"

"I wouldn't be surprised," Ryan said. "I'd like to know why, though."

"Because they're obviously interested in wolves." Piers kept up with them along the sidewalk, with Rocky leading the pack. "And dislike them. But it doesn't make sense that they endanger themselves unless they have some other motive to cause the wolves to look bad. Getting rid of them in this area, sure—but why is it that important to them?"

"Yeah, we need to find out their motive, and also which wolf or wolves are involved."

"Which, as in whether they're shifters?" Maya fortunately kept her voice low. She looked between Ryan and Piers as if unsure which would answer.

"That's right," Ryan responded even more softly. "But we don't talk about that here."

Not that anyone was close enough to hear, certainly not the media behind them. But Maya needed to understand that there'd been a reason he had only spoken with her in a remote area of the park.

Secrecy. It was extremely important, especially to Alpha Force. The world wasn't to learn about the covert military unit. Especially not on his watch.

"I get it," she said. "But—look, I want to stress that I need more information, too. I want WHaM to help protect the wolves around here. *All* the wolves, even if the rest of my group isn't…well, aware."

He could have hugged her. She was willing to do what she could to help shifters as well as feral wolves, and was listening to him, not being specific in what she said.

He had even more of an urge now to explain his own background and reason for being here. Piers's and Rocky's, too.

That meant he had to leave her presence for a while, right now, to make sure he followed all necessary protocols.

"We really appreciate that," he said, looking at her. "And—well, we're going to walk you back to the hotel, then Piers and I need to go find a place to make a phone call."

Her expression turned wry. "A private call, I take it. That's fine. I know you're full of secrets." She grinned, then grew solemn again. "But just don't forget that we're on the same side. I just want to help."

He had an urge to grab and kiss her right there, despite Piers being beside them and a whole slew of locals and media still following them. He hadn't turned to check out how many were there, but he could hear the footsteps—some that sounded uneven, so they were probably the Frittses keeping up despite their limps—and irritated comments. It might be hard to get away to find a quiet and private location. But hopefully his group's heading into the hotel for a while would get the others bored enough to leave.

In addition, some cars on the road beside them slowed as drivers gawked at the parade behind them. Some shouted questions, too, and a few got responses from the gang—explaining they were trying to get more information about dangerous wolves.

Ryan was relieved when they finally reached the

hotel. He turned to face their pursuers. Carlo Silling still pushed the wheelchair, but Vinnie was no longer in it. "Thank you all for caring about wolves," Ryan said. "Now, we're heading to our rooms for a little privacy." There was some grumbling, and the Frittses appeared ready to limp inside and confront them, but Ryan turned away.

The lobby wasn't extremely busy, fortunately. Though Maya said she'd be fine here, Ryan insisted on accompanying her upstairs to her room. Piers led Rocky to the rear of the first floor, where their rooms were.

The stairway was empty except for them as they walked to the third floor. No one followed, not even the Frittses.

After Maya used her key to unlock the door, Ryan pushed it open, then followed her inside, instinctively wanting to make sure no one waited for her there—like another anti-wolf protester.

Was that really his reason? After checking the place out, he returned to her side near the door.

"What's that about?" she asked. "Do all Fish and Wildlife people act like police or security people and look for intruders—wolf or human?"

"Maybe not all," he said with a laugh, and then, knowing he had to leave, he grew serious. "Just be careful. And I don't only mean keep away from wolves in the woods."

"I promise that—"

She didn't finish, since he took her in his arms and gave her a quick—yet hot—kiss. It felt better than he wanted to think about to have her curvaceous body snugged up against him—making parts of him stand at attention. He quickly let go.

"See you later, for dinner," he said.

"Yeah, see you later," she responded with a grin so sexy he considered staying for a while.

But he didn't. He left the room, closing the door behind him—and looked forward to seeing her again in a few hours.

Maya had an urge to dash right back out the door.

To kiss Ryan again? Yeah, right. But she didn't think she'd be able to just hang out here for the few hours until they met up for dinner.

One of these days, she'd head to places like the local animal shelter or, better yet, city hall, to discuss the wolves and their reception by citizens other than those like the Frittses, or people who showed up at her talks. How about the rest of the locals? What did they think?

How had Trev learned about what happened to Vinnie? Or had he simply seen, and joined, the crowd and found out about it then? She might ask him next time she saw him, but she wasn't about to try to contact him now. Despite his initial appearance of being a wildlife lover interested in WHaM, he'd seemed to vacillate a bit when they'd spoken. She wanted him, and the other wolf fanciers in town, to stay that way no matter what had been going on with the Frittses.

Yes, she'd have to start mingling again soon. Asking questions phrased to encourage people to recognize that wolves were wonderful representations of wildlife— stressing the *wild*.

But not now. She was too keyed up, plus she wanted to at least pretend to obey Ryan this time. And since today was Sunday, no one would be at city hall anyway.

Heading into the woods at night after hearing a wolf howl was an entirely different matter.

She sat down on the edge of the lacy coverlet on

her bed, crossing her jeans-clad legs and holding her cell phone, which she'd extracted from the small purse she'd been carrying. She pushed a button to call a person whose voice might help calm her: Cheryl Jaker, a fellow WHaM member who also lived in Colorado.

Cheryl answered right away. "Maya! Good to hear from you. How are things in the state of Washington?"

Maya stared at a picture on the hotel room's wall, a representation of a train with an old-fashioned engine at the base of a mountain. She had wondered, on seeing it for the first time, where that area was located—and whether there were wolves around at the time.

"Not great," she said. She proceeded to give her friend a rundown on her talks here and the people she'd met, the existence of wolves—some of which she'd seen—and the apparent attacks on people by them.

Her only reference to Ryan, Piers and Rocky was a mention that some US Fish and Wildlife folks happened to be there, too. She didn't say anything about shapeshifters.

Even if she hadn't promised to stay quiet about them, she wouldn't want her good friend and colleague at WHaM to think she'd gone crazy.

"That's terrible!" Cheryl exclaimed when she was done. "What are you going to do to help protect the wolves?"

"I'm fortunate to have the Fish and Wildlife guys around. They're aware of the situation and seem to be taking charge. Fortunately, with the protected status of wolves in this area, they're not just giving a license to the people who've been hurt, or anyone else, to kill the animals."

A license like that under the circumstances could

be an even bigger mistake than usual, if the attacking animal happened to be a shifted human...

"Well, that part's good, at least. Keep me informed. And you take good care of yourself, understand? I know how you love to go meet the animals you're just supposed to view from a distance and count for our census. If some around there are particularly likely to harm people..."

"I get it. And as I said, I've been telling everyone to avoid the wildlife to be safe."

"Are you heeding your own warnings?" Cheryl knew her too well.

"I will from now on," she said—crossing her fingers as she had before when making promises to Ryan. She would take care of herself—but she would do what she needed to do.

"You have a better idea?" Ryan asked Piers. They were in the rental car, with Rocky lying on the backseat, still in the hotel parking lot. There was no particular place they needed to go, but this was certainly a private location.

A good place, Ryan thought, for them to make their phone call.

"No, but I thought we were getting into the car to drive somewhere to call HQ. I'd have brought a cup of coffee or something."

This guy certainly liked his java. "We could drive to a coffee shop, if you'd like."

"Why not?" Piers was in the driver's seat and immediately backed out of the parking spot. The hotel had an adjoining coffee shop, but a big-name chain was only a block away, and had a nice-sized parking lot, too.

About ten minutes later, they were back in the same

positions in the car, this time with hot drinks in the cup holders between them.

A few patrons got into their cars nearby, and others exited a vehicle parked in the row facing them. None looked interested in a couple of guys sitting in a car sipping coffee. The air outside was cool enough that the inside of their car felt pleasant, so no problem about the windows remaining closed.

"Ready?" Ryan asked his aide.

"Go for it."

Ryan immediately pulled his phone from his pocket and pushed the button to call Drew. He also put the phone's speaker on since they weren't hooked up to any Bluetooth in this vehicle.

Drew answered immediately. "I've been waiting for your update. What's going on there?"

"A lot of interesting stuff." Ryan began by informing their commanding officer that there were indeed other shifters around. Then he got into the apparent attacks on humans by wolves. "I don't know yet if they're shifters or not."

"I've heard something about that in the news," Drew said.

"I'm still trying to figure it out," Ryan said. "In the meantime I'm also getting to know members of one family of shifters—both parents and their son, who's in his early twenties. I met the parents in shifted form on the night of the full moon." He quickly summarized how he had shooed them away when they had started harassing the representative of WHaM who was out trying to find the source of some howls that night. "And guess what?"

"I have a feeling you're going to tell me that there

are other shifters around besides you who're changing on nights when the moon isn't full."

"You got it." Ryan told Drew more about the Sharans, and how their son, Pete, who focused on science in school and apparently did a good job of it, had come up with some kind of formula that allowed shifting on other nights, as well. "We haven't talked about it in any detail since, though I've told them I know about shifters and hinted I might be one, too, I wanted to get your okay before I mentioned Alpha Force under these circumstances. And I'm hoping, when things settle down here—and I figure they will—that I can convince Pete to come visit our Alpha Force headquarters. He might make a good addition to our unit."

"Maybe so. And, yes, consider this your okay to mention it to them as long as you get their promise of secrecy—and you reasonably believe they'll comply with it."

Piers chimed in then. "If he hints at what could be in store for Pete based on the family agreeing to confidentiality, I'm sure this group will keep things quiet for their own sakes. Ryan'll have to figure out who else around here are shifters, though, and determine whether it's good for Alpha Force for information about us to go any further."

"Good point," Drew said.

Ryan looked at his aide and nodded. "I was going to mention that, too, but glad you beat me to it. I got a sense from the Sharans that they weren't the only ones who came to town because the situation wherever they'd been living was getting tense, and I have an idea who some might be. I don't see any as potential recruits yet, but who knows?"

"We'll see," Drew said, "but I at least like the idea of the Sharans' son."

Some people got into the car nearest Ryan's side, and for a minute he talked about the weather around this part of Washington, taking a sip of his cooling coffee.

Drew's laugh echoed through the car, thanks to the speaker on the phone. "I take it you have company."

"Not sure if they could hear anything outside our closed car," Ryan said, "but just in case…"

"Got it."

In another minute, that car drove off. "Okay, back to our subject," Ryan said. "Telling other people about Alpha Force."

"Other people—as in shifters or nonshifters?" Drew asked.

"You guessed what I'm about to get into." Ryan had been a member of Alpha Force for less than a year but he had come to not only like their commanding officer a lot, but to highly respect his intelligence.

Not to mention who he really was. The guy was married to a nonshifter, a veterinarian, and they had a couple of kids who were too young for a determination of whether they, too, would be shifters, but Drew, and even his wife, Melanie, often expressed their hope that they'd have that in common with their dad.

Drew obviously trusted some nonshifters, *some* being the operative word. And could Ryan be certain that Maya was as trustworthy as Melanie Connell?

He had a sense she would be. After all, she already knew what he was, had seen him shift and hadn't gone crying to the world or even hinting at it to the media. She seemed to be willing to protect him the way she protected nonshifting wolves.

He said to Drew, "There's someone else here I want to tell about Alpha Force."

"That WHaM representative?" his CO immediately guessed.

"That's right. She's seen me shift—accidentally—and fortunately she has been discreet about it. Her appreciation of wildlife, especially wolves, seems to be what drives her." Not necessarily any appreciation of him, he told himself—notwithstanding the kisses they had shared, the way they sometimes looked at each other...

"Well...under those circumstances I guess you have to trust her some anyway. Just lead into it like you did with those Sharans, getting promises of secrecy before saying more. But I don't really think it's as critical that she learn about Alpha Force. You're not going to recruit her or anything like that."

"No, but someone else who gives a damn and looks at the situation of those attacks from another angle might be helpful." He described in greater detail how Morton Fritts had been attacked on the night of the full moon, and his nosy and careless wife had done as he had, apparently chased after whatever wolf was howling in the distance last night and had also been injured. He just hoped it wasn't Pete Sharan.

He had continued to ponder that possibility, often replaying in his mind his meet-ups with Pete that night, and still didn't believe the attacking wolf had been Pete. He had seen the Frittses on the hillside around that time, but not close to either instance when he had been with the wolf that was Pete. The wolf he'd seen had run off in a different direction from those humans, and Pete had said he'd shifted back right after Ryan and he had met up.

Therefore, it was more likely a feral wolf—or another shifter with some way to shift outside the full moon. He'd keep the possibility in mind but for now wouldn't let it deter him from possibly recruiting the smart young shifter.

"We need to prevent that from happening with anyone else," he finished.

"Yeah," Drew said. "You do. Okay, I'll trust your judgment about the WHaM lady. I just hope you're thinking with your head and not any other part of you."

Ryan felt his eyes widen. He looked over at Piers. Had his aide mentioned anything about the apparent attraction between Maya and him to Drew? But Piers just shrugged.

This could just be another example of their commanding officer's intelligence and intuition.

"Well, I can admit that the woman is attractive in ways beyond just her appreciation of wolves," Ryan said. "But I'm not giving in to any impulse—or I won't unless I think it'll help me protect shifters or other wolves, and that would be a stretch."

"Yeah, it would," Piers agreed, grinning at his superior officer.

"Well, okay. You've got your orders. Revealing a bit to shifters, and this one particular nonshifter, as long as you receive believable promises of secrecy, is okay, but only if you really think they'll keep things to themselves."

"Yes, sir," Ryan said, still looking at Piers. "We'll report in again soon, let you know how things are going."

"No need to send any other representatives of Alpha Force there now, right?" Drew asked.

"Right," Ryan replied, and Piers expressed his agreement. They hung up a minute later.

Ryan didn't say anything to Piers at first. His mind was churning.

Could he trust the Sharans? He still felt fairly certain that Pete hadn't been the attacking wolf. The Sharans had an agenda of their own, and all three of them would want not only to protect the idea of shifting, but also potentially help Pete find a new and highly appropriate career. The answer, therefore—as long as he was right about Pete's innocence that night—was yes.

And Maya? Was Ryan thinking with body parts other than just his brain, as Drew had suggested?

"What do you think?" Ryan asked Piers. "You've been with Maya when I've been shifted. Can we—should we—trust her with more?"

"I've got a feeling that she is one smart and trustworthy woman—but it's up to you, sir."

"I'll sound her out when I get her alone, soon, and decide then," Ryan said.

But he was fairly certain he knew what the answer would be.

Chapter 18

Dinnertime. Maya felt more antsy than hungry, but she was ready to eat—or at least meet Ryan and Piers for dinner.

Walking down the stairway to the lobby, she thought once more that it was a shame they were staying in a hotel like this. She enjoyed cooking and wouldn't mind putting a meal together for them.

Only—what did people like Ryan really enjoy? She'd seen him eat steak as well as breakfast food. Red meat might be his favorite kind of meal, but maybe not.

Maybe it was just as well that they were eating out and he could order whatever he wanted.

They were waiting in the nearly empty lobby for her. Rocky the wolf-dog was with them and made Maya smile.

Would she smile as broadly if that was Ryan sitting there on the floor in his own wolf form?

To her own surprise, she thought the answer was yes. But she remained a bit confused. Not that she expected a bunch of detailed websites on the reality of shape-shifters and how they lived and shifted and all, but she had spent an hour or so that afternoon online after her conversation with Cheryl researching as much as she could about what Ryan truly was.

All the sites referred to the whole idea as myth or legend, or horror movies—nothing with any truth to it. But she knew full well that shifters were real. She'd seen it, more than once.

Kind of admired it…

She also admired how shifters had apparently been able to keep who and what they were as secret as they did. For surely Ryan wasn't the only one, and he had hinted at others.

"Hi," she said immediately as she reached them. Ryan and Piers sat on chairs in the center of the lobby with Rocky lying on the floor between them. "You guys hungry?" She looked directly at Ryan as if to ask if he was ready for some meaty food—and found herself flushing. He did appear hungry—but the kind of hunger she thought she saw in his hot glance toward her didn't suggest he was ready to eat a meal.

Instead, she had an urge to invite him to her room. Into her bed.

Which was ridiculous. She wouldn't do that with any guy she was interested in without knowing him better. And getting more involved with someone with—well, secrets— like Ryan made no sense at all.

"I'm definitely hungry," Piers replied. "We thought we might try another restaurant tonight, if that's okay with you."

Not the steak house? "Where did you have in mind?" Maya asked.

"The local pancake house, Griddle Junction. It's just a few blocks from here."

Pancake house? For dinner? Well, the ones Maya was familiar with served other meals besides breakfast. There might even be steaks there, if that was what Ryan—and Rocky—wanted.

"Fine with me." Maya wondered why they had chosen that place. From what she had gathered, these two didn't do anything without a reason. Was there something there they could learn about wolves? Or shifters like Ryan? She might never find out, and she knew better than to ask questions here, in the hotel lobby. Or there, at the restaurant.

Well, maybe as they walked there. But when they got on their way and she started asking questions, Ryan, who strode beside her, said, "Look, there's a lot I want to talk to you about. But it'll have to wait for now. We need to find a place with no one else around again."

Back at the park? Maybe. But that wasn't going to happen tonight.

Just be patient, she ordered herself, though that wasn't in her character. Yet if she wanted answers to her questions, she needed to wait.

And, yes, be patient.

Ryan let himself enjoy walking with Maya to the restaurant despite the frustration she apparently felt, too, though for different reasons. She didn't talk much on this stroll, just appeared to look around and take in the sights, such as they were, of the downtown area of this small city.

He'd already told her he wanted to talk with her but

hadn't said when or where. Yet despite his receipt of permission to tell her more, this wasn't the time. Not that everyone on downtown Fritts Corner sidewalks was a shifter with hearing acute enough to eavesdrop on what he said, but he didn't want to take any chances with the few regular people who were also out there, shifters or not.

Not when it came to talking about his covert military unit, Alpha Force.

For one thing, Piers, now walking behind them with Rocky, had done additional research online about the Sharans, such as when they had arrived in Fritts Corner—about ten months ago—and who else had moved here around the same time.

He had learned that Buck Lesterman, owner of Berry's Bar, had arrived around the same time. Plus, the owners of Griddle Junction had bought a home here, as well as the restaurant, at nearly the same time as the Sharans. Their names were John and Georgia Maheus, and there had been no indication they had lived here prior to that time. Ryan hoped to meet them this evening.

Had they and Lesterman come with the Sharans? For similar reasons? He would try to find that out, and hopefully learn if they, or anyone else in the area, were shifters, though he might not get all that information tonight.

And if they were, could they shift the way Pete did? Had he shared his formula?

Had any of them shifted—and attacked the Frittses?

For now, it would be a bonus to share another dinner with Maya. He certainly wouldn't be able to talk with her in private at the restaurant, but he'd find a way to do so as soon as possible since he now had permission to tell her more. Maybe they could walk Rocky together after they ate, not around the park but someplace a lot more private than the sidewalks of downtown Fritts Corner.

He already had plans in mind for tomorrow. He'd decided he'd remain hungry after breakfast, a good time to visit the Corner Grocery, buy some snacks and find a way to speak with the Sharans again, especially Pete. They, at least, had a private office.

But for now—well, he'd find a way to talk with Maya, if not tonight then tomorrow.

After passing Berry's Bar, some clothing stores and a couple of gas stations, they soon reached Griddle Junction, a single-story restaurant with lots of windows that occupied nearly half a block. He listened as they headed inside and heard a lot of conversations, as with a typical restaurant. He also inhaled scents typical of a pancake house at dinnertime—including sweet syrup and eggs, as well as hearty red meat. And that wasn't all.

"Cute place," Maya said. "I even see a couple of other dogs here."

Ryan had smelled them, too. Both were small and lying on the floor inside the place, perhaps not permitted by law here but no one was complaining, which made Ryan like the place immediately.

"Hi," said a fortysomething woman carrying menus and smiling her welcome. Her graying hair was caught up in a clip on top of her head. Ryan caught another scent as she approached.

One that suggested she could be a shifter.

"Hi," he returned. "Are you one of the owners of this place?"

He wasn't surprised when she said she was Georgia Maheus. "Have you eaten here before?" she asked.

"I haven't," Maya said, "but I'm sure I'll enjoy it tonight." She looked toward Ryan for his response, her expression somewhat quizzical as if she realized he had an ulterior motive for coming here.

"We're just visiting town," he replied, "but we've heard good things about this place."

Georgia showed them to a table in the middle of the moderately busy restaurant, notwithstanding the fact they had a large dog with them. That emphasized Ryan's belief that they might have good reason to welcome canines here.

So did their hostess's scent.

It wouldn't hurt to meet her mate, too. "Is the rest of your family involved with this restaurant?" he asked. "I travel a lot and enjoy seeing how families work together running businesses in so many locations. I'm with the US Fish and Wildlife Service, by the way."

The woman's brown eyes widened as she regarded him. "I'll bet you have an interesting job," she said, then added, "Are you here because people around this area have been seeing wolves?"

"That's right." He continued to watch her reaction, which she clearly attempted to keep blasé.

"And I'm with WHaM," Maya added. "That's Wildlife Habitat Monitoring. I'm interested in learning more about the wolves, too. What do you think about them?"

Ryan was both amused and pleased that Maya seemed to work as a team with him, and with Piers, too, who was watching them all.

"Oh, we like wild animals," Georgia said, "But I've heard some people were hurt by the wolves. That's truly sad, from both the people's and the wolves' perspectives, I'm afraid."

"Do you know of anyone who's going after the

wolves?" Piers asked, his tone just as Ryan hoped to hear it—interested, but not too interested.

"No—but if I do, do you gentlemen have a card so I can let you know? I assume Fish and Wildlife would be interested."

Ryan nodded at Piers, who took a card out of his pocket. Fortunately, as part of their cover, they'd gotten phony identification for just this kind of situation.

He noticed Georgia motion to someone behind a nearby table. A man approached, tall and thin, with a wary expression on his face.

"John, these people are with US Fish and Wildlife, and with WHaM." She turned back toward Ryan and said, "I've got to get busy now, but I wanted to introduce you to my husband."

"Good to meet you," John said. "Sorry I don't have time to talk to you, but welcome to Griddle Junction." He reached his wife's side and they walked away together quickly.

"So what was that about?" Maya asked immediately.

"I think you can guess," Ryan responded.

"Something else we'll talk about some other time?" Her tone was sweet, her expression irritated.

"You got it. Now, are you in the mood for breakfast food for dinner, or what do you have in mind to eat?"

"I saw someone eating a really huge and great-looking omelet," Piers said. "That's what I'm getting."

"I need to look at the menu," Maya said. "I might go for an omelet, too. And I assume you'll at least consider the steak." She smiled and batted her eyes at Ryan.

"I'll consider it," he confirmed.

Dinner was over. Maya had enjoyed her omelet. She'd enjoyed the company even more. But now they

were walking back to the hotel. There was no indication they were going to do anything when they arrived
except to all head for their beds.

She didn't want that. She wanted to chat with Ryan.
He'd already said he had things to talk to her about, too.

Why not tonight?

They reached the door to the lobby. They'd taken
their time somewhat to make sure Rocky was able to
accomplish all the sniffing and relieving himself that
he wanted, and now the dog seemed quite happy to
come inside.

Maya was, too—maybe. "I'm not really tired," she
said to her two male companions as they entered. "And
we discussed the possibility of talking about some of
the stuff that's going on around here. Why not here
and now?"

She anticipated Ryan's reaction. He'd only talk to
her when he felt comfortable no one else would be able
to listen in.

Then, as she'd said, why not here and now? The hotel
lobby was empty except for the senior guy at the registration desk. He most likely wouldn't be able to hear
what they said as long as they kept their voices low.

"Not here," Ryan said. "But just a minute."

He motioned for Piers to join him off to the side of
the empty room. Maya didn't know what they were
talking about but she had an idea. She approached the
guy at the registration desk and asked some questions.
Then she hurried back across the lobby to where the
men stood. Apparently their quick conversation was
over since they both just looked at her.

"Okay," Ryan said as she reached them. "Here's what
we can do. Piers will take Rocky to his room to bed,
but you and I will go for a ride to talk."

"Sure," she said, her mood lightening. She'd been concerned they would just tell her they were tired and no one really wanted to talk to her, after all. "Or, we can go to my room." She told them she'd seen the people on either side of her leave with luggage earlier, and she'd just confirmed that they had checked out—and that no one else had checked in. "No one'll be close enough to hear anything if we talk there."

"So we've got two good possibilities." Ryan's smile looked relieved. Good! He must really be serious about wanting to tell her…something. What? She already knew what he was.

Still…

"So which will it be?" Maya asked.

"Let's look at your room first," Ryan said, "and if all seems as quiet and private as you indicated, it'll be fine not to run around anymore tonight."

"Great." Maya felt her heart rate accelerating.

She shouldn't feel at all excited that she might be alone with Ryan in her bedroom for an unknown length of time.

They were going there to talk, for him to tell her even more, she believed, about the kind of person he was, and how he melded into the regular world of regular people.

If nothing else, that should be a huge turnoff. In fact, she had a sudden urge to change her mind and say they should go for a drive to talk.

But she didn't. And in another minute Piers and Rocky were heading down the hall toward their room… and Maya was leading Ryan up the stairs toward hers.

Chapter 19

She'd invited him into her room—to talk, Ryan reminded himself. She had confirmed that the nearest rooms were unoccupied, and as they reached her doorway and she opened the door with her key, he listened carefully.

Sure, he'd have felt even more comfortable that no one was around if he'd been in his wolfen form listening with his superior sense of hearing. But his hearing in human form wasn't bad—and the only things he heard on this floor were a couple of television sets turned on down the hall, a conversation between a man and woman nearby but not in the closest rooms, and apparently the sound of a mother reading a book to a kid who giggled and talked about the doggy in the story.

If he only knew what other kind of doggy stood nearby...

But Ryan had the answer he wanted. Even so, as they

entered the old but well-maintained room and Maya put her purse down on a chair near the door, he listened once more.

Then he said, "Okay with you if I put the television on? I'll keep the volume low but it should help drown out our conversation in the unlikely event that someone is listening."

Of course if that other person happened to be a shifter, too, then drowning out what they said would be unlikely. But it was better than nothing.

"That's fine. Sorry I don't have anything here I can offer you to drink unless you'd like a bottle of water."

Like his room and Piers's, hers had a small refrigerator.

"No thanks. I'm fine." He looked around. The only chair in the room was the wooden one with a woven cane seat where Maya had put her bag.

The most inviting place for him to sit was her bed, with its attractive lacy coverlet. But...the bed?

Heck, he was here to talk. Nothing else.

He could tamp down the sexual attraction he felt for Maya. It was totally inappropriate. And he really did want to talk with her.

That was all.

He planted his denim-clad butt on the bed and patted the area near him—but not right beside him. Maya gave a silly smile that he wanted to kiss right off her face but didn't.

He'd need to see if she was still smiling after he'd told her what he wanted to...

"Okay, here's the thing," he said, looking straight into her face. She was really beautiful, and her hazel eyes looked intense, interested—and maybe a bit turned on. But he was probably just imagining that. "Piers and I don't actually work for the US Fish and Wildlife Service."

Her grin as she laughed only made her look sexier. "Tell me something I don't know—like who you really do work for."

He'd already figured she was smart, and it wasn't much of a stretch for her to determine, from the way he'd been acting, that he'd told a few lies for expediency's sake. And for the secrets he needed to keep.

"That's exactly what I intend to do, but I only got permission based on securing from you a credible promise that anything I tell you will be kept utterly confidential. That you won't repeat it, or even hint at it, to anyone else—except in the highly unlikely event that I give my consent."

"Whoa," she said, still smiling. "Sounds pretty hush-hush...and important."

"It is. Part of the reason is national security, and you'll see why." He reached over and took her hands from where they'd been propping her on the bed. She remained seated there but allowed him to hold on to her hands. They were warm, and her grip, as she turned her arms so she could hold his hands as well, was as tight as his.

And sexy. Very sexy.

He continued looking at her eyes, not touching her anywhere else, and said, "So, Ms. Maya Everton, do you agree that everything we discuss tonight will be kept utterly secret by you, that I can rely on you not to disclose anything to anyone?"

"That sounds pretty restricted and important," she said. "And hopefully at least partly in protection of animals, not just national security?" She made the last a question, and he couldn't help just a hint of a smile as he nodded.

"I think you and I will make a pretty good team as things continue," he said. "And, yes, some of what I'm about to tell you involves protection of animals. And people."

"And people who are also animals, like you." She made that a statement, as if she was already reading his mind.

"You got it. So…?"

"Of course I promise. Do we need to do a pinkie swear to prove it?"

"No. But as I indicated, national security is involved. If you breach your promise, there could be some pretty nasty consequences."

"What, you'll have me thrown in federal prison?" Her tone sounded scornful—but her expression was troubled, as if she understood completely that what she said could in fact be true.

"Let's hope it doesn't come to that," he said. "And if it helps you to agree, we can pinkie swear if you'd like."

That should at least take some of the pressure off this conversation, though it could seem to minimize its importance.

He had a sense that she knew better.

"All right, I swear I won't tell anyone what you're about to tell me, not without your approval. Pinkie swear. Okay?" She pulled her hands away from his only long enough to extend her right hand so her pinkie finger pointed toward his.

With a laugh, he wrapped his finger around hers. "Okay," he said. "So here it is. I happen to belong to a highly classified, totally covert military unit called Alpha Force."

Her eyes widened, but she didn't pull her finger away from his. He had an urge to use it to pull her closer, but didn't.

"Are all members of your Alpha Force like you?" Her tone suggested awe, which only made him want to hug her even more.

"Some are," he said. "Piers is a member who isn't a shifter, though. He's my aide. The shifters all have aides and cover animals who look like them while shifted."

"Then Rocky's your cover dog. I thought he looked like the way you were when I saw you in werewolf form." She looked delighted now. "Are all your shifters wolves?"

He started giving her more of a rundown on the shifters comprising Alpha Force, who were mostly wolves but also included other kinds of animals, as well.

"Wow!" she said when he was done and had released her finger. "What kinds of military assignments do you get involved with? And why are you here? Is this area in danger?"

"This was more of a hunting expedition on my part," he said. "With the sudden influx of wolves to this area, I was given the assignment of checking whether any were shifters—both for their protection and, possibly, recruitment into Alpha Force."

"And you have found shifters, right? Are any of them going to join your force?"

"Still looking into who around here might be a shifter, though I know a few for certain. So far I haven't tried to recruit anyone, though I hope to."

"Wow," she said again. "Wow, this is just so amazing. Werewolves, more like you and part of our military. Wow!" Suddenly, she launched herself along the bed toward him.

In moments, she'd wrapped her arms around him and pulled him down onto the coverlet. Her mouth suddenly captured his.

And he was engaged in one amazingly hot and sexy human kiss that he wanted never to end.

This wasn't what she'd had in mind…was it?

How could she know, even ponder that, now that she was in Ryan's arms and he lay on top of her with his amazing, hard body, kissing her like he was? While she was kissing him back. Enjoying every moment.

Yet a shapeshifter. Many shapeshifters. A military—

Oh, my, he was running his hand under her shirt, reaching toward her breasts. Her bra miraculously seemed to disappear—or was it simply pushed up and out of the way by his searching fingers?

In fact…he moved a bit and suddenly her shirt and bra were missing. Was that a special act of a shapeshifter?

Heck, no, for she used the opportunity of his no longer keeping her in place with his body to yank off his T-shirt, as well.

But he moved back on top of her once more, holding her more tightly so she could feel the warmth of his skin against her now-naked breasts, the hardness of his ripped muscles, as he again sought her mouth, surrounding it with his for an incredible new kiss.

She wasn't about to let things stop there, though. Or should she? She wasn't exactly thinking things through with all her logic as a human being when she moved her hands around to his back, first squeezing his butt through his jeans, then reaching around to the front— still outside his pants, but, oh, how his erection grew to fill her grasp and then some.

He moaned her name. "Maya. Do you know what you're doing?"

"Hell, yes," she said. And then she stopped still. "Don't I? I mean, can you do what…what people do when you're in the shape of a man?"

His laugh sounded so damned sexy she felt the moistness that had started to gather below increasing. But had he meant he couldn't do what regular men do? Or—

"I'm not about to take the time to give you a rundown on what could happen if we continue," he whispered against her mouth.

And then he pulled away.

Maya felt lost suddenly. Well, not entirely, since this way, as he stood, she could see him—the hard muscles of his bared chest rippling as he first reached into his jeans pocket. He pulled out his wallet. What? There'd be no money involved if they—

No. She heard the crinkling of plastic as he pulled out a condom.

The guy wasn't only sexy, he was considerate. And smart. But she knew that.

She used the time to grab the remote on the nearby nightstand to turn off the TV.

"But I damned well want to continue," he said. "As long as you do. And what I can tell you briefly is that this'll give the kind of protection we need to ensure that there'll be no other result if we go on with our lovemaking."

"Then let's do it." She gasped as, smiling, he pulled his pants down till they crumpled onto the floor.

His erection was every bit as large and thick as she'd anticipated, and it was pointing toward her.

"Wow," she whispered, even as she reached down to

remove the rest of her own clothes and remained lying on the bed. Enticingly, she hoped.

Must be, since in a moment, after he'd sheathed himself, he was back beside her. He reached over, first stroking her breasts once again and then reaching lower. Touching her moistness, reaching a finger inside her and pumping it slowly as if informing her what else he would be doing in a moment.

"Please," she whispered.

In moments, he was on top of her. Inside her. Moving slowly at first, then more heatedly and faster and—

She swallowed her cry, knowing he didn't want anyone to hear them. Sure, no one was in nearby rooms, but—

He groaned at the same time, then dropped quickly back on top of her, gently enough not to hurt her. His breathing was erratic.

Well, so was hers.

Neither said anything for a long moment. Then Maya heard herself say "wow" again.

"Oh, yeah," Ryan added. "Wow."

"So that's how shapeshifters do it?" Maya asked a long moment later when her own breathing was somewhat tamed.

"That's how shapeshifters do it," he confirmed, once more sort of repeating what she'd said.

"Then shapeshifters are amazing," Maya whispered hoarsely into his ear. "And I wonder. Would this shapeshifter—" she reached around and hugged him closely again "—like to stay the night?"

His laugh was husky and sounded amused. "Yeah, this shapeshifter accepts that very welcome invitation."

He did stay. And he had brought more condoms. Maya lost count of the number of times they made love, possibly because what they did sometimes resulted in fulfillment and sometimes just tantalized her enough to touch him even more. Taste him even more. Enjoy his tasting her…

It didn't all result in consummation, but it did make her feel absolutely wonderful.

Then there were those fantastic times when they did it all…

In between, well, she did sleep some. Snuggled up against his hot body beneath the soft sheets, feeling his flesh touch hers, his arm often around her, as he slept, too—or at least seemed to.

She wasn't sure how long she had slept the last time when she was awakened by Ryan's movement beside her. She smiled and turned toward him, to find his head on the pillow, his gaze on her, his sexy lips that she had felt on her—how many times and places?—now smiling in a way that suggested satisfaction.

Satisfaction? Not total. Not yet. Not if she could help it. And so she smiled back, and moved her hands, then her mouth, until they once more experienced the kind of sex she had only dreamed about.

Even that drew to an end eventually. She was out of breath when he started to get out of bed after kissing her once more.

"It's still early," she whispered teasingly.

"Yeah, and that's why I'm leaving now, so hopefully no one will know I was here. This has been one hell of a night, but I don't want it to end with your being embarrassed about it."

"I won't be," she responded quickly. But how would she feel if the people she needed to impress, so they'd be supportive of the local wolves, knew what else she was up to?

Probably fine…since none would know who and what Ryan really was. Right?

Well, Piers knew. And he was part of Ryan's strange and secret military force. What would it mean to Ryan if it got back to his commanding officers that he was having sex with a normal human female?

"I hope not," Ryan said, "but let's make certain of it." He'd already pulled on his undershorts and had his jeans and shirt in his hand. He bent down and kissed her on the cheek before heading toward the bathroom.

Well, fine. She'd had a simply amazing night. One she could—and would—remember for a long time. And those memories would include not only that she'd made love with one amazingly sexy man. Emphasis on *man*. She might know what he really was, but nothing she'd experienced that night was different from how it would have been with a regular human.

Except how astoundingly wonderful it was…

She heard the sound of the shower and lay back with her head on her pillow, eyes closed for the moment as she inhaled and still smelled the aroma of their love-making.

Someone like him would smell it even more intensely, she imagined.

Someone—something—like him…

Would she want to repeat this sometime? Sure. It had been wonderful.

And they had agendas that were at least somewhat similar, in learning about the wolves around here and making sure they remained safe. Ryan and she could work together, and play together.

For now.

But that was all. They couldn't possibly stay together. He had to go back to wherever his strange military unit was headquartered—outside Washington, DC, he'd previously indicated. She would return to her WHaM headquarters.

And that would be that.

So…could she, would she, ever make love with him again knowing their time together was, and needed to be, quite limited?

She hoped so.

He popped out of the bathroom then and bent over her. He was dressed, and now he smelled of the soap supplied by the hotel. His hair was wet.

And once more he gave her one amazing kiss.

"Let's get together for breakfast in a while," he suggested, "after I get back to my room and change clothes and hook up with Piers and Rocky. Okay?"

"Okay," she said, and as he left she felt both a slight bit of relief and a lot of regret.

No matter what or who he was, she'd had a fantastic experience.

But would it be the only time?

She would think about it long and hard—and just have to see how things worked out.

Chapter 20

What a way to end one day and start another, Ryan thought once he had returned to his room. Now, he was standing by his bed—with a lacy coverlet like Maya's—getting dressed. And thinking.

And remembering what an amazing night he'd just had.

Well, this day promised to have some very interesting aspects, too. But nothing would compare with what he and Maya had shared.

As he enjoyed the memory, he pulled his neutral navy T-shirt on over his jeans. He liked his ability to dress casually most of the time here, even while claiming to be an employee of the federal government.

He hoped Maya had found last night as good as it had felt to him, and that it would be the first of many such nights—as long as she remained receptive not only to who he was, but also to keeping secret his identity and the existence of Alpha Force.

And as long as they shared an affinity to wolves—although clearly for different reasons.

Shirt on and wallet in his pocket, he got ready to leave. He'd already called Piers, and now he hurried from his room and out through the hotel's lobby to catch up with his aide and dog. He needed to share with Piers that he had informed Maya about Alpha Force and what her reaction had been.

Everything else could remain private between Maya and him.

He spotted them on the next block, Piers on the sidewalk and Rocky sniffing nearby grass.

All three were about to meet Maya for breakfast—again. And when they had finished, Piers and he absolutely needed something from the grocery store.

It was time to let the Sharans in on their little secret, too—as long as they also promised to keep what he revealed to themselves.

"Hey," Ryan said as he caught up with Piers. Rocky had spotted him first and pulled on his leash in his direction. Ryan strode toward his wonderful wolf-dog and ruffled the thick fur on his head, scratching behind his erect ears.

And thinking about how it would feel if someone patted him the same way when he was shifted…

"Morning, boss." Piers joined Ryan at Rocky's side. He looked quizzically toward Ryan as if he sensed something was different, but he was tactful enough not to ask. Even so, Ryan wondered if his pleasure was evident on his face.

Instead Piers asked, "What's on our agenda today?"

"I've already followed through on letting Maya know

our background," Ryan said, starting to walk toward
Andy and Family's restaurant. He purposely didn't look
at Piers as he spoke, not wanting to see any amusement
there if his aide knew what that had led to. "Since we've
got Drew's okay, next thing I want to do is approach the
Sharans and see how that comes out."

What he hadn't done with Maya, though, was to invite her to walk to breakfast with them. He'd wanted
to bring Piers up-to-date about his revelation to Maya
and plans for the Sharans.

He felt certain that telling Maya had been the right
thing. In fact, he hoped he would find ways to utilize
her knowledge and assistance.

They reached the restaurant. Ryan squared his shoulders before proceeding inside after Piers and Rocky.
Heck, he was a professional, as well as a shifter. He
would do what was right for his military unit, fellow
shifters and even wild wolves.

If that permitted more interaction with Maya, all
the better. But if it didn't, he would do what he had to.

Breakfast at Andy and Family's was becoming a
pleasant habit, Maya thought as she saw Ryan, Piers
and Rocky enter and head for the table she'd saved for
all of them just outside on the patio.

Interesting that she had arrived before the others
did this time. But, though Ryan and she had talked
about when they'd meet for breakfast, she hadn't tried
contacting him to see if they should all walk together
once more. In fact, after the night they had shared, she
needed a little space.

To think more about it? That hadn't been her intent,
but it was what she'd done nonetheless.

To fixate on it as she walked alone in this direction.

To recall the most delightful moments, with Ryan's hands on her, with her hands on him. And more. Much more...

Enough. She could certainly move her mind off it now, out in public, while they ate. She had to.

Plus—well, she'd have to follow Ryan's lead in how to act with Piers. She now knew Piers was Ryan's aide in his odd but appropriate military unit. Presumably, Piers wouldn't criticize his superior officer. Or could he in these circumstances?

"Good morning." Ryan smiled down at her as he pulled his chair from beneath the table.

"Hi." She leveled a neutral grin first on him, then Piers and finally Rocky. She reached over to scratch the wolf-dog behind his ears, watching him and not the men who accompanied him. But she looked again toward Ryan as he sat down. "Hope you slept well last night."

Was that a stupid thing to say? Had he already revealed to Piers what they'd been up to? She managed a sideways glance at the other man. His pleasant expression gave away nothing.

"Well enough." Ryan raised his dark eyebrows for an instant as he regarded her. Even that fairly neutral expression was enough to heat her insides once more, but she ignored it. "I'm pretty hungry this morning. Hotcakes and sausage sounds good to me. How about you?"

Their conversation glommed on to food possibilities. Nice and nonchalant, Maya thought. A server came over to bring drinks nearly immediately. Maya chose coffee, since she needed caffeine to keep her going after her lack of sleep.

They soon placed their food order, as well. Everything seemed nice and calm and not much different from their prior breakfasts together.

How could that be? Maya had an urge to stand and dash toward Ryan and take him into her arms, covering his face with kisses. Touching as subtly as possible those parts of his body that had given her such pleasure last night.

But she of course stayed still.

"So what are your plans today?" she asked Ryan, as neutrally as she could manage.

"We have some official business to take care of first thing," he said. His slight smile had some kind of message behind it. She probably wasn't supposed to ask questions.

Even so, she would ask anyway, though she would maintain the cover story.

"Then Fish and Wildlife has you out and about today?" She opened her eyes wide as if fascinated by whatever answer they'd give. And she truly would be interested.

She would be even more interested in having them tell her the truth. If they had an official assignment today, it wouldn't be something US Fish and Wildlife ordered them to do.

But that fascinating Alpha Force Ryan had told her about? It was another story. She felt certain that whatever they were up to, it would result from the covert military unit he had described. And she wanted to know more about it. A lot more.

"That's right," he responded.

"This is a great area to deal with wildlife issues," Piers said, backing Ryan up. "We've got more ideas about looking into the wolves around here before we go back to our headquarters."

Piers looked at her with an expression that appeared

to give her orders, maybe even more than his commanding officer did.

"Well, if there's anything I, or WHaM, can do to help you protect those wolves, just let me know," Maya said.

They seemed to agree, but she doubted they'd follow through. Bringing her closer, giving her more knowledge, wasn't something either was likely to do. She'd need to figure out a way to do it herself.

But for the moment, she would just play along—first enjoying her breakfast and, later, determining on her own just what they were up to.

Maya apparently had administrative work to do for WHaM that held some urgency but could be accomplished online, or so she told them as they finished their breakfasts. That sounded fine to Ryan, especially since she said goodbye at the restaurant door and headed back to their hotel after insisting on paying for breakfast for all of them. He'd let her—this time. She now knew he wasn't being funded by Fish and Wildlife, but he was still an employee of the federal government.

Even so, he appreciated her insistence on taking care of things herself. She was independent. She loved wolves.

She was the sexiest woman he had ever met...but he couldn't keep thinking about that.

As they separated, he, Piers and Rocky headed toward the Corner Grocery Store. They had a meeting to conduct.

Ryan wasn't especially pleased that Maya was joined on the next block by that guy Trev, but he trusted her not to say anything.

He just didn't trust that guy, geek though he appeared to be, to avoid coming on to Maya. Hopefully,

they would just discuss wolves—nonshifting ones—
and WHaM.

It was around 10:00 a.m. by then, but the store wasn't
particularly busy when they arrived. There were a few patrons in all the aisles but no big crowd, and only a couple
of people waited in line to check out. Someone who wasn't
a Sharan, presumably an employee, was helping them.

A strong aroma of hazelnut coffee permeated the
place, and Ryan assumed that some beans had just been
ground somewhere in the back to brew a large urn for
patrons. Other aromas he inhaled included fruit muf-
fins—sweet and tart and sugary. Good thing he'd already eaten breakfast, but his mouth watered anyway.
There were a lot more scents around here in the morning than later in the day.

The Sharans might not think having so few patrons
was a good thing, but Ryan was glad. He hoped he'd
get all three of them to invite his group into their office to talk.

Burt was nearest the door, refreshing some shelves
with pastries including the ones Ryan had smelled. Ryan
approached him first. "Good morning." He smiled as if
all was well between them. Hopefully, it was.

"Hello. What can I help you with today?" Burt's
skeptical expression suggested he didn't want to hear,
whatever it was.

Ryan kept his voice low. "Are Kathie and Pete
around? I'd like us to get together in your office. I've
gotten approval to let you in on something I think you'll
want to hear about."

Burt lifted his chin, staring at Ryan down his long
nose, his apparent skepticism building. "Why would
we want to hear about it?" he asked, keeping his voice
muted as well, his eyes darting around as if to make

sure no one was close by. "We already know too much about each other."

"But there's something I can reveal to you soon that I think you'll want to hear. Something good. Something that might make Pete especially happy."

As they'd been talking, Ryan had spotted Pete approaching along the nearest aisle. He'd raised his voice slightly—not that someone like Pete wouldn't have been able to hear him anyway.

"Why is that?" the younger man asked as he reached them. He appeared somewhat interested, his shaggy brows raised but his dark eyes not radiating the same skepticism and mistrust as his father's.

"Why don't we go into your office and talk?" Ryan countered. "Then you can be the one to judge whether what I have to say can change your life the way I think it potentially will."

That clearly got Pete's attention. He first obtained his dad's reluctant okay for the meeting Ryan suggested, then went off to get his mother.

Soon, after Burt talked to their few employees on duty, the Sharans headed to the office at the back of the store with Ryan's group. Ryan had scoped it out before for its privacy, and the walls were thick enough to contain some insulation. Perfect soundproofing? Unlikely, but with the store patrons talking outside only shifters were apt to be able to hear anything from the office, and Ryan would make sure they kept their voices low.

"Okay," Ryan said as they all settled into the small room. Burt Sharan had the main seat behind the desk this time, with Kathle on a chair beside him and Pete standing behind him.

Ryan took another chair, and Piers sat at his side with his hand on Rocky's head. The wolf-dog soon lay down on the floor, obviously not stressing about what the people around him were up to.

"So what the hell are you talking about?" demanded Burt right away. "You've got our attention. We all know that most of us except a couple—" he looked toward Piers, then at Rocky lying on the floor "—have something in common. Is that what this is about? We've already discussed it."

"Let's keep our voices down," Ryan directed him, muting his own voice. "And, yes, we've discussed some aspects of it." He looked beyond Burt and up toward Pete, staring him straight in the eye. "But Piers, Rocky and I are here for some very special reasons. We have been sent by a particularly special organization to learn about local shifters as well as feral wolves—but primarily the former."

He stood, maneuvered around the desk and placed himself directly in front of Pete.

"First things first, though," Ryan said, still speaking softly. He turned to Pete. "I don't know whether you've heard, but Vinnie Fritts was attacked by a wolf the way her husband was—the night you and I ran into each other in shifted form. Did you have anything to do with that?" He hoped he knew the answer.

"Really? No!" Pete exclaimed. "Like I told you, I shifted back right after you and I saw each other. And—in case you're wondering—I do remember images of what I see while shifted so I'd know if I attacked a human. Which I'd never do."

"How dare you—" Kathie began, but at least she also kept her tone low. She'd started to stand up at Ryan's question.

"I hoped, and believed, that would be the answer," he said. He looked Kathie in the eye, and although she still looked troubled she sat down again. Her husband, too, regarded Ryan suspiciously but said nothing—for now. "And I accept it," Ryan continued, "although if any of you happen to hear of other shifters in town who might have been involved, or any rumors of wild wolves who could have attacked, please let me know." He wanted answers, actual answers, but intended to do what he could to protect whatever wolf was involved. One of the other Sharans? He doubted it.

And could he really believe Pete? He wanted to. *Did* believe him. Could he be wrong? Sure, but he didn't think so.

Besides, Vinnie Fritts should have known better than to confront any canine, especially after what had happened to her husband.

"Okay, now," Ryan said next. "Let's get to what I really wanted to talk about. Pete, I recognize that this is now your home and respect that. And before this goes any further, I need to get a promise from each of you that what I'm about to reveal will be kept utterly secret by you, that you'll talk about it only among yourselves and even then in circumstances when no one will be able to hear you—not even other shifters, so you'll have to be particularly careful that you're not within their hearing distance while shifted or human."

"What is this all about?" This time Kathie stood up completely, facing Ryan and her son. Her voice was somewhat raised now. Her usually fluffy light hair was now styled close to her face, and her deep brown eyes were even wider than usual beneath brows that gave her a particularly troubled look. "Are you playing games with us? With Pete?"

The movement stirred Rocky's attention, and the dog now rose, looking from one human to another. "It's okay, boy," Piers told him, scratching behind his ears. Though the dog sat back down again, he remained alert—and looked even more like Ryan's cover dog, taking on a more concerned expression than the smart canine usually did. Ryan couldn't help smiling at him before responding to Kathie's questions.

"Not at all," he finally said, once more acting as an example by lowering his voice. "And this is what I actually came here for today. I might be wrong about Pete's ambitions, but I think he'll appreciate the choice of whether to remain here helping to run your store for the next years, or giving something else that could be part of who he is a try."

"What's that?" Pete's expression remained neutral, but something flashed in his eyes that suggested to Ryan that his interest had been piqued.

"Like I said," Ryan continued, "do I have promises of secrecy from all of you?"

He saw the parents exchange glances first with each other, then with their son.

Even if they agreed, could he trust them? Probably, since they, too, were shifters. But somehow he felt that the promise he had obtained from Maya would be worth even more.

Was that just because of what they'd shared? He didn't think so. He trusted her and her love of wildlife—of all kinds.

But these people, if they agreed to stay quiet, would have more at stake if they didn't.

"Yes," Pete finally said first. "I promise to keep it secret."

"Me, too," said Kathie.

"I will, too," Burt finally added.

Ryan traded glances with Piers, whose smile looked wry yet genuine. "Go ahead," his aide said.

"Okay." Ryan grinned broadly at each of them, then continued, "We, my friends, are members of a very special covert US military unit, Alpha Force."

For the next few minutes, Ryan explained a bit of what Alpha Force was about—how it had been started, how it continued with shifters and cover animals and aides, and some of the amazing and productive goals it had achieved to help the United States. All was done undercover and achieving only the kudos of the few members of the government trusted with knowing what they were about.

"We're always checking into the potential existence of other shifters," Ryan said, "and looking to recruit additional qualified members." They'd all regained their earlier positions by then, but he rose once more to face Pete directly. "That," he said, "might include you."

"Really?" Pete sounded like an excited child told he was about to meet Santa Claus.

Swallowing a chuckle, Ryan said quite seriously, "Really. I'll want to talk to you more about your qualifications. And I'd also like you to interview and audition for us, starting tonight if possible."

The young man had the decency to look once more at his parents, although his excitement remained written on his face. "I don't want to do anything to make things harder for you, Mom and Dad," he said to them.

"And we want the best for you," Kathie said. "Keep us in the loop, okay? But go ahead and do your interview and all, if it's what you want."

"Thanks!" He bent to give each of his parents a kiss, then he looked back up, first at Rocky and Piers, then at Ryan. "And is Alpha Force the best?"

"The absolute best," Ryan said with a smile of his own.

Chapter 21

Ryan could almost hear what Kathie and Burt Sharan weren't saying as their brief meeting closed and they all shook hands and headed back into the store. Pete's parents kept looking at each other, and at their son, and back again.

Were they concerned about how the store would do with just them around to run it? Maybe, but they had already taken on help. Ryan was curious whether any of the clerks were also shifters. He hoped to find that out.

In any event, he figured the Sharans were worried about how their son would potentially do far from here, in a military unit no one was permitted to talk about much. Would he be in danger? Possibly, but he might be in danger here as well, where some people were pleased to have wolves around…and others weren't.

Perhaps the unknown aspects of the situation were also worrying them. He could understand that. But if

Pete's testing went well, and if the young man remained interested, Ryan would invite them to come along when he took Pete to introduce him to the other unit members. If Pete was then recruited, Ryan himself would reassure the Sharans about how wonderful that was and make sure they had his contact information. After that, they, as shifters, could come visit the Alpha Force headquarters in Mary Glen, Maryland, as often as they wanted to talk to others in the unit, as well.

Yet they were parents—apparently caring ones. He had wondered now and then how his parents had coped, living in a remote part of Wyoming that nevertheless contained not only shifters but regular humans, as well. He still had a loving family, and Ryan knew his mom and dad and grandparents worried about him, but they clearly were proud of what he now was doing.

Would he ever marry and have kids—presumably shifters? How would he feel if they integrated into partially nonshifter society, as he had?

And who would he marry? Maya's face popped into his mind even as he placed himself in the main grocery store aisle to say goodbye. He immediately erased the image. Sure, they'd shared wonderful sex, but that was all.

That had to be all, considering the many differences between them.

"So," he said softly to Pete, who had stayed beside him. The store was more crowded now, filled with an undercurrent of voices though fewer tempting aromas. "I'll come by around nine tonight and we'll go have a… drink. And I'll interview you." He got even closer so he could whisper into the young man's ear. "The formula you've developed to…well, you know. Please bring it for a demo, okay?"

"Fine." Pete smiled, even as Ryan turned to leave—and stopped.

Just entering the store were the Frittses, both of them. Morton and Vinnie had come through the door and were now side by side, looking around.

Vinnie's eyes lit on Ryan first. He could still see the healing scratches on her face, and she was bent over as if it remained difficult to walk.

For Morton, too, although his healing scabs were now turning into scars.

Both glowered at Ryan, then at Piers, who was now beside him—and, of course, at Rocky, who resembled a wolf. Then they started walking toward Ryan.

"Hello," he said, painting a big, caring smile on his face. "You look better, both of you. I assume you're healing well, or at least I hope so." He gestured around the store. "I just came in for some snacks. You?"

"Yeah. Snacks. And more." Morton looked as if someone had attempted to shove crispy graham crackers down his throat. "I don't suppose you feds have come to see the light and have decided to round up the wolves?"

"I don't suppose so." Ryan kept his voice as friendly as possible. He wanted to shout out, ask these injured people again just how they'd both happened upon wolves in the middle of the night—shifters or not—and put themselves into positions to be attacked.

He still suspected they'd somehow done it on purpose so they could wind up looking this damaged and pitiful. But if so, why did they hate wolves that much?

If it truly had been two separate and unfortunate confrontations…well, again, how and why?

And surely Pete Sharan hadn't been involved either time…

"Well, we really just need some stuff for dinner tonight, that's why we're here." Turning so his gaze no longer met Ryan's, Morton maneuvered his way around him in the aisle, still coming close enough to bump into him as if asserting nonverbally who was in charge.

Which might have made Ryan laugh if the circumstances here weren't so challenging. He wouldn't be surprised if the Frittses knew, or suspected, that there were shifters around.

Either way, they clearly weren't thrilled. Or at least there was no indication they'd be more accepting if the wolves were genuine wildlife. Or if, perhaps, they preferred shifters, after all.

As both Frittses meandered farther from him, Ryan looked at Piers and nodded toward the door, essentially telling his aide it was time for Rocky and him to leave.

And Ryan? He decided he was in desperate need of some supplies to bring back to the hotel. At least he wanted it to appear that way. He hurried to the entry, got a plastic basket to drape over his arm, then began wandering after picking up a loaf of bread so it appeared he actually was shopping.

But what he really was doing was attempting to subtly observe the Frittses.

What kind of game were they playing? He knew what kind of game *he* was playing: watching this unfathomable couple and how they appeared to interact with others who were shifters, the Sharans.

Did they know or suspect that, or was their visit to this store completely innocent?

Ryan was interested when the Frittses both approached Pete, who appeared to be restocking a refrigerator case with red meats. Ryan inhaled the enticing aroma and figured that Pete was doing so, too.

"Is there any fresh meat in this store?" Vinnie asked,

her expression sardonic. "Like, anything we should carry so we can throw it far from us if a wolf approaches to get it away from us?" She didn't move her gaze from Pete's face, and the young man appeared amused— though not without some effort.

"I'd suggest you just stay inside at night, far away from where any wolves might be. You were attacked at night, both of you, right?"

"That's right. And do you have any other advice?" That was Morton talking, and both the Frittses took further steps toward Pete as if attempting to back him into a corner.

Which Ryan didn't like at all. He maneuvered toward them and pushed between the two Frittses, bending over the refrigerated counter. "Hey, this stuff looks good. I think I'll buy some for tonight." He turned slightly to face Vinnie. "Maybe that's what you should do, too. Cook at home to let yourself heal better, go to bed early and all that. And so far everything I've bought here is good, so load up now." Ryan picked up a package of raw T-bone steak figuring he wouldn't have anyplace to cook it at the hotel, but its cost, even if he just left it in his room's refrigerator, would be worth it to calm this situation.

"Mind your own business, Mr. Fish and Wildlife," Morton growled.

"Oh," said Ryan, "I am." He slipped the steak into the basket he held and continued to stand there, moving his gaze from one of the Frittses to the other until they apparently grew uncomfortable enough to move.

"Here." Vinnie shoved the basket she held at Pete. "Put this stuff away. I've changed my mind. I don't want to buy anything in this filthy, nasty store." She grabbed Morton's hand, and they both stomped out of the place.

"Thanks, I think," Pete said softly. "I already wondered if they thought…knew…you know."

"They clearly aren't fans of wildlife," Ryan agreed. "And I think it would be best if all of us who are wolf aficionados stayed out of their way."

He soon paid for his steak and other stuff, then, bags in hand, once more sought out Pete. "We're on for tonight still, right?"

"Can't wait," Pete replied.

Why was it, Maya wondered, that she felt certain Ryan and Piers, and maybe even Rocky, had a very different agenda from hers that day?

She'd been a bit surprised when Trev had caught up with her during her walk back to her hotel, but fortunately he had mostly just said hi, asked how she—and WHaM—were doing that day and mentioned not hearing any wolves last night.

Not a surprise to Maya. She hadn't heard any, either.

But she had certainly had a wonderful time with one of those entities who could have been on the hillside howling…in a different form and under different circumstances.

Trev had seemed a bit pushier about the wolves, giving her his phone number and asking her to call if she heard them again. But then, fortunately, he had left her, crossing the street as she reached the hotel.

Now, sitting on her hotel room bed with her computer open on the coverlet in front of her, she'd started to work practically the instant she had returned after breakfast. It was all essential stuff, and she was glad to work on it.

Even as her mind floated off now and then to wonder where Ryan and his gang were, and what they were doing.

Oh, she knew she had a unique assignment, speaking with her fellow WHaM executive Cheryl Jaker on the phone, then working with her on the group's remote assessment of the origin of the wolves now in Fritts Corner and where she might be able to observe some more. She was the only WHaM representative in the area, sure, but her organization had developed a computer program that helped to predict where wolves that had been seen and listed in their census had come from and where they might roam in the next weeks.

Always accurate? No. And Maya figured that its accuracy would be even less when it came to predicting where shifters might go.

On the other hand, shapeshifters would most likely remain in the areas where their human selves had set up their homes.

While talking on the phone with Cheryl, Maya thought that, if nothing else, demonstrating what she was seeing online might be a good reason to approach Ryan and all, in case they were interested.

It at least gave her a good excuse to contact Ryan.

But first, she had additional administrative items to attend to despite her distance from headquarters, and so she dug into that. And eventually realized it was midafternoon.

She had pretty well finished all she needed to do—for WHaM. But what about for herself? Or the local wolves?

She made a few other small entries into the computer, placed another brief call to Cheryl to substantiate some items she had seen and wanted to confirm, then decided to call it a day, at least with reference to her professional association.

It was nearly four o'clock, late enough to consider plans for the evening.

Not that tonight would be anything like last night—although she could dream, couldn't she?

No. Last night's experience with Ryan was a once-in-a-lifetime event. Now, she had to get back to being totally professional with him.

Work with him in preserving the wolves that had shown up around here.

Maybe even get him to reveal which were like him. If so—well, she'd have to work with him, and maybe his Alpha Force to some extent—to determine the best way for WHaM to ensure the wildlife's ongoing existence without violating her promise of secrecy.

Alpha Force. What an amazing-sounding military unit. She hoped to learn more about them. A lot more.

But not right now.

Closing her computer, she got off the bed. She'd sat there most of the time during the last few hours, so she was stiff. She walked around for a minute or two, then hurried back to the bed where she had left her phone.

She called Ryan, and he answered right away—a good sign. "Hey," she said, "I've been working all day and need a break this evening. Are you free for dinner? All of you, if you'd like."

He didn't answer immediately, which troubled her. If he was as enthusiastic as she was, surely he'd jump right on her invitation and agree. But his answer, only a few seconds later, was positive. "Sure," he said. "But we'll need to eat early. And, just so you know, we've got some other plans later tonight so it'll have to be a relatively quick meal."

."That's fine," she said, maybe a little too brightly. He was trying to be kind while pulling away from her.

Or maybe they really did have other plans for that night. If so, what were they?

Hopefully she would find out at dinner.

But dinner turned out to be a lot earlier, and a lot quicker, than Maya had hoped for. Plus, Piers and Rocky were with them. That was no surprise. She had included them in her invitation.

Even so—well, she felt irrationally, or perhaps rationally, disappointed when all three of them met up in the hotel lobby not long after she'd spoken with Ryan and walked to the House of Steak together. It didn't help that she got to walk Rocky there. Not that she didn't enjoy holding the wolf-dog's leash and teasing him, and the men, as they hurried along. After all, they all had their own relationships with wolves, whether or not they could talk about it.

But right or wrong, she really wanted to be with Ryan.

It was early enough that the restaurant wasn't overly crowded. "I'll bet you're in the mood for a nice, big, rare steak," Maya gibed at Ryan after they'd been seated inside but near the patio door.

"Maybe I'll have a chicken sandwich tonight," he countered, his raised brows suggesting the picture of innocence on his utterly handsome face. But then he smiled. "Or not."

They ordered. Maya decided on a steak, though a smaller one than either of the men. None of them asked for wine or any other drink.

Maya again wondered what they were up to this evening, and whether that had anything to do with the guys choosing not to have alcohol.

Her curiosity led her to avoid any, too. Could she get them to reveal what was going on?

Could she find out some other way? Maybe she was reading things all wrong, but her curiosity was stoked.

She couldn't help wondering whether whatever it was involved Ryan shifting that night...

"Don't know what you three did today, but here's what I was up to." Maya began describing the wolf-tracking and prediction program used by WHaM.

"Really? Does it actually work?" Piers in particular looked impressed.

"Somewhat, though it's not perfect." Maya told them how well it had appeared to work in another location, in Alaska, when it was being tested, and in some Colorado locations, as well. "And there are some factors about...well, certain wolf characteristics that haven't yet been programmed in, and probably will never be."

She caught Ryan's eye as if to assure him she was talking about shifters, and that she'd never reveal anything, as promised.

Soon, dinner was served, and they all enjoyed their meals, even Rocky—or at least the dog received samples from each of the humans.

And eventually it was over. As always, Maya attempted to pay her share, which seldom worked, and she was almost never permitted to treat the others. This time, Piers insisted, and Ryan backed him up.

They walked back to the hotel together. Maya was able to maneuver things so that Ryan and she followed Piers, who had Rocky on his leash.

"This was a very pleasant evening," she told Ryan, smiling at him with just a hint of suggestion in her smile to see his reaction.

"It was. Sorry it has to end this early, but as I said we have some plans that can't be changed."

"Oh." Maya hesitated, then said, "Don't suppose I could tag along, could I?"

"Sorry. Not tonight." He actually did appear somewhat sorry, as his mouth curved into a grimace. "Hopefully we'll get more time together soon—to talk more about that program, for one thing."

Then he wasn't suggesting another night of passion, or even hinting there could be one. Oh, well. It was better that way.

But Maya remained curious. What were they really up to that evening?

Could she figure out a way to find out?

She was definitely going to try.

Chapter 22

Any regret Ryan had about shrugging Maya off that night had disappeared—well, mostly—as he and Piers drove to the lot at the far side from the park, at the base of the hillside. They'd brought Rocky along, too, in case Ryan needed extra cover, though they considered that unlikely.

Ryan intended to shift. But he particularly wanted Pete Sharan to shift first, using his own formula so Piers and Ryan could observe what occurred. They were also meeting his parents there because the senior Sharans wanted to be kept in the loop as much as possible, and they already knew about the existence of Alpha Force.

Their rental car, which Piers had driven, was the only vehicle there, a good thing even though it was expected. They had arrived earlier than they'd told the Sharans to meet them, and their meeting place was the clearing partway up the hillside. That family could approach it other ways.

"So, you ready?" Piers asked as he removed the key from the ignition switch.

"I'm always ready." Ryan tried to sound as if he meant it. But Piers knew him well enough to recognize when he was acting fine but had a few qualms inside.

They opened their car doors simultaneously, and while Ryan got Rocky out of the backseat Piers used the key to pop the trunk. He extracted the large backpack he used to carry his Alpha Force supplies, including light and elixir.

Ryan wondered what kind of concoction Pete had put together to aide him in shifting, if it contained any ingredients also within the Alpha Force elixir. He might never learn that with certainty, but if he was able to recruit Pete the guys with the scientific backgrounds in their military unit who kept improving the elixir would undoubtedly figure it out.

The few lights on poles in the parking lot emitted only a dim glow, as if it was nearly a given that no one would really park here after dark. Well, in his short time in Fritts Corner, Ryan had learned otherwise. They'd parked in a darker area where the car would not be beneath the glow of any light. If anyone else happened to come by, they might even think the car had been abandoned here, at least overnight. After all, who in his right mind would be hiking up the thickly forested hillside after dark?

Never mind that it had been done before.

"You ready?" he asked Piers once the trunk was shut and he'd helped his aide fasten the bag over his shoulders.

"Yeah. Let's move."

Piers made it look easy to carry all that heavy stuff. They'd both donned black athletic clothes to allow them agility while keeping their visibility at a minimum. In seconds, all three of them were on the worn path up the hillside, and only then did Piers remove a light from his pocket to illuminate their way.

Though Ryan would have preferred moving more briskly, they kept their pace slow, mostly to minimize how much they could be heard by regular human ears if anyone, as unlikely as it was, happened also to be hiking in the dark.

If they were heard by shifters, in either form, that was most likely okay.

They maneuvered around trees and bushes, and Ryan listened for sounds of any life around them. He heard rustles of creatures of the night and confirmed by their scents that they included raccoons, possums and skunks, and other nocturnal beings that were longtime natives to this area. Then there were the owls and other birds he anticipated, as well. Rocky put his nose into the air often but didn't slow them down.

No wolves. Not yet.

"Almost there," Piers whispered. In addition to holding the flashlight, he'd been peering at his phone's GPS. The area was somewhat familiar to Ryan since they'd been there before, but even someone with his enhanced senses needed some assistance in finding places in the dark that were hidden by canopies of trees.

In another minute, the trees gave way to an opening, and Piers shone his light around. The clearing was vast, and they stayed along its periphery—but only for a moment.

Three people stepped out of the darkness off to their right and approached. It was the Sharans.

"What kept you?" The broad smile on Pete's face told Ryan he was just joking. "Hey, we just got here, too. So—what magic are we going to create tonight?"

He looked directly at Ryan, and his parents were right behind him. All of them, too, were dressed in dark clothes, right down to their athletic shoes. Kathie Sharan appeared concerned, or at least Ryan saw a big frown on her face in the glow now emanating not only from Piers's flashlight but hers and Burt's, too.

Pete held a large brown duffel bag in his right hand. Was that where he stowed his equivalent of an elixir? Ryan figured they'd find out soon.

"Magic?" Ryan repeated. "I don't think any of this is magic, but it's certainly stuff that regular people might consider, well, supernatural, or at least different."

"I'll say." Pete put his bag on the dirt ground around them. "So where do we start?"

"Okay, as I first said before we decided on this meeting, you've already made a promise of secrecy. Do you confirm that promise?"

"Of course," Pete said, and his parents agreed. But then Pete added, "Can you tell us more now about Alpha Force?"

Good request. If he really was a potential candidate for recruitment, he would want to hear a lot more about the highly specialized military unit.

"Sure," Ryan said. "Hey, let's sit down here first for just a few minutes and get as comfortable as we can." The others followed his suggestion, and when they were all seated on the hard ground in a circle, he stopped to listen to make sure they remained alone. He again heard the sounds of some nocturnal animals but nothing stood out as presenting any danger, so he continued. "Okay, here it is—the short version. We do whatever is required of us by the military, going undercover a lot in various circumstances and, yes, getting involved in some combat, too. I'll tell you about some of our successes. And no, there haven't been any failures at all that I'm aware of."

For the next twenty minutes or so Ryan revealed some of the missions Alpha Force had been involved in, even going up against anarchists and training a similar unit of shifters in Canada.

"There's more," he said when he was done. "And as I indicated before, we're always eager to recruit other shifters who can jump in and help our unit—possibly including you, Pete."

"Heck, yes!" The young man jumped up. "I'd love to join Alpha Force. What do I have to do?"

"First thing, that formula that helps you shift—tell us more about it."

"Our son was always great at science in school," Burt said proudly.

"I was interested in science because I started shifting when I was a young kid and wanted to learn more about it, even though I couldn't talk about it to many of my school friends—only those who were also shifters. But I wanted to do more than be forced to shift, like it or not, under full moons. It took me a long time and a whole lot of experimentation, but I finally came up with something that lets me shift whenever I want to even outside a full moon."

"How does it work, and how long do you stay shifted?"

"It's far from perfect," Pete grumped. "But I shift about five minutes after I take a spoonful and stay shifted for about half an hour for every dose I take. Do you want to hear the ingredients?"

"If all goes well, I'll need for you to tell some of the unit members who get all the technical stuff better than me. But I want to observe you now, and then, when you're done, I'll give you a brief look at how Alpha Force's very special elixir works."

"That's how you changed the other night—an elixir?" Again, Pete sounded utterly excited. Ryan explained that the elixir was the basis of the unit, that it allowed shifting outside a full moon as Pete's medicine did—which he already knew after seeing Ryan shifted since he apparently recognized and recalled it from when he had been shifted, too—and that it permitted shifters while in shifted form to maintain their human cognition.

"Really?" Now even Burt sounded excited. "And can shifters outside the unit use that stuff?"

"Unfortunately, no—though we might be able to make occasional exceptions for family members."

"Okay, son, we're with you," Burt said to Pete. "Go for it." He glanced toward Kathie, who nodded.

Pete reached into his duffel and pulled out a plastic bag. His parents helped him place a dose of his liquid onto a spoon from a small bottle. He removed his clothes, then Kathie held him as, in a few minutes, Pete's shift began. He groaned and was clearly in pain as it went on, but it didn't take long despite there not being a full moon.

Soon, she was hugging a wolf. It was a larger wolf than Rocky. It backed off some, knocking at her with his muzzle and acting somewhat like a tame dog like Rocky, now sitting calmly beside Piers, who held his leash.

Rocky was definitely used to seeing people shift, though not exactly this way.

"May I?" Piers asked and at Burt's nod drew closer. "Okay, Pete, sit."

The wolf just looked at him without obeying.

"Do you understand what I'm saying?" Piers continued, but again, though he didn't run, the wolf stayed standing where he was.

Piers and Ryan took turns talking to him for the next ten minutes, but Ryan was certain that the wolf had no more human cognition than Rocky and most likely remained around only because he recognized his tie to his parents on some level.

Pete had said before, though, that he recalled what he saw while shifted, even if he couldn't use his human thinking abilities then.

Soon after that, his shift back began and then Pete lay naked on the ground, panting as he withdrew from his discomfort.

"Very impressive," Ryan said when he figured Pete could understand him. "Do you let other shifters use it?"

"Burt and I do, a little," Kathie said, "and some of our friends do, too, just for the fun of it—if you can call it fun."

"I can," Ryan said, "when I use the Alpha Force elixir. Do you want to see?"

"Sure," Pete gasped.

It was Ryan's turn to strip. He took a vial of the elixir Piers handed him and drank it, then waited in the light his aide shone on him that resembled that of the full moon.

Soon his own discomfort began, and in minutes he was wolfen in form.

He looked at the others, nodding his head. Then Piers, who had told an obedient Rocky to stay where he was, began talking to Ryan.

* * *

Sit. Piers had said that, and so Ryan sat.

Shake hands. He held out his paw.

When Piers told him to touch the ground as many days as they had been in Fritts Corner, he scraped it six times. The others looked somewhat impressed— although that could have been some of his training.

But then Piers told him to use his paw to scrape the loose dirt in the form of the moon that night, only a few nights after the full moon, he did that, too.

He heard all of those around him, shifters, too, gasp their amazement.

"I want that!" Pete exclaimed.

And Ryan believed he would soon introduce a new recruit to Alpha Force.

Maya hurried onto the tree-shrouded upward path before turning on her flashlight.

She had parked her car on the opposite side of the lot from Ryan's, in a corner as dark as possible at the foot of the hillside. She had left her purse in the trunk, although she'd stuck her cell phone into her pocket. She could use it to take pictures, but she hadn't brought her camera.

Before, certain Ryan and Piers were up to something that night—something important, she figured, since Ryan had let her know they had plans without revealing what—she had sat in her car in the shadows at the hotel parking lot for almost an hour, waiting.

Was Ryan shifting again? Maya felt certain of it. But why couldn't she watch this time?

She might just watch without their consent, if all went as she hoped.

Maybe they were walking to wherever their *plans* took them, but she somehow hadn't believed so. And her conjecture was proved correct when they arrived at their car around 9:00 p.m. and headed out.

She'd followed at a distance, not surprised at all when she saw they were heading toward the far side of the park and its forested slopes.

Where she knew full well that Ryan had shifted before.

She drove by the entry then, turning around and returning a while later when she figured they'd had time to leave their car and head up the hillside. Sure, they could be heading toward a different clearing for this night's shift, and in any event she'd have to be as careful as possible not to be heard by Ryan in either form or allow him to see a glow from her flashlight.

If she was lucky, she could pretend to be a creature of the night and make only the sounds an animal might create while hunting prey this late—the lightest footsteps possible. Her work at WHaM, and her prior visits to this hillside, gave her at least a little hope of achieving that.

She finally returned, and had again parked her car in those shadows, this time as far from the other car as she could in the extended but empty lot, got out of her car and secured her purse in the back. She did it all quickly and carefully to minimize the possibility that the lights, or sound of the car door or trunk closing, would capture Ryan's attention. In moments, she'd reached the threshold of the path up the hillside to the clearing.

Sure, she'd had to turn on her flashlight then, but hoped that the cover of the trees and other flora here would keep her from being spotted by Ryan or Piers. Ryan's extra senses were more focused on scents and sounds anyway.

She took a few steps, listening. Yes, she did hear

some distant noises like animals stepping on the forest's dried leaves, and she attempted to imitate them with her own steps.

She hoped she remembered all the turns on the upsloping path. There were branches away from it, after all, but the main path was the one she wanted.

She hoped it was the one Ryan and Piers wanted, too.

She hated going so slowly, but would hate it worse if she was discovered.

But she would hate it worst of all if she didn't arrive at the clearing in time to see Ryan shifted. She figured that, if he was already there, he would have changed into wolf form by now, but even if he ran into the woods he would return there, where he was likely to have left Piers, before shifting back—right?

Well, she'd just have to see.

For now, she attempted to curb her impatience and continued upward—also hoping she recalled enough to avoid getting lost up here in the dark. At least she wasn't cold, since she wore a hoodie—charcoal in color, and her pants and athletic shoes were dark, as well. She'd learned from Ryan that keeping a low profile at night included wearing drab and unexciting clothes that wouldn't grab the attention of any person who happened to be around, let alone any animals.

She figured she was about halfway there by now. Just a little farther and—

A moan sounded off to her left. A *human* moan.

And then a gasp, and a "Sshh."

What was going on? Was this Ryan's important task of the night, something to hurt a person? Had he attacked someone while shifted?

Which made her wonder again if it had been a shifter

who'd attacked the Frittses—and whether that shifter was, indeed, Ryan.

Okay. She didn't want to get lost, but she had to check. Still attempting to sound like a stalking wild creature, she moved off the path and in the direction of the sounds.

Which were followed by more sounds, like hisses and a "damn," which was also shushed.

What was going on?

Still trying to go slowly enough not to attract the attention of a person or creature, she continued forward. The aromas of blossoming trees and other plants seemed mushed together, and she didn't actually sense by smell or hearing any creatures like those she tried to emulate.

But were there wolves around? Shifters?

Suddenly, she saw a light ahead of her—and stopped walking. She moved behind a tree, though, to gaze forward into the small clearing that was ahead.

There, in the middle, beneath a light on what appeared to be a portable pole, sat Carlo Silling. His friend Morton Fritts knelt in front of him with some kind of gadget in his hand that appeared to resemble a claw of some kind. No, not a claw. It was like scissors with curved teeth—and Morton leaned forward and raked the thing against Carlo's face, which was already torn and bloody.

And resembled how Morton's, and Vinnie's, had looked after their apparent wolf attacks.

Apparent was now the operative word. They must have done this themselves, setting it up to look as if wolves had hurt them to garner sympathy—and more.

They undoubtedly wanted someone to go find the wolves, perhaps themselves, and kill them, using the attacks as an excuse.

And now they were performing a third one to help make their point.

Maya wished she could confront them. Better yet, call the authorities to confront them.

But for now she could do neither.

Except…she reached very slowly into her pocket, where she'd stuck her silenced phone. She needed to take a picture of this—and then get away. Far away.

She pulled it out and checked to make sure the flash wasn't on—a shame, since the picture wasn't likely to turn out well. But she didn't dare do anything to call attention to herself.

She aimed it toward her view of the supposed attack and pushed the button, moving the camera as she took several shots, glad the sound was off so there'd be no clicks to indicate photos were being taken.

She stuck her phone back into her pocket, took a few breaths, then turned to leave.

And felt her arm and neck being grabbed as she was thrown to the ground.

"What are you doing here, bitch?" yelled Vinnie Fritts's shrill voice.

"Hey, let her go," said a voice from behind Maya.

But it wasn't Ryan's voice, or even Piers's.

No, it was Trev. What the heck was he doing here?

And how, Maya wondered, was she going to get out of this?

Chapter 23

Still lying on the ground, Maya managed to look up toward Trev. He had a gun, and he stood there aiming it not toward Vinnie, but at her.

What was going on?

"Trev?" she said, hating the quaver in her voice. "Have you come up here looking for wolves? I haven't seen any. Or heard any. But I'd certainly like to see them." And please don't shoot me, she thought. Or any wolves. What was going on? Was he somehow a worse threat than the Frittses and Carlo?

"Yeah, I want to see them, too," Trev said. "I want to get rid of them—as many as I can." His face was an ugly sneer now, his voice angry.

"Really?" Vinnie, who'd been standing near Maya, now edged closer to Trev. "Who are you?"

The nearby illumination grew brighter suddenly, and

Morton and Carlo joined them. Morton held the pole with a light attached, probably battery powered.

"Yeah," Morton said, facing Trev. "Who the hell are you, and what are you doing here?" He didn't look nervous about the gun that Trev whipped around to aim on him.

Maybe that was because Carlo also had a gun—a larger one, and he had it pointed toward Trev.

"Hey," Trev said, holding up his hand so his gun was aimed toward the sky. "I'm on your side. You want to get rid of the wolves, don't you?"

"Yeah, we do," Morton said. "But you're not from around here. Why do you care if there are wolves in this area? Tell you what. You sit down right there and explain to us." He motioned to the ground below where Trev stood. It was covered with dead leaves like the rest of this woodland. Above, the tall trees obliterated any view of the moon or stars in the otherwise clear nighttime sky.

Vinnie knelt now beside Maya, binding her hands together. "This is getting more interesting all the time," she muttered.

Interesting, yes. And also frightening. Maya's wrists hurt beneath the ropes. The rest of her, lying on the ground, was uncomfortable, too. But she wasn't about to complain.

She just wished she understood what was happening, and why.

And who, really, was Trev?

"Okay, okay," Trev said, still holding his gun but not pointing it at anything. He obeyed and sat on the ground—too near Maya, she believed.

What was this supposed wildlife aficionado doing here, threatening wolves?

Threatening people, too. Only now, he was being threatened.

And so was she.

"Here's my story," Trev said. "And why I'm determined to get rid of wolves, or other protected wildlife, wherever it happens to be. And yeah." He glared toward Maya. "I'm against your wonderful WHaM. Like I told you, I came here because I heard someone from that damned organization was going to give a talk. I wanted to hear you, learn all about you. Figure out a way to turn you, and your group, into an example. Put an end to your organization and do the opposite of what you're saying. All those damned beasts out there, they should be killed by anyone who wants to."

"Then you're a hunter?" Maya ventured. Was that what this was about? He just wanted to kill animals for the fun of it?

She wished then that she was in a better position to rise, to run away from here.

To hopefully find Ryan, and get Piers and him and maybe their military organization to grab this guy, take down this entire group.

And make sure that wildlife remained protected from horrible people like him.

But...

Oh, Ryan, she thought. Would she even see him again?

Would she survive what was happening to her here?

"Yeah, I'm a hunter—now," Trev said. She saw him look toward Morton, then Carlo. "You guys, too?"

"In a way," Morton answered. "But we've got reason. Do you?"

"Of course." He looked back at Maya. "Did you by

any chance think enough about me to try to find me on the internet?"

She had but didn't want to admit it. Besides, she hadn't located anyone with his name.

"Not at all," she said, shooting him a disdaining grin.

"Well, it wouldn't have mattered if you had," he said. "See, my name's not Trevor Garlona. It's Tim Grant— so even if you knew that and tried looking me up, you'd find a lot of guys with my name."

"Why'd you do that?" Vinnie asked. She was now sitting on the ground beside Maya, no longer touching her.

"I needed a new name for what I intend to do," he said.

"Kill wolves?" Carlo asked scornfully. He was still standing, beside Morton.

He was still holding his gun.

"Exactly. And more wildlife, too. Anything I can— especially grizzly bears. But with all the publicity that's now being given to wolves coming back to Washington in large numbers, and mostly getting protection, especially in this part of the state—well, I just figured I could make a statement by killing a bunch of them, then explaining why. But I needed to do it under another name, another appearance, before going public."

"Why is that?" Maya asked. Keeping these people talking might give her time to figure out what to do. She couldn't get her phone out of her pocket with her hands bound, even if she had a way to call Ryan. But if he was up here on the hillside, his special wolflike abilities would let him hear human voices.

Assuming he was close enough.

"What do you care?" He sneered toward her. "You like those damned animals more than you like people, right?"

"No," she said quietly. Then, more defiantly, "Of course it depends on the people."

His laugh sounded bitter. "I'll bet it does. Well, what about if a person is the brother of a really cool, smart guy who was studying to be a doctor, who loved people and taking care of them—and even liked animals enough to go hunt them, not to shoot them but to take pictures? You might like that cool, smart guy with the camera, but what about his brother?"

"You're the brother?" Maya ventured. She shifted slightly on the dirt, trying to see him better—and get more comfortable. She succeeded a bit in the former, but not the latter.

"Yeah, the brother of that poor, smart, *dead* guy named Jerry Grant who was up on a mountain like this in another part of the state and happened to run into a grizzly bear. A damned *protected* grizzly bear, in that area."

Oh. This was starting to make at least a little sense now. Horrible sense. But Maya still didn't know what to do.

"That's why I came here to learn more about WHaM, to figure out how to put an end to it and its damned animal-loving members at least as an example to other groups who'd rather see vicious creatures live than people."

"I'm very sorry," she said quietly. Then, to all of them, she said, "Look, I know we have some major differences of opinion. Could we all just go back to town? I can leave tomorrow, not give any more talks favoring wildlife. I can even go public with something in addition to my advice to remember that wildlife is wild, something sympathetic to those who have been hurt by wild animals. Because I certainly am sympathetic."

She moved slightly to look toward Vinnie—and then realized she had seen, upon arriving here, the most likely way that Vinnie and Morton had been "attacked" by wolves.

The same way they had been goring Carlo with a fake claw.

No, she wasn't sympathetic toward them. But she didn't mention that.

"Sorry," Morton said. "That's not going to happen. But Trevor, or Tim, or whoever you are, we're really sorry for your loss, too. I can't even tell you how sorry we are, and with good reason. But I'm especially glad to hear that you hate lots of wild animals. Since you're here, you're going to get your wish to help bring down wild animals, to help us make our case against wolves. You see, I just had a damned good idea. You're going to be attacked by wolves, too. Like your brother was with a grizzly. And when people see one—or better yet two—people have been killed by them, then their protection is bound to end."

What was he talking about? Maya tried not to panic, but her breathing sped up. People being killed? Trev—or Tim—being killed?

Her being killed as number two?

"Now wait a minute," she began, but it was too late. Morton leaped down to where Trev sat on the ground, yanking the gun from him and throwing it to the side. He then pulled out that same gadget he had been using to wound Carlo, thrust the sharp claws hard into Trev's neck and yanked it sideways, as Trev gagged and coughed, till blood spewed from his throat.

"Then you really can think like a person while shifted? That's so cool! I love that you can count, and

make shapes on the ground, and all of it!" Pete, who had also shifted before but remained in human form now, pranced all around Ryan as he responded to Piers, eyeing him, clapping his hands.

"No hand clapping," Piers whispered sharply to Pete. "There aren't likely to be other people around but we don't need to make noise that could draw attention to us, just in case."

"Sorry." Pete dropped his hands to his sides.

Piers looked deeply into Ryan's eyes, his expression a question. Ryan nodded his head. Then Piers again faced Pete and said, "He wants you to come with him through the forest. He'll show you more of who he is, what he can do. Are you interested?"

"Am I!" Pete nodded vigorously, but then he turned to his parents as if seeking their consent.

Both nodded, too.

"Then go ahead. Follow Ryan. But be careful, and obey whatever he conveys to you. He'll give you instructions even without talking. You okay with that?"

"For sure."

"Here's a flashlight. Ryan's unlikely to need it since there is some brightness to tonight's moon, but you can use it. We don't want you tripping and hurting yourself."

"Thanks." Pete took the flashlight and turned it on. Good guy. He aimed it toward the ground and not into the trees.

And then Ryan slowly began stalking into the woods.

He could not go very fast with a human at his side, though he liked to bound through the brush in areas like this. But his current mission was to show this young man that not only was he a shifter, but that the Alpha Force elixir gave him powers and insights that only members of his unit had.

After a short while, he stopped and put his nose into the air. He captured the scent of a squirrel. He stalked carefully in that direction, then stood on his back legs with his front paws on that tree, looking toward the large knothole where he knew the small rodent resided, and most likely nested with young ones in the spring. He looked at Pete, barely visible in the light, and nodded.

Pete got the message. He examined the ground around them, picked up a fallen branch and knocked it against the trunk.

Nearly immediately, the squirrel shrilled its scratchy call and dashed outside onto the branch nearest to the hole. The animal looked down at them, made further noises, then disappeared upward into the thick branches.

A true wolf might do as he did, Ryan knew, but not necessarily at this hour, and only if seeking prey to eat. He instead got back down on all fours, looked at Pete and nodded his approval of what he had done.

Pete laughed. "Cute. I might be able to find us something else to scare but I'd do better if I was shifted, too."

Once more, Ryan nodded. Perhaps he could find a fox or a snake next time to play with using methods that were even more human. He headed in a different direction now, making certain Pete followed.

What could he do next to make it clear to the young man how much human cognition he maintained? He sniffed at the air, figuring he would head toward the flat lawn of the park, perhaps demonstrating something near the podium where Maya had spoken.

Maya. What would she think if she saw him now and recognized who he was?

Too bad that he could not have agreed to allow her

to participate. It was an important exercise for Alpha Force and needed to remain classified.

For the next minutes, he allowed his nose to lead him downward and in the direction of the park—until he suddenly heard a very soft but shrill noise, like a human cry of terror.

He stopped only for an instant to look up at Pete. Had the young shifter heard it, too?

Maybe. His expression appeared puzzled.

Ryan uttered a low growl and nodded his head in the direction from which the noise had come—just as he heard another one.

"What is that?" Pete asked softly.

With a small woof, Ryan began running in that direction, knowing Pete's footsteps would be louder and more conspicuous here than his own. But if a human was in trouble—well, there could be no better demonstration of the usefulness of the Alpha Force elixir than for him to use his human cognition to help that person.

Did he hear sounds from behind him? Perhaps Piers had indeed followed, despite agreement not to. But having backup here might be useful, and he undoubtedly would have Rocky with him.

Although—might it be someone else? There seemed to be more than one set of footsteps, and not just from one human and dog. Surely the older Sharans weren't following, as well.

Ryan could not stop to check now. He could only hope that, whoever it was, they did not add to what he suspected could become a dangerous situation.

As he ran, he listened and continued to smell the air. It would be better if he was alone. He did not want to lead Pete into danger.

And when he heard further sounds, voices and

moans, he had no doubt that there was danger ahead of them.

There was also someone in trouble. It might be his human imagination, but the voice that moaned sounded like Maya, though that could not be. She was in her hotel room for the night.

But he knew her well enough to recognize that she was wherever she wanted to be—although of course, if it was her in danger, that had not been her goal.

"Please, just let me go. I won't tell anyone."

Damn. That was Maya's voice from somewhere in front of them. Ryan halted and turned to face Pete, to make him not only slow down and cease the sounds of human running footsteps through these woods, but also to stay back while Ryan scoped out what was there.

What was happening to Maya?

Who was with her, and who she was pleading with?

He quickly shook his head when he met Pete's eyes, gently knocking the hand that held the flashlight to convey that it needed to be shut off. When Pete understood and obeyed, Ryan sat down, nodding his head to convey that Pete was to do the same.

He was glad in many respects when Pete obeyed that, as well. This was a young man who was a shifter, who was smart and followed orders well. He recognized Ryan's human cognition and respected it.

He would make a fine asset as a member of Alpha Force—depending on what happened now.

While Pete sat there, Ryan turned back and crept forward on all fours, close to the ground. He continued to listen and take in the smells around him.

He heard nothing from Maya now. Was she all right? Had whoever it was listened to her and let her go?

Ryan wasn't naive enough in either form to believe that.

Slowly, slowly, he moved forward, wishing he could run until he saw what was happening. But that might be more dangerous to Maya if he was heard or spotted too soon. He needed to surveil her situation before determining how to act.

He slid along the dead leaves among the trees, trying to make as little sound as possible.

A small clearing opened in front of him.

There, off to his right, sat Maya. She must have been bound, since her hands were behind her.

In front of her was Morton Fritts, leaning down as if he wanted to strike her.

Carlo Silling stood beside Morton. His face appeared to be sliced open, and Ryan smelled the scent of blood.

But it probably wasn't Carlo's he smelled. No, lying off to Maya's side was someone else. Someone whose throat had apparently been cut—gnawed?

He wasn't sure, but it appeared to be that Trev guy.

Fortunately he saw no injuries on her...yet.

He didn't even try to speculate why she was there. That information would come in time.

But for now he had to determine the best way to save her.

Vinnie Fritts was there as well, watching the men close to Maya.

What would be his best course of action? Were those men armed?

Might they shoot Maya first if he leaped in to try to help her?

He hated to stay where he was, even for a few precious seconds more. But if he wanted to do things right, he had to observe and think and plan.

Could he use Pete's help?

Maybe. But he hated turning back to tell the young man to join him.

For now, he would wait. And watch.

Maya was terrified. What could she do?

Trev was clearly dead. The marks at his throat did look astonishingly like bites. Wolf bites. And blood puddled on the ground beneath him.

Vinnie had aimed a gun at her while they finished killing Trev. She had made Maya sit up afterward and checked that her wrists were tightly bound. She wasn't sure what they intended for her—but considering what she had seen, she could guess.

Her phone remained in her pocket, but it was useless. She'd screamed once as they killed Trev, but Vinnie had kicked her and she'd immediately grown silent.

That had been a while ago now. The two men were huddled together over Trev's body, still arranging it, she thought. Clawing it more so it would appear the wolf had attacked other parts of him before going for the throat.

If only she could contact Ryan somehow, tell him what was happening, work with him to find an effective way after this to protect him and his kind, as well as feral wolves. Even before killing Trev, these miserable people had been creating injuries on themselves so they could blame wolves, the better for making claims that the animals should be killed.

And now they would have a dead body to demonstrate the worst that wolves could do.

If anyone deserved to really be attacked by wolves, it was these three. But she was the one in danger of being killed now.

Why wouldn't they kill her, considering that she'd seen what they had done to Trev? She knew the answer.

She knew what was coming.

Now she sat on the hard ground with her hands bound behind her back. She tried to keep her trembling from fear at a minimum. She didn't want to give any of them a further sense of triumph over her. In fact, they hadn't won...yet. She might be captured, but she wasn't done fighting.

She watched as Vinnie stood and joined Morton and the apparently injured Carlo. The group huddled together. Maya wished she could hear what they were saying.

Even more, she wished she could take this opportunity while none focused on her to run away. But though her legs were free, even if she managed to stand she recognized that at least Carlo, who faced her, would see it.

And they had guns. They probably didn't want to use them, since the wolves they wanted to blame for everything didn't shoot people, but she figured they would anyhow if she attempted to run. Even if they didn't shoot her, she doubted she'd be fleet enough, at least at first, to escape so far into the woods that they'd be unable to find her.

Those woods were dark despite the moon, though not quite full anymore, glowing above them. The light they had brought to this clearing wouldn't reach far. And she'd need her hands for balance.

Still, she worked on trying to pull them loose from the cords that bound them. She also attempted to look defeated as well as scared, even as she kept fidgeting slightly to try to find a way to stand and run.

At least the temperature was bearable, though chilly.

She kept listening for sounds in the forest, any kind of distraction—like the appearance of a wolf.

Right.

Oh, sure, she heard some noises, like an owl hooting in a nearby tree, and some rustling thanks to rodents running on the dried leaves on the ground. None of those would help her.

If only she had some way of communicating with Ryan. She'd no doubt that he would try to help her. But just because she now had reason to believe in something she had considered unreal and supernatural just days ago—shapeshifting—she didn't yet believe that all such supposedly paranormal things were true…like extrasensory perception. She'd already considered recently if ESP could be real but doubted it. And she'd need ESP now to get through to Ryan.

Uh-oh. The conclave among her enemies appeared to be over. All three were standing, facing her, staring at her. And grinning.

That couldn't be a good sign.

Vinnie broke away from the men. Maya wished she could wipe the smugness off the woman's face. The woman's *scratched and scarred* face. Maya wasn't a malicious person, but right now she wished she was able to add to Vinnie's injuries, scratch her face up even more to distract her and the others, then run away.

But for now she couldn't, didn't, move.

As Vinnie approached Maya, her hands weren't visible. Was she hiding a gun? Did she intend to shoot Maya, then bury her out here where no one would ever think to look for her?

They would still have a body to show the world, one that arguably had been attacked by a wolf.

Boy, had she been dumb, Maya thought, not to at

least have told Ryan what she was up to. But hindsight was, as usual, twenty-twenty.

She had to deal with things as they were now.

She had to survive, no matter what.

But then Vinnie pulled her hands from behind her back. She now grasped that clawlike gadget Morton had been using to maul Carlo—and that he'd then used to murder Trev. Of course.

Vinnie thrust it toward Maya, manipulating its handle so the claws at the end, mock nails as sharp as knives, opened and closed ominously.

"You know," Vinnie said, "I'd already figured it was a terrible shame that the wolves around here attacked first Morton, then me and poor Carlo, too. And after that, they even managed to kill that Trevor/Tim guy." She turned slightly in the men's direction but immediately faced Maya once more. "But they're not done. They're dangerous. Very dangerous. So dangerous that the one about to attack you will go for your throat, bite and claw it till you bleed to death just like Trevor did. Not just one death here tonight, but two. It won't be hard at all for us to convince the authorities that all wolves, no matter what their origin, have to be rounded up and killed."

As scared as Maya was, her thoughts focused momentarily on Vinnie's words *no matter what their origin*.

Then this group knew about shifters? Believed in them?

Wanted to get rid of them along with any feral wolves?

Why?

They should at least answer her questions, shouldn't they, before they killed her?

And as she got those responses, maybe she'd come up with answers to the even more pressing problem: How was she going to get out of this?

"I don't really get it, Vinnie," she said quietly. "I know you feel strongly against wolves, but I'd like to know why, so I can fully understand why you killed Trev and intend to kill me, too. Surely, you can grant me that, can't you? And...well, what did you mean by 'no matter what their origin'?"

"You know!" Vinnie spat furiously, taking more steps toward her intended victim. "Don't try to play games with us. You've gotten close to that guy Ryan. I can't be sure he's a shapeshifter, but some of the people who moved here recently are shifters."

Would playing dumb help or hurt her? Maya determined to approach the subject as carefully as she could. "Shapeshifters? Even if there are such things, why do you dislike them so much?"

She was growing extremely uncomfortable kneeling there—physically. Mentally she knew she was a mess but had to keep smiling in a sympathetic manner.

"You mean you don't know?" shouted Vinnie. "Didn't you do your research on this area before you came like the eco-monster you are and began patting yourself and all other tree huggers—no, make that wolf-huggers—on the back for encouraging those killers to hang around here?"

"Sorry." Maya tried to sound humble as she looked down at the ground. She actually had researched the area both before and after her arrival and had no idea what Vinnie was talking about.

At least the two men stayed where they were, taking in this conversation without approaching. But that still didn't mean Maya could do anything to help herself.

"I'll tell you what they did. And it wasn't here in Fritts Corner but a distance away, up in the mountains overlooking the Pacific. I've got something in common with that Trevor guy, and not just because I was sliced with our little claw gadget here. No, it wasn't just my brother but the rest of my family, too—my parents and brother, Odell—who got killed a few years ago, not long after wolves started to be seen more in the western part of the state. My dear Morton was very close to my family, too, and Carlo was their neighbor. We'd thought Odell was crazy when he told us he'd seen a person turn into a wolf under a full moon, just like the old tales said. He wanted to prove it was true and my parents, though they thought him nuts, promised to go along…and they were all killed. No pictures or anything but they were mauled to death under a full moon."

That didn't necessarily mean the animals were shifters, Maya thought, though she wasn't going to say anything now. It could have been coincidence—or not.

And as she had been telling people in her talks, wild animals were wild. Even shifters, apparently.

It was safer to avoid all of them…right?

"We did some more research," Morton said from where he still stood. "Learned that it was likely that those damned shifters did exist, were present in that area, but it really doesn't matter. Her family was found mauled, sure, but their bodies were at the base of a cliff and the authorities said it was just a bad accident, a fall, that caused their injuries and death. We knew better thanks to the types of wounds they had. Wolves, bite marks and more, and the coroner didn't deny it exactly, just came up with multiple explanations."

"That's right," Vinnie added. "We kept pressing, saying we knew it was wolves, but people kept laughing at us, said we were crazy to make such allegations. They may have all been shapeshifters themselves, damn them."

"Wolves, whether human in origin or not, are dangerous," Morton said. "They kill people. The ones who mauled our family are probably still out there and we never learned who they are. So people should kill all wolves first." He paused, but only for an instant. "Go to it, Vinnie!" he exclaimed.

And Vinnie, still several strides away, rushed toward Maya with the claw gadget pointed toward her throat.

Chapter 24

"No!" Maya screamed as she tried wildly to yank her wrists loose, attempting to get free to push the claw away—or, better yet, run.

Fruitless. She wanted to close her eyes as the inevitable happened. She was about to die. Painfully.

And then, she heard a bark followed by a growl and opened her eyes as a large gray wolf leaped onto Vinnie, grabbing her neck in his mouth and closing his teeth into it.

Ryan. It had to be him in shifted form.

He was here to save her.

But she saw, beyond him, that Morton and Carlo had rushed toward them, both brandishing guns.

"Ryan!" she screamed. "Look out!"

Fortunately he was too connected with Vinnie for them to shoot without fear of hurting her, or so Maya believed. But they'd find a way. She was certain of it.

Meantime, Ryan had clearly heard her warning. Without lifting his mouth from Vinnie's throat or his body from partly covering hers now on the ground, he managed to look in the men's direction.

What was he going to do? Oh, lord, he couldn't die because of her.

He had reacted immediately because he'd no choice. He would not allow them to harm Maya. He would not allow them to kill her.

But now they would kill him, and if so they might yet do the unthinkable with Maya.

Wouldn't they be thrilled? A second dead human along with the corpse of a wolf, assuming he didn't change back. They would get away with all this and still be able to make claims that could lead to the murders of shifters as well as the death of feral wolves.

Revenge? Maybe. He had been listening before leaping in. But they should have found those who had killed Vinnie's family, not taken out their fury against all wolves...or shifters.

At least now he could harbor no further doubt that Pete wasn't the one to attack Vinnie Fritts.

What could he do? If he stayed as he was, they might not shoot since they would hit the human woman with whom he had entwined his body. But this could not last forever.

Even with his human cognition, he did not come up with an immediate solution. Yet this sort of standoff could not last long.

But then—he saw another form bound out of the forest, a wolf who resembled him. No, a wolf-dog. Rocky.

His cover dog had no weapons to fight off the attackers except his teeth, which would do no good against guns. Yet maybe he could act as enough of a distraction...

"Get them!" That was Piers, who now appeared at the edge of the forest from which Rocky had emerged. He was a soldier, a member of Alpha Force, yet he probably had brought no weaponry here into the forest. Why would he? But he was giving Rocky commands that might lead to the dog's death.

"Yeah, get 'em," cried another human voice. Pete was suddenly there at Piers's side, still in human form, holding up a phone to take pictures.

But the photos would only show him, in shifted form, and possibly Rocky attacking humans—unless Maya could turn and show how she was bound.

The situation was pure confusion now. Who would get hurt—or killed? Who would survive?

He had to pull away, take charge, act like the Alpha Force member, the alpha member of his allied pack, that he was. Yet what would happen if he moved away from this miserable excuse for a human who now smelled like terror but would undoubtedly do all she could to kill him if he backed off?

And then—two more wolves appeared from behind the two human men, leaping into the clearing, each heading straight for those miserable humans with guns.

The Sharan parents, shifted? The scent told Ryan the answer. He appreciated that they wanted to help. Without human cognition, they would hopefully follow the lead of other members of this canine pack, including Rocky...and him.

But would they, too, get killed?

He could not allow that. He could not allow any of his current pack to be harmed in any major way.

He had to ensure that Maya remained all right.

The guns were suddenly pointed away from him. Oh, yes, he had to take charge immediately to save those brave older shifters. With a growl, he bit down once more before releasing the throat of the woman beneath him, hoping he had provided enough of an injury, and a warning, to stay where she was.

He sprang into action.

Thanks to Piers's commands, Rocky was now behind the men they all had to bring down. The men now facing the Sharans with their weapons.

Ryan began barking as he leaped forward toward the armed thugs, causing Rocky to bark, too, even as he followed Ryan's lead and bounded toward their enemies from behind.

They turned and fired their guns. Ryan felt a pain in his right side as he soared sideways to minimize their ability to target him. No matter. He was alive. And he saw no indication in that fleeting moment that anyone else had been hurt—except for Trev.

He crouched down momentarily as if badly injured, while Rocky hurled himself onto Morton's back and brought him down.

Ryan showed their other shifted pack members what to do, jumping up once more and grabbing Carlo's gun hand in his mouth, biting down. Hard. Shaking his head until the man, bloodied and shouting, released the gun.

One of the Sharans—Kathie?—hurled herself onto Carlo's back, ensuring that the man could no longer rise.

The other, Burt, jumped on top of Morton, holding him facedown.

Had they won?

No—Vinnie had not accepted his warning. She now

had her arm around Maya's throat. "Let them all go!" she screamed. "I'll kill her!"

"You'll do it on camera," Pete yelled, aiming his phone toward her.

Vinnie appeared not to care. Maya was clearly attempting to break away, sagging and twisting as her eyes looked furious and frightened. But Vinnie's hands moved to clutch her throat.

At least that clawing weapon was on the ground, out of the way. But Vinnie obviously intended to choke the life out of Maya.

He had to count on the shifted Kathie and the fact that Piers was near them, crouching as if picking up one of the guns.

Ryan broke away from Carlo, feeling the injury he had suffered in his side and ignoring the pain. He wished for this moment that he was not in shifted form, that he could grab a gun and aim it at the fiend who was hurting the woman he loved.

Loved? He dared not think about that now.

He crouched once more as if in pain and crawled along the hard ground covered with leaves—and blood. His blood. But no matter.

He drew closer until—

"Stay there, you filthy creature!" Vinnie shrieked, obviously tugging harder at Maya's throat. Maya appeared ready to lose consciousness.

To die?

No!

Ryan lay on the ground for another second, as if giving in, obeying, giving up—

And then he sprang forward right at Maya, who, wonderful woman, had also been playing at submission. She pulled sideways and down, allowing Ryan to

*leap right at Vinnie, grab her throat once more in his
teeth and go into worrying mode, shaking and tearing
more at the flesh and what was inside.*

*He did not want to kill her, but one human here had
already died thanks to injuries to his throat.*

*"No!" Vinnie's scream turned into a choked wail.
She suddenly released Maya, clutching at her own
throat even as she fell to the ground gagging and crying as Ryan held on.*

*In moments, Piers was there. He held a gun so its
muzzle touched the top of Vinnie's head. "I've got her,"
he told Ryan. "It's okay to let go."*

*Ryan gave one more shake, then obeyed. He backed
off slowly, making sure he saw what he hoped to: Piers
in control of Vinnie.*

*The other canines were obeying commands Pete
yelled at them, restraining one of the two formerly
armed men: Carlo. Pete had put down his phone and
had grabbed a leash—Rocky's?—and bound Morton's
hands behind his back.*

All was under control...now.

*Only then did Ryan allow himself to fall to the ground
and lose consciousness.*

No. Oh, no. It was all supposed to be over. The bad
guys were now under control, and sirens sounded in
the distance. Pete must have already called the cops,
and they'd be here soon to arrest the people who'd attacked her—and Ryan.

But Maya was a wreck. Her hands now free, she sat
on the ground beside poor Ryan. At least he was still
breathing. Still alive, with his eyes closed.

But how could his wounds be tended to? What phy-
sician would know what to do with a shapeshifter in

animal form? Or should it be a veterinarian? And how could they keep it all a secret?

"We'll be back soon," Pete said and led two of the wolves back into the woods. The way he had been talking to them, they had to be his parents. Was he a shapeshifter, too? Maya would find out later, she figured. Right now, Pete held his phone in his hands and seemed to be looking at the screen even as he led the shifted wolves away.

Piers remained there, at least, holding what must be one of their own guns on the three evil people who'd started all this: Vinnie, Morton and Carlo. Rocky sat on the ground beside him, ears up and head edged forward, clearly ready to spring if any of those horrible humans dared to move.

Sirens drew closer as if cop cars raced toward the parking lot below them. As the noise stopped, Piers looked toward Maya.

"We need your help," he said.

"Of course."

In moments, she was the one to hold the gun aimed at the Frittses and Carlo. Piers dashed off for a very short while and returned with a backpack in his arms. He removed some rope from it, quickly bound the arms of their captives, then tied them together. Finally, he made them sit down, tied their legs together as well, then bound them tightly to a nearby large tree—not far from Trev's body.

"I'll leave Rocky with you. We'll be back soon."

He pulled a large lantern from his backpack and turned it on, and the light in the clearing was immediately enhanced. Then he put the backpack over his shoulders, hefted Ryan the wolf carefully into his arms, and hurried off into the forest, another, smaller light tied to his chest leading the way.

What was Piers doing? Would he leave injured Ryan hidden around here when the authorities arrived so as not to show anyone the truth of what Ryan was?

Could Ryan survive?

Maya wanted to cry, but of course she didn't dare do anything to keep her attention from the people in front of her. Sure, they were tied up, but that didn't mean they couldn't escape.

No way would she let them. They'd killed a man. They had tried to kill her.

They'd shot Ryan, the hero who had saved her from them.

She was relieved when a short time later Pete returned. With him were his parents—in human form.

Instead of staring at his cell phone now, Pete lifted it to his ear although Maya hadn't heard it ring. Maybe it had vibrated. He spoke into it, turned to tell his folks to remain there and help Maya if she needed it, and handed his father a gun—presumably the other one that had been aimed by either Morton or Carlo.

"I'll be back in a few minutes with the cops," he said.

Kathie and Burt stood beside Maya, and Burt kept his gun trained on the others despite their still being bound. Sweet and obedient Rocky stayed there, pacing a bit behind them, and Maya felt sure that he was as scared as she about what was going on with Ryan.

She had no idea about how much time passed, but soon Pete was back, leading some uniformed officers from the Fritts Corner PD. "Okay," said the tall man in front who appeared to be in charge. "Tell us what's going on here."

"These people jumped us, Officers," cried Vinnie

from where she was tied on the ground. "They brought some wolves here, said they were werewolves. One of them mauled poor Carlo and then killed Trevor."

She motioned toward the dead body lying on the ground as Carlo, that supposedly poor, mauled man, jutted his head forward, obviously hoping to emphasize the cuts on his face.

"The gadget they used to make all the cuts, including the fatal ones, is over there," Maya said, nodding toward one side of the clearing. "They did it themselves to make it look like wolf attacks. Then they tied me up and said they were going to use it to slash my throat, to kill me in a way to look like a wolf did it."

"No way, Officer," Vinnie cried out. "She's just saying that to protect herself. It's them that—"

"I've got some photos on my phone to help show what happened here," Pete said. "And before you ask, yes, this wonderful dog, Rocky, is in some of them. He was trying to help us stop those jerks from hurting Maya or any of us."

Maya wondered if he'd done anything while taking his parents away to shift back to human form to edit the photos on his phone—or put them in another file or somehow conceal evidence that there had been four canines here instead of one. There hadn't been much time. But in her very limited experience, she'd been impressed to see what shifters did to protect themselves and each other.

If only that could have helped Ryan...

"Officers, so glad you're here," said a familiar voice from the edge of the forest. She couldn't help looking in that direction and smiling. Could her thoughts of him actually have conjured up Ryan?

He stood there in human form. Very human form,

standing tall and straight, his face a bit pale but perhaps that was just the minimal illumination from the moon above and the fading artificial light.

He must have shifted back after Piers carried him off. Had the shift somehow cured his wounds, as well?

She doubted it, but at least for this moment he appeared okay.

Piers stood behind him on his right side, the side that had been shot. They must have intended to hide that he'd been a shifter in wolf form who'd been shot by this group of horrible people.

Sure, they might have a reason to hate certain shifters but to take it out on as many shifters, or even regular wolves, as they could put themselves in contact with?

To take it out on the perfectly innocent Ryan?

Horrible!

"Okay, look," said the officer in charge, who called himself Sergeant Pass. "We aren't going to be able to sort this all out here in the middle of nowhere. We've already called the medical examiner's office to send someone for the body. One of us will stay here, and all the rest of us will head to the station." His fellow cops started herding everyone together, weapons drawn, after slicing off the ropes binding the Frittses and Carlo.

The Frittses and Carlo. They were locals. Would they receive special treatment?

But at least some of the photos Pete had taken would show what those horrible people had been up to.

The ones that could be shown to the cops and become evidence, though, would only show Ryan in wolf form, possibly injured.

He had saved her.

With the help of the others, he'd brought this group of crazed anti-wolf people down.

He'd therefore potentially saved a lot of wolves, both the usual type and shifters.

No matter what else happened, Maya would do all she could to make sure the world, including WHaM members and everyone else, knew what a hero Ryan Blaiddinger really was.

As long as she could do it without revealing any secrets.

Chapter 25

His side hurt like the devil. But Ryan knew that Maya, the angel, was waiting for him in this medical office's waiting room, so he simply gritted his teeth while the doctor finished cleansing his wound and bandaging it. He tried not to inhale deeply since the room smelled of antiseptics and other medical aromas—including the odor of his own wound—and he definitely did not want to throw up.

At least now, since he was in human form, his wound was probably easier to deal with than if he'd still been shifted.

Plus, he'd be able to control better when he took the necessary antibiotics to prevent the injury from festering and becoming infected.

The Sharans had brought him here, to a medical doctor they'd been using since their arrival in Fritts Corner, a good guy who only cared about his patients becoming, and staying, healthy. The Sharans hadn't been the only ones to use his services, either. Apparently this nice, skilled Dr. Delmert had a perfect bedside manner with people, even though he'd asked questions of the Sharans—and now Ryan—indicating his suspicions that they weren't just run-of-the-mill human beings. But he was kind and discreet, and clearly wanted to help cure his patients and keep them healthy while doing no harm—or revealing his suspicions to the world.

When he first looked at Ryan and his wound, he'd suggested a hospital visit but had been willing to treat Ryan here when the injured man had requested that instead.

"There." Dr. Delmert had dark-toned skin and gentle hands, and he hadn't asked questions about the wound. Fortunately, the bullet had passed through Ryan while he was shifted but had caused an ugly, painful and bloody wound. "This should start healing now. Just make sure to keep it clean and don't do any heavy lifting for a while."

Then he wouldn't be able to lift Maya in bed—not that she was particularly heavy.

And not that he would really get another opportunity to be alone with her the way he had a few nights back.

"Sure thing," Ryan responded. "Thanks, Doc."

Then he left, heading for the waiting room, where he'd pay his bill—and meet up with Maya.

Maya sat on a small, stiff chair in the compact and nearly empty waiting room. She'd picked up a magazine from an end table and had been thumbing through it, though she wasn't interested in the private lives of celebrities.

She'd much rather they had reading material about wildlife.

The reception desk was along the far wall and opened into the area containing the medical facilities. A couple of women governed it, checking in the arrivals and taking payment from those who were through.

Piers was with her, too. He had driven Ryan and Maya here, then took Rocky back to the hotel. He'd just returned alone, and Maya had to keep biting her tongue to avoid asking all the questions she had about what had really happened back there on the hillside, and what was going to happen now.

Assuming Ryan did all right. He'd clearly been in pain since he returned as a human, and it had been a while before they'd been able to come here. First, they'd needed to head down to the parking lot, then drive to the police station and answer questions. Fortunately, that hadn't taken too long and the cops had released them—for now. They'd said they would have more questions.

Through all of that, Ryan had been brave—not surprising, of course. And that pain…he had pretended it wasn't there, but she could see it in his eyes and slow, precise movements. At least his bleeding hadn't been heavy or the cops would have noticed. But he wore a jacket over his shirt so no one could easily see the bulge beneath it where he held things against his wound to absorb the blood.

Maya knew his wound had still been bleeding. When the interrogation was over she had quietly offered her hoodie to help staunch the flow of blood. Before that, he and Piers had used a T-shirt Piers had had in his backpack along with Ryan's clothes—and the other stuff he carried. Her hoodie had been larger and had absorbed a lot more blood than the shirt—but could only be used when they weren't around the cops any longer.

When they had finally come here.

But even if she couldn't talk about what she wanted to while waiting, there were a few questions she could ask Piers now that they could discuss. "Piers, do you know where the Sharans are now? Did they just go home?"

"No, they said they were staying at the police station for now in case there were more questions. They said a few friends were on their way for backup, if needed."

Most likely more shifters. Even so, they were probably recent arrivals at Fritts Corner, too. Would the cops continue to accept the word of newcomers instead of members of the Fritts family, as they seemed to be doing?

Pete's photos helped with that, she knew. She also hadn't had an opportunity to check to see whether they'd been pared down to not show how many canines had actually been present before the cops' arrival, but she hoped so.

Questions about that would be hard to answer.

Piers didn't seem inclined to talk. In fact, he picked up a magazine from a nearby table, too—one on sports.

Muffling her sigh, Maya started looking once more through the magazine still on her lap. Maybe she could stand reading about a TV news reporter's elevation to anchor on the national network. At least it was better than who was sleeping with whom.

But she looked up when, from the corner of her eye, she noticed the door into the medical area open.

Ryan walked out. He was smiling.

She stood immediately and started walking toward

him, as did Piers. She wanted to run, to hug him, to tell him how happy she was to see him.

Instead, she kept her pace moderate and then just stood there. "How are you?" she asked.

"Real good." He grinned at her, then turned it toward Piers. "Let's get out of here."

Ryan stood in the hotel parking lot, putting the last of his belongings into the rental car's trunk.

It was daytime now, a pleasant Friday in late September, several days since the bringing down of the Frittses and Silling. He had learned that they would be charged with the homicide of Tim Grant, as well as assault with a deadly weapon and more. Ryan had given his initial statement, and so had Piers, Maya and the Sharans. He'd have to return to this area eventually to testify at their trial—and he would be happy to do it.

It was cool today but not too cold. A good day to drive, and to fly.

He looked around the parking lot. Only a few cars were parked there right now but he figured more hotel guests would arrive later in the day to spend the weekend in Fritts Corner. Probably not a lot, though. The town hadn't exactly turned into a tourist spot, which remained a good thing.

At the moment, he was the only person in the lot. Piers had already finished packing his stuff and stowed it in the trunk, including his prized backpack and its vital contents. Now, he was giving Rocky a final walk before they left.

The Sharans had managed to put together a very brief meeting in their office yesterday, where the other people in town they knew to be shifters—Buck Lesterman and John and Georgia Maheus—were invited and told the truth about the Frittses and how they'd "claimed" to be trying to harm shapeshifters, of all things. No one gave them any credence, of course.

Of course. But that was enough information for those in that room, and they all promised to stay in close touch without talking about any secrets that had resulted in their invitation there that day.

And they weren't informed about the biggest secret of all: Alpha Force.

Now, Ryan kept looking around. Maya had said she was leaving later that day. He'd told her what time he'd be packing up his car, hoping she would come to say goodbye.

She hadn't.

Maybe it was better that way but he nevertheless felt a bit...well, hurt. This was likely to be the last time they would see one another, unless they made plans otherwise. Piers and he were about to drive to Sea-Tac Airport to return the rental car—and to head back east to Fort Lukman, the military headquarters of Alpha Force.

They'd see the Sharans again, though. All three members of that family would meet them at the airport and join them on the flight and beyond. Once they were at the military base on Maryland's Eastern Shore, Ryan would introduce all of them to his commanding officers who would then also interview Pete.

He remained clearly eager to join the covert unit. Ryan believed he would be a great asset. The young man was smart, had even developed his own version of a shifting formula. Sure, it was far from perfect, but it worked enough for Pete and his parents the other night. They'd changed to help Ryan save Maya and bring down those bad guys who'd been collaborating to remove federal and state protection of wolves and get them all killed, shifters or not. The Sharans might not have had human cognition while shifted but their canine cognition was enough to get them to follow their son's commands.

Plus, Pete had been wise enough not only to take pictures of what had been going on during the tumult up on the hillside, but also to quickly download them onto a tablet computer his parents had carried into the woods. He'd left only those that would be helpful against the Frittses and Carlo on his phone, which he'd turned over to the cops as evidence after their promise to return it soon.

He'd told Ryan and the others later that he'd also fixed things so that there'd be no evidence he'd taken those additional photos. Good guy—a whole lot more tech savvy than Ryan.

Well, some good had come out of this trip. Quite a lot, actually. Wolves—and most likely some shifters—had been saved. There would still be some observation of the area by Fish and Wildlife and other organizations thanks to all the newly arrived wolves that most people wouldn't know included shifters.

A new member of Alpha Force may have been recruited, one who was not only a shifter but also had some pretty valuable skills.

Ryan supposed that was enough. Yet—

There. He'd glanced toward the rear door of the hotel just as Maya came out. She peered around as if looking for someone, and when her gaze caught his she smiled and began hurrying in his direction.

Okay. They'd at least be able to say goodbye.

That would be enough. It had to be.

"Hi," she said breathlessly as she reached him. She looked up with her hazel eyes aglow, and he wanted in the worst way to bend down and give her a kiss that wouldn't quit.

But that would only make their parting harder. He'd give her a quick kiss goodbye as Piers and he got ready to go.

That had to be enough.

She looked dressed for traveling, too—a pale green shirt tucked into beige pants, dressy but flat brown shoes, nicer than hiking garb. But she looked good in everything. Too good.

And in nothing…

He nearly shook his head with disgust at himself.

"Hi," he said. "Glad to see you. I'm just waiting for Piers and Rocky, then we're going to leave."

A look of sadness seemed to cross her lovely face, making him want to reach out to comfort her. But then it disappeared.

"I'm leaving soon, too. But I wanted to invite you and any members of—you know—to come visit our facility in Colorado. We don't rescue wolves per se, though we help support organizations that do, and we've a lot of educational materials and classes available. Plus, there's all the information we collect and share with appropriate parties."

"Sounds good," he said. "Maybe someday…soon." He hoped.

But the reality of it was most likely different.

"Okay. Great." Her tone suggested she recognized that he was just being kind without committing. Then she perked up but kept her voice low. "So how are you feeling?" She glanced toward his side, which remained bandaged beneath his clothes. Most of the world didn't know he'd been hurt, and he needed to keep it that way. His wound had been cleaned well by that doctor, Ryan was on antibiotics to avoid infection and he seemed to be healing fine.

"Quite well, thanks." And he really did owe her thanks for helping him that night.

"So—any word about what's going to happen next with those horrible anti-wolf people?" She didn't mention what kind of wolves, which was a good thing, but he already knew she was tactful as well as caring.

Even so, he had to keep himself from pulling her close.

Instead, he said, "Things aren't resolved yet, whether it'll be the feds or locals who prosecute them, or maybe both. They're all still in custody here at the Fritts Corner Police Department but will be moved soon to the Tacoma authorities, at least for a while. It's hard to keep people whose names are the same as the town in jail there."

"I figured. But—well, since they murdered Trev, I assume they'll be imprisoned for a long time, maybe the rest of their lives. Justice should be served, and that should also prevent them from ever going after or hurting wolves or other wildlife. Right?"

"That's what I think, too. And besides our testimony, there's a lot of evidence against them for other crimes. Apparently they may even have admitted to leaving a patch of blood up on the hillside when Morton was first mauled but still claimed it was a wolf who attacked him. There's been some media coverage of their arrest and why, so that might help to at least keep the public's interest in protecting, and not harming, wildlife. Plus, though I'm not really with US Fish and Wildlife," he said softly, "some of my…er, bosses, have connections that will allow me to testify as if I am. I am an employee of the federal government, after all."

"What kind of charges besides murder will be brought against them?" She looked concerned, as if nothing could be punishment enough.

"That's the big one, of course, but the rest is still being worked out, too. They might be tried locally for conspiracy to commit fraud, thanks to their fake attempts to appear like they were injured by protected wolves. And they certainly can be brought up on charges for assaulting you, and your testimony then would be crucial. They could even be charged by the federal government for killing protected wildlife."

"Killing?" Maya asked, clearly worried.

He quickly mentioned the injured wolf whose body hadn't been found—actually, him—that had been the subject of some of Pete's pictures. Rocky and he both had been in some of them. But Pete had purposely not taken pictures of his parents. "He's got lots of other good photos of that night, too, that could help bring those SOBs down for any or all of those charges. Then there's the crime of fraud and false statements, claiming some of the wolves they were after to be shapeshifters." He kept his tone light but maintained a somewhat serious expression as Maya looked at him skeptically. "As long as the truth isn't revealed," he whispered, which made her smile again.

"It sounds as if they should get what's due to them," she said.

Ryan saw Piers enter the far end of the parking lot with Rocky. They would leave soon.

He had to say goodbye. Now.

He couldn't say goodbye.

A thought crossed his mind. He pulled his phone out of his pocket and checked the time.

"I think we can spend another ten minutes here," he told Maya. "Can you join me for coffee?"

"Sure." Her face lit up with what appeared to be hope. Or was he the one who was seeing things because he was hopeful?

"I'll let Piers know."

Which he did after striding across the parking lot to his aide and cover dog.

"You saying goodbye to her?" Piers looked dubious, as if he expected Ryan to do something else.

Actually he wasn't sure.

But he had an idea.

He would suggest it to her during coffee, which he'd buy and they'd carry on a private walk around the hotel area.

He hoped the result would make his goodbye temporary, at least for now.

Coffee with Ryan, and a last walk with him before they said goodbye.

It was better than nothing, Maya thought. At the coffee shop near the hotel she ordered just some brewed stuff with cream, hoping to somehow coat her insides to help alleviate the sorrow she knew she'd feel.

But as they walked back onto the street and headed around the block in the opposite direction from the hotel, she listened carefully and pondered the possibilities of what Ryan suggested.

When he stopped talking and looked down at her as they still strolled, she didn't return his gaze for a minute while she thought. And then she stopped walking and looked up at him. "I think it'll work," she said. "In fact, I love it!"

"And I love you," Ryan said. His eyebrows rose as

if he was shocked at what he'd said. But then they lowered, and his smile grew wide and sexy and definitely inviting.

How could she resist? Especially because it was the truth.

"I love you, too."

Chapter 26

Maya was excited. She was thrilled.

A week had passed since she'd last seen Ryan, and they had stayed in close touch.

She was now in the main administration building at Fort Lukman.

The home of Alpha Force.

Ryan had picked her up at BWI Airport in Baltimore. He was dressed in military fatigues in camo style, greens and browns and altogether official-looking.

He looked great in it, though no better than he'd looked in the casual clothes he'd worn around Fritts Corner.

She had dressed up a bit, in a gray suit and heels. This was, after all, going to be an interview of sorts. She had checked a suitcase with several additional outfits in case more than one day was needed here to get things settled, which was what she hoped. It was now in the trunk of Ryan's car. He'd said he had booked her a room in nearby Mary Glen.

Ryan had driven her here to Maryland's Eastern Shore. He'd talked nearly all the way about who she would be meeting, and what she should expect.

Lots of interesting people she gathered—some who were shifters.

And lots of questions, too.

They'd eventually reached the facility, and Ryan had pulled his car up to a kiosk at a gate beside a large black metal fence that undoubtedly kept the place private. He talked to a guard there whom he appeared to know and was permitted to drive inside and park. Then he'd led Maya into this small but official-looking building.

Now, they were in a waiting room of an office on the top floor. Piers joined them with Rocky, who leaped over to Maya and wagged his tail. "Great to see you, guys," she said, patting the wolf-dog on his head and behind his ears. And it was.

Not just because he reminded her of a shifted Ryan, either. She simply loved canines that were, or resembled, wolves.

"And great to see you," Piers said. "Ryan told me what's going on, and I think the idea's a good one."

So did Maya. But would these guys' commanding officers agree?

Another soldier in camo, probably in his early forties, entered the reception area from the office door. He was tall, with dark hair that had lines of silver within it. His eyes were golden, his eyebrows dark and he had a hint of dark beard on his nice-looking face.

She couldn't be sure, but Maya believed he could be a shifter. He at least had some features with coloration resembling a wolf.

Ryan and Piers both rose to greet him. No salutes, but Ryan had said that generally Alpha Force tended to be less formal than most military units, at least in that way.

"Maya, I'd like you to meet Major Drew Connell," Ryan said, motioning for her to join them, which she did. She offered her hand, and the major shook it. "Drew, this is Maya Everton."

"Ah, yes. I've heard a lot about you, and I've liked WHaM for a long time." That statement somehow convinced Maya even more that this man was a shifter.

She'd anticipated meeting quite a few of Ryan's kind here.

They all went into the room behind the door, and she was introduced to the man whose office it was—and quite an office it turned out to be, with bookshelves lining the wall behind the main desk. Its featured contents appeared to be classics, and in the center, under glass, was what appeared to be an original script of the movie *The Wolf Man*, starring Lon Chaney, Jr.

It belonged to General Greg Yarrow, who apparently was the driving force in the military behind Alpha Force. He knew and helped to select its members, even though Maya gathered that he wasn't a shifter himself.

The general sat behind the desk, rising to shake her hand. Like the other military men here, he wore a camo uniform. He also appeared fairly senior.

"Welcome, Ms. Everton," he said. He introduced the other men who sat in chairs facing his desk.

Then Drew introduced her to Lieutenant Patrick Worley, his second in command at Alpha Force, as well as Drew's wife, Dr. Melanie Harding Connell, a veterinarian—and, apparently, not a shifter, Maya gathered.

"Welcome," Melanie said. "I think we'll have lots to talk about if all goes well here."

Which it seemed to do.

Ryan's idea had been to form an alliance between Alpha Force and WHaM. Although the fact that many of Alpha Force's troops were shifters was definitely private, its reputation was now being allowed to grow as a unit that used K-9s and other animals for military purposes.

Many of them appeared to be wild animals, like wolves and cougars and birds of prey.

Having an organization like WHaM as an unofficial partner in the protection of wildlife seemed like an excellent idea.

Giving one of the founders of WHaM an office at Fort Lukman could only add to the cover story. That's what Ryan had suggested, and his commanding officers seemed willing to give it a try.

They seemed to like and respect Ryan. In fact, he'd promised that Pete Sharan would meet them when they left here. His parents had come, too, but had left for home. Pete definitely was joining Alpha Force in the near future.

It didn't take long before an initial agreement was reached with the others in the room with her. They'd need to come up with a more detailed plan before putting it into effect, but everyone seemed pleased with the idea of an alliance, at least to some extent, with WHaM.

Maya soon said goodbye to her new friends here, except for Ryan, who walked out the office door with her.

She felt a bit overwhelmed, but definitely delighted.

Especially since she would get the opportunity to see more of Ryan. Potentially a lot more.

As they exited the building, Ryan said to her, "This is a great beginning."

"It sure is," Maya agreed, grabbing his hand and

squeezing it, but only for a moment. They both had to act professional, especially here.

"Now, I'd like to show you more of Fort Lukman," Ryan continued, "like the kennels and training facilities for our cover dogs, the labs where our elixir is made and improved, and more."

"Sounds wonderful," Maya said.

"We can grab dinner a little later at the cafeteria—and then, if you'd like, I'll show you around our Bachelor Officers Quarters, my apartment in particular."

His smile grew wide and suggestive, and Maya could only grin back. "I'd love to see it now—and visit it in the future when I move here, too."

"Count on it," Ryan said, putting an arm around her shoulders and, despite the fact that other soldiers were out there on the grounds of the military facility, he pulled her close.

She didn't object. In fact, she did the same with him.

And definitely looked forward to the future.

* * * * *

Need an adrenaline rush from nail-biting tales
(and irresistible males)?

Check out **Harlequin® Intrigue®**
and **Harlequin® Romantic Suspense** books!

New books available every month!

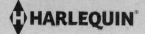

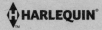

HARLEQUIN™

Save $1.00

on the purchase of any

Harlequin® series book.

Available wherever books are sold, including
most bookstores, supermarkets, drugstores
and discount stores.

✂

Save $1.00

on the purchase of any Harlequin® series book.

Coupon valid until July 31, 2018.
Redeemable at participating retail outlets in the U.S. and Canada only.
Limit one coupon per customer.

52615203

Canadian Retailers: Harlequin Enterprises Limited will pay the face value of
this coupon plus 10.25¢ if submitted by customer for this product only. Any
other use constitutes fraud. Coupon is nonassignable. Void if taxed, prohibited
or restricted by law. Consumer must pay any government taxes. Void if copied.
Inmar Promotional Services ("IPS") customers submit coupons and proof of sales
to Harlequin Enterprises Limited, PO Box 31000, Scarborough, ON M1R 0E7,
Canada. Non-IPS retailer—for reimbursement submit coupons and proof of
sales directly to Harlequin Enterprises Limited, Retail Marketing Department,
225 Duncan Mill Rd., Don Mills, ON M3B 3K9, Canada.

U.S. Retailers: Harlequin Enterprises
Limited will pay the face value of
this coupon plus 8¢ if submitted by
customer for this product only. Any
other use constitutes fraud. Coupon is
nonassignable. Void if taxed, prohibited
or restricted by law. Consumer must pay
any government taxes. Void if copied.
For reimbursement submit coupons
and proof of sales directly to Harlequin
Enterprises, Ltd 482, NCH Marketing
Services, P.O. Box 880001, El Paso,
TX 88588-0001, U.S.A. Cash value
1/100 cents.

5 65373 00076 2 (8100)0 12314

® and ™ are trademarks owned and used by the trademark owner and/or its licensee.

© 2018 Harlequin Enterprises Limited

HSCOUP0318

Looking for more satisfying love stories
with community and family at their core?

Check out **Harlequin® Special Edition**
and **Harlequin® Western Romance** books!

New books available every month!

CONNECT WITH US AT:

Harlequin.com/Community

 Facebook.com/HarlequinBooks

Twitter.com/HarlequinBooks

Instagram.com/HarlequinBooks

Pinterest.com/HarlequinBooks

ReaderService.com

**ROMANCE WHEN
YOU NEED IT**

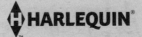

LOVE
Harlequin
romance?

Join our Harlequin community to share your thoughts and connect with other romance readers!

Be the first to find out about promotions, news, and exclusive content!

Sign up for the Harlequin e-newsletter and download a free book from any series at

www.TryHarlequin.com